THE DARKER SIDE

Also by Cody McFadyen

SHADOW MAN

THE FACE OF DEATH

THE DARKER SIDE

Cody McFadyen

BANTAM BOOKS

NEW YORK   TORONTO   LONDON   SYDNEY   AUCKLAND

THE DARKER SIDE
A Bantam Book / October 2008

Published by Bantam Dell
A Division of Random House, Inc.
New York, New York

All rights reserved
Copyright © 2008 by Cody McFadyen

Book design by Carol Malcolm Russo

Bantam Books is a registered trademark of Random House, Inc.,
and the colophon is a trademark of Random House, Inc.

Library of Congress Cataloging-in-Publication Data
McFadyen, Cody.
The darker side / Cody McFadyen.
p.   cm.
ISBN 978-0-553-80694-6
1. Government investigators—Fiction. 2. Women detectives—Fiction.
3. Serial murderers—Fiction. I. Title.
PS3613.C438D37 2008
813'.6—dc22   2008028095

Printed in the United States of America
Published simultaneously in Canada

www.bantamdell.com

BVG   10 9 8 7 6 5 4 3 2 1

THIS ONE IS FOR HYERI, AND ALL HER GENTLE WAYS.

ACKNOWLEDGMENTS

THANKS AS ALWAYS TO LIZA AND HAVIS DAWSON FOR SUCH able and enthusiastic representation. Liza, thanks for listening all the times I needed to bitch and moan. Continuing thanks to Chandler Crawford for lugging my works across the ocean to other countries and getting them excited too. Big thanks to both Danielle Perez and Nick Sayers for the excellent editing; they never fail to make me make it a better book. And to all the readers who've e-mailed or written, you're the fuel for the engine. I'll keep writing as long as you'll keep reading.

THE DARKER SIDE

PART ONE

THE CALM BEFORE

1

DYING IS A LONELY THING.

Then again, so is living.

We all spend our lives alone inside our heart of hearts. However much we share with those we love, we always hold something back. Sometimes it's a small thing, like a woman remembering a secret but long-gone love. She tells her husband she's never loved anyone more than him, and she speaks the literal truth. But she has loved someone as *much* as him.

Sometimes it's a big thing, a huge thing, a monster that cuddles up next to us and licks us between the shoulder blades. A man, while in college, witnesses a gang rape but never steps forward. Years later that man becomes the father of a daughter. The more he loves her, the worse the guilt, but still, still, still, he'll never tell. Torture and death before that truth.

In the late hours, the ones when *everyone's* alone, those secrets come knocking. Some knock hard and some knock soft, but whispering or screeching, they come. No locked door will keep them out; they have the key to us. We speak to them or plead with them or scream at them and we wish we could tell them to someone, that we could get them off our chest to just one person and feel *relief*.

We toss in bed or we walk the halls or we get drunk or we get stoned or we howl at the moon. Then the dawn comes and we shush them up and gather them back into our heart of hearts and do our best to carry on with living. Success at that endeavor depends on the size of the secret and the individual. Not everyone is built for guilt.

Young or old, man or woman, everyone has secrets. This I have learned, this I have experienced, this I know about myself.

Everyone.

I look down at the dead girl on the metal table and wonder: What secrets did you take with you that no one will ever know?

She's far, far too young to be gone. In her early twenties. Beautiful. Long, dark, straight hair. She has skin the color of light coffee, and it looks smooth and flawless even under these harsh fluorescents. Pretty, delicate features go with the skin: vaguely Latin, I think, mixed with something else. Probably Anglo. Her lips have gone pale in death, but they are full without being too full, and I imagine them in a smile that was a precursor to a laugh; light but melodic. She's small and thin through the sheet that covers her from the neck down.

The murdered move me. Good or bad, they had hopes and dreams and loves. They once lived, like all of us, in a world where the deck is stacked *against* living. Between cancer or crashes on the freeway or dropping dead of a heart attack with a glass of wine in your hand and a strangled smile on your face, the world gives us plenty of chances to die. Murderers cheat the system, help things along, rob the victims of something it's already a fight to keep. This offends me. I hated it the first time I saw it and I hate it even more now.

I have been dealing with death for a long time. I am posted in the Los Angeles branch of the FBI and for the last twelve years I have headed up a team responsible for handling the worst of the worst in Southern California. Serial killers. Child rapists and murderers. Men who laugh as they torture women and then groan as they have sex with the corpses. I hunt living nightmares and it's *always* terrible, but it's also everywhere and inevitable.

Which is why I have to ask the question.

"Sir? What are we doing *here*?"

Assistant Director Jones is my longtime mentor, my boss, and the head of all FBI activities in Los Angeles. The problem though, the reason for my maybe-callous query, is that we're not *in* Los Angeles. We're in Virginia, near Washington, DC.

This poor woman may be dead, the fact of her death may touch me, but she's not one of mine.

He gives me a sideways glance, part thoughtful, maybe a little bit annoyed. AD Jones looks exactly like what he is: a veteran cop. He exudes law enforcement and leadership. He's got a square-jawed, strong face; hard, tired eyes; and a regulation haircut with no nod to style. He's handsome in his way, with two past marriages to prove it, but there's something guarded there. Shadows in a strongbox.

"Command performance, Smoky," he says. "From the Director himself."

"Really?"

I'm surprised by this on a few levels. The obvious is simple curiosity: Why here? Why me? The other is more complex: AD Jones's compliance to this unusual request. He has always been that rarity in a bureaucracy, someone who questions orders with impunity if he feels it is warranted. He said "command performance" but we wouldn't be here if he didn't feel there was a valid reason for it.

"Yeah," he replies, "the Director dropped a name I couldn't ignore."

The door to the morgue swings open before I can ask the obvious question.

"Speak of the devil," AD Jones mutters.

FBI Director Samuel Rathbun walks in alone, more strangeness; Even before 9/11, FBI Directors traveled with an entourage. He walks up to us and it's my hand he reaches out to shake first. I comply, bemused.

Looks like I'm the queen of this ball. Why?

"Agent Barrett," he says in that trademark, politically handy baritone. "Thank you for coming on such short notice."

Sam Rathbun, otherwise known as "sir," is a tolerable mix for an FBI Director. He has the necessary rugged good looks and political savvy, but he also has real experience behind him. He started as a cop, went to law school nights, and ended up in the FBI. I wouldn't go so far as to call him "honest"—his position precludes that luxury—but he lies only when he has to. This is integrity incarnate for a Director.

He's reputed to be pretty ruthless, which would not surprise me, and is supposed to be a health nut. Doesn't smoke, doesn't drink, no coffee, no soda, jogs five miles in the morning. Hey, everyone has their faults.

I have to angle my head to look up at him. I'm only four-ten, so I'm used to this.

"No problem at all, Director," I say, lying through my teeth.

Actually, it was a problem, a big fucking problem, but AD Jones will catch any fallout I generate by being difficult.

Rathbun nods at AD Jones. "David," he says.

"Director."

I compare the two men with some interest. They're both the same height. AD Jones has brown hair, cut short in that way that says "I don't have time for this." The Director's is black, flecked with gray and styled, very handsome-older-man, mover-and-shaker. The AD is about eight years older than Director Rathbun and more worn around the edges for sure. The Director *looks* like the man who jogs in the morning and loves it; the AD looks like he *could* jog in the morning, but chooses to have a cigarette and a cup of coffee instead and fuck you if you don't like it. The Director's suit fits better and his watch is a Rolex. AD Jones wears a watch that he probably paid thirty dollars for ten years ago. The differences *are* notable but really, in spite of all of this, it's the similarities that strike me.

Each has the same tired look to the eyes, a look that testifies to the carrying of secret burdens. They have card-players' faces, continually holding things close to the vest.

Here are two men that would be hard to live with, I think. Not because they're bad men, but because they'd operate on the assumption you knew they cared, and that would have to be enough. Love, but no flowers.

Director Rathbun turns to me, again.

"I'll get right to it, Agent Barrett. You're here because I was asked to bring you by someone I'm not prepared to say no to."

I glance at AD Jones, remembering his comment about how the Director had "dropped a name."

"Can I ask who?"

"Soon." He nods at the body. "Tell me what you see."

I turn to the body and force myself to focus.

"Young woman, in her early twenties. Possible victim of homicide."

"What makes you say homicide?"

I indicate a series of bruises on her left upper arm.

"The bruises are red-purple, which means they're very recent. See the outlines? Those bruises were caused by a hand. You have to grip someone pretty hard to cause bruising as defined as that. She's cool to the touch, meaning she's been dead at least twelve hours, probably more like twenty with the visible bruising. Rigor hasn't left the body, meaning she's been dead less than thirty-six." I shrug. "She's young, and someone grabbed her arm hard enough to bruise it not long before she died. Suspicious." I give him a wry smile. "Oh yeah, and I'm here, which means she probably didn't die of natural causes."

"Good eyes, as expected," he says. "And you're correct. She was murdered. On a commercial airliner as it headed from Texas to Virginia. No one knew she was dead until after the plane was empty and the flight attendant tried to rouse her."

I stare at him, certain he's pulling my leg.

"Murder at thirty thousand feet? Is that a joke, sir?"

"No."

"How do we know she was murdered?"

"The nature of how she was found made it clear. But I want you to see it all fresh, with no preconceptions."

I turn back to the body, truly intrigued now.

"When did this happen?"

"Her body was discovered twenty hours ago."

"Do we have a cause of death yet?"

"The autopsy hasn't been done." He glances at his watch. "In fact, we're waiting for the ME now. He's probably held up signing non-disclosure forms."

This oddity brings me back to my original question, and I ask it again. "Why me, sir? More appropriately—why you? What is it about this woman that warrants direct involvement from the Director of the FBI?"

"I'm about to tell you. But first, I want you to see something. Humor me."

Like I have a choice.

He goes over to the body and lifts the sheet away from her chest. He holds it up.

"Take a look," he says.

AD Jones and I move to the head of the table so we are looking down her body from top to bottom. I see small breasts with brown nipples, a flat stomach. My gaze travels down her young form, arriving at her pubic area with impunity, one of the many indignities of the dead. And there I stop, shocked.

"She has a penis," I blurt out.

AD Jones says nothing.

Director Rathbun lets the sheet fall back. He does this with gentle care, an almost fatherly gesture.

"This is Lisa Reid, Smoky. Does that name mean anything to you?"

I frown, trying to make the connection. I can only find one that accounts for the Director's presence here.

"As in Texas congressman Dillon Reid?"

"That's right. Lisa was born Dexter Reid. Mrs. Reid asked for you specifically. She's familiar with your—ah—story."

I'm amused at his discomfort, but I hide it.

Three years ago, my team and I were hunting a serial killer, a true psycho by the name of Joseph Sands. We were very close to catching him when he broke into my home one night. He tied me to a bed and raped me again and again. He used a hunting knife on the left side of my face, carving himself into me, stealing my beauty and leaving me with a permanent relief map of pain.

The scarring starts at my hairline in the middle of my forehead. It goes straight down to between my eyebrows, and then it rockets off to the left, an almost perfect ninety degree angle. I have no left eyebrow; the scar has replaced it. The puckered road continues, across my temple, arcing in a lazy loop-de-loop down my cheek. It rips over toward my nose, crosses the bridge of it just barely, and then turns back, slicing in a diagonal across my left nostril and zooming one final time past my jawline, down my neck, ending at my collarbone.

There is another scar, straight and perfect, that goes from under the middle of my left eye down to the corner of my mouth. This was a gift from another psychotic; he forced me to cut myself while he watched and smiled.

Those are just the scars that are visible. Below the neckline of whatever blouse I happen to be wearing, there are others. Made by Sands's knife blade and the cherry-end of a burning cigar. I lost my face that night, but that was the least of what Sands stole from me. He was a hungry thief, and he only ate the precious things.

I had a husband, a beautiful man named Matt. Sands tied him to a chair and made him witness my rape and torture. Then Sands forced me to watch while he tortured and murdered my Matt. We screamed together and then Matt was gone. It was the last thing we ever shared.

There was one final theft, the worst of all. My ten-year-old daughter, Alexa. I'd managed to get free and had come after Sands with my gun. He yanked Alexa up as I pulled the trigger and the bullet meant for him killed her instead. I filled Sands up with the remaining bullets in the gun and reloaded, screaming, to do it all again. I would have kept firing until the end of the world if they'd let me.

I spent six months after that night teetering on the knife-edge of suicide, wrapped in insanity and despair. I wanted to die, and I might have, but I was saved because someone else died first.

My best friend from high school, Annie King, was murdered by a madman for no other reason than he wanted me to hunt him. He raped Annie with abandon and gutted her with a fisherman's skill. When he was done, he tied Annie's ten-year-old daughter, Bonnie, to Annie's corpse. Bonnie was there for three days before she was discovered. Three days cheek to cheek with her hollowed-out mother.

I gave the madman his wish. I hunted him down and killed him without a twinge of guilt. By the time it was all over, I just didn't feel like dying anymore.

Annie left Bonnie to me, as it turned out. It should have been a doomed relationship; I was a rickety mess, Bonnie was mute as a result of the horrors she'd witnessed. But fate is funny sometimes. Curses can blossom into blessings. Apart, we were broken; together, Bonnie and I helped each other to heal. Bonnie began speaking again two years ago, and I'm happy to be alive, something, at one time, I thought would never happen.

I have learned to accept my disfigurement. I've never considered myself beautiful, really, but I used to be pretty. I am short, with curly, dark hair down to my shoulders. I have what my husband used to call "bite-sized boobs," along with a butt that's bigger than I'd like but which seems to have its own appeal. I had always been comfortable in my own skin, at peace with the physical hand dealt me. Sands's work had made me cringe every time I looked into the mirror. I had kept my hair brushed forward after the attack, using it to obscure my face. Now I keep it tied back in a ponytail and tight against my head, daring the world to look and not giving—as my dad used to say—a "good God damn" if they don't like it.

All of this—my "ah—story" as the Director had put it—had appeared in various papers, and it had given me a grisly celebrity with people both good and bad.

It had also established a ceiling for me at the FBI. There was a time when I was being considered for the Assistant Director's job. Not anymore. My scars gave me a good face for a hunter, or even a teacher of hunters (I'd been offered a teaching position at Quantico, which I'd turned down), but as far as being the administrative face of the FBI? Photoshoots with the President? Not going to happen.

I'd come to terms with all of this years ago. I won't say that I enjoy my job—*enjoy* is not the right word—but I am proud of being good at what I do.

"I see," I reply. "Why did you agree?"

"Congressman Reid is friends with the President. The President is nearing the end of his second term. Reid is the front-runner for the Democratic nomination, as I'm sure you're aware."

"President Allen's party," AD Jones says, observing the obvious for me.

The puzzle pieces fall into place. The name the Director had dropped, the one that AD Jones couldn't ignore, had been the President's. And Dillon Reid was not just the President's friend, he was potentially the next President himself.

"I didn't know that," I muse.

The Director raises his eyebrows. "You didn't know Dillon Reid was a shoo-in for the Democratic nomination? Don't you watch the news?"

"Nope. It's all bad, so why bother?"

The Director is staring at me in frank disbelief.

"It's not like I don't vote," I add. "When the time comes, I find out who the candidates are and what they're about. I'm just not that interested in all the stuff that comes before."

AD Jones smiles a little. The Director shakes his head.

"Well, now that you do know, listen up," he says.

Introductions are over, time has come to hand out the orders.

"At no time in this investigation are you to let politics or political considerations keep you from doing an honest investigation. You are expected to be considerate and to exercise discretion. I'm going to fill you in on some important facts. You're going to keep these facts to yourself. You're not going to write them down anywhere, not a note, not an e-mail. You're going to relay these facts to the members of your team that need to know, and you're going to make sure they keep their mouths shut. Understand?"

"Yes, sir," I reply.

AD Jones nods.

"A transsexual child is political dynamite for anyone, but especially so for a Democratic congressman in what's historically a Republican state. The Reids dealt with this by essentially cutting ties with their son. They didn't disown him, but whenever they were asked, they made it clear that Dexter wasn't welcome at home as long as he insisted on pursuing a transgender path. It got its fifteen minutes and that was pretty much that."

"But it was bullshit, wasn't it?" AD Jones says.

I glance at him, surprised. Director Rathbun nods.

"The truth is, the Reids loved their son. They didn't care if he was gay, transgendered, or Martian."

And now I understand.

"They helped pay for the sex-change, didn't they?"

"That's right. Not directly, of course, but they provided money to Dexter whenever he needed it, knowing it would be used for sex-change necessities. Dexter has also secretly attended every Reid family Christmas."

I shake my head in disbelief. "Is the lie really that important?"

The Director's smile at me is the smile you give a child who's just charmed you with their naivete. *Her so cute!*

"Haven't you seen the culture war going on in this country? Well, magnify that by ten when you hit parts of the South. It could be the difference between being President or not. So yeah, it's important."

I consider this. "I understand," I say, "but I don't care about any of that."

Director Rathbun frowns. "Agent Barrett—"

"Hold on, sir. I'm not saying I won't keep the confidence. What

I'm saying is that I won't keep it because the congressman wants to be President. I don't give a rat's ass about that. I'll keep it because a family that lost a son wants me to." I nod toward the body of Lisa. "And mostly, because Lisa seemed content to keep it herself."

The Director stares at me for a moment. "Fair enough," he replies, and continues. "Mrs. Reid is going to be the family contact. If you have to speak to the congressman, she'll arrange it. Any permissions needed in terms of searching Lisa's condo—anything—she's the one you'll talk to. Stay away from the congressman unless it's absolutely necessary."

"And what if this ends up pointing at the congressman?" I ask.

His smile is mirthless. "Then I know I can count on you to ignore political necessity."

"Who's going to handle the press on this?" AD Jones asks.

"I'll deal with that. In fact, I don't want any of you speaking to the press, period. No comment and that's it." He glances at me. "That goes double for Agent Thorne, Smoky."

He's referring to Callie Thorne, a member of my team. She's known for saying what she wants when she feels like it.

I grin at him. "Don't worry, sir. She's got other fish to fry."

"How's that?"

"She's getting married in a month."

He does a double take. "Really?"

Callie is somewhat infamous as a serial non-monogamist. I'm getting used to the disbelief.

"Yes, sir."

"Wonders never cease. Give her my best. But keep an eye on that mouth of hers." He glances at the Rolex. "I'm going to take you to see Mrs. Reid now. The ME should be arriving shortly. The autopsy results go to me and your team and that's it. Any questions?"

AD Jones shakes his head.

"No, sir," I say, "but I think I should see Mrs. Reid by myself. Mother to mother."

He frowns. "Explain."

"Statistically, men are more ill at ease with transsexuals than women. I'm not saying the congressman didn't love his son, but if Lisa had a champion, someone she was really close to, I'm betting it was the mom." I pause. "Also, I think there's another reason she asked for me."

"Which is?"

I look down at Lisa. She represents a new secret now, one the dead reveal, the old know, and the young will always ignore: life is too damn short, however long it is.

My smile at him is humorless. "Because I've lost a child too. It's a members-only club."

2

I WATCH AS THE CAR PULLS UP BEHIND THE MORGUE. IT'S
black of course; preferred color of the government and its employees,
almost comforting in its continuity. The back windows are tinted to
prevent anyone outside from looking in.

It's half past four in the afternoon, and dusk is beginning to make
itself known here. This part of Virginia huddles close to DC while still
retaining its own identity. It is quieter than the capital and whether
true or not, feels somehow safer. There is a mix of suburb and city
that provides an illusion of comfort. Like so many places in the East,
it has a certain weight to it, a unique blend of character and history.

It's late September here in a way I'll never see on the West Coast.
The air has teeth, a bite that promises a winter with snow. Not as bad
as, say, a Buffalo, New York, winter, but not one of those wussy California winters either.

There are trees everywhere, young and old. Their sheer volume
tells me they are cherished by this city, and I can see why. Fall is an actual season in Alexandria, Virginia. The leaves are on the turn and,
well—it's pretty spectacular.

The car stops, the side door opens, and I climb inside. Time to focus on why I'm here.

I'd been given the basic facts about Rosario Reid by the Director.

"She's forty-eight years old. She had Dexter when she was twenty-
six, a year after she married the congressman. They've known each

other since high school but waited until a few years after they finished college to marry.

"Her great-grandfather came to the U.S. from Mexico, and built a small cattle empire back when that was a difficult thing for a Mexican in Texas to do. He seems to have passed his gumption along to his progeny—Mrs. Reid is one tough cookie. She's a Harvard-trained lawyer and she has a taste for the jugular. While Mr. Reid was building up a head of political steam, Mrs. Reid was busy championing the underdog. She won a number of high-profile cases, none of which I have the details on, all of which basically stuck it to various corporate bullies. When Mr. Reid decided to run for Congress, she rolled up her tents as a lawyer and managed his campaign." The Director had shaken his head in admiration. "People in Washington who know better are afraid of crossing her, Smoky. She's one of the nicest women I've met, but she can be ruthless if you mess with her husband."

I find all of this intriguing, even admirable, but high-profile people can become mythological fast if you let them. I want to get a sense of Rosario Reid for myself, because understanding the mother will help me understand the child. I need to figure out if and how much she's going to lie to me, and if she does lie, for what reasons. Love for her child? Political expedience? Just because?

MRS. REID NODS TO ME as I close my door. She knocks on the partition window for the driver to go and pushes a button that I surmise turns off the intercom. The car starts driving and we take a moment to appraise each other.

Rosario Reid is undeniably attractive. She has the classic lines of an intelligent Latin beauty; sophisticated, yet sensuous. As a woman, I can tell she's taken measures to tone this beauty down. Her hair is short and all business, and she's allowed strands of gray to remain untouched. There's no mascara thickening her lashes. Her son got his full lips from her, but she's used liner to make less of the cupid's bow. She's wearing a simple white blouse, a navy jacket, and matching navy slacks, all tailored to perfection but sexually muted.

These superficial things highlight her political savvy and tell me a lot about her loyalty to her husband. Rosario is doing the opposite of what most women do. She's playing down her native sensuality, leavening her beauty with understated professionalism. Tweed, not silk.

Why? So that she remains palatable to the congressman's female constituency. Powerful women can be attractive, but never sensuous or sexy. I don't know why this is so, but it is, even for me. I trust a woman in a position of power who looks like Rosario more than I would one who looks like a Victoria's Secret model.

Go figure.

She's strong too. She's keeping herself composed, but the intensity of her grief is obvious when I look into her eyes. She won't weep in public. Grief is private to this woman, another thing we share in addition to our dead children.

She breaks the silence first. "Thank you for coming, Agent Barrett." Her voice is measured, quiet, neither low nor high. "I know this is unusual. I've made a point, over the years, of not using my family's political position for personal favors." She shrugs, and her grief gives it a terrible elegance. "My child is dead. I made an exception."

"I'd do the same in your position, Mrs. Reid. I'm very sorry for your loss. I know that's a clichéd thing to say and I know it's inadequate under the circumstances, but I am sorry. Dexter—" I stop, frown. "I'm not familiar with the etiquette here, ma'am. Should I say 'him' or 'her'? Should I use Dexter or Lisa?"

"Lisa spent her life wanting to become a woman. The least we can do is treat her like one now that she's dead."

"Yes, ma'am."

"Let's do away with the titles in private, shall we, Smoky? We're just two mothers of dead children here. No men around with their peacock worries or chest-puffing." She pauses, fixes me with a fierce gaze. "We need to put our heads together and do some dirty work, and that requires first names and no pleasantries, don't you agree?"

We women, we're the ones who bury the children, the ones who drag the hems of our dresses through the cemetery dirt, that's what she's saying.

"Okay, Rosario."

"Good." I see her eyes appraising my scars. "I read about what you went through. In the papers and so on. I've been an admirer of yours for years."

Her gaze remains level as she says these words to me. Her eyes don't flinch at the scars on my face, not even a little. If she's at all un-comfortable, she hides it better than the Director did.

I've inclined my head to Rosario in acknowledgment.

"Thank you, but there's nothing all that admirable about being the one who wasn't killed."

She frowns. "That's very uncharitable. You went on. You contin-ued to do the job that put you in harm's way. You continue to do that job well. You continue to live in the house where it happened—which I understand, by the way. I'm sure many don't, but I do." She smiles a sad smile. "Your home is your tree, the place where your roots are buried. It's where your daughter was born, and that memory is more powerful than all the painful ones, yes?"

"That's right," I reply, quiet.

I find myself taken by this woman. I like her. She is honest. Her in-sightfulness speaks to her character. This is someone who under-stands: family is home, family is the roof against the world. Love may be the glue, but the string of moments shared, that's the soul of things.

We're driving at a leisurely pace, a big circle with the morgue at its center. My eyes are drawn to the turning leaves again; it's as if the trees are on fire.

"Like you," Rosario says, continuing to look out the window, "I married the man I kissed in high school. Have you seen pictures of my Dillon?"

"Yes. He's handsome."

"He was then too. And so young. He was my first love." She gives me a sideways glance, a small grin. It makes her seem eighteen for a moment, a brief, bright flash. "My first everything."

I smile back. "Matt was for me too."

"We're a dying breed, Smoky. Women who marry their high school sweethearts, who can count their lovers on just a few fingers. Do you think we're better off, or worse?"

I shrug. "I think happiness is the most personal thing there is. I didn't marry Matt to make a statement about chastity or anything. I married him because I loved him."

Something about what I just said shakes that composure, a little. Her eyes get wet, though tears don't fall.

"What an excellent way to put it. Yes. Happiness *is* a personal thing. That was certainly true for my daughter." She turns in the car seat so that she is facing me. "Did you know that it's more dangerous to be a transgendered person than any other discriminated minority? You're more likely to be a victim of a violent hate crime than a gay or a Muslim, a Jew or an African-American."

"Yes, I did know."

"And they are aware of this, Smoky. The boys and men who become women, the girls and women who become men—they know they're going to be shunned and reviled, maybe beaten, maybe even killed. Still, they do it. Do you know why?" Her hands shake and she grips them in her lap. "They do it because there's no other way for them to be happy."

"Tell me about Lisa," I prod her.

Because that's what she really wants to do. That's why I'm here. She wants to make me see Lisa, to care for her. She wants me to understand what's been lost, and to feel it.

She closes her eyes for a moment. When she opens them, I can see the love. This is a strong woman, and she'd loved her child with all of that strength.

"I'll use the name Dexter first, because that's how he started. Dexter was a kind, beautiful boy. I know all parents think their children walk on water, but Dexter really did not have a mean bone in his body. He was small and slight, but never weak. Gentle, but not naive. You understand?"

"Yes."

"I suppose the stereotype would have him as a momma's boy, and that was true to a degree, but he didn't hide behind my skirts. He spent his time like any boy—outside, in the sun, getting into various types of trouble. He played in Little League, started learning the guitar when he was ten, got into a fight or two with bullies. No reason to think or assume he was going to do anything other than grow up to be a wonderful man. I rarely had to use his first, middle, and last name at the same time."

She assumes I know what she means, and she's right. It's universal mother-speak. Every child knows, when Mom uses your first and last name together, you're in trouble. First, *middle*, and last? That particular triumvirate is reserved for the worst offenses, the greatest angers. Duck, cover, and hold.

She looks at me. "How old was your daughter when she died?"

"Ten."

"That's a great age. Before they start keeping secrets from you." She sighs, but it's more wistful than sad. "I thought I knew Dexter inside and out, but of course, no mother really knows her son once they hit puberty. They begin to get distant. Horrified by the idea that Mother might know they masturbate about women—Mother is a woman after all. I was prepared for that, it's the way of things, but Dexter's secrets were different than my assumptions."

"How did it come about? Realizing he had a problem?" I stop myself. "Sorry—is it wrong to call it a 'problem'?"

"That depends. To those who oppose the whole concept of a transgendered person, it's the change that's the problem. To the transgendered, the problem is that their body doesn't match their interior sexual identity. Either way, I suppose 'problem' is accurate enough. To answer your question, Dexter probably felt ill at ease as a boy for a very long time. He first started . . . experimenting when he was fourteen."

"Experimenting how?"

Those hands, shaking again, finding each other in her lap. She doesn't speak for a moment, and I see the struggle.

"I'm sorry," she says, "it's just . . . Dexter's personality, the things I loved so much about him, were so evident in the *way* he handled his first forays into exploring his gender identity. It was bras and panties, you see."

"Wearing them?"

"Yes. I found them one afternoon in the bottom of his underwear drawer, buried and hidden. My first assumption was that they were mine, but they weren't, which is what I mean about his personality. You see, we gave Dexter an allowance, and he also did odd jobs in the neighborhood. Mowing lawns and so on. He took his own money and bought his own underthings. Do you understand? He was fourteen, he was conflicted about what was happening, I know from later conversations that he felt guilty, dirty—but he simply didn't feel it would be right to steal my things. He felt the only honorable thing to do was to take his money, walk into a Kmart or some such and buy them himself. He was very embarrassed about it, he told me that later, but he was stubborn with himself when it came to right and wrong."

I can see it in my mind. A young, slight boy, buying a pair of panties and bra, cheeks burning as he did it. Doing it because it just *wasn't right* to steal from his mother.

I picture myself at fourteen. Would I have been that straight arrow, if I'd been him? Embarrassment before dishonor?

Uh-uh. Hell, no. Mom would have lost a set of underwear.

"I understand," I tell Rosario. "What happened then?"

She grimaces. "Oh God. Three terrible years, that's what happened. You have to understand, I come from a Mexican-American family. Catholic, very conservative. On the other side of that, I was a lawyer, used to rules and structure—and keeping secrets. The first thing I did was keep this between Dexter and me."

"Understandable."

"Yes. It took me some time to pry it out of him, and to be fair, it was pretty formless for Dexter. He was confused, still sorting through what was happening himself. He told me that he felt 'weird' sometimes, like when he looked in the mirror, he wanted to see a female body, not a male. I was scandalized. I confiscated the underwear and the bra and sent him packing to a psychologist."

"But things continued to change."

"The psychologist said that Dexter had gender dysphoria, also known as gender identity disorder. Fancy words meaning that Dexter strongly identified with the opposite sex."

"I'm familiar with the subject. It can range from a light obsession to a certainty the individual is the opposite sex trapped in the wrong body."

"That's right. He 'treated' Dexter. He wanted to use psychotropics as a part of his therapy, but I forbade it. Dexter was bright, considerate, alert, kind, he was a straight-A student who'd never been in trouble with the law—why in the world would I let him be drugged?" She waves a hand. "It was all useless. Treatment boiled down to assigning the label and working with him to 'behave against the compulsion.' It changed nothing."

"When did he decide to go the route of sexual reassignment?"

"Oh, he told me about it when he was nineteen. But I imagine he'd decided before that. He was simply trying to figure out how to do it so that it would hurt his father and I the least. Not that we made it easy, regardless." She shakes her head. "Dillon went ballistic. We'd kept this from him for so many years, and he was enjoying the political game so much. It blindsided him in the worst way."

"How did Dexter handle that?"

She smiles. "He was calm. Calm and ordered, with that quiet certainty." She shrugs. "He'd decided and that was that. His father's strength."

Yours too, I think to myself.

"Go on."

"He told us that he understood this was going to be a problem for us, particularly for his father, and that his solution was that we publicly disown him. He said that it was important to him that his decision impact us as little as possible. Can you imagine?" Her voice is full of grief and amazement. "I remember, he said: 'Dad, what you do is valuable. You help a lot of people. I don't want you to have to give that up for me. But I'm not going to give this up for you either. This is the best compromise.' I think that's what got through to Dillon. That his son was willing to be publicly castigated so that his father could continue doing what he loved. I'm not saying it was smooth sailing, but . . ."

"Dexter got through."

"Yes." She looks at me, and all I see now is a deep, deep pain tinged with regret, maybe a little bit of self-loathing. "The details aren't important. What's important is that like the good political family we'd become, we did exactly what Dexter proposed. We set up a trust, and he moved out. When he began to actually live as a woman—do you know about that part of the process?"

"Part of the procedure for getting approval for the surgery is living for a year as the sex you are becoming—something like that?"

"Exactly like that. You don't get to have any surgical alterations done until you've lived as a woman or a man for a full year. For Dexter that meant attending work dressed as a woman, going out in public, etc. It's designed to ensure that you're certain."

"Makes sense."

"I think so. So did Dexter, for that matter. Anyway, when that began, we gave our wonderfully perfectly worded statement. About how we still loved our son but couldn't agree with his choices. It was a masterpiece of deception." She pauses, searching for words. "You're not from the South, Smoky, so I don't think you can truly understand how deep the differences run. Don't misunderstand, there are plenty of liberal intellectuals in Texas, but I would not put them as a majority."

"Sure."

She shakes her head. "No. You have an idea of it, perhaps a stereotype. There's no way you can appreciate the truth of it unless you grew up there. You probably imagine tobacco-chewing rednecks with gun racks in their trucks. We have those, it's true, but the more complex picture is of a well-educated, very intelligent, likeable individual who preaches that homosexuality is an abomination without blinking. That person will have a friend, a best friend, someone he grew up with, who thinks gays should have more rights. The two can still be friends across this divide—still be good friends." She lifts an eyebrow. "But if the liberal friend was *actually* gay? Oh no. And transsexuals? Oh my. Freaks of nature, perhaps to both of the friends in that example. We've made great strides in the South, and I love the place. It's my home. But it's a creature of habit, resistant to great changes."

"I get the picture."

"Meanwhile," Rosario continues, "as you know, Dexter still came for Christmas, but on the sly." She pauses. "Horrible, don't you think? Giving up our child for professional ambition?"

I think about this. This woman deserves a real answer, not something trite and clever.

"I think," I say, cautious, "that anything else would have hurt Dexter. He felt that he had to do what he was doing, but he was worried about how it would affect your husband's career. I mean, he said 'publicly disown.' Did he ever seem to expect that either of you would actually disown him?"

She's startled by this concept. "No. No, I don't think so."

"So he was secure in being loved by you. I'm not saying it excuses everything, but it's certainly not nothing, Rosario."

Grief is sometimes simple, but often complex. It encompasses self-doubts, what-ifs, if-onlys. It resembles regret, but is more powerful than that. It can disappear in an instant or settle in till death. I see versions of all these things run across Rosario's features, and I'm happy for it, because it means I've given her a truth. Lies can hurt, but nothing moves us like truth.

It takes her a moment to get herself under control. Still no tears.

"So, Dexter got through that year, and that year was the end of Dexter. A son died, a daughter was reborn. Such a beautiful daughter too. Lisa blossomed, both inside and out. She'd always been a happy child, but now she seemed to glow. She was . . . content. Content-ment is hard to come by, Smoky."

I notice how easily she's slipped into using "Lisa," "she," and "her." Dexter became Lisa, not just to himself, but to his mother.

"How did the congressman adjust?"

"He was never really comfortable with it. But I don't want to paint a picture of him as a stereotypical intolerant, Smoky. Dillon loved Dexter and he was trying very, very hard to love Lisa. He considered any difficulty in doing so to be his failing, not Lisa's."

"I'm sure Lisa saw that too."

Rosario nods and smiles. "She did. She was—happy. The hor-mones took very well, and she was wise with her breast augmentation, fitting it to her frame, not going too big or too small. She took to makeup like a fish to water, walked like a woman without any real ef-fort, had a good sense of style. Even her voice lessons, which can be the most difficult for some, went easy for her."

Men have lower voices because their vocal cords elongate during puberty. This elongation is not reversible, requiring that men who transition to women learn how to pitch their voices higher.

"Was she planning on . . . going all the way with it?"

Not all transsexuals elect to change their genitalia.

"She hadn't decided."

"Why was Lisa in Texas?" I ask. "I understand she lived here, in Virginia. Was she visiting you?"

"She came down for her grandmother's funeral. This was Dillon's mother."

"Did you and the congressman attend the funeral?"

"Yes. It was small and private. We're not in the middle of a cam-paign right now, so there was no media. We held the service and Lisa left the next day to go back home. She was supposed to be working tomorrow."

"What did she do?"

"She ran her own travel agency. A one-woman show, but she did fine. She had a very profitable niche, coming up with vacations designed for the gay, lesbian, and transgendered community."

"Are you aware of any enemies she had? Anyone she might have mentioned bothering her?"

"No." Emphatic. "I'm not brushing off the question or operating in denial, Smoky. It's the first thing I considered, and nothing came to mind."

But you might be surprised, I think.

All those late night secrets, the big and the small, the ones that come knocking when the moon goes behind a cloud—children have them too, and the parents are usually the last to know.

"What about you or the congressman? I realize you both have enemies, all high-profile people do, but is there anything specific, anything recent or in the recent past that stands out?"

"I wish I could say so. Dillon gets the occasional crazy letter, and I read them all before passing them on to the Secret Service. The last one like that came in six or seven months ago. Some kook threatened to kill Dillon with his mind or some nonsense. We're not straddling any contentious issues on the moral front at the moment. Rarely are, truth be told. Avoiding that type of confrontation is how Dillon's managed to hold a Democratic seat in Texas."

I search for more to ask her, but can't think of anything at the moment.

I choose my next words with care. "Rosario, I want you to know that I'm going to do everything I can to find the person responsible for this. I can't promise I'll catch them—I learned not to make promises like that a long time ago—but my team and I are very, very good. We are going to need access in order to do our jobs. I'll bow to a certain amount of political decorum, but in the end, I'm not working for you or for your husband, I'm working for Lisa."

"Lisa is all that matters."

"I'm not trying to be insensitive. I just want to ensure I make it clear what my priorities are."

"Your priorities are reassuring." She reaches into her jacket pocket and hands me a slip of paper. "All of my numbers. Contact me any time of the day or night for the smallest thing."

I take the paper from her. She knocks on the partition again, a signal to return us to the morgue. The sun is setting and the blood in the sky mingles with the fire-trees of fall.

Winter is coming. Winter here is still, like death.

"Can I ask you a question, Smoky?" Rosario says.

"You can ask me anything you want."

She looks at me, and I see, finally, the tears. Not a sobbing grief, no hysteria here, just a stream from the corner of each eye, evidence of the deepest ache.

"Do you ever get over it?"

Truth, truth, nothing but truth, that's what this woman deserves. I give it to her.

"Not ever."

3

Jones tells me. "They should arrive in a few hours."

We're outside the autopsy room, watching through a pane of glass as the medical examiner disassembles the body of Lisa Reid in order to help us catch her killer. It's the final outrage. There's no soul to an autopsy, just the reduction of a human being to their lowest common denominator: meat.

It's now after seven o'clock and I am beginning to feel the disconnection from home.

"Pretty weird to be here," I remark.

"Yeah," AD Jones replies. He's silent for a moment. "My second wife and I actually talked about moving out here once."

"Really?"

"You saw those trees? They have four real seasons here. White Christmas, things coming to life in the spring." He shrugs. "I was into it. Then the marriage went south and I forgot about it."

He goes quiet again. This is the story of our relationship. He doles out personal information at unexpected times in little dollops. They're often bittersweet, as now. He'd loved a woman and they'd talked about moving someplace where they could rake fallen leaves and build snowmen. Now he is here because of a corpse. Dreams evolve, not always for the better.

"Dr. Johnston is a strange one," I mutter, changing the subject.

"Yeah."

Dr. Johnston, the ME, is in his mid-forties and he is *huge*. Not fat—muscular. He's got biceps it would take both of my hands to fit around. His legs are so big he probably has to get his pants tailored. His hair is bleach blond and shaved close to his head. His face is square jawed and brutal looking, with a big nose that's bent from past breaks and a vein that throbs away in his forehead like a living metronome, mesmerizing. He could be a professional bodybuilder or a mob knee-breaker.

He's all business with Lisa, putting those muscular arms to good use as he cuts through her rib cage. Even through the window, the sound is unsettling, like someone stepping on a series of Styrofoam cups. I can't hear what he's saying, but his lips are moving as he dictates his findings into the microphone that hangs above the table.

"How did it go with Mrs. Reid?" AD Jones asks me.

"Fine. Terrible."

I fill him in.

"You were right. About why she asked for you."

"Yep."

Johnston is leaning forward to peer into Lisa. Looking *inside* her. I've seen much worse, but for some reason this makes me queasy.

"What's your take on this so far, Smoky?"

I know what he's asking me, what he wants. He wants me to do what I'm best at. To exercise my gift.

I do what I do because I have an ability to understand the men I hunt. It's not immediate, and it's not clairvoyant, but give me enough data and a picture *will* form. It will have three dimensions. It will have emotions and thought processes. Above all, it will have *hungers*. Hungers I can almost taste inside my own mouth, dark flavors so tangible I can almost swallow them.

I have worked with talented men, AD Jones among them, who helped me to hone this gift. I came to understand that the crux of it is my ability to do the most unnatural thing; I look closer when normal people would turn away.

It's like diving into oil; you can't see through the murk while immersed, but you can feel its slickness covering you. Sometimes, I dive too deep. Sometimes, this scars me on the inside, and gives me secrets all my own.

Five years ago I was hunting a man who murdered only young, beautiful brunette women. None of them were over twenty-five, and all of them were striking. Even in death, and even to me, as a woman, they were lush and beautiful. Made to cloud men's minds.

The man killing them felt the same way. He raped them and then he killed them with his fists. He beat them to death slowly, methodically with focused dedication. It's an intimate, personal way to kill another human being.

I stood over one of those victims and I *looked*. I looked and I saw *him*. The killer. I kept looking until I *felt* him. He was a man in a frenzy, an overwhelming mix of sexual desire and anger. In the end, I realized, he wanted his sex with them to shake the moon loose from the sky.

I'd stood up, dazed, and had found to my horror that I was a little bit wet between the legs. I had dived too deeply, felt what he felt too strongly.

I found the nearest bathroom and puked my guts out.

Bad as that was, it helped. I knew we were looking for a man who was organized and smart, but who couldn't control himself if the right trigger occurred.

We caught our man, we had DNA, but because of my deep dive, we got a confession as well. Stacy Hobbs was a new agent in the LA office, and she was exactly what I needed. Twenty-four, brunette, a distraction to all the men in a thousand-foot radius.

I had her dress as the women he killed had dressed, had her make herself up. I told her how to stand in the corner, how to stare at him, how to cock her hip and smile seductively. I told her she wasn't to say a word.

His name was Jasper St. James, and he couldn't take his eyes off her. I watched his fists clench. Watched as his mouth fell open, just a little. His lips actually plumped up before my eyes, like the lips of a vampire. He began to sweat and he muttered under his breath.

"Bitch. Bitch." Over and over.

In prior interviews, he'd been cool as a cucumber.

I crossed my legs, a signal to Stacy. She did what I'd told her to do: she looked right into Jasper's eyes and licked her lips, long and slow, smacking and obscene and wet-sounding. Then she turned, abrupt, and left without a word.

Jasper actually screamed with frustration when that happened. It was just a single screech, a high-pitched keen, as if someone had squeezed his balls with a pair of pliers. I leaned forward over the interrogation table.

"It must have felt so so so so so so good," I said, pitching my voice low and breathy, "to watch them realize they were going to die."

I remember his look. Horror and fascination and hope. Could almost hear his thoughts.

Could she actually understand? Was it possible?

It was, God help me, though not in the way he thought. I felt it, I understood it, but in the end, my understanding was synthetic. I was unfaithful; only Jasper's love was pure.

He blabbered and blathered and sweated and shook and he talked. He told me his secrets. He was happy to share, grateful to finally have an audience. I listened and nodded and pretended empathy.

It occurred to me that Jasper had probably used false empathy to lure those women. Did this make him my victim? Our aims weren't that much different. He wanted to destroy those women; I wanted to destroy him. The difference between us is that he deserved it.

None of these thoughts had shown on my face. I'd given him my full attention. At one point, I even held his hand when he cried. Poor Jasper, I had whispered. Poor, poor Jasper.

I went home that night and soaked in the tub till the water turned cold.

AD Jones is asking me to dive into that oil, to begin the process, to start feeling the man who did this.

"I don't have enough data yet," I say. "No emotional component. The act itself is incredible. Audacious. That has meaning to him. It's either a message or it heightens the excitement, or both."

"What kind of message?"

It pops into my head from nowhere, a shallow dive. "I'm perfect. Or the reason for what I'm doing is perfect."

AD Jones frowns. "How's that?"

"It's like . . . murder in a locked room. He killed her midair. He was trapped and surrounded by witnesses. I think he killed her early in the flight too, so he could sit there next to the body and feel that excitement. It would have been tantalizing. Would someone notice? If they did, there was no way out. Only someone who was perfect could do this, could have the courage, could master that fear. He felt protected, either by his own ability, or because what he was doing was right."

"What else?"

"He's very smart, very organized, capable of long-range, meticulous planning. He'll be older, but not too old. Late forties."

"Why?"

"He's too confident to be young, too practiced." I sigh. "We'll interview the other passengers, but I can almost guarantee any description we get will be inaccurate."

"You think he used a disguise?"

"Yes, but it will have been subtle. Hair color, tinted contacts, things like that. The greatest difference will be personality. He'll have adopted a characteristic that will stand out in the witnesses' memories, something that caught their eye and drowned out other observations."

"What makes you sure about this?"

"Anything less wouldn't be perfect. Only perfection would do."

JOHNSTON BEGAN TO PEEL LISA'S face down from her skull so he could open her head and get to her brain. I decide this is a good time to do something else. I place a call to Bonnie. It's almost eight-thirty here, which means it's dinnertime in California. She answers the cell phone I'd gotten for her on the first ring.

"Hi, Smoky!"

"Hi, sweetheart. How are you?"

"I'm fine. Elaina made macaroni and cheese."

Elaina Washington is the wife of Alan, a member of my team. She's one of my favorite people, a Latin woman who was born to provide love and support to those in her life. Not in some sugar-sweet, overly sentimental way; Elaina can love you as much by chastising you when you need it as by hugging you. She was the first to come visit me in the hospital after Sands's attack. She held me in her arms and got me to cry, and I'll always love her for that.

Elaina watches Bonnie when work situations like this one pop up. She also homeschools my adopted daughter.

"That's great, babe."

"Alan left. Does that mean you're going to be away longer?"

"It looks like it. I'm sorry."

"You need to stop doing that, Momma-Smoky."

Bonnie has been aged well before her time, both by circumstance and her own gifts. Her mother's murder and what came after scarred her inside, gave her a terrible emotional maturity. Her gifts lie in her art—she is a painter—and in the depth of her insight. But "Momma-Smoky," the title she bestows on me when she tries to comfort me, or sometimes for no reason at all, never fails to make me smile inside. It's evidence of a younger heart, the voice of a child.

"Doing what, babe?"

"Apologizing for something you can't control anyway. People don't get murdered on a schedule, you catch people who murder, so your life isn't on a schedule. I'm fine with that."

"Thanks, but some Momma-things just don't bow down to logic. I'm still sorry for being away."

I hear the sound of AD Jones's shoes against the tile and turn to see him looking at me. He nods his head toward the observation window.

"I have to go, sweetheart. I'll call you tomorrow, okay?"

"Smoky?"

"Yes?"

"Is Aunt Callie *really* getting married?"

I grin.

"She really is. Good night, honey."

"Night. I love you."

"I love you back."

DR. JOHNSTON POINTS TO A pan containing Lisa Reid's heart.

"Her heart was punctured. The hole was small, on the right side of her rib cage." He points this out to us. As he said, the hole isn't very big, but the bruise it created is the size of both of my hands put together. There are vertical slits above and below the hole. I'd missed the wound earlier in my shock at finding out Lisa was Dexter.

"That makes sense," AD Jones says. "Lisa had a window seat and her killer was seated on her right."

"What could do that?" I ask.

"Anything long, cylindrical, and sharp. The killer would need strength, determination, and some basic knowledge of anatomy." He makes a fist and pumps it once by way of demonstration. "One clean thrust, through the lung, up into the heart, and it's done."

"She'd have to be drugged for him to do that on a plane," I murmur.

Johnston nods his massive head in agreement. "Yes. Death would be very quick, but it would be very painful too. It would have been to his benefit to anesthetize her in some way."

I consider this. "He would have wanted something he could administer orally," I say. "Nothing that would have required a hypodermic, nothing that would induce seizures. Any theories?"

"GHB, ketamine, or Rohypnol would all work, but they all pose problems. All can bring on vomiting. Ketamine can induce convulsions." He crosses his gi-normous arms. "No, if I were him, I would have gone old school. Chloral hydrate."

"Mickey Finns," AD Jones opines.

"It works best with alcohol, and I smelled some in her stomach contents. It's fast, and he could have given her an overdose amount to induce unconsciousness quickly."

"True," I say. "He wouldn't have been worried about her dying of an overdose. You'll check for all of this on tox?"

"Yes. I'll rush it through. I should have it tomorrow afternoon, along with my findings."

Something else occurs to me. "I wonder how the hell he got whatever he stuck her with onto the plane?"

Dr. Johnston shrugs. "Not my department, sorry."

I give him my cell phone number. "Call me when the findings are ready and I'll send someone to come get them. Make a single copy for yourself and put it in a safe place." I look him in the eye. "This is a federal case for three reasons, Dr. Johnston. One, because it happened while flying the friendly skies. Two, because it involves a congressman and could be a precursor to an attack on Dillon Reid himself. Three, because it could be a hate crime. But the cloak-and-dagger is a courtesy to the Reids, not a cover-up. I want you to know that. My priority is catching whoever did this."

His smile is a little tired. "I appreciate the candor, Agent Barrett, but don't worry. I'm not conspiracy-minded. I've dealt with three other politically connected deaths, including one that involved a powerful man and a male prostitute. I'm familiar with the territory."

It occurs to me that Dr. Johnston is pretty damn competent. I shouldn't be surprised; most of those I've met who deal with the dead take what they do very seriously.

"I appreciate that." I look down at Lisa Reid, lying on what we still call a slab, though it's been made of steel for a very long time. "Anything else probative?"

"Oh yes. Something very, very unusual. I was just getting to that." He grabs another pan and holds it out. "I found this inserted into her body. He widened the wound on her right side. You noticed the cuts?"

"Yes."

"He was smart; he cut her postmortem, after the blood flow had stopped. Then he stuck this inside her."

I peer into the pan and see a medium-sized, silver cross.

"Where are your gloves?" I ask.

He nods to a box of latex gloves on a nearby counter. I grab a pair and slip them on. I reach into the pan and pick up the cross.

"It's heavy," I say. "Dense. Probably a silver alloy."

The cross is a humble one, simple. It's approximately two inches tall and one inch wide. I turn it over in my hand and squint. There appears to be an engraving on the back, but it's far too small to read with the naked eye.

"Do you have a magnifying glass?"

Johnston finds one and hands it to me. I place it over the cross. I see a symbol, very small, very simple: a skull and crossbones, patterned after the universal sign for poison. It's been engraved into the back of the head of the cross. Along the crosspiece are some numbers.

"Number one forty-three," I say out loud.

"What the fuck does that mean?" AD Jones asks.

"I don't know." I place the cross back in the pan. "Let's make sure we withhold this particular detail, Doctor, if anything does end up getting to the media."

"Of course."

"Anything else?"

He shakes his head. "Not at the moment."

AD Jones glances at his watch, points a finger at me. "Then let's head to the airport. Your team should be arriving shortly and I need to get back to California."

We say our good-byes to Dr. Johnston and head down the hall toward the front of the building. Our shoes click-clack on the linoleum, eerie in the context of our surrounds.

"What's your game plan?" AD Jones asks.

"The basics. Forensics on the plane where Lisa was killed, interviews of the passengers, start working up a profile. From there . . ." I pause. "From there we need to get on to identifying other potential targets as quickly as possible."

I don't state the obvious and most worrisome thing:

A death's-head and "#143"—there's only one thing a killer would count.

Leading, of course, to the next concern: how high will the counting go?

4

IT'S PAST ELEVEN O'CLOCK AT NIGHT, AND IT'S FREAKING *cold.* I hate the cold.

The wind isn't fierce, but it is steady and it blows across the tarmac in short gusts that have numbed my cheeks.

The moon is huge and bloated in a sky devoid of clouds. It has that look to it, the look that says it's the same moon that shone on the cavemen: it was here before me, it'll be here long after I'm gone.

It took us about an hour to make our way to this private airport near Washington, DC. It's small and lonely, just a single hangar and a landing strip. My team and I will make our way from here to Dulles International Airport, where the plane Lisa died on awaits.

I hug myself as we watch the private jet taxi on the runway. It's a white Learjet and I've been on it many times.

AD Jones seems unmoved by the temperature. He's smoking, a habit I gave up but still miss, particularly when I see someone smoking my old brand, as he does. I had been loyal to my Marlboros and in return they had always been there for me. They gave me comfort, I gave them years off my life. It was an equitable arrangement until it wasn't.

"Listen, Smoky, I need to talk to you about something." He sucks in smoke, holds it, blows out a cloud. I watch and wait and envy. "I want you to keep me in the loop. Daily. This is a different playing field than you're used to. Rathbun is decent enough for a Director, but in the end, he'll cover himself and feed you to the lions if it will help him." His gaze is penetrating. "Don't be fooled. You're expendable to him."

"I can take care of myself, sir."

"I know. Keep your eyes open anyway."

"Aye, aye." I click my heels and give him an exaggerated salute.

He's unamused. "This isn't a joke, Smoky. People at the DC level make a career out of hanging each other out to dry. You're a gifted agent, and God knows you're tough enough, but you're inexperienced on that playing field."

"Okay, okay. I understand."

"The area where he can really help you out is with the media. Do exactly what he says—don't answer any of their questions and refer them all to the Director. You've dealt with the media before, I know, but if this leaks it will be huge. The FBI has people that live for that shit, let them handle it."

"Scout's honor."

"Keep a gag on Callie."

"I can control her."

The look he gives me is doubtful. He flicks his cigarette into the night.

"Plane's done taxiing. Let's go."

"**GOOD GOD, HONEY-LOVE, IT'S TOO** cold here," Callie complains the moment her high-heeled feet hit the tarmac. "Why are we here and not back in a place with civilized weather planning for my upcoming wedding?"

I smile, as always. I'm never immune to Callie. I don't think many people are.

Callie is a tall, skinny, leggy redhead, with model looks that only seem to deepen with age. She just turned forty, and if anything, she's more attractive now than she was five years ago.

Callie is aware of her beauty, and she's not above using it to her advantage, but appearance is unimportant to her in the larger scheme of life; it's her mind she's honed the sharpest. She holds a master's degree in forensics with a minor in criminology and has been hunting killers with me for the last decade-plus.

Callie has a sense of humor that not everyone appreciates or understands. Her use of "honey-love," for example, a favored phrase, is a total affectation. It comes from the South; Callie comes from Connecticut. I imagine she adopted it to poke fun at herself and annoy others, emphasis on the latter. Local legend says that she has a reprimand on file for calling the Director of the FBI, Mr. Rathbun himself, honey-love. It wouldn't surprise me in the slightest.

Callie's humor isn't mean-spirited. It simply says: *If you take yourself too seriously, you'll have a hard time around me, so lighten up—*honey-love.

Then there is the other side of Callie, a darker part, the side the criminals get. She is ruthless in her search for truth, because truth is everything to her. If I were to commit a criminal act, Callie, who loves me, would hunt me. She might grieve as she did it, but she'd take me down. To do otherwise would be to deny her basic self and that's one thing Callie is not about.

She's set to marry Samuel "Sam" Brady, the head of the LA FBI SWAT. It's a move that's caught everyone by surprise. Callie has been chasing men for years and enjoying them to their fullest for the pleasure they could give her, a kind of female Lothario. Emotional longevity has never been a part of the picture.

Callie is intensely private about the serious goings-on inside her, but I know some of her secrets. Like her current addiction to Vicodin, the legacy of a spinal injury she got two years ago that nearly crippled her. Like the fact that she hadn't allowed herself to be close to a man for so long because she got pregnant when she was fifteen and was forced to give up her child. She's since reconciled with her long-lost daughter, and maybe that's a part of this sea change inside her. I don't know. I only have glimpses of her secret self, small treasures she's entrusted me with over the years.

Callie's greatest gifts to me have been her unswerving demand that we enjoy the moment, the *now* of life, and the invulnerable constancy of her friendship. I can count on her. It was Callie who found me in the aftermath of Joseph Sands, Callie who took my gun away and pulled me to her without a second thought, Callie who held me as I shrieked and screamed and ruined her perfect suit with my blood and tears and vomit.

"Political hoo-hah," I say in response to her questions. "And I don't like the cold either."

"It's not so bad," a low voice rumbles. "Least there's no snow. I hate snow."

Alan Washington is the oldest member of my team and the most seasoned. He didn't go straight into the FBI, but spent ten years working homicide as a member of the LAPD.

Alan is African-American. He's a big man, as in the startling "big" of a linebacker or a great oak, the kind of man who might make you cross to the other side of the street if you saw him coming your way late at night. His form hides the truth: Alan is a deep thinker with a big heart and a meticulous nature. He can sift through details for days, patient, never getting exasperated, never looking for shortcuts, sticking with it until he's broken a complexity down into its component parts. He's also the most skilled interrogator I know. I've watched him reduce the hardest of the hard to quivering, blubbering messes.

The best testaments to the soul of Alan are that he's married to Elaina and that he loves her so obviously, so unashamedly, with a mix of wonder and pride. I was loved that way by Matt; it's nice, and it speaks to the character of the man who does it.

Alan smiles at me and tips a nonexistent hat.

"Thank God for small favors," I reply, smiling in return.

The next voice I hear is sour with disapproval.

"Why are we here?"

This question comes from the last member of my team. The tone of it—blunt, unfriendly, impatient—irritates me, as always.

James Giron is brilliant, but he is about as unlikeable as a human being can be. We sometimes refer to him as Damien, after the son of Satan from *The Omen*. He has no social veneer, no interest in softening the blow, no visible regard for the feelings of others. He takes the concept of thoughtlessness to new heights.

James is a book of blank pages. I don't know if he even has a personal life. I've never heard him talk about a song or movie he enjoyed. I don't know what TV programs he watches, if any. I'm not aware of any personal relationships he's had. James doesn't bring his soul to work.

What he does bring is his mind. James is a genius in the fullest sense of the word. He graduated high school at fifteen, got a perfect score on his SATs and finished college with a PhD in criminology by the time he was twenty. He joined the FBI at twenty-one, which had been his goal all along.

James had an older sister, Rosa, who was murdered by a serial killer when James was twelve. He decided what his path would be the day they buried her. The fact of this is the only real evidence I have of James's humanity.

In most ways, James and I grate against each other, two positive poles repelling, a zero attractant. There is one exception: he shares the ability I have, to peer into the minds of those who murder for pleasure.

"Because someone's dead and someone with the power to do so has ordered us to deal with it," I answer him.

He frowns. "This is out of our jurisdiction. It's not our job to be here."

I glance at AD Jones. He's glaring at James with a mix of resignation and mild disbelief.

"Stop whining," Callie tells James, "or you're not invited to my wedding."

He sneers. "Is that supposed to be a threat?"

"I can see how you might not consider it to be one, but"—and at this Callie smiles—"your mother would be very disappointed. We had a wonderful talk on the phone, Damien, and she's looking forward to meeting the people you work with."

James scowls at her. "Don't call me that."

I hide a smile and allow myself some secret satisfaction at Callie's end run around James. I've never met his mother, but I know he visits Rosa's grave with her every year on Rosa's birthday, so in theory they are close.

"You want to brief us here?" Alan asks, cutting through the banter.

"Hold that thought," AD Jones says. He turns to me. "Remember what I said. Keep me in the loop."

"Yes, sir."

One nod and he walks away without another word.

"We have a car waiting over there," I say. "Let's get inside and fire up the heater and then I'll brief you."

It's a big Crown Vic, a little battered but serviceable. Alan takes the driver's position, with me riding shotgun. James and Callie squeeze into the back.

"Heat, please," Callie says, rubbing her arms and giving off an overdramatic shiver.

Alan starts the car and puts the heater on high. The big engine rumbles on idle as the heated air blasts out from the vents like wind from the mouth of a cave.

"How's that?" Alan asks.

"Hmmmm," Callie purrs. "So much better."

Alan gestures to me. "Floor is yours, then."

WHEN I FINISH TALKING, EVERYONE is silent, thinking. James looks out the window in the back. Callie, next to him, taps her front teeth with a red-painted fingernail.

"Pretty theatrical," she says after a moment. "Killing that poor woman mid-flight."

"A little too theatrical," Alan replies.

"Yes," I muse, "but he pulled it off. He killed her on the plane—"

"Her?" Alan snorts.

I frown. "Legally, yes. It says 'female' on her driver's license. What's the problem?"

He reaches his hands up, grips the steering wheel on either side, and squeezes, once. Blows air out of his mouth, a noisy sigh.

"Look," he says, "I don't like transsexuals. I think it's unnatural." He shrugs. "I can't help it. I dealt with a few tranny murders when I worked in the LAPD, and I did my job and I felt for the families—a person is a person—but it doesn't change the truth. They disgust me on some level. Sometimes it slips out."

I gape at my friend, shocked. Absolutely, one hundred percent poleaxed. Am I really hearing this from Alan? Outside of an interrogation room, Alan is the calmest, fairest, most tolerant person I know. At least I've always thought so.

"My, my, my, where have those clay feet been hiding?" Callie asks, echoing my own thoughts.

"He's a homophobe," James says, the venom in his voice surprising me. "Right? You don't like fags, do you, Alan?"

Alan rotates in his seat so he can look at James. "I'm not a fan of seeing guys kiss, but no, I'm not a homophobe. I don't care who you screw. There's a big difference between that and cutting off your breasts or chopping off your cock." He scowls. "This is my 'thing,' okay? I'm not saying it's right or that it makes sense, and frankly, I don't want a bunch of crap about it. Elaina's given me a piece of her mind on the subject already, and it just doesn't seem to change. It won't affect how I do my job."

"Tell us the truth," Callie says, her voice solicitous. "Was it a woman you picked up one time? Lots of tongue-kissing and then you reached down and found sticks and berries?"

Alan groans. "Fuck this. I shouldn't have said anything."

"You're right," I say. "You shouldn't have. If you let that kind of comment slip around the family . . ."

He nods, chastened. "Yeah. I'm sorry."

"Not homophobic, huh?" James says.

I glance at him, surprised. His face is angry. He's not letting this go.

"I already said I wasn't."

"Bullshit."

Alan looks ready to get angry, but sighs instead.

"Fine. Don't take my word for it. Doesn't make it less true."

James stares at Alan. He's scowling and shaking. I have no idea what's going on here.

"Really? Then tell me . . ." He stops, hesitating, breathing deeply, in and out. "Then tell me what you think about this: *I'm* gay."

Silence fills the car. I can hear the heater blowing and the sounds of breathing.

"Oh boy," Callie says. She mimes eating from a bag of popcorn. "Go on, don't stop now, honey-love."

For myself, I'm speechless.

James, gay?

It's not the revelation itself that shocks me. It's the fact that he's revealing anything at all. It's just too personal. It would be as disconcerting if James told me what his favorite flavor of ice cream was.

I am, on some level, surprised at how well he's managed to hide it. We've dealt with gay victims before. He's never let the slightest hint or opinion slip.

Of course, neither had Alan.

"Why are you telling us this now?" Alan asks.

"I don't know!" James snarls. "Stop stalling. Answer the fucking question."

Alan gives James a long once-over. The slightest smile tugs at his lips. "Then I'd say . . . I *still* don't like you."

Callie snorts and begins to giggle. She sounds ridiculous.

Some of the anger drains away from James's face. He scrutinizes Alan, looking for deception.

"And that's all you'd have to say?"

"That's it."

Something happens that rocks me. Alan reaches his arm out over the seat and places a hand on James's shoulder. It's a gentle gesture, full of reassurance. What shocks me though is James's reaction. No twitch or flinch or turning away. I see a hint of something else, a kind of . . . *what?*

Relief, I realize, amazed. It's relief. What Alan thinks matters to him.

"Really, son," Alan says again, his voice as gentle as the gesture.

The moment hangs. James shrugs off the hand. "Fine," he replies. He glares at Callie and me. "I don't want to hear anything more about it, okay?"

I hold my fingers up in the "scout's honor" salute. Callie nods, but slides herself across the seat, putting as much space between her and James as possible.

"What the hell are you doing?" he asks, suspicious.

"Don't worry, honey-love," she says, "I have no problem with you being gay, really I don't. But I'm getting married soon, and, well—they say those gay cooties can be catching. Better safe than sorry."

I manage to keep the smile off my face. James gives her a speculative look before sighing and saying: "You're an idiot."

Again, there's a certain relief there. Callie is treating him the same as ever and this annoyance is comforting to James in the wake of his revelation.

What about me? I wonder. What did he expect from me?

I glance his way, but James is staring out the window again. He seems relaxed.

I realize he wasn't worried about how I'd react. James knew I'd accept him.

This makes me feel good.

"Now that we've gotten the Jerry Springer moment out of the way," Callie says, "can we get back to the business at hand? Let's not forget our priority: planning my wedding."

"What does the business at hand have to do with that?" I ask, bemused.

Callie rolls her eyes at me. "Well, it looks like we have to catch a killer first. So, chop-chop."

I grin at her. She's not actually worried about her wedding. This is Callie's way; she lives to lift the somber, to light the dark.

"Let's head to Dulles," I say. "They're holding the plane for us. We can talk on the way."

Alan gets the car moving and I reflect that this is the thing about life that's so different from death. Life is in motion. It's always *happening*, always going somewhere, forcing its way through the cracks, moment-opportune or not. Alan's unexpected ugliness regarding transsexuals, James's sudden reveal, good or bad, both mean *alive*, and the often uncomfortableness of living is always preferable to the always tidy peacefulness of dead.

5

way to the airport. A local cop who'd been waiting got our car hurried through a security checkpoint and pointed us in the right direction. It's after midnight now, but like all international airports, Dulles lives off the clock. As Alan drives, I can see planes taking off, jumping from a sea of light into the night sky.

The plane Lisa was killed on had been moved to a maintenance hangar. The hangar is large, made of metal and concrete, which means it's cold. The temperature is continuing to drop and I realize I'm really not dressed for this weather.

Lights are on in the hangar, big and bright. The late hour and the stark utility of the place combine with the cold to create a feeling of solitude.

"Guess we're supposed to just drive right in," Alan mutters, and does so.

"Who's that?" Callie asks as we pull up.

We're being met by a blonde woman I've never seen before. She's about my age, and she's wearing a black jacket, black slacks, and a white shirt. Simple, but it fits her too well to be off-the-rack. She's neither tall nor short, about five-five, pretty without being beautiful. Her face, which is a study in blankness, frames intelligent blue eyes.

"Smells like an exec to me," Alan mutters.

She walks right up to me as I get out of the car. "Agent Barrett?"

"Yes? And you are?"

"Rachael Hinson. I work for the Director."

"Okay."

"You have the plane for up to twenty-four hours," she says, skipping any preamble. "No one will be allowed in this hangar until then. You won't be bothered." She points to a rolling cart near us. "Forensic field kits are there, including cameras, evidence bags, and the file created by the police before we took over. I'll be supervising."

I thought this might be coming.

"No," I say, keeping my voice mild.

Hinson turns to me with a frown. "I'm sorry?"

"I said no, Agent Hinson. This is my investigation. My team and I will be the only ones on that plane."

She steps close to me, very close, using her height advantage to try and intimidate me. It's a smart move, but an old move, and I'm unfazed.

"I'm afraid I'll have to insist," she says, glaring down at me with those blue eyes.

She's fairly scary looking, I'll give her that.

"Call the Director," I say.

"Why?"

"Because he's the one who can resolve this. This isn't a power play, Hinson. Okay, maybe it is a little. But the truth is, you'll just be in the way, and your motives for being there would be a distraction. We don't need someone looking over our shoulders right now."

She doesn't so much step back as shift her weight onto her right leg. I can see her considering what I'm saying, weighing whatever directive she'd been given regarding keeping an eye on us against the wisdom of bugging the Director. She's not worried, she's thinking it through. Hinson is used to exercising her own discretion.

"Look," I say, to help her along, "You know I'm not here just because the Director ordered me to be."

"Functionally, you are."

"Functionally, but not *actually*. I'm here because the congressman's wife asked for me."

The smallest of smiles ghosts her lips, a slight softening of that all-business blankness. It's a smile of respect, an appreciation of my not-so-subtle name-dropping.

"Fine, Agent Barrett," she says, stepping back now. She reaches into her inside jacket pocket, giving me a glimpse of a weapon held by an under-the-armpit shoulder holster. She produces a simple white business card and gives it to me. The card says: *Hinson* in black type, followed by a phone number and e-mail address. Nothing else.

I glance at her. "We're into brevity, I see."

She shrugs. "I can count on two hands the number of times I've handed that card out. Please call if you need anything. You can reach me twenty-four seven."

She turns and walks off without another word, pumps clacking against the cold gray concrete of the hangar.

Round one to me, but I remember AD Jones's warning and I'm sure now he was right to give it.

"Hm," Alan rumbles, "how do you describe someone like that? Scary? Tough? Both?"

"Describe her as she lives to be," I murmur.

"Which is?"

"Useful. Useful is her higher power. Now let's check out our crime scene."

"I'VE NEVER BEEN ON A totally empty plane before," Callie says. "It's odd."

"Too quiet," Alan observes.

They're right. Under normal circumstances, planes have their own noise, a kind of murmuring crowd sound. This one is a tomb.

"What is this, a seven twenty-seven?" Alan asks.

"This is a seven thirty-seven eight hundred," James replies. "Medium-sized, narrow body, seats one hundred sixty-two passengers in a two-class layout—which is what this plane has. It's one hundred twenty-nine feet long with a wingspan of a hundred twelve feet. It weighs ninety-one thousand pounds empty, can travel over three thousand nautical miles fully loaded, and has a cruising speed of roughly mach point seven."

Alan rolls his eyes. "Thanks, Encyclopedia Brown."

"Where was she seated?" I ask.

Alan consults the file. "Twenty F. Window seat."

I frown. "One question to ask: How did he ensure he had a seat next to her? That requires prior knowledge of her seating arrangements. We need to find out how she booked her flight."

"There are too many variables here," James says.

I glance at him. "Meaning?"

"Look, the way he killed her *required* that she have a window seat." He pulls the file from Alan's hands and removes a photograph. "He left her leaning up against the window, with a blanket pulled over her, like she was asleep. He wouldn't have been able to do that if she was sitting in the middle seat, much less an aisle."

"So?"

"My point is, there's various ways he could have found out what her seating assignment was. He could have bribed someone, or hacked into the system. From there, he could have requested the seat next to hers, or talked the person who was originally supposed to sit there into giving it up to him, any of a number of things. But post nine eleven, there's virtually no way he could have *guaranteed* she'd have gotten a window seat. No way to plan or arrange that."

I understand now what James is saying. "Killing her on the plane wasn't a given."

He nods. "Right."

It's a tiny thing, but, as always, it is a piece of the overall puzzle, a part of seeing the man who did this.

He started out with the decision to kill Lisa Reid, not the decision to kill her on a plane. He stalked her, watched her, gathered information about her life. He found out she was going on a trip, found out somehow that she had gotten a window seat, and only then planned and arranged killing her here. If events hadn't fallen into place the way he needed them to, he would have killed her somewhere else.

"Location interested him," I murmur, "but it was an aside, a novelty, a 'see what I can do.' She was the most important factor, not the location. Lisa was the key."

"Wait," Callie says. "There's another possibility, yes?"

"Which is?"

"That it was a random killing. Perhaps the location *was* the key factor for him. He got himself a middle seat and planned to kill whoever was unlucky enough to be sitting next to him, and that just happened to be Lisa. Maybe he has a problem with this airline, or air travel in general. I've wanted to kill off an obnoxious fellow passenger myself once or twice."

"Possible and definitely disturbing," I allow, "but unlikely. The fact that it was Lisa Reid—transgendered person and offspring of a congressional family?" I shake my head. "That's not a coincidence. He likes planning and control. Victim choice would be an integral part of that. I could be wrong, but . . . this doesn't feel random to me."

Callie considers this, nods in agreement. "Point taken."

We move down the single aisle. The 737-800 has the classic seating arrangement, rows of three seats on either side. The air is cool but not cold yet. Airplanes hold heat well. We arrive at 20F.

"How far did their Crime Scene Unit get, Callie?" I ask.

She flips through the file. "Full photographs, with good coverage both before and after removal of the body. They collected her luggage, which is down there in the hangar. That's about it."

"Someone jumped on this one fast," Alan observes.

I take a moment and look. Nothing fancy, nothing psychic. This is it, right here, the place where one human being murdered another. A life ended in that seat by the window. If you believe in the soul, and I do, this is the location where the *essence* of the *who* of Lisa Reid disappeared forever.

I'm struck, as always, by how inadequate the location of death is when compared to the truth of death itself. I saw a pretty young woman once, staked out in the dirt. She was naked. She'd been strangled. Her tongue lolled from her swollen, beaten mouth. Her open eyes stared at the sky. She still had some of her beauty, but it was fading fast, being eaten around the edges by the coming entropy. Dead as she was, she still put the dirt to shame. There was no forest, no ground, and no sky, there was only her. No canvas exists that can really add to an ended life; death frames itself.

"I see blood on her seat cushion," Callie observes, jarring me from my thoughts. "Easiest thing to do will be to just take the whole cushion. Take hers, take his, then search for prints. That's a good avenue. It would have stood out if he'd worn gloves. Then vacuum everything for trace. That's pretty much going to be it."

"I think he would have taken something," James notes.

I turn to him. "What?"

"A trophy. He left something in her, the cross. He's into symbols. He needed to take something."

Not all serial killers take trophies, but I agree with James. It feels right.

"Could have been anything," Alan says. "Jewelry, something from her purse, a piece of her hair." He shrugs. "Anything."

"We'll go through her belongings, see if something obvious is missing," I say.

"It's only getting colder, so what's the game plan, honey-love?"

Callie's right. I've started to get the smell of him but there's nothing else here that's going to help me.

"You and James are going to stay here and finish processing the scene. Call me when you're done. Alan, I want you to drop me off at Lisa's place, and then I want you to interview the witnesses. Flight attendants, passengers, anyone and everyone. Follow up on how he bought his ticket as well. Did he use cash? A credit card? If he used a credit card, it was probably a false identity. How'd he make that happen?"

"Got it."

Callie nods her assent.

I take a final look at the window Lisa had died next to, turn, and walk away from it forever. It'll fade eventually, I know. Someday I'll be sitting at a window seat on an airplane and I won't even think of Lisa Reid.

Someday.

6

andria. We don't have much company on the road; just a few other
night-drivers who, like us, probably wish they were in bed.

Alan is silent as he drives. We have the heaters blowing full tilt to
deal with the cold. Darkness has really settled in, darkness and silence
and *still*.

"What is it about the cold that makes things seem more quiet?" I
wonder out loud.

Alan glances over at me and smiles. "Things *are* more quiet. You're
used to Los Angeles. Doesn't get cold enough there to drive people
and animals inside, usually. It does here."

He's right. I've experienced this before. Between the ages of six and
ten, before my mom died of cancer, we used to take family driving
trips. Mom and Dad would synchronize their vacation time and we'd
spend two weeks trekking halfway across the U.S. and back.

I remember the hard parts of these trips; the unending sound of
the wheels on the road and the world rushing by, the intense, almost
painful boredom. I also remember playing car games with my mom.
I-spy, counting "pididdles" (cars with only one headlight working).
Raucous, off-tune car songs. Most of all, I remember the destinations.

In a four-year period, I saw great parts of Rocky Mountain National
Park, Yellowstone, Mount Rushmore. We crossed the Mississippi in a

few places, ate gumbo in New Orleans. We rarely stayed in hotels, pre-ferring to camp instead.

One year, Dad got especially ambitious and drove us all the way to upstate New York in the fall. He wanted us to see the Catskill Mountains, where Rip Van Winkle was supposed to have snoozed. It was an unbearably long trip and we were worn out and cranky by the time we arrived. We pulled into the campground and I got out of that car as fast as I could.

The trees were incredible, either evergreen or with leaves on the turn, short and tall, young and old. It was cold, cold like it is here, and I remember the bite of it on my cheeks, my breath in the air.

"Not only do I have to pee in the woods," my mother had groused, "but I have to get goose bumps on my ass while I do it."

"Isn't it beautiful, though?" my dad had said, a little bit of awe in his voice, oblivious to her anger.

That was one of the things I loved about my dad. He was eternally young when it came to viewing the world. My mom was more careful. Like me, she had a cynical edge. Mom kept our feet on the ground, which was important, but Dad kept our heads in the clouds, which had its own value.

I remember her turning to look at him, ready with some smart quip that died on her lips when she saw the actual joy on his face. She'd pushed her grumbling away and turned to look as well, finally seeing what he was seeing, getting infected with his wonder, stum-bling into his dream.

"It is," she'd marveled. "It really is."

"Can I explore?" I'd asked.

"Sure, honey," Dad had replied. "But not too far. Stay close."

"Okay, Daddy," I'd agreed and had bounded off, heading into the trees.

I'd kept my word and stayed close. I didn't need to go far; fifty steps and I had found myself alone, more alone than I'd ever been. I'd stopped to take this in, not so much afraid as interested. I'd arrived in a small clearing, surrounded by a number of tall trees with dying leaves that hadn't given up the ghost just yet. I'd spread my arms and tilted my head all the way back and closed my eyes and listened to the stillness and the silence.

Years later I'd find the body of a young woman in the woods of Angeles Crest and remember that stillness and silence and wonder what it was like to be killed in the middle of nowhere, to have that solitude as a cathedral for your screams.

I was ten years old on that trip to New York, and it was the last trip we took before my mom got sick. When I think of my parents, I always think of them then, at that age, just thirty and thirty-one, younger than I am now. When I think of being young, I remember those trips we took, I-spy and pididdle and are-we-there-yet and my mother's complaints. I remember my father's wonder, my mother's love for him, and I remember the leaves and the trees and the time when stillness held beauty instead of the memories of death.

LISA'S CONDO IS NEW CONSTRUCTION, located near the center of Alexandria. The buildings are nice, but don't really fit their surrounds.

"Kind of like California in Virginia," Alan observes, putting voice to my thoughts.

The condo is brown wood and stucco on the outside, with its own small driveway. No one has entered yet; there's no yellow crime scene tape on the door. We pull in, exit, and walk up to the front door. Alan will clear the condo with me before leaving to go chase up on witnesses.

We'd swung by the morgue so I could grab Lisa's keys. I am fiddling with them in the bad light from the streetlamps to find the one we need.

"Probably that one," Alan notes, indicating a gold-colored key.

I fit the key into the deadbolt lock and it turns with a click. I put the key ring into my jacket pocket and we both pull our weapons.

"Ladies first," Alan says.

THE CONDO HAS TWO BEDROOMS, one of which doubles as a home office. We clear these as well as the guest half-bath and the master bathroom before holstering our guns.

"Nice place," Alan observes.

"Yeah."

It's decorated in earth tones, muted without being bland. Catches of color appear throughout, from maroon throw pillows on the couch to white cotton curtains with blue flower trim along the edges. It's clean and odorless, no smell of pets or dirty clothes or food left out. She didn't smoke. The wooden coffee table facing the couch is covered in a happy disarray of magazines and books. Lisa was tidy but not fastidious.

"Okay if I go?" he asks.

I glance at my watch. It's now 5:00 A.M.

"Sure. Before you get on to chasing down witnesses or following the money, get a search going for murders with a similar signature."

"The cross, you mean?"

"The cross, or just the symbols he left on the cross. I don't think we're going to find any really old crimes, but we might find some new ones."

He frowns. "You think he's been operating for a while and only just decided to come out into the open?"

"I do."

"Bad idea on his part."

"Let's hope so."

ALONE NOW. I LEAVE THE lights off. The dawn has arrived and I want to see the living room as Lisa would have seen it. I sit down on the couch, brown microfiber, a couch like a thousand others, except that this one had been hers. She'd sat here, time after time. I'm able to pick out her favored spot, a cushion that's just a little bit more worn than the others.

A medium-sized flat-screen TV faces the couch, placed a comfortable distance away. I imagine her sitting here, lights out, shadows dancing on her face. I see a bottle of nail polish on the coffee table and smile. Watching TV while painting her nails. I find a book on a side table, a silly romance novel. Guilty pleasures, maybe reading while her toenails dried.

This place was a sanctum, a refuge, and I'm going to root through it with impunity. I reflect that in this way, I'm very like the killers I hunt. I will move through this home and open her drawers, read her e-mail, peer into her medicine cabinet. Cross all boundaries of privacy until there's nothing left to find.

Once upon a time, Lisa could turn the lock and keep the world outside from finding out her secrets, but not anymore. The killers I hunt are empowered by this concept.

My motives are purer, obviously, but I learned a long time ago that I won't survive doing what I do if I am dishonest with myself, and the truth is, I feel just a little hint of that power when I go through a victim's home, the slightest thrill of the voyeur. I can look where I want, touch what I want, open any door I want. It's heady and I can understand, just a little, why it has such a draw for psychopaths.

I get up and move into the kitchen. It's small but functional and very clean. Brown granite countertops. Stainless steel refrigerator with matching over-the-counter microwave, stove, and dishwasher. I open a few cabinets and peer inside. White china, neatly stacked.

The refrigerator is nearly bare. I see a note/shopping list posted on the refrigerator door. It says, *Need bottled water, napkins, mac and cheese.*

Never going to happen now, I think.

The kitchen drawers reveal nothing. Silverware, a phone book, some pens and Post-its. I'm not really surprised. Lisa was someone used to having to hide in public. She wouldn't keep her secrets out here where a guest could find them by accident.

I move to the bedroom. It's medium-sized, with a lush beige carpet. The bed dominates the room, a California king. The earth tones continue here. Lisa had found her own sweet spot in terms of décor; feminine without being girly.

I move to the common repository of secrets for women: the nightstand. I open the top drawer and am not disappointed. There's a plastic bag of marijuana with some rolling papers. I also see some baby oil and a magazine filled with photographs of well-muscled naked men. I glance around, note the CD player.

I can imagine Lisa, putting on a CD, lighting up a joint and inhaling while she flipped through the pages of the magazine to find the right visual spark. Finding it, lying back, grabbing the baby oil . . .

And that's where we part ways, Lisa.

My fingers, when they travel down there, arrive at a different tactile experience. I've never had a penis, never wanted one, but I've held them in my hands. I know what they feel like, smell like, taste like, but I don't know what it's like to hold one and feel it being touched at the same time.

Did that bother you? You were attracted to men, you longed to be a woman. When your hand found a penis, was it alien? Did you transform it in your fantasies to something else?

I strain to arrive there, to feel it as she would have felt it, but the experience eludes me.

I close the drawer and open the one below it, find only some paperbacks.

I move to her dresser and rummage through the drawers. I could be looking through my own. There are no male items here at all. Bras, panties, some T-shirts and jeans. The closet reveals the same, a mix of dresses, slacks, and a ton of shoes. She had good taste, just to the left of classy, a muted flair. Hinting at mischief without giving away the store.

I leave the room and enter the bathroom next to it. Again, I'm struck by the fact: this is a woman's place. Makeup, loofah, lavender-scented soap. Bath beads, pink razors, a hand cream dispenser. Even the toilet seat is down. Did she sit to pee, or stand?

The medicine cabinet belongs to a healthy person. I see aspirin, bandages, the basics. No antidepressants or prescription painkillers. In fact, no medication of any kind, which puzzles me until I work it out. She would have taken her medication with her on her trip to Texas.

The area under the sink provides another contrast. No tampons there in that easy-to-reach-while-sitting-on-the-toilet position. Just a hand cloth and some tile cleaner.

There's a digital scale on the floor, and I step onto it out of habit, still trying to be Lisa. I ignore its lies, as I imagine she would have. A last pause and look around and I leave the bathroom to go check out her home office.

The office is decorated in the same earth tones as the rest of the condo. There's a desk placed under the window. She'd have been able to look outside when she felt like it, but her flat-screen computer monitor would have been protected from the sun's glare. The desk itself is made of dark wood, neither substantial nor rickety, something in between. Lisa liked wood, I think. I've seen very little metal in the furniture here.

There's a file cabinet next to the desk. A six-foot high bookshelf leans up against an opposing wall, more dark wood. I glance at the titles on the book spines. They're almost all travel guides with a gay/lesbian emphasis. *Gay Travel in Italy, Madrid—Simply Fabulous,* stuff like that.

A check of the file cabinet reveals nothing of immediate interest. We'll have to go through it all, but that's not why I'm here right now. I'm looking for something, anything, that jumps out, that could help put us on the right path.

I examine the desktop. It's clean, just a slate cup-coaster and a pen. I close my eyes, try to imagine her morning routine. I slip off my shoes, because that's how she'd have walked around in here, that's why she had these plush carpets.

I imagine her waking up, walking to the coffeepot, pouring a hot cup of coffee and heading over to sit, bleary-eyed, in front of the computer . . .

No, that's wrong.

There had been a crucial difference between Lisa and me. When I wake up in the morning, my hair might be a mess, I may have bags under my eyes, I might even think I need to wax my upper lip, but I never have to worry about someone coming to the door unannounced and finding out I'm not a woman.

Lisa would have had that worry, a constant concern. I close my eyes, and retrace my mental steps.

I imagine her waking up. First stop would have been the bathroom. Shower, shave her legs if needed, brush her teeth. Do her hair. Do her makeup—nothing fancy, just making sure that it is a woman's face looking back at her. We're all slaves to the mirror in some fashion, but it would have had a whole new dimension for Lisa.

Clothes could have remained casual, a T-shirt and sweatpants were fine, but she would have done her face before getting her coffee. She would have woken up and prepared for the possibility of being seen by the world.

Now the rest of it feels true; cup of coffee, walking into this office in her bare feet.

I sit down in the chair and start up her computer. Her wallpaper is a striking photograph of the pyramids of Egypt silhouetted against a cloudless blue sky.

I open her browser and look through the history to see what sites she visited. It's a mix of business and shopping. I find her own website, Rainbow Travels. There's a photograph on the first page. Lisa, smiling, beautiful. I'd never know, from this picture, that she hadn't started her life as a woman.

Pictures . . .

I stand up, walk out of the office, and go back through the living room, the bedroom. I was right—there are no photographs on her walls. No pictures of her family, of Rosario or Dillon, or even of herself. There's a Picasso print and an Ansel Adams black and white, but that's it.

I wonder about this. Why no photographs? Had the idea of seeing her parents' faces every day been painful to her? Or was it simply a continuation of her protecting them from her life, of keeping visitors from making the connection?

I walk back into the office and continue going through her computer. I check out her e-mail. Lots of business e-mail, e-mail relating to online purchases, but again, the oddity—nothing personal. It's the cyberspace version of no family photos.

I'm starting to get an idea here that belies Rosario's vision of Lisa's contentment. The condo was nice, Lisa ran her own business, she had her flat screen and her weed and baby oil and that was all great, but I think this was a place of solitude, of daily routine and loneliness.

I don't see any e-mail to or from friends, any visits to dating sites, no evidence of any outreach at all.

I sigh and lean back in the chair. I feel dissatisfied. Where is Lisa in this place? Where's her soul?

My foot kicks against something underneath the desk. Frowning, I move the chair back, crouch forward, and pick it up. When I see what it is, my heartbeat speeds up a little.

It's a brown leather book, embossed with the gold letters *Journal* on the front.

"Now we're talking," I murmur.

The first entry is dated about a week ago. Lisa has nice handwriting, a looping, legible script. I read.

I'm not sure why I keep these journals. Maybe to record my own loneliness. I don't know.

It helps, I guess, just to sit here every now and then and write the words: I'm lonely, I'm lonely, I'm so damn lonely.

I was reading Corinthians yesterday in the Bible. I read it and started weeping. I cried and cried and cried. I couldn't help it. Here's what it said:

> Love is patient, love is kind. It does not envy, it does not boast, it is not proud. It is not rude, it is not self-seeking, it is not easily angered, it keeps no record of wrongs. Love does not delight in evil but rejoices with the truth. It always protects, always trusts, always hopes, always perseveres.
>
> Love never fails.

I read that and I felt for a moment like I couldn't breathe. Like I hurt so hard I'd fly apart.

It was the question, you see, that it brought to my mind: Will I ever have someone to say those words to? Will I? Will anyone ever feel that way about me?

Is there a man out there who's going to kiss me and find out what I am and keep kissing me anyway and forever? And if there is, will I recognize him when he appears?

I know, I know, I'm on a journey, and it's a marathon, not a sprint. But sometimes, I doubt. I doubt myself, I doubt my decisions. Sometimes, I'm ashamed to say, I even doubt God.

How could I doubt God? God is the only one who's always been there for me.

I'm sorry, God.

Sometimes I just get so damn lonely.

I finish this passage and clear my throat. I move to the next, written two days after the first one.

Nana's dead. No surprise, but still, it hurts. Nana was a racist, Nana wouldn't have accepted me the way I am now, but I loved her anyway, I just can't help it. After all, Nana always kept my secret. THE secret. She kept on loving me even after that terrible thing I did, the most shameful act I ever committed, when I

I frown. It ends there. I run a finger along the inside and realize that pages of the journal have been removed, ripped out. I flip through the later pages.

Then I see it.

And I freeze.

My hands tremble a little bit as I open the journal wider to look, to make sure I'm seeing what I'm seeing.

At the top of one page, a hand-drawn symbol.

A skull and crossbones.

Below that, a single line:

What do I collect? That's the question, and that's the key. Answer it soon, or more will die.

I drop the journal onto the desktop. My heart is racing.

Him. He'd been here. The man on the plane.

The man who killed Lisa.

1

Alan phrases it as a statement, and not a happy one.

"And he's set a clock. Catch me or I kill again."

The moment I know, for certain, that a killer is serial, everything stops. It's a moment of total silence, an indrawn breath. The earth stops rotating and a low hum fills my head and thrums through my veins.

It's a terrible pause, a necessary minute where I accept the burden of my profession: until I catch him (or her or them), the killing rolls on. Anyone who dies now is my responsibility.

It's one thing to know that they don't stop until we catch them. It's another thing entirely for them to say outright that they're already homing in on the next victim. A whole different level of pressure.

"Fuck." He sighs. "I sure get tired of these guys. Don't they know they'll never be original?"

"It's always new to them."

"Yeah. What do you want to do?"

I'd called Alan first, without really giving it too much thought. I'd needed to talk to someone, to tell them what I'd found. The shock of adrenaline is fading now.

"What are you working on?" I ask.

"He used a credit card to buy his plane ticket. It's a valid card, turns out it was issued a few years ago. I got an address and I'm headed over there now."

My heart sinks.

"What was the name on the card?"

"Richard Ambrose."

"The real Ambrose, whoever he was, is dead, Alan."

"Yeah."

If our perp had manufactured this identity from whole cloth, the credit card would have been issued recently.

"He probably found a guy that came close to his own physical description," I muse. "That will help, at least."

"You want me to continue with what I'm doing, or come to you?"

"Get over to Ambrose's place. I'm fine here. It was just a shock."

"Ned and I will take a look and I'll call you."

When Alan was being trained for homicide, his mentor told him that a notepad was a detective's best friend and that a friend should have a name. Alan gave his pad the name Ned. It's stuck to this day. I've seen many incarnations of Ned pulled from an inside jacket pocket. Ned's been a faithful friend.

"Okay."

"You sure you're fine?"

"I'm sure. Keep doing what you're doing."

"MY, MY, MY," CALLIE MUSES after I fill her in. "Our very own crazy Hansel, leaving us a trail of bloody bread crumbs."

And James had been right, I think. He is taking something from his victims. He told us he is.

"How is it going there?" I ask.

"We finished vacuuming for trace. I won't know how helpful that is until I get it back to a lab. I haven't found any prints, but I did find some smudged areas on the arm rest where prints should have been."

"He probably wiped them down."

"Not a stupid Hansel, but then, we expected as much."

"I bet it means he's in the system."

"Why?"

"He's leaving us clues, Callie. He wants us to know he's there and that we should chase him. Why bother wiping his prints? I think it's because he knows they would lead us right to him."

"Hm. If so, it's not immediately probative, but helpful. It means he either has a criminal record, is a government employee, or has been in the military or law enforcement."

"It's something. What else?"

"Nothing, yet. We're about to remove the seat cushions. I still need to print the overhead luggage compartment and then we're done."

"I want you to come over here next. We need to process this condo."

An overdramatized, long-suffering sigh. "No rest for the bride-to-be, I see."

I chuckle. "Relax. Marilyn is still working on the wedding logistics, right?"

Marilyn is Callie's daughter.

"It's not Marilyn I'm worried about. It's her helper."

I frown. "Who?"

"Kirby."

I raise an eyebrow. "Beach bunny Kirby?"

"Is there any other?"

Kirby Mitchell is an eccentric bodyguard I'd hired a few years back to help protect a potential victim. She's in her early thirties, about five-seven, blonde, with all the plucky personality and chipper talk you'd expect from a California stereotype. The truth of Kirby is something a little different, however. Kirby is ex-CIA "or something like that" as she likes to say. The rumors are that she spent many years down in Central and South America as an assassin for the U.S. government. I have zero doubt about this. Kirby, for all her thousand-kilowatt smiles and "gee-whiz" exclamations, is as deadly as they come.

She's also loyal and funny and has managed to insinuate herself into the lives of the team.

"Why'd you pick Kirby?"

"She's got wonderful taste for a killer, Smoky. Exquisite, actually."

"I see."

"But she needs supervision, you know?"

"Oh yeah, I know."

Kirby is unapologetic about satisfying her impulses, and her moral compass needs a little nudge sometimes.

Callie sighs. "Oh well, I'm sure it'll be fine. I told her not to hurt anyone too much if they tried to overcharge me."

" 'Too much'?" I query.

I can almost hear Callie's smile. "What's the use of having an assassin help with your wedding planning if you can't use her to scare the vendors a little?"

I PLACE A CALL TO Rosario Reid and fill her in on what I found. She's silent for a moment.

"He—he was there? The man who killed my Lisa?"

"Yes."

More silence. I know what she's feeling. Grief, rage, violation. An impotent desire to destroy the man who did this, who not only took her child from her, but walked through Lisa's condo, Lisa's life, with impunity.

"Rosario, I have to ask—do you have any idea what Lisa was talking about in her journal? The big secret she mentions?"

"I haven't the slightest, I really don't."

Is that true? Or are you lying to me?

I let it go, for now.

She sighs. "What are you going to do now?"

"When my team is done with the plane, they'll be coming over here. They'll be processing the condo from top to bottom."

"I see." Yet more silence. "Thank you for keeping me up-to-date, Smoky. Please call me if you need anything."

She hangs up, and I realize that she hadn't asked me what else Lisa had written in her journal.

Perhaps you're capable of dishonesty after all, Rosario. Maybe you know you'll find that Lisa wasn't as happy as you told yourself she was.

I can't blame her for this. I want to remember my Alexa as perfect too.

My phone rings. Alan.

"Not only is Richard Ambrose dead," he begins without preamble, "his body is still here."

I curse to myself. This is getting out of hand.

"Give me the address," I say. "I'll find a cab and meet you there."

8

IT'S NOW NEARING TEN IN THE MORNING, AND I'M START-
ing to feel like someone who has missed a night's sleep. My eyes
are gritty, my mouth tastes bad, and I have aches I'm not usually
aware of.

I concentrate on the weather and the sky to shake myself awake.
The cold has cleared the air and the sky is incredibly blue. When I step
out of the cab the wind bites into me, not unpleasant. The sun burns
cold, nothing more than a source of light.

Richard Ambrose lived in a medium-sized older home. It's built
with the sloping roof houses have in places that get snow. The exterior is mostly gray stone, lightened in places by blue and white trim. It
sits on a large yard that's covered with the leaves of fall.

It's a quiet neighborhood, very charming. I have visions of hot apple cider on Halloween, kids raking those leaves into a pile so they
could jump into them. I'm not one of those Californians who think
California is superior, or the only place to be. I can understand the
draw of a place like this, the character of it. I could even consider living here, if it weren't for the snow.

I don't do snow.

I pay the cabbie and send him on his way. I crunch through the
leaves until I reach the concrete porch, noting the neighbor on the
left peeking through a curtain. The front door is cracked. I open it
and am assaulted by the sweet and sour smell of death.

"Jesus," I mutter. I swallow hard, forcing down something wet and gooey that's trying to climb up my throat.

I force myself to enter, closing the door behind me.

The inside of the home is warm—warmer than it should be, like the heat has been cranked up.

Is this a little present you decided to give us? Turn the house into a sweat lodge so that the body would get nice and stinky?

I breathe in deeply through my nostrils, fighting the urge to gag as I do. I don't have a mask to put on or any menthol to rub under my nose. This is another trick; draw the scent in deep and overwhelm the olfactory receptors. Nothing really works one hundred percent, other than a gas mask. The smell of death is too profound.

The inside of Ambrose's house matches the outside, rich in its oldness. I see dark hardwood floors everywhere, and although the wood shines, it's scuffed and worn in a way that makes me think it's original. The walls are actually plaster and the light fixtures are old enough to be authentic as opposed to tacky.

"Alan?" I call out.

"Upstairs," he answers.

The stairs to the second floor face the front door. They're narrow, walled on each side. I walk up, clacking and squeaking all the way, more of that old wood. The smell of rotting flesh keeps getting stronger.

I reach the top landing and find myself facing a wall. A hallway stretches to the right and the left.

"Where are you?" I ask.

"Master bedroom," he calls out, his voice coming from the left.

I turn left and listen to the wood protest being walked on. It sounds like a cranky old man, or maybe a mother laying on a guilt trip. I pass a print on the wall, a Picasso sketch, a study of Don Quixote on his horse.

I reach the master bedroom and turn in.

"Wow," I say, grimacing.

Alan is standing at the foot of the bed, staring down at something that used to be a living person.

Ambrose was laid on his back, his arms arranged next to him. He's past the point of being bloated. His skin has a creamy consistency in some places, is black in others, and body fluids have run over the mattress on both sides to drip onto the floor. The smell in here is overwhelming. I struggle to keep my mouth from filling with saliva. Alan seems unaffected.

"State of decay, he's been dead between ten and twenty days," Alan notes.

I nod. "Alone too. No insect activity to speak of means this house has been locked up tight. Any obvious cause of death?"

Alan shakes his head. "I don't see any bullet holes, and there's been too much slippage and decomp to tell if he was strangled or had his throat cut."

"This was purely functional," I murmur. "There's no joy here. The killer needed his identity, that's all."

"Speaking of that, check this out."

Alan hands me a photograph in an eight-by-ten frame. I see a good-looking man in his mid-forties with dark hair and an easy smile. Ambrose was not movie-star handsome, but I doubt he had many problems attracting women. Most interesting, however, is the fact that he sports a full moustache and beard. I hand the photo back to Alan.

"He chose Ambrose because they're roughly the same age, height, and appearance," I say. "He knew he'd be on a plane, in an enclosed environment. He couldn't afford to get too clever or complex with his disguise. I'm betting he went clean shaven to the airport and used Ambrose's driver's license. He'd tell security personnel that he'd just shaved the moustache and beard." I shrug. "If he was confident and charming enough, and the basic physical similarities were there, he could pull it off."

"I don't know. Seems risky. What if he got a really alert attendant, someone that did a double take?"

"He killed on a plane, mid-flight. I don't think risk is an issue for him."

"Good point."

"Besides, the truth is, with adequate social engineering, it's just not that hard."

The problem with decent people is that they are decent people. They tend to assume decency in others by default. If he says he's a plumber and he's in a pair of coveralls, then he's a plumber, not a serial killer in disguise. Ted Bundy wore a cast on his arm and asked a girl for help moving a couch into his van. He was handsome, charming, and she, being decent, helped him without a second thought. He, being evil, killed her without a second thought. I'm sure she still couldn't believe it, even as it happened.

The funny thing is, people assume we're more careful now, that Bundy's broken arm trick wouldn't work today. They're wrong. It would work today, and it will work a century from now. It's just the way we are.

"What's the plan?" Alan asks.

I sigh. "We're getting spread too thin. We have the plane as a crime scene, and now Lisa's condo and this house. Callie and James aren't going to be able to handle it all." I shake my head. "I'm calling AD Jones."

"IT'S TIME TO START PLAYING this by the book, sir," I tell him. "We've got three crime scenes now. Legally, the Ambrose murder belongs to the locals. If I try and contain it I'm not only getting into sketchy legal territory, I'm putting the need for confidentiality above the need for a speedy investigation. I can't do that."

Investigation of murder is a full-court press, always. It's a blitz, no finesse. You pull out all stops, use every resource available, because if you don't come up with something in the first forty-eight to seventy-two hours, it's unlikely you're going to come up with anything at all. I had remembered this as I stared down at the rotting corpse of Richard Ambrose and realized I was solving someone else's problem. Like I told Rosario—I work for the victims. Not her, not her husband, certainly not political expedience.

I hear AD Jones sigh. "Any other way around this?"

"Not ethically, no, sir. We've got a murder scene here, a pretty big one. The whole house needs to be gone through. We've got identity theft, interviews still to be done of plane passengers, ticket counter personnel, flight attendants. Not to mention the distinct possibility that other past victims are going to pop up *and* his promise to kill again until we catch him. If we're going to do a good job of this, we need to bring in local law enforcement."

A long pause. "Agreed. But we hold on to the Lisa Reid murder directly. We have legal reason to do so. I don't want anyone else in her condo, and I want the ME report to continue being suppressed. If the details about the cross leak, it'll impair your investigation."

"Right."

"Before you call in the cavalry, though, I want you to arrange a little air cover, Smoky."

"Such as?"

"Call Rosario Reid. Explain to her that keeping this in-house is no longer practical or feasible. Get her to understand that it'll impede finding Lisa's killer. Appeal to her as a mother and the wife of a politician. I'll deal with the Director."

"Yes, sir."

"You made the right call on this, Smoky."

I'M IN THE FRONT YARD, leaves blowing around my ankles, that crisp, cold wind numbing my cheeks and hands. I welcome it for now; it's clearing the smell of death from my nostrils.

"I trust your judgment, Smoky," Rosario tells me. "I meant what I said in the car—Lisa is your priority."

"I appreciate that. I didn't think otherwise, but you deserve a heads-up. Also . . ." I hesitate.

"Yes?"

"To be honest, it would be helpful if you conveyed your confidence in my decisions to the Director."

"I'll talk to him personally."

"Thanks. I ran into his assistant, and she made me a little nervous. I'm not used to this particular playing field."

"Rachael Hinson?" She sounds amused. "She's formidable, true, but so am I. And I have ten years on her. Do whatever you need to."

"I will."

She disconnects and I turn to Alan, who's waiting on the front porch, hands in his jacket pockets. I nod. "Call in the locals."

9

coordinating with local law enforcement at Ambrose's home. I don't
feel a need to be there. Ambrose was used and thrown away; he wasn't
important to the killer. As callous as it sounds, that means he's not
immediately important to me.

James is walking through the condo. Doing the same thing I had
done, I imagine, soaking in Lisa's personality. She was important to
our madman. Know the victim, know the doer.

Callie looks tired. I watch as she pulls a bottle of Vicodin from her
jacket pocket and pops a pill dry.

"Yummy," she says, rolling her eyes in faux joy and rubbing her
stomach with exaggerated motions.

"How are you doing with that?"

"Still addicted," she quips. "But then, that's something you're going to help me with before my wedding. You and I locked in a room
together, sweat and barf."

"Sounds fun."

"Monkeys, barrels of them. So, what do you want me to do?"

I explain about the diary, what I'd found.

"He spent time here, Callie. I think he stole some pages from her
diary. I want you and James to go through this place with a fine-tooth
comb."

"Do you think we'll find anything?"

I hesitate, then shrug. "I don't know. Maybe. He wanted us to know he was here, and he left the cross in Lisa's body as a clue. He's pulling us down a trail, but he hides his fingerprints . . ." I shake my head. "I can't quite pin him down. I don't have enough to work with yet."

James has reappeared and has been listening.

"I agree," he says. "All I can really tell about him, so far, is that he's older, he's organized and accomplished, fearless without being insane about the risks he takes, and that he wants us to know he's out there."

And that he's going to kill again, soon, I don't add.

"Anything else from the plane?" I ask.

"No," Callie says. "We still have to go through the trace we vacuumed up, and we have the bloody cushions, but that's all."

"The most telling evidence then," James says, "continues to be the fact that he wiped down his prints. He's in a database somewhere."

"Yes. That and his behavior are the best leads we have." I sigh. "Which isn't saying much."

"Pish," Callie says. "We're only twenty-four hours in. He's already made the biggest mistake of all—he attracted our attention."

James shakes his head. "Yes, but it's not looking like we'll catch him before he kills again."

Callie shrugs. "Not under our control. This is. So let's get to work."

I'm about to chime in with agreement, but my phone rings. Alan.

"Bad news," he says.

"What?"

"Remember you told me to put out a search for similar crimes?"

My heart sinks. "Uh-huh."

"I did that before I went to Ambrose's place. We've already got a hit. Get this—it's a fresh crime. Happened ten days ago."

"Are you kidding me?"

"Wish I was. He's on the move. Man with a plan."

I close my eyes, rub my forehead. This bad news seems to bring all my exhaustion crashing down on me.

"Give me the details," I say.

Interlude:
THE DEATH
of
ROSEMARY SONNENFELD

10

ROSEMARY WAKES UP AT SIX-THIRTY TO THE SHRILL BLAST OF her alarm. She considers turning it off and going back to sleep. It's Saturday, after all. The thought is seductive, but the rebuke is instant and fierce.

No, that's not how this works. Not how you work. Discipline, day in, day out, from now till death. It's the only way.

So she forces herself to a sitting position, legs dangling down from the side of the bed. Her feet touch the wood floor once, tentative, curling away from the cold as a reflex.

Coffee. I need coffee.

She stretches once and marvels, as she often does, that she could feel this achy and sluggish. She's only thirty-four and it's been four years since she straightened her life out.

That's the price you pay for the wages of sin.

She glances out the window of her apartment. She's living in Simi Valley, California, has been since she fled here four years ago to restart her life. It's a nice apartment, two bedrooms, décor that's comforting in its absolute lack of edginess. Beige carpets and off-white walls, wood floors in the bedroom and kitchen, she could be happy with that forever.

There's a chill in the morning air, not that common for September. She's naked, and the chill gives her goose bumps and makes her nipples hard.

She stands up and pads into the bathroom. She yelps once as she sits down on the toilet seat; it feels like ice against her ass. She pees, knees together, wipes, stands, flushes. Before leaving the bathroom, she takes stock of her body in the mirror.

Looking good, as always. Too bad that's never been a helpful thing.

Rosemary observes that her breasts are still perky, a perfect 38C. Her belly is still flat, no stretch marks or scars. Her five-five frame isn't slender, but it isn't fat either. She has muscular thighs and a firm ass. Her pubic hair is brunette, just like the waist-length hair on her head. She likes not having to shave down there anymore.

Perfect body, but then, why wouldn't it be? I always aborted when I got pregnant, didn't I? Eight times, yes, sir. My uterus is so scarred now, it's doubtful I'll ever have any children. Which is probably a good thing. Kids deserve better than me.

She turns away from this thought by turning away from the mirror, and heads back into the bedroom. She grabs the necklace and hangs it around her neck; a small silver cross on a thin silver chain. She kneels down next to her bed, knees on that hard, cold wooden floor, bends her head forward, closes her eyes, and prays as she does every morning.

"God, thank you for another day of freedom from the sinful life I used to live. Thank you for giving me the force of will to stay away from the temptations and the hungers that still plague me. They're better, Lord, but they still bother me. Sometimes I think about drugs and fucking and I just want to get up and go out and score some coke and booze and suck a nice big cock. Even saying it now makes my pussy a little bit wet. But every day, with your help, I manage not to give in. I turn away from those temptations and I thank you for helping me find the strength to do that, Lord."

When she first started praying, years ago, she never used that kind of language. She used cleaner words, tried to be more pure. She found it unsatisfying. She'd talked to Father Yates about her problem in this area.

Father Yates was in his fifties, but he was pretty cool. He'd give anyone a chance—ex-hookers, recovering drug addicts—as long as he felt your intentions were genuine, he was there for you. Nothing seemed to faze him.

"Rosemary, the things you find yourself wanting to say to God—the unclean things—tell me how you feel when they come to you."

"Like urges, Father. When I need a drink or a fuck—sorry, Father—real bad, it's like a bunch of black waves washing over me, one right after the other. If I hold them in, the urges just get stronger. But if I talk about them, if I put words to them, I get some relief."

"Give me an example."

She'd stared at him. "You want me to say it like I think it?"

"That's right."

"I don't know, Father. I'm talking about some pretty dirty stuff here."

He'd chuckled. "Rosemary, I've heard every profane word that exists. I've heard things in confession that would curl your toes—confessions about bestiality, the fantasies of child molesters—I promise you, I can deal with whatever you want to say."

Looking at him then, she believed what he was saying, but it was still hard. The things she felt, the words to describe those things, were secrets. There was a time when she lived those words, when she said them without a second thought. Times had changed.

On the other hand . . .

She could sense that there might be a certain relief to be had by putting voice to the dark things that bubbled up inside her.

But, what if . . .

It was the big concern, the greatest one of all, the one that keeps us from owning up to our sins.

"Father, if—if I do . . ." She bit her lip, which trembled. "Do you promise to still like me afterward?"

She couldn't look at him. He grabbed her chin and forced her to raise her eyes. The kindness she saw there made her want to cry with relief.

"I promise, Rosemary. On my love of God."

She'd cried a little, and he'd waited while she did. Then she'd wiped her eyes and had started talking, telling those secrets. The words were like a flood, dark and awful, but so needing to be spoken.

"Sometimes, Father, I just want to fuck, you know? Not make out or make love or any of that stuff. I want a cock in my mouth and in my pussy and I want them there after I've swallowed a bunch of booze and snorted as much coke as I can get my hands on. I want it and even while I fight wanting it, I get turned on, and that makes the wanting even stronger, you know?

"It's always been like that. People think girls like me are victims, and some are I suppose. But I've *never* been able to get enough. Never. The dirtier the better. Spit on me, piss in my face, make me a fucking whore, it'll all make me come that much harder and stronger. I want it for days, I want it for weeks, I want to be fucked till I stop breathing."

The words had rushed out, uncensored, and then she'd been done. She'd snuck a glance at Father Yates, had been relieved to see no shock or judgment on his face. Perhaps even more precious, in its own way, even more important, was that she didn't see the slightest hunger there. No hint of voyeuristic thrill.

"Thank you, Rosemary. How do you feel, having said all that?"

"Better," she'd replied without hesitation. "The wanting goes away. Kind of like . . ." She searched for a metaphor. "Like squeezing a big old whitehead zit. Hurts to do it, thank God when it pops, you know?"

He'd smiled and nodded. "Yes, I do." His face got serious. He put a hand on her shoulder. "Rosemary, I think saying it is better than doing it, don't you?"

She'd blinked, surprised by this concept.

Was it better? In this society, sometimes it didn't seem so. Say the words *suck a cock* in public, and you might as well be sucking one on an escalator, you know?

Still . . . there was a big difference between talking about drinking and fucking and waking up from a blackout with a stranger's come in your ass.

"I guess so, Father. Yeah."

"Then my advice, when you pray? Say what you need to say. Don't worry. God can handle it."

It had seemed like strange advice, and to be honest, it had been hard to implement, but she got the hang of it. Some might find it blasphemous, but you know what? Fuck them and their high horses. Truth was, it worked. She talked to God without a censor, and she had almost five years on the straight and narrow as a result.

She figured God knew what was up. God knew her love for Him grew every day she made it through without fucking a stranger or drinking a beer or snorting a gram.

She figured God had watched when she turned tricks at seventeen and started making porno films at eighteen. Figured he'd seen her all-black gang bang under the bright lights (*Big black cocks in a tight white hole!* The cover of the video had proclaimed) and her foray into dog-fucking for the bestiality black market. God had seen her toward the end too. Like when she was on her knees in a hotel room that could only be described as grotesque, as some fat fuck spit on her face and called her a "meat puppet" and she smiled and agreed because she needed some money for blow and because it kind of turned her on too.

God had been there the Day It All Changed, she was sure of that. She'd been lying in bed in another shitty room. She was sick with the flu, was sweating and cold, but the guy fucking her didn't care. He'd paid extra to do her without a condom, he had sores on his pecker, but she really didn't give a shit, she'd pretty much accepted that she was on her way out.

He was there above her, his tongue literally hanging out, panting like a dog, and then his face had changed. It had contorted into a look of pure hate. He'd raised a fist and started hitting her.

He didn't stop until he'd broken her nose in three places, broken her jaw, knocked out a tooth or two, blacked her eyes shut, broken her left arm, and cracked a few ribs. Then he fucked her again and she passed out.

She woke up in the hospital, and Father Yates was there, sitting next to her bed. He hadn't said anything. He'd just moved closer, had taken one of her hands into his, and had looked down on her with those gentle, gentle eyes.

She'd started crying then. She cried, on and off, for days. Father Yates and others from the church stayed by her bedside until she was ready to be released. They didn't preach or judge or even say much of anything at all. They were just there for her.

She'd come to understand that God was present for the good and the bad, and it wasn't that He was cruel, but that He knew—goodness was a choice. Rightness was a choice. Free will was the road to salvation, and God wasn't going to make you do the right thing. God's job was to be there if you chose Him, there if you didn't.

Father Yates and the church had helped her get onto her feet. Helped her clean up, find an apartment and a job. Were there for her in the beginning when she strayed, twice.

She remembers all of these things now, as she often does, and adds some final words to her prayer.

"Thank you God, for helping me, and for listening to my bad fucking mouth and my dirty thoughts, and for letting me say what I need to say so I can stay on the path. Amen."

Dirty words and evil thoughts were her secret things, and you can't stay clean with secrets so God let her spew her bile and never blinked, however raunchy things got.

She stands up and goes to shower. No work today, but discipline was the key to her life now. Waking every day at the same time, not letting herself sleep in or be slothful. Sunday through Friday she ran a mile. Saturday she let herself off on the running, but she still got up, showered, had her coffee, and then went to the church to volunteer.

All of which, she reflects, helps keep the real secret, the true dirtiness inside her, at bay. That one terrible thing when she'd—

A knock at the door startles her from this thought. She frowns.

Who the hell is that?

She grabs a bathrobe and checks her face in the mirror, chastising herself immediately for this vanity, knowing that this is one habit she'll never break.

She opens the door without peeking through the peephole. It's Saturday morning, and this is Simi Valley, after all. One of the safest cities in the nation.

The man has a gun and a smile. He levels the gun at her face and walks forward, causing her to backpedal.

"Scream and I'll shoot you dead," he observes, calm, cool, collected. He closes the door to the apartment.

"Who the fuck are you?" she asks, voice trembling.

He puts a finger to his lips.

"Shhhhhh . . . I have something for you, Rosemary."

He reaches into a jacket pocket and lifts out a bag. She recognizes it right away, of course.

Cocaine, sweet, beautiful, delicious cocaine.

"It's okay, Rosemary. God will forgive you for this, so long as you give yourself up to Him before I kill you. Remember: God is love."

She feels the old familiar demon rise inside her, even now, even after all these years, even with a gun in her face. She feels the truth that she so often reflects upon: she was a Jezebel born, not made.

Dear God, I'm scared, I'm so fucking scared, but even so, I want that coke so fucking bad, and (she can't be dishonest talking to God, not now not ever) it won't really be my fault because he's making me do it so that's kind of a relief because it sort of lets me off the hook, you know? Forgive me for that.

On the heels of this, puzzlement:

How does he know I'm a coke addict?

She struggles to remember if she'd seen his face at her Narcotics Anonymous meeting, or at her church.

No, she thinks. I would have remembered those eyes. Those awful eyes.

"Come now, Rosemary," the man says, his voice almost gentle. "We have work to do."

Does it matter, Lord? Does it matter that I never would have done this coke by myself? Even though I really want what he's giving me, doesn't it make a difference that I didn't go looking for it?

Rosemary had always felt the presence of God while praying, but never His voice. This time was no different. God didn't speak to her, but, as always, God was there.

He was there when she snorted the coke at gunpoint, He was even there when the end came, with all its darkness.

God never spoke, but He was there, and it was enough. She knew He heard her last thought, her final revelation.

Yeah, it does. It does make a difference. In fact, it makes THE difference. Our Father, who art in heaven, God oh my God, I love you so.

She would have died smiling if she hadn't been in so much pain.

11

Jones.

"Similar crime?" he asks. "Here?"

He doesn't groan, but I know he wants to because I feel the same way.

A killer who hops municipalities is a whole new monster. A man dedicated to his craft, a traveler, spreading the wreckage of his acts across multiple jurisdictions. It creates problems. Locals who don't want us playing in their sandbox. The potential for incompetence on the part of forensics or pathology increases by virtue of increasing the per capita of law-enforcement involvement. Not to mention the simple truth that some victims will fall through the cracks. VICAP, the Violent Crime Apprehension Program, which provides a national database of cross-referenced violent acts, is a voluntary program. Unless a local homicide cop decides to enter the crime into VICAP, it's not there to search for and find in the database.

"It's a headache," I agree.

"What do you want to do?"

I think about it. The truth is, I'm tired, my team is tired, and there's no way we'll be able to keep up our current pace for very long.

But . . .

The time he's most likely to err is in the commission of the crime itself. The longer he has to cool down, the more opportunity he has to cover his tracks, and worse, to refine his technique. The first murder, in most cases, is the sloppiest.

But this isn't his first now, is it? Maybe not even his tenth or his hundredth.

I sigh. "We'll continue blitzing it for now, sir. I'll fly back and check out the Sonnenfeld murder. The rest of my team will stay here."

"What's the division of labor?"

"Callie and James are processing Lisa's apartment personally. Alan is coordinating with the locals on the Ambrose scene."

"Is he really needed there?"

I consider this. "Probably not. I was going to have him do the passenger interviews, but the locals could do that. I'm sure Virginia forensics will pass muster and, besides, I think Ambrose was a throwaway."

"Big assumption."

"If Lisa wasn't random—and I feel strongly that she wasn't—then Ambrose was a means to an end, not the reason why." I sigh. "He was incidental. He's not going to give me any real insight."

"Then take Alan with you. Have him turn over the Ambrose scene and the passenger interviews to the locals." A pause. "I want you to have a partner with you when possible, Smoky. This guy seems to be pretty intent on getting law enforcement involved. That means he's going to be watching."

I'd already thought of this, but having AD Jones say it out loud sends a small icy shiver down my spine. On at least three occasions now the men I hunt have taken a personal interest in me and my team, and while we're all still alive, we've never walked away from those encounters unscathed.

"Roger that, sir."

"Keep me briefed."

He hangs up without saying good-bye. I dial Alan.

"Let me guess," he says without preamble. "We're going back to LA."

"How telepathic of you."

"Nah. If you hadn't asked me to come I would have insisted."

"I'll come pick you up," I say. " 'Bye."

I've been standing outside of Lisa's apartment to make these calls. I poke my head in.

"Callie!"

She walks out of Lisa's bedroom, digital camera held in gloved hands.

"What is it, honey-love?"

I explain about Rosemary Sonnenfeld. She raises an eyebrow.

"Busy boy."

"Yes. Alan and I are going to fly home and check that out. I need you and James to continue here. Collect everything you can find. When you're done, call for the plane and bring it all back with you."

"Do we get to sleep after?"

"If not, I'll buy the donuts."

Callie is addicted to miniature chocolate donuts. Loves them, really. It's a passionate affair.

"A fair trade," she says. "I accept."

"See you soon."

"Oh, and, Smoky? Say hi to my man if you see him. Tell him I expect sex when I return. Lots of it."

"I'm sure he'll be pleased to hear it."

She tosses her hair and smiles. "I just want to give him adequate time to prepare for the coming storm."

ALAN AND I ARE SITTING in the car waiting for the jet to arrive. He glances at his watch.

"We should get there by about six o'clock. I already talked to the Simi Valley cops and let them know we're coming. Some guy by the name of Atkins is the primary on the case."

"Where are they at with it?"

"All the forensic work is done, including the autopsy. They don't have any leads."

"Have they released the apartment yet?"

"Yeah."

"Damn."

I won't get the same opportunity I had with Lisa Reid.

"What do you want to do?"

"Let's meet with Atkins, find out everything we can about Rosemary Sonnenfeld, who she was and how she died. See if it takes us anywhere."

"Think it will?"

I glance at my friend and shrug.

"It will take us somewhere. Hopefully that's somewhere helpful."

He stares off and nods. I wonder if he hears it like I do, the humming in the stillness. Three newly dead, and more in the oven. My stomach is sour with worry and dismay, and I feel like cicadas are buzzing through my veins.

"ARE YOU COMING HOME TONIGHT?"

We're mid-flight and I'm on the plane's phone with Bonnie.

"I hope so, sweetheart. I miss you."

"I miss you too, but I'm okay. If you need to work, I won't mind."

"Thanks, babe. But I'm really going to try."

A pause.

"Smoky?"

"Yes?"

"I know you're busy, but I want you to make some time to talk with me about something soon."

My antennae go up. I can't remember Bonnie ever making a request like this. All kinds of things run through my head, good, bad, and banal. Mostly bad. I keep my voice calm.

"What's up, sweetheart?"

Another long pause, also uncharacteristic.

"Well, I've been thinking. You know I love Elaina. And I really did need to be homeschooled while I got better, but . . ."

"But?" I coax her.

She sighs, and it makes my heart hitch a bit. It's the sound of a little girl carrying a big weight. "Well, I think it's time for me to go to a normal school. You know, with other kids and stuff."

Now it's my turn to pause.

"Hm," I manage.

"I'm not asking you to decide right now, Momma-Smoky. I just wanted you to know. That I want to talk about it."

I clear my throat and force myself to sound reassuring and understanding.

"Sure, honey. Of course."

"Okay. Thanks." She sounds relieved.

Too relieved. What's she so worried about? Me? If so, not good.

I continue with the whole reassuring and understanding thing, in spite of my inner turmoil. Some things you never forget how to do as a parent. Calm and smiling while it storms inside, no problem, like riding a bike.

"I'll talk to you later, babe. Too much."

"Way too much," she replies.

We spend a lot of time together, but we also spend a lot of time apart by virtue of what I do. We've developed an emotional shorthand that works wonders for us. "Too much" is one of our phrases, the answer to the unspoken question, "how much do I love you?" It was super sappy and absolutely appropriate.

God, I love this girl.

" 'Bye, sweetheart," I murmur.

" 'Bye."

I hang up and stare out the small window, watching the clouds go by. I search for a level place inside myself, but I'm having trouble. Fear is my oldest friend and he's taken advantage of my unease to cuddle up close.

"Something wrong?" Alan asks, startling me from my reverie.

I shrug. "Bonnie. She wants to talk about going to public school."

He raises both eyebrows in surprise.

"Wow."

"Yeah, wow."

"Scares you, huh?"

His eyes are gentle, patient, kind. Alan knows me pretty well, and a lot of that is because I trust him so much.

I sigh. "It terrifies me. I mean, I understand. She's twelve. I knew I couldn't keep her inside a cocoon forever. But it scares me to think about her . . . *out there.*"

He nods. "Understandable. She's been treated rough. So have you."

"That's the problem. Every parent worries about sending their child out into the world. But not every parent has seen what I have. The possibilities aren't just theoretical for me."

"Yeah." He is silent for a moment. "I love Bonnie, Smoky, you know that. Truth is, the idea scares me too. Not just for her—though that's the biggest part of it, of course—but also for Elaina, and for you. Bonnie is your second chance at being a mom, and probably Elaina's only chance to experience a little of what that's like. You and Elaina are the most important women in my life, and if something happened to Bonnie . . . I don't know. I don't think either of you would make it back from that."

He smiles, rueful. "But on the other hand, I'm happy about it. Because it means that that little girl really is okay." He looks at me, his gaze intense. "You understand? She's not afraid to venture out into the world again. That's *progress,* Smoky. It means we've done good by her. And that's pretty cool."

I smile at my friend. He hasn't taken away my fear, but he has tempered it, a little. Because what he's said is true. Bonnie was almost lost to the world after a visit from a monster. Her soul had been flickering out there on the edge of forever, a tiny candle in a rainstorm. The essence of her had nearly been snuffed out.

Now she was telling me that she was strong enough to want to start building a life with more than just me in it. It was terrifying, it might even make me a little bit jealous, but yes, it was also pretty cool.

"Thanks, Alan. That helps."

"No problem. Just don't expect me to be all wise and understanding when she starts dating."

I grin at him. "Dating? There will be no dating going on."

He grins back.

"Amen to that."

12

SIMI VALLEY, LIKE MUCH OF VENTURA COUNTY, IS MUCH NICER than LA proper. It's younger, smaller, and safer. The 118 freeway connects Simi and the San Fernando Valley, but the drive between the two takes you through undeveloped country, rolling hills and mini-mountains.

The easternmost side of Simi Valley is older, with homes that date back to the sixties. As in all things USA, the more west you go, the newer things are.

This is what California used to be, I think. Clean air, unending sun in the spring and summer, a horizon you could still see. Simi is a fair-sized city, but it lacks the congestion and traffic snarl that has been a staple of Los Angeles for many moons.

Traffic is annoying but not crippling and we arrive at the police station around 7:00 P.M.

"That must be Atkins," Alan says.

I see a middle-aged man with a receding brunet hairline in the parking lot of the station, leaning up against his car. He's wearing a charcoal gray suit, not off the rack but not Armani either. He spots us and comes up to greet us as we park.

"You must be Agent Washington," Atkins says to Alan, putting out his hand with a smile. "No offense, but you're pretty hard to miss."

"I get that a lot."

"I'll bet." Atkins turns to me. "And you're Agent Barrett."

His eyes dance over my scars, something I'm long used to by now. I don't mind certain subsets of the population examining my face. Homicide cops like Atkins, for example. His interest is genuine and quizzical. He looks, shrugs inside, and lets it go, no disgust or horror evident. Most physicians do the same. Small children run the gamut from "is that your real face?" to, in the case of nine-year-old boys, "wow, cool!"

"Thanks for meeting us this late," I say, shaking the hand he's offered.

"Hey, anything that will help me crack this case." His eyes go flat, expressionless. "This one bothers me."

He doesn't elaborate. He doesn't have to. You see a lot of dead people, doing what we do. None of it is good, but some of the corpses become ghosts.

"Tell us about it," Alan says.

Atkins inclines his head. "I can tell you about her death, and I will, but first I thought I'd take you to see a man who can tell you about her life."

"Who?" I ask.

"Father Yates. Catholic priest in the Valley who almost literally pulled Rosemary out of the gutter."

Alan looks at me and raises an inquiring eyebrow.

"In for a penny, in for a pound," I quip, using humor to push aside my exhaustion. I gesture to Atkins's car. "You drive. You can fill us in on the way there."

IT OCCURS TO ME THAT American carmakers are unlikely to go out of business as long as police forces exist. The car is a fixed-up Crown Vic, no longer black and white, just black and sleek with a growl under the hood.

It's dark out now, the moon is up, and we're headed back down the 118 freeway again. It's rush-hour light at the moment; there are other cars around us, but the distance and speed are companionable. The sky is cloudless and the moon is full. Silver, not yellow. It makes some of the rocky hills in the distance look like they have snow on top.

I'm in the front seat with Atkins, Alan is in the back.

"Rosemary Sonnenfeld. Single white female, age thirty-four, five-five, approx. one hundred twenty-five pounds, in good physical shape. She was found dead in her apartment with a bag of coke on the nightstand next to her. On first glance the thought was that Rosemary had reverted to type. She was an ex-prostitute, ex-porn girl, ex-coke and sex addict. I thought she'd probably decided to get high and maybe was a little out of practice on her coke usage and over-dosed."

"Makes sense," Alan says. "What changed your mind?"

"A closer look. Tox screen showed she had enough coke in her system to kill a horse, but she'd also been stabbed in the side."

"Interesting," I allow, not yet willing to give up data on Lisa Reid.

"Yeah. Then, of course, there was the cross. Silver cross, about two inches high and one inch wide. Engraved with a skull and crossbones and the number one forty-two on the back. It had been inserted into her."

The same as Lisa Reid, I think. *And one forty-two? Lisa was one forty-three.*

"If all that wasn't enough to call it a homicide," Atkins continues, "the icing on the cake is that the cross was inserted postmortem."

"Yeah, that's pretty definitive," Alan says.

"Then there's Father Yates."

"What do you mean?" I ask.

"Yates is a priest who does a lot of good, but he's no fool. He made Rosemary do a piss test once a month at a local clinic."

"Really?" I ask, surprised. "Sounds like a pretty distrustful priest."

Atkins smiles. "Father Yates is a realist. He's a true believer, and he does good work. But he has a three strikes rule. If he takes you in and helps you get clean, you get three relapses and then you're gone."

"So I take it Rosemary had stayed clean."

"For over four years. I checked her record. Nothing during that time. She'd held a steady job, she volunteered at the church every weekend. Everything says that she really had gone on the straight and narrow."

"I can see why this one got to you," I say.

Most people think that cops are cynics. There is truth to that stereotype. We see the worst that people can do or be. It makes us . . .

attentive. But we're people too. Most of those I've known in law enforcement, however hardened they may be, still harbor a willingness to believe that someone could—maybe—turn their life around. A bad guy or girl could—maybe—wake up one day and decide to become a good guy or girl. It's just that—a maybe—but it never really goes away. No one can live with the idea that man is basically evil and stay happy.

"Yeah," Atkins says. "Anyway. It was a homicide, but everything dead-ended. Forensics came up with nada. We couldn't find any past known associates that were still alive. Ten days later, no viable suspects." He shakes his head in frustration. "I've been doing this for a while, Agent Barrett. I know when a case is going to go cold. This had that feel to it—until Agent Washington called me."

"Was there any evidence of sexual violation? Any ejaculate near the body?"

"No."

"How was her body positioned? Were her legs together or apart?"

"Together. Arms folded over her chest."

"Interesting," I murmur.

"What?" Atkins asks.

"Our other victim was a transsexual. Rosemary was an ex-porn actress and sex addict. Based on our victims, I would have expected a sexual component to these crimes, but it's been absent both times. The only commonality we know of is the cross. Strange."

"What's it mean?" Alan asks, prodding me.

I shake my head. "I don't know yet. Let's see what the priest can tell us."

"ROSEMARY WAS ONE OF MY favorite successes. One Rosemary could make up for ten failures. You understand?"

Father Yates is a very fit fiftyish. He has rough-hewn, handsome features, close-cropped salt and pepper hair, and dark, intelligent eyes. They are what I used to call "priest eyes" to my friends. Too full of kindness to get self-righteous with, too full of an understanding of the ways of sin to hide anything from. I grew up Catholic, though I am long lapsed, and I recognize the type of priest Yates is: hands-on, approachable, devout without being out of touch with the realities of life.

Perhaps if more priests were like him, I wouldn't have lapsed.

He's a tall man, about six foot five, thin without being gangly. He wears a short-sleeve shirt with the white collar at the throat. His hands are restless. This is an energetic priest, a man of action. Working for God, to him, means *working* for God.

I like him.

"I do understand, Father. We enjoy similar victories, sometimes, and they make up for the failures. Mostly."

Those priest eyes fix on mine and I feel the old, familiar flush of guilt. He knows, he knows. He knows I masturbate sometimes with the help of a vibrator. He knows I take a secret pleasure at making a man come with my mouth.

Sweet Jesus—and there's another one, blasphemy—I thought I was past all this!

I know, at some level, that it's all in my head. Father Yates is no mind reader. I even recognize the phenomenon; put a civilian in an interrogation room with me, and he'll feel exactly the same way.

"Yes," he replies, nodding. "I imagine there are a lot of parallels in what we do."

"I'll bet," I agree. "We both know about the dark side of people. You've probably heard about most of the crimes I've seen."

He waves a hand. "I've heard everything in confession. Pedophilia. Incest. Rape. Murder. The difference, I suppose, is in our methods."

"I jail them, you try and set them free."

It comes out sounding a little bit sarcastic. I hadn't intended it to.

He gives a faint, amused smile. "And which do you think is more effective?"

I spread my hands. "They can find God in prison too, Father. But at least in prison, they can't hurt anyone else."

He chuckles. "Fair enough, Agent Barrett. I won't press the point. I believe the truth of a person can be found in their actions. It may not be the party line for the church at the moment, but I care more about how you live your life than about how often you receive Communion." His expression becomes more grave. "I'm familiar with your story, and with some of the men you've put away. You're a force for good, I think."

I laugh. I don't take offense at his use of a caveat; I can tell that he's teasing me.

"I appreciate that, Father."

Alan and Atkins are sitting a few pews back. They're keeping quiet, remaining unobtrusive. This is an interview, not an interrogation. Intimacy is all.

"Tell me about Rosemary," I prod.

"I've been the pastor here at the Redeemer for twenty years, Agent Barrett. As I think you know, Los Angeles is a temperamental city, full of contrasts. Within the surrounding five blocks you will find upstanding, middle class families, teenage prostitutes, honor roll students, gang members—all sharing the same pavement."

"Yes."

"When I was called by God, I always knew that He would want me to be a hands-on priest. My gifts don't lie in giving a Mass. I do the job, but I'm not a tremendous public speaker. God knew that what I had to offer was an ability to witness the evil in others without losing faith in the possibility of redemption." He smiles a wry smile. "He knew, of course, that I was also blessed with a big mouth and a questioning mind. Don't misunderstand, I stand behind my church with all my heart, but I lack political dexterity. If I think an ecclesiastical law should be reviewed, I'll say so."

"I understand," I reply, amused.

It's interesting to me to find that even within the confines of the church, there is a divide between the "suits" and the men on the ground, between the officers and the sergeants.

"I was relegated to this tiny church because they had to put me somewhere. They knew it would be wrong to cloister me away—the church is not always blind, in spite of what some think—but they didn't want me in the limelight either." He grins and I can almost see him twenty years ago, vibrant, a rebel. "I was overjoyed. This was, and has always been, where I wanted to be."

A question occurs to me. "Father, if I can ask—what did you do before the priesthood?"

He nods in approval. "Very germane, Agent Barrett. Before I was a priest, I was a troubled young man. I spent time in reform school for petty theft, I had careless affairs with women, I drank, and I engaged in casual violence."

He says it all with such ease, without the slightest hint of shame. Not proud of his past, but not apologizing for it either.

"What changed?" I ask.

"I met a very tough old priest by the name of Father Montgomery. He grabbed me by the scruff of the neck and set me straight. He impressed me. Here was a man of God—a profession I'd always considered for suckers—who didn't blink at the sight of blood, or turn up his nose at a young girl who came in to pray wearing her leather mini skirt and platform shoes. He'd give her Communion even though he knew she was going to walk out the door and sell her body afterward. He had a saying: 'Leave your knives at the door, and you're welcome here.' "

"Where was this?"

"Detroit." He shrugs. "He turned me around. I got the calling, and as I said, I knew that God wanted me to emulate Father Montgomery. Which I have tried to do."

"Rosemary," I prod again.

"Rosemary was a very troubled young woman. Her story wasn't exactly original. A difficult teen, she ended up doing drugs and selling her body. What made Rosemary different, more complex, was the component of addiction. She truly enjoyed the combination of drug use and depraved sex. I don't mean that she thought it was right or good. But it gave her great pleasure. She sought it out. Rosemary was not the innocent victim of a smooth-talking pimp. She had no family history of abuse." He shakes his head, remembering something. "She told me once, she was 'just born bad.' I was alerted to her arrival in the ER by a nurse who is a member of my congregation. That nurse's words, essentially: 'This girl has hit rock bottom, Father. She will either turn around or she will die.' "

"Had she? Hit rock bottom?"

"Oh yes. She had been beaten nearly to death by a john while she was high on cocaine, and she had chlamydia, syphilis, and gonorrhea raging through her—along with a touch of the flu."

"Wow."

"Yes. She'd escaped HIV infection, thank God, and the syphilis was recent. The Holy Spirit must have been watching over Rosemary."

I think this is debatable, but I keep it to myself.

"Go on, please, Father."

"I was there when she woke up. She couldn't stop crying. I asked her the question I always ask: Are you ready for my help? Rosemary said that she was. I arranged a place for her to stay, members of the church helped her get clean, we prayed together." His eyes get sad. "We prayed together a lot." He looks at me. "This was the thing about Rosemary that you have to understand to really care about her, Agent Barrett. Not every detail of her recovery, not even every detail of her sins. But that somehow, from somewhere, this hopeless girl found inside herself a tremendous strength. It never got easier for her. She told me she still thought about drugs and sex almost every day. The longing grew more distant, but it never disappeared. Still, she held on." He clenches his hands in frustration. "She had been living in God's grace for five years. No drugs, no reversions to former behaviors. I hate to use the word, but it applies here—Rosemary had been *saved*."

"I see." I am not convinced, but I'm willing to accept the possibility that Rosemary's change had taken. Father Yates is not operating with blinders on, after all.

"There was also the fact that . . ." He hesitates.

"What?"

"I take confession, of course. I can never tell you what she said, but I can tell you this: She trusted me with the worst parts of herself. She held nothing back."

I am intrigued. *Way* more than curious. But I know this man will never give up Rosemary's confidence. I find an unexpected comfort in this certainty.

The roots of the Catholic tree run deep, I muse.

"Is there anything else you can tell me, Father? Anything you think might help?"

"I'm sorry, Agent Barrett. I'm afraid the only thing I can really provide is a memory of Rosemary at her worst and her best."

I reach into my purse, pull out my card, and give it to him.

"Call me if you think of anything, Father."

"I promise." His gaze lingers on mine for a moment. "And what do *you* think about prayer, Agent Barrett?"

I stare at him, caught by surprise. "Personally, I've found it to be overrated and the results underwhelming."

The words snap out, uncensored. I regret their vehemence. I shrug in apology.

"Sorry."

"Not at all. If you're mad at God, that means you still believe He exists. I'll take that for now."

I don't know what to say to this, so I just mumble, "Thank you, Father," like a six-year-old and head toward the front doors of the church. Alan and Atkins follow.

Damn those priest eyes. Sometimes the holy really do annoy me.

13

IT'S AFTER EIGHT-THIRTY. ALAN, ATKINS, AND I ARE SEATED
in a booth at the back of a Denny's. It's a slow night and our waitress
is tired. She manages a halfhearted smile as she tops off our coffee
cups but doesn't try to chat us up. I guess she's used to serving cops.

Vinyl and formica as far as the eye can see, I muse. Is there anything more American?

Atkins has given us a copy of the case file, replete with crime scene
photos. Now that our waitress is at a safe distance, I open it up and
examine the photographs.

"Ugly," I observe.

"But neat," Atkins replies.

It's an insightful comment. He's right. I'm looking at a photograph of Rosemary. She had been a pretty woman. In the photograph
she is nude, lying on her back on her bed. Her legs are closed. Her
arms rest on her chest. Her head is thrown back and her eyes are
opened wide. A line of dried blood runs from her right nostril at an
angle, following her cheek to her jawline. It's a terrible image, but not
as terrible as it could be. There's no evidence of sexual abuse. Other
than the blood from her nose and the puncture and bruise on her
right side, Rosemary's body is almost pristine.

"No rage here," Alan says.

"Yes," I reply.

Sexual psychopathy is not an act of simple anger. It is an act of violent, mind-bending rage. Penetration is not enough; it's destruction that is required. I don't see any of that in these photographs. Sex doesn't seem to be the motive. I close the file and take a sip from my coffee cup.

"The Crime Scene Unit found nada," Atkins says.

"I'm not surprised," I tell him. "This perp is very organized and very experienced. He had a job to do and he did it, no muss no fuss. He got in and got out. You always see less transference in those circumstances."

"Then how do you catch him?"

Sometimes you don't, the cicadas buzz.

"By figuring out why he does what he does. And by hoping, as time goes on, that he'll slip up and leave us a clue."

"That's not real comforting."

I give him my bleakest smile. "We don't do comforting in this line of work, Atkins. You know that."

He returns the smile, just as bleak, and raises his coffee cup in agreement.

ALAN AND I ARE ON the highway again, headed home. Alan is driving. We had left Atkins with promises, but not much reassurance.

"You want me to take you by my place to get Bonnie?" he asks.

I look at my watch. It's almost ten-thirty.

"No. Drop me off at home. I'll come get her tomorrow."

I consider dialing Callie and James, but realize it's after 1:00 A.M. where they are. If they are asleep—and I hope they are—I don't want to wake them.

"Been a pretty crazy few days," Alan says.

"Sure has."

He glances at me. "Any insight to offer yet?"

I shake my head. "Not really. I need to get some sleep and let it percolate. There are things that bother me a lot about this one, though."

"Like?"

"Like I think this perp has been killing for a long time, and I think he's gotten pretty good at it. I think he's methodical and organized and that he's not going to slip up any time soon."

"He's already slipped up. He let us know he's there."

"True, but that was purposeful. We're still playing catch-up."

Alan smiles a faint smile. "You always start out cynical on a case. We still end up getting our guy when it's all over."

"Then, by that logic, let me stay pessimistic for now."

He laughs. My cell phone rings. My heart lifts a little when I see who it is.

Tommy Aguilera has been my boyfriend for a little over two years. Tommy is an ex–Secret Service agent who now does private security and investigation work. I had met him when he was still in the Service. He'd been assigned to guard someone who turned out to be a serial killer. Tommy had found it necessary to shoot the young man at one point and in the ensuing firestorm, my testimony kept him from being hung out to dry. He'd been very grateful and had told me to let him know if I ever needed anything.

He left the Service a few years later. I still don't know why. He would probably tell me if I asked, but I have never asked, and he has never offered. It's not that Tommy's cold, he's just laconic in extremis.

I had taken him up on his offer of help during a case. He'd come over to my home to sweep for bugs (which he found, along with a GPS tracker on my car). It wasn't planned, but I ended up kissing him, and he'd surprised me by kissing me back.

My husband had only been dead for six months, my body was scarred, I felt ugly inside and out, and I hurt. Tommy took me in his arms and made me feel desirable again. This was satisfying on levels both spiritual and venal. Tommy is a lovely man; he's also a hunk and a half.

He's Latin, with the requisite dark hair, tan skin, and brooding eyes. He is not a pretty boy; he has a scar at his left temple and a strong jawline. He has the rough hands of a construction worker and the body of a dancer. Tommy is a delicious sight when his clothes are off, and sex with him can be rough or gentle or languorous; he's a sweaty joy beneath the sheets.

"Hey," I answer.

"Hey," he replies. "You still out of town?"

"Nope. I'm heading home right now, as a matter of fact."

"Want company?"

"Yes, please. Are you up for giving me a foot massage? I need to unwind a little."

"Sure. See you soon."

I hang up and find myself humming a little. I stop, mortified, and sneak a glance at Alan. It looks like he has all his attention on the road, but then he speaks.

"That guy seems to make you happy."

"He's okay," I say.

"Hm."

I look at my friend. "What, 'hm'?"

"It's not my business, Smoky, but you might want to consider taking the qualification off that. You deserve to be happy, and he probably deserves to know that he makes you feel that way."

I am surprised at the sudden surge of annoyance running through me. I feel a retort ready to trip off my tongue, but I manage to choke it back.

"I'll take it under advisement," I mumble.

"Hey." It's a soft rebuke, like a friendly hand under the chin lifting my reluctant gaze to his. "I'm just talking here. I like seeing you smile over a guy again, that's all."

The annoyance vanishes. I sigh.

"Me too, I think."

14

I TURN THE KNOB AND OPEN THE DOOR AND FIND WHAT I'D expected: the stillness and quiet of an empty house.

This is the home that Matt and I bought together. It is the home where I learned about being a wife, a mother, and where all of that was lost to me. This is the home where I was destroyed and where I rebuilt myself again.

Three years have passed since my Matt and my Alexa died. I no longer wake up screaming, I no longer stare at my gun in the middle of the night wondering if it would hurt when the bullet took the top of my head off, I no longer walk through my life with my soul in a deep freeze. I have Bonnie now, and Tommy, and of course I have my team. I have learned to start enjoying life again. The cynic in me hesitates to say that life is *good*, but I am allowed to say that life is *better*.

Even so . . . loss can come at oblique angles. It is the contrasts that still have power.

Matt was a perfect fit for me, for us, for the way our life was. It wasn't unusual for me to arrive home at nine o'clock in the evening, soul-tired and smelling of the dead. I'd hesitate before opening the door then too. I'd stop, key in the lock, and I'd try to shake off the dark stuff, to make sure I didn't drag it into the light and love of my home. It didn't always work, but I always tried.

I'd open the door and all the lights would be on because Matt liked light. He'd usually have the TV going or maybe the stereo because he was comforted by the background noise. The smell of something yummy would be in the air. Matt was a fabulous cook. If there was a cookbook for it, he could make it happen.

He'd always come to greet me when I got home. This is something that never changed, not after years and years and years of marriage. It didn't matter if we were fighting or loving each other.

Welcome back, traveler, he'd always say. That was our phrase, as necessary and natural as the sun or the rain.

In the days before Alexa was born, he'd feed me some good food and maybe a small glass of wine and he'd listen to me bitch and moan about my day and then I'd listen to him bitch and moan about his and we might watch some TV together. We'd usually end up having sex before falling asleep. We had a lot of sex in those early times. Good sex, okay sex, even some bad sex (though, as Matt pointed out, there was really no such thing as a bad orgasm).

As the marriage progressed, the frequency of the sex changed, but the great thing about being married to Matt was that the marriage *progressed,* it never *wore on.* We stopped being novelties to each other, but we never really lost our wonder.

Alexa was born and that added a new dimension to coming home. When she was younger, I came to her. As she grew older, she came to me. She picked up her father's phrase, and I would hear it in stereo sometimes.

Welcome back, traveler, kick off your boots, the weather outside may be fair to partly crappy, but in here it's all sun all the time.

The cliché becomes a cliché because it was true enough to be repeated often enough: there's a difference between a house and a home.

Things are not the same now. When I walk in, the lights are off. The place is a little bit chilly. No food smells dancing around. No TV noises, no stereo playing.

The other thing missing is the plants. Matt maintained a small indoor jungle. Me? I am death on plants. I don't just kill them, they commit suicide in my presence. They slash their little planty wrists the moment they find themselves under my care.

Welcome back, traveler.

But it's not the same.

I remember what Rosario said to me in the car, about this place being where I had my roots, and I wonder at the truth of that. I've moved on, but will I ever really let go of the past, living in this home?

I close the door behind me and move through the living room and into the kitchen, flipping on lights and the TV as I pass. A news anchor chatters away and fills the emptiness a little. I pop some macaroni and cheese into the microwave. This is another difficult area for me—I can't cook. I could burn water.

I pour myself a glass of wine and grab my mac and cheese when it's done and I take them with me to the couch. Matt always insisted we eat at the dinner table like a civilized family.

Then change it, dummy. You have Bonnie now. You have Tommy. Start eating at the dinner table. Hell, put the TV on a timer if you like so you have some noise to come home to.

My spirits lift a little. Pragmatism has always been my strength. I like to fix things when they break. Crying in my beer (or wine, as the case may be) goes against my grain. I've spent more than enough time weeping in the last few years. Less tears, more sweat. Giddyup.

Good idea, Mrs. Barrett, I say to myself. Hear, hear.

I giggle at this internal interchange. I no longer worry about being crazy because of it. I figure this either means I've changed for the better or really *have* gone crazy.

I watch the news as I polish off the pseudo-food. Nothing new; civilization continues to teeter on the precipice, as it has been doing since the reporting of news began. There's no mention of Lisa Reid yet.

When the knock comes, a tingly little happiness jolts through me. I dump the empty macaroni and cheese container into the trash and find myself hurrying to the door.

I open it and smile at the man in my life. He's wearing a dark jacket and slacks, and a white shirt with no tie. His hair is a little rumpled, but he looks, as always, like a very edible million bucks.

"Hey," he says, one word suffused with warmth and backed with a big smile. He's as happy to see me as I am to see him.

I angle my head up for a kiss and he gives me a long one.

"Welcome back, traveler," I murmur.

He raises an eyebrow. "I think I should be telling you that." He smiles. He comes in and flops down on the couch. "You've been a busy lady."

I sit down next to him and put my feet on his lap. It's an unspoken demand for a massage. Tommy complies, and I almost arch my back as those strong hands begin rubbing the tension away.

"Yeah," I reply. "Too bad you can't get frequent flier miles on a private jet. Jesus, that feels good."

"You want to talk about it?"

It occurs to me that this is one of the big differences between the relationship I have with Tommy and the one I had with Matt. I didn't talk with Matt about my cases, not often. I kept that out of my home, away from him and Alexa. Tommy is different. He understands death and murder, and, like me, he's killed people. I can talk with him about my work and it won't damage him, because, well, that damage has already been done.

"Sure," I say, "as long as you don't stop giving me those foot orgasms."

I give him a lengthy recap of the last day and a half. He listens, nodding at spots, without ever once missing a beat on the massage.

"Wow," he says when I'm done. "Complicated."

"No kidding." I count off on my fingers. "Let's see: I have the transsexual daughter of a congressman—said congressman also happens to be a favored presidential hopeful—murdered mid-flight, pulling me and my team out of our usual jurisdiction and onto a political minefield. I have a born-again ex-addict-hooker-porn girl killed back here. Both of them had crosses stuffed into their bodies by the killer, and the numbers on the crosses are in the one hundreds—which, by the way, I don't think is symbolic at all. I have no leads to speak of yet. In the middle of it all, Callie is getting married, and James dropped the bombshell that he's gay." I run a hand through my hair. "Craziness." I force a smile. "At least it's not boring."

He smiles back but it's a smile with a quality to it that I can't quite place. His massage of my feet has become automatic, almost absent-minded.

Nervous, I realize. Mr. Stoic is nervous.

I pull my feet away. "Something you want to tell me?"

Silence. He leans back, looks at the ceiling and sighs. "Yeah."

"Well? You're starting to give me the jitters."

He gives me a very, very speculative gaze. It does nothing to alleviate my nervousness.

"You know that I have a little integrity problem, right?" he asks.

"Is that a joke? You're a total Boy Scout. You don't even curse."

"Yeah, well. That's what I'm talking about. I understand compromise, okay? It's a part of living, and it's for sure a part of living *with* someone. My problem is, when it comes to integrity, I can't compromise. Not even a little, not ever. It's created real problems for me in the past. There were times in the Service when people wanted me to see a little more gray, a little less black and white."

"I'm sure, but I think that's a good quality."

He smiles and shakes his head. "We'll see about that. I realized a few days ago that there's something I need to say to you. That I have to say to you. It might not be the best time to say it, compromise might be the better part of valor, and so on, but—" He shrugs. "It's a point of integrity."

My stomach is a gold-medal gymnast, *flip flip flip flip flip*.

"What I said earlier? About making me nervous?" I punch his arm. "We're heading toward terrified here."

"Then I'll just say it." He takes a deep breath and looks me right in the eyes. "I'm in love with you, Smoky. I told you a couple years back that I knew it would happen, and that I'd let you know when it did. Well, it has. I've fallen in love with you. The moment I was sure, I realized I had to tell you." Another shrug, a little weaker this time. "One of those integrity things."

I am speechless.

He loves me.

Wow.

He loves me?

Say something, stupid. But try not to say something stupid.

I clear my throat. It comes out in a stammer. "I—I—wow, I'm not sure what to say."

I regret these words the moment they come out. This man, this wonderful man, has just said that he loves me, and that's the best I can do?

"Oh, for fuck's sake, Tommy. I'm sorry. That was lame as lame can be."

He amazes me by smiling.

"Relax. I'm smart enough to understand that you need some time to process this. I'm not insecure enough to need an answer right

away. I just had to tell you, had to cross that bridge and burn it behind me. It was time."

I look at him and take care to choose the words I'll say next, because I know what I say next is very, very important. I opt in the end
for good old-fashioned bare naked honesty. I grab his hands in mine.
I want the contact.

"I do need time. I wish I didn't, but I do. That doesn't mean I'm
saying I don't feel the same way. It just means . . ." I search for the
words that fit what I'm feeling. "I'm scared."

He brings my hands up to his mouth. He gives each one a soft kiss,
two benedictions. His eyes are full of a gentle compassion that I've
never really seen in him before. I have seen kind Tommy, angry
Tommy, thoughtful Tommy, deadly Tommy. This is a new Tommy;
understanding and empathy without the sometimes saccharine false-
ness of sympathy.

Ahh, I realize, this is loving Tommy.

"You loved one man, Smoky. You met Matt when you were both
still teenagers, and you knew he was the one. You never doubted it,
you never wondered about it, you never longed for something else.
You lost him because of a tragedy, not by choice. It makes sense that
this would knock you for a loop. I can understand you not having an
answer right now. I just need you to think about it and figure out
what the answer is."

The words, their compassion, their complete lack of agenda, are a
punch to the gut. They squeeze the breath out of me. A lone tear rolls
down the unscarred side of my face. Tommy reaches out a thumb and
wipes it away as gently as he can.

"Don't cry, baby."

He's never called me that before, *baby*, never used such a personal
term of endearment, and it undoes me for reasons I can't quite grasp.
I have no idea why. I move into his arms and bawl my eyes out against
his chest. It's not a bad grief, there's no despair in it. It's a thunder-
storm that's rolled in, clouds that have to cry. I pound against his
rocks for a few moments, he takes it, the tears eventually stop and
turn into sniffles, he is quiet and strokes my hair. It occurs to me
that I could stay right here forever, if this moment was all he wanted
from me.

But there's the rub. He doesn't just want this, he wants everything.

I pull away from him, and wipe my cheeks with the palms of my hands.

"Where does that leave us in the meantime?" My voice is husky from the tears.

His eyes are a little bit sad. "We need to spend some time apart. You need to process this and I need to not sleep with you until you do."

"What? Why?"

It's the question of a child. The truth is, I know why.

"I can't sleep with a woman after I've told her that I love her until I know she feels the same way. It's not a punishment or an ultimatum, Smoky. I just can't be with someone who feels less for me than I feel for her."

I stare at him for a long time and then I sigh. "Yeah. I couldn't be with you either, if the shoe was on the other foot."

He leans forward and he takes my face in his hands. They are strong hands, rough hands, soft in places, callused in others. He brings his lips to mine and the kiss is perfection. Deep, passionate, *Casablanca* all the way. It leaves me breathless and teary-eyed again.

He stands up.

"You know where to find me."

"Hey, Tommy," I call after him as he walks toward the door. "That integrity thing? You're right, it's a real pisser."

No reply.

"Tommy?"

He stops, turns his head to look at me.

"Yeah?"

I manage a smile.

"I still think it's a good quality."

He returns the smile, tips an imaginary hat with his fingers, and then he's gone.

I am left alone again with all my contrasts. They're like bats that chuckle as they tangle in my hair. I pull my knees up to my chin and wrap my arms around my shins. I rock back and forth.

"Fuck fuck fuck fuck fuck." The tears are coming again, hot galloping horses behind my eyes.

And me without any ice cream.

Hey, that inner voice says, a little sly. You still got some Jose Cuervo hidden away in the upper kitchen cabinet.

I ignore myself and stick with my most faithful friend: the *good cry*. AMA—After Matt and Alexa—I've spent a lot of time with my good buddy grief. We hang out together for a few minutes, a worthy jag, and then I send him on his way.

I lean back on the couch and stare at the ceiling while I sniffle. I feel drained and miserable.

What is your problem, anyway? Tommy's a good man. No, scratch that—Tommy is a great man. He's honest, he's loyal, he's sexy as hell, he loves you. Like you have so many other choices?

But it's not about Tommy, I know this. It's not about the present. It's about the past.

Sure, there was a time when the idea of being with another man felt like a betrayal of Matt. Matt's ghost used to be everywhere; here in the living room, standing in the kitchen, lying in bed next to me. But Matt's just a lovely memory now, not a phantom.

Besides, I know Matt would want me to be happy again.

So? Then what?

Well, there is Bonnie . . .

I shake my head.

No. Don't you put it on her.

One of the last holdouts of Bonnie's childhood is her penchant for Saturday morning cartoons. She never misses them and when Tommy is here, he gets up and they watch them together. I don't share their love of early mornings, but I have stumbled down the stairs toward the coffeepot on a number of occasions to find them laughing together as horrible things happen to Wile E. Coyote. I don't know if I would call it a father/daughter bond that they have, not yet, but Bonnie cares for Tommy, and she knows that he cares for her.

The truth is, I realize, I can't pin this terror on anyone but myself.

So why?

A word bubbles up from the darker parts of me, like brimstone from a crack in the earth.

Punishment.

I turn the word over in the mouth of my mind, tasting its bitterness and wondering at the slight hint of terror it seems to bring.

Punishment? For what?

You know what. For that unforgivable thing you did after Matt and Alexa died. That thing that no one knows about, not even Callie.

I clap my hands together. The sound is startling in this quiet house. A rifle crack. I do it again. *Crack!*

We're not thinking about that right now! Not now, maybe not ever. NO way.

Inner me pauses. I sense sadness now, not slyness.

Well, fine. But it's why you're afraid to love him: you don't think you have the right to love anybody.

I have no reply to this; none is needed. Truth tends to get the last word.

I stand up and head for the kitchen. I need a distraction, now now now. Jose Cuervo will do just fine, thank you.

I grab the bottle from its hiding place in the upper cabinet and I pour myself a shot. I lift the glass in an angry toast.

"To the truth that the truth doesn't always set you free."

The tequila goes down like the paint stripper that it is. The heat blossoms in my belly and brings a rush of focus and contentment with it. I put the bottle back and clean the shotglass, making sure to leave no trace of this little secret. I'm too disciplined to be a drunk, but I only drink tequila in such moments of weakness. This never fails to deliver a prick of shame and a need to conceal.

The bitterness, that jittery taste of terror and dismay, has not been so much expunged as blurred. Its sharp edges are now covered in foam rubber and that'll work for now.

"For my next trick," I mutter, padding back to the living room, "I will turn to my most long-term and beloved addiction."

Work.

Work, work, sweet glorious work. One of the fine things about having a job with real purpose is that you can use it to replace yourself when you need to. That cicada buzz can be seductive as well as stressful.

I grab the yellow legal pad and pen from the coffee table. I keep this pad there for one of my own rituals. Late at night (like now) when

I am alone, I curl my feet under me and try to bring order to the jumble of data in whatever case I'm working on.

It helps me focus and has led to any number of useful epiphanies over the years. It's also a pretty good talisman. Scratching away on that yellow pad helps beat back thoughts I don't want around.

There are certain axioms I've developed over the years about homicides. Pragmatisms. Insights. I concentrate on these and jot them down to get the wheels turning in their grooves and dispel Tommy and the ghosts he brings.

The Victim is always everything. Even when the murder is a random event, remember: the thing we choose on the spur of the moment can be the most revealing.

A killer once told me he chose his strangling victims by watching for the first woman who made eye contact with him. I pointed out that, somehow, these first women were always blonde. He thought about this, laughed, and admitted that his mother had been a blonde. ("Mom was a real cunt," he had added without prompting.)

Method tells us what drives him, or what he wants us to think drives him.

Another killer I caught beat his victims until they had no face. He had been driven by a hatred so intense that it could actually induce a minor fugue state. "A couple times," he'd told me, "I remember starting to hit a whore, but I don't remember nothing else till it was over. Which is a real shame. 'Cause honestly, that's the best part." He really had been regretful about it.

Insanity is not the same as stupidity.

The truth is, they're all crazy in their own way, but some of them are also brilliant.

Sex as a component, or the lack thereof, is key when considering motive.

This last one gets me thinking.

Both victims we know of—Lisa Reid and Rosemary Sonnenfeld—were murdered but not sexually abused. Lisa was a pre-op transsexual, which in itself points toward a sexual component. Rosemary's past points to sex as well, and yet he didn't abuse her.

I chew on the pen, thinking about this. I come to the same conclusion as I had earlier.

It's not about sex for him.

This is rare. It's almost always about sex.
Not this time.

Okay, then what's it about? Victims are everything. What are the commonalities?
Both victims were women.

I scratch that out. Lisa Reid was not a woman. The distinction might be unfair to her, but it would have been significant to the killer. This is not a commonality.

Look for similarities in method then.

Both victims were killed in the same way. A sharp object was thrust into their right side and angled up and into the heart.
Both victims had a cross placed inside the resulting wound.

I consider the cross. After sex and general insanity, religious mania plays a big part in serial homicides. Only parents get hung with more blame than God. Satanic elements are a popular choice, but there are plenty of instances where the killer felt that he was saving his victims, that he was working for the man upstairs, not the one in the nether-basement.

Is that the deal here? Is he saving his victims from something?
I doodle on the pad:

What do you save someone from?

One answer:

The consequences of their actions.
From a religious standpoint, you save them from damnation.

Yeah.

What damns someone?

I rattle my brain, trying to jar loose old memories of catechism. Something about mortal sins, venial sins . . .

I take my notepad with me as I pad up the stairs and into my oft-used home office. I sit down in front of my computer and open the browser to a search engine.

In the search field I type: *mortal sin defined.*

The first choice is *Mortal Sin—definition*

"Ask and ye shall receive," I mutter. I click the link.

The *American Heritage Dictionary* definition of mortal sin appears:

A sin, such as murder or blasphemy, that is so heinous it deprives the soul of sanctifying grace and causes damnation if unpardoned at the time of death.

There is a treatise farther down on the page that relates to Aquinas.

A mortal sin destroys the grace of God in the heart of the sinner. In order for a sin to be mortal, it must meet three conditions:

A. Sin must be of a grave matter.

B. Sin is committed with the full knowledge of the sinner.

C. Sin is committed with the full and deliberate consent of the sinner.

Thus a mortal sin cannot be committed by accident, as two of the qualifying components are knowledge and consent. In other words, the sinner knows what he or she is doing is an offense against God, but does so anyway, and with premeditation. The sinner is aware that he is rejecting God's law and love.

In Galatians 5:19–21, St. Paul gives a list of grave sins: "Now the works of the flesh are manifest, which are these; adultery, fornication, uncleanness, lasciviousness, idolatry, witchcraft, hatred, variance, emulations, wrath, strife, seditions, heresies, envyings, murders, drunkenness, revellings, and such like: of the which I tell you before, as I have also told you in time past, that they which do such things shall not inherit the kingdom of God."

And in 1 Corinthians 6:9–10: Paul also tells the Corinthians, "know you not that the unjust shall not possess the kingdom of God? Do not err: neither fornicators, nor idolaters, nor adulterers, nor the effeminate, nor liers with mankind, nor thieves, nor covetous, nor drunkards nor railers, nor extortioners shall possess the kingdom of God."

It continues in this vein. I go back and click some of the other links the search engine gave me. I'm not surprised to find that the specifics of what constitutes a mortal sin is a widely debated subject. The Catholic Church has views and definitions that are distinct from Protestants. Orthodox churches in places such as Eastern Europe have different views than those in the west. Strict traditionalists classify the so-called Seven Deadly Sins as mortal, while others dispute this.

There are definite points of agreement. Everyone allows that murder is pretty bad. Homosexuality is universally considered to be a quick ticket into hellfire.

"Sorry, James," I murmur. "No one likes a godless sodomite."

The most general consensus, from what I can see, is: you know it is a grave sin, you know it denies God's love and law, and you do it anyway. If you don't take responsibility for that mortal sin prior to death, you're fucked. Get ready to burn like an indestructible marshmallow over an eternal campfire.

I lean back in the chair and consult my notepad again.

Okay, let's roll with this. So . . . if he's saving them from damnation then—what? He gets them to confess before he kills them?

The other and obvious possibility occurs to me.

Maybe he is not saving them. Maybe he is damning them.
If he's aware of something they've done, something he considered

a mortal sin, and he kills them before they have the opportunity to repent, then, within his paradigm, he'd be sending them straight to hell.

Why would he want to do that? I doubt it's based on a personal connection with the victims, so direct revenge is out. It would have a broader base. Vengeance in absentia? Sending a message? Will of God?

"Are you saving them, or damning them? Do you care about their souls?" I toss the pad down on the desk in frustration. "Do I have any idea if I'm even on the right track?"

I think about this. Yeah, I do. It's not something I can prove, it is something that I feel. This is the way it goes.

He is not killing them for sexual gratification. He is killing them because their deaths matter in a religious sense, and sin is the hub of the wheel on which all religion turns.

I grab the notepad back and return to the living room. I stare at it as I think and I begin to write again.

He asked us a question: "What do I collect? That's the question, and that's the key."

I'm pretty sure I know the answer, or at least the answer for now, based on the information I have and what my gut is saying.

Sins. He collects sins. That's the victimology. That's the commonality. Not hair color or boob size or maybe even gender. His victims are sinners (or he thinks they are).

This feels right. It resonates. The tuning fork inside me quivers, telling me that I've hit the right note.

One question, though, remains.

Does he think he's sending sinners to their just rewards, or the redeemed to sit at the hand of God?

The next question comes without my wanting it to, a return of the yammering I've been trying to quash.

What about your sin? Does it qualify as mortal?

Oh yeah. You bet. Good thing I don't believe in heaven or hell.

Right?

Silence to that, blessed silence.

"Praise God," I mutter, with all the sarcasm and bitterness I can muster.

God does not reply, as is His wont.

A wave of exhaustion hits me like a truck, so fast and heavy that my eyelids close of their own accord. I let the notepad slip from my fingers and curl up on the couch as sleep drags me down into darkness.

15

THE PHONE WAKES ME UP AND I WAKE UP HARD. I FEEL
hungover, though it's not a result of last night's alcohol. This is about
my age. In my early twenties I could pull an all-nighter or two, sleep
for one night and wake up refreshed. Now it can take me days to
bounce back. The crick in my neck tells me that sleeping on the couch
hadn't helped.

I pull myself to a sitting position and groan. Last night I was
lonely. Right now I'm just glad that no one is here to witness this. I
push away the fog through sheer force of will and answer.

"Barrett," I croak.

"You sound chipper, honey-love."

"What time is it?"

"Eight-thirty A.M."

"What? Dammit."

I stand up and rush to the kitchen while I hold the phone against
my ear. I forgot to set the timer for the coffee last night, so I hit the
button now and wait for the blessed brown nectar to start flowing. I
have the patience of a junkie when it comes to getting my first cup of
coffee in the morning. Bonnie always wakes up before me and knows
this; she starts pouring a cup for me the moment she hears my feet hit
the stairs.

"Lazy, lazy," Callie teases. "Up too late having various forms of
acrobatic sex?"

She means well, but the question brings back memories of last night.

"No."

The terseness of my answer makes her pause.

"Hmmmm . . . is that bark of a no due to a lack of caffeine or problems on the home front?"

"Both, but I don't want to talk about it right now. What's up? Where are you?"

"Nearer than you think."

A knock at my front door.

"Little pig, little pig, let me in."

I groan again. I don't feel like dealing with Callie—or anyone else—this morning.

"Hang on." I sigh.

WE ARE SEATED AT MY dining table. I'm about halfway through my coffee and life seems a little more hopeful.

Callie sits across from me enjoying her own cup. I study her and marvel, as always, at her ability to look good in any situation. I'm the one who got some sleep last night and I'm sitting here in rumpled clothes and hurricane hair. Callie looks like she just came from a day at the spa.

She reaches into her jacket pocket and pops a pain pill. This brings me back to reality. I sip at my coffee and examine her eyes. It's well hidden, but the exhaustion is there, swimming in the shallows, visible in just the right light.

"Is grumpy-bunny feeling better?" Callie asks.

"A little. When did you get in?"

"Damien and I arrived about two hours ago. We'll be using the lab facilities at the Bureau to examine our little treasure trove of evidence." She raises her cup in a mock toast. "And I'll be able to get my wedding back on the rails."

I raise an eyebrow. "Is it off them?"

"Nothing disastrous, but it's possible that Kirby needs a little more . . . oversight."

"What happened?" I have a vision of Callie's florist waking to Kirby sitting in a chair next to his bed, twirling a stiletto.

"There were some problems with the cake. Kirby lobbied on my behalf a little too enthusiastically. She didn't actually *do* anything, but she showed too much of her true face."

"Ah," I say.

Kirby's true face is terrifying. She's all happy-go-lucky and charming until she decides to let the humanity drain away from her eyes. Then you feel like you're in a staring contest with a very hungry leopard.

"They were going to return my deposit, but Sam charmed them again. The point being, when the cat's away, the assassin will play." She puts the cup down and leans forward. "Now, tell me what happened with Tommy."

I consider telling Callie to mind her own business but realize this would be futile. Laughable, really.

"He told me he loved me."

"Really?"

"Yes."

Callie leans back in her chair. Her mood is introspective.

"Well," she says, after a moment. "I can see why that would be difficult for you."

This is the other face of Callie and one of the reasons she is my friend. She is quick with the quip and irreverent as hell, but she also knows when it's time to be serious.

"The thing is, I don't know why it's so difficult. But it is."

This is only a partial lie.

"Is it about Matt? Because you know, Smoky, Matt would have zero difficulty with you and Tommy."

Callie knew Matt and loved him. She would invite herself to dinner a lot. She couldn't get enough of Matt's tacos.

"I know. That's the thing, I really do know that. I'm in a good place when it comes to Matt and Alexa, as good as I'll ever get. I remember them now and I'm glad to. It doesn't kill me anymore."

Her voice is gentle. "It's time to move on, Smoky."

I examine my friend. Callie has been there with me through everything. She doesn't know the one secret, the one I've kept for myself, but she knows all the rest.

"Can I ask you something, Callie?"

"Of course."

"Why are you getting married? I mean, I know why people get married—but what changed? You've always been a lone wolf."

She runs a burgundy-painted fingernail around the rim of her coffee cup.

"A lonely wolf, not a lone wolf. There is a difference. And I needed to be sure, very, very sure. Wolves mate for life, you know."

"And are you? Sure?"

Her gaze at me is almost wary. Callie is one of the most private people I know. If there is anyone that she trusts with her inner self—other than Sam—it is me, but she doesn't often throw caution to the wind, even so.

"Yes. I'm sure."

Then she smiles and it catches me by surprise. I realize that for Callie, this—being *sure*—has made her happy. Callie was never what I would call depressed, but there is a difference between contentment and joy. This is joy.

"Feels good, huh?"

"Yes it does."

She puts the smile away and retreats back behind that familiar wall of mischievous irony.

"Now," she says. "You and I will never be *Sex and the City* girls, so let's change the subject and get to work."

I tip my cup to her. "I'll drink to that."

16

"WHY DON'T THEY EVER REPLACE OUR CARPETS?" ALAN grouses as we head down the hallway to our offices.

"Because no one is allowed up here that the Bureau is trying to impress," I reply.

Callie and I had run into Alan on the elevator.

"If that's true," she says, "then the carpets can stay. I prefer them to the media."

The truth is, there's nothing much wrong with the carpeting. It's a thin tight weave, built for heavy traffic, a little worn but more than serviceable. But we'd had to pass through reception on the way to the elevators, and Alan had noticed they were replacing the marble backdrop behind the large reception desk for the second time in five years.

"Be fair, Alan," I say. "The last time they had to fix the lobby was because of us."

Two years ago a man burst into reception and lobbed a few grenades. He followed this up with automatic-weapons fire before making his escape. He had been connected to a man that we were hunting, so it was kind of our fault.

"Yeah, yeah. But look." He points to a small stain with a hint of outrage. "New marble down there, but I have to see that stain every time I walk to my office for the last four years. It's not right."

"I didn't know you were such a priss," Callie teases.

We take the final left to get to our offices, known within the building as "Death Central."

The current title for my position is NCAVC coordinator. NCAVC stands for the National Center for the Analysis of Violent Crime. It's headquartered in DC. Each Bureau office has a person in charge of NCAVC activities for that geographical area. Death's representative, so to speak. In Podunk that might be a single agent who also carries numerous other responsibilities. Here in Los Angeles we rate a full-time coordinator-in-charge—me—and a multi-agent team. I guess serial killers are like the rest of us: they enjoy the sunny California climate.

"Speaking of not being let up here," Alan remarks.

Kirby is standing outside the door to the offices, twirling a lock of blonde hair around a finger. Her eyes light up as she sees us.

"Hey, guys! How's it going? How was it out East? Too cold for this girl, I can tell you that. I need to know I can have beer on the beach when I want it, you know? Anyway, I have to confer with Callie-babe about some wedding stuff."

This is how Kirby talks, like a runaway freight train without a care in the world.

"How'd you get up here, anyway?" Alan asks.

"Hey, I have my ways, remember?" She winks at him and makes to give him a friendly punch, but he puts up a hand in protest. "Don't need another bruise there, Kirby."

She's only five-seven but her "playful punch" apparently packs a wallop. She grins at him.

"Don't be a wuss. But okay, because your wife makes a heck of a cupcake. I had a few yesterday and—"

"What?!" Callie cries.

"Relax, Callie-babe, they were just the test run. I didn't down any of the chosen ones."

"Hm," Callie says. "And stop calling me that."

She's wasting her breath. Kirby will call her that and "Red Sonja" and whatever else she feels like. She's just not afraid of Callie. Or anyone else, for that matter.

"Hey, sorry about the cake guy." She rolls her eyes. "Who knew that an accidental flash of my weapon would make him so jittery?"

"Accidental, huh?" Alan asks. The disbelief in his voice is stark and mirrors my own.

"Hey," she says, reproachful, "I'm not a barbarian." She smiles till she dimples. "I just know how to hold a negotiating position."

He smirks. "Is that what they're calling it now?"

Kirby's fist shoots out and lands a pretty good one on Alan's biceps. He winces and rubs it as he glowers at her.

"Men are such babies." She turns her attention to Callie. "So the reason I'm here. The tailor wanted to charge us an extra five hundred dollars because of the color changes on the bridesmaid dresses. I told him that just didn't seem fair, but he wasn't budging, so then I told him I would really appreciate it if he'd learn some better manners, and you know what? He agreed." She smiles like a child who's just handed you an A+ report card.

"Just like that?" Callie asks.

"Well, no, that's the abridged version, but I think the details of diplomacy are pretty boring, don't you? As long as no one's killing each other or going to jail, mission accomplished, I always say."

Callie decides to let it go. "What else?"

"The florist is cute. I mean super cute. I've been curling his toes for the last few nights—and he's been curling mine too, let me tell you. Anyway, point is—he's giving us a deeper discount now. I don't want to brag or anything, but"—she bumps her hip into mine—"I'm pretty sure it's because of the deep discount I've been giving him." She giggles, almost girlish. "Deep discount. Get it?"

Alan groans. I shake my head and smile. Callie takes it in stride; the pragmatism of a bride to be.

"Slut it up if it will save me another few hundred dollars," she chirps. "Anything else?"

"Nope."

"Thanks for the update. Keep me apprised, please."

"Yep." She turns away and heads back down the hall.

"Oh, and, Kirby?" Callie calls after her. "Keep the gun out of sight for any expense under a thousand dollars."

"You got it, Callie-babe."

Alan shakes his head. "Doesn't it bother you that she's fucking your florist for a discount?"

Callie reaches up and pats him on the cheek. "Alan. Flowers are expensive."

"NICE OF EVERYONE TO SHOW up."

James is glaring at us all in disapproval.

"Don't get your pink panties in a twist," Callie replies, breezing past him. "I got as much sleep as you did. Besides, it's Smoky's fault."

"And?" he challenges Alan. "What's your excuse?"

"Same answer as always: none of your business."

"I imagine the AD is going to be calling soon," I say, interrupting this friendly chatter, "so let's have a meeting in five minutes."

James glowers, but shuts up. I head to my office.

Death Central is really just two big rooms. The largest is a wide open space where James, Callie, and Alan have their desks. I rate a small office with a door. The arrangements are spartan but functional.

I sit down in my chair and dial Bonnie's cell phone number.

"Hi, Smoky!"

Bonnie's voice gives me the lift I had searched for last night in work and a tequila bottle. She sounds so happy to hear from me, her pleasure is so genuine and unconditional. Men can come and go, but your child is forever.

"Hi, honey. How are you?"

"Pretty good. Elaina and I are about to start my math lesson. Bo-ring."

"Hey, no dissing the three R's."

I can almost hear her eyes rolling at my attempt to speak the lingo. Dissing, indeed.

"Are you going to come and get me today? I want to see you. Besides, we're supposed to try that steak recipe thingie."

Bonnie and I made a pact a few months ago. We agreed that the microwave, while wondrous, was a limited tool when it comes to food. We decided we would take a night a week—it didn't matter which one—and try to actually cook something. I purchased a bunch of cookbooks and we've had a good time filling the house with smoke and the smell of burning meat. We've even managed to create something edible a few times.

"I'll get the steaks before I come and pick you up, sweetheart."

"Cool."

"Back to math, honey. I'll see you this evening."

A noisy sigh. I am heartened by it, as I am by any sign of normal behavior in Bonnie. When she's an official teen and starts to talk back to me, I'll probably rejoice.

"Okay. 'Bye."

I consider giving Tommy a quick call, but decide against it. I want to talk to him just a little too much right now.

I leave my office and head into the main room. We have a large dry-erase board that we use when we're brainstorming. I uncap a marker while the others look on.

"First let's go over what we know," I say. "We know we have two victims: Lisa Reid and Rosemary Sonnenfeld." I write their names on the board. "We know that they are in different geographical areas."

"Means he travels," Alan says. "Question is, why?"

James nods. "Right. Does he travel because he likes to spread his destruction over a wide area, or because he followed his victims there?"

"I think it's the latter," I say. I tell them about my theory, the sin collector.

"Creepy," Callie offers. "But interesting."

"Strip away the non-commonalities," I say. "One was a woman, one was a man transitioning into a woman. Lisa Reid was the daughter of a wealthy, connected family, while Rosemary was an ex-prostitute ex-drug addict. Rosemary was a blonde, Lisa was a brunette. The only things they had in common were manner of death, and, perhaps, things from their past."

"Explain that again?" James asks.

"Lisa's diary. She mentions some big secret, is about to reveal what it was, and then the pages are torn out. He leaves his little message. We already know that Rosemary led a questionable life before her conversion."

"You're saying the only thing they have in common is that they were sinners?" Alan asks.

"Well, that narrows the victim pool," Callie mutters.

"What about forensics?"

"I have bupkes at the moment. We have a bag of trace we vacuumed up from the plane. We have the bloody cushions, but I imagine all the blood will turn out to be Lisa's. We have smudges but no prints from the armrests. Perhaps the trace will show something, but . . ."

"Probably not," I say. "He's older and he's practiced. I don't see him making stupid mistakes."

"I'm going to have the cross analyzed," she continues. "Metallurgy is virtually untraceable, but it is our most direct connection to the perp."

She's right. The cross is his symbol. It's important to him. When we touch it, we are touching him.

"Good. What else?"

"You know," James muses, "going with the religious motivation—which I agree with, for now—there's another 'known' that's very significant. The manner of death."

"Stuck in the side," Alan offers.

"Stuck in the right side," James corrects. "From a religious perspective, that's relevant."

I stare at him in sudden understanding. I wonder why I hadn't thought of it myself.

"The lance, Longinus," I say.

"Very good," James replies.

"Sorry," Callie says, "but you've lost me. Can you explain it for the heathens in the room?"

"Longinus was the Roman soldier who pierced Christ's side with a lance to make sure he was dead," James explains.

" 'But one of the soldiers pierced his side with a lance, and immediately there came out blood and water,' " Alan intones.

I look at him and raise an eyebrow.

He grins. "Sunday school, Baptist-style. My friends and I liked Revelation and the story of the crucifixion the best. Dramatic and bloody."

"Kind of missing the deeper meaning," I say.

"I was ten. Sue me."

"Yes, yes, yes," James continues, impatient. "The point is, it's generally agreed that Longinus pierced the right side of Christ with the lance."

"Just like our victims," Callie observes.

"The biggest question remains," he continues. "Why is he killing them?"

"Easy," Alan offers. "Because they're sinners."

James shakes his head. "But they're not if they confessed. Which, per the debrief you gave us on your interview with Father Yates, Rosemary did."

"Whoa," I say. "Lot of assumptions there. Maybe he just thinks Rosemary was a sinner because she used to be a hooker. Lisa Reid was changing her sex, which I'm pretty sure is a universal abomination."

"True," James says, "but that doesn't fit with his methodology. If he's outraged by their actions, why is there so little violence? The killings are neat, functional, and symbolic. They lack passion."

"No torture either," Callie muses. "It's almost as if the victims were *necessary* more than anything else. Props in the play."

The lack of anger continues to resonate. Sex crimes violate the victim; our victims were not violated. Rosemary was posed, but not in a degrading way. The fact of their deaths were more important to him than anything else.

"So," James says, "different victim types, not sexually motivated, religious theme, what does that tell us?"

"If it's not about sex," I muse, "then it's either about revenge or sending a message. He's either getting back at someone, or he's telling us something by killing them."

"It's not revenge," James says. He delivers it as a flat statement of fact.

"I agree," I say. "There'd be more anger."

"So what's he telling us?" Alan asks.

"I don't know. Something important to him, though. Did anything else come up on the VICAP search for similar crimes, Alan?"

"No."

Callie whistles. "Wow. We're nowhere."

I scowl at her. "Very helpful."

"I call it as I see it."

My frustration is not caused by Callie so much as the truth of what she's saying. And its consequences.

"You know he's already picked his next victim," James remarks, reading my mind. "Maybe the one after that."

I give him a sour look.

"You and Callie should hit the forensic bricks."

"And us? Or me?" Alan asks.

"I need to fill in AD Jones and do a follow-up call to Rosario Reid. After that you and I are going back to see Father Yates. I want to interview anyone and everyone that knew Rosemary and had anything to do with her in the last few years."

He gives an approving nod. "Good detective finds his own leads."

"That old chestnut," Callie says with faux scorn. "You two have fun. Damien and I are going to the lab."

"Stop calling me that, you drug addict," James says.

It's hard to tell with James. Is he poking fun at Callie? Or really trying to skewer her?

Callie takes it in stride.

"Touché, Priscilla. Now get those ruby slippers in gear and let's go to work."

They head out the door insulting each other.

"He seems to be adjusting to Callie harassing him about being gay," Alan observes.

"I think he'd be more disturbed if she didn't. This way he knows she really couldn't care less. Besides, he knows she'd never do it around anyone but us."

"Yeah. You going to run those other errands?"

"Give me fifteen minutes and I'll meet you in the lobby."

17

"NOTHING'S HIT THE NEWS YET ON LISA REID," AD JONES tells me.

"I'm impressed. Even without the fact of her being a congress-man's kid, murder mid-flight should have gotten someone's attention."

"Director Rathbun knows how to handle the press. It won't last forever, though. Where are we at?"

I fill him in on everything that's happened since we last spoke, including the various theories that we're batting around.

"What's your feeling on this?" he asks me when I'm done.

AD Jones got where he is by working his way up the ranks. He's done the work, put in the time. He'll never be a "suit." When he asks a question like this, he asks it because he respects my views and he wants the unvarnished truth.

"I think we're going to hit a dead end very soon unless we find a new lead or . . ."

"He kills someone else," AD Jones finishes for me.

There it is again, that pause in the earth's rotation. The killer is out there, and he's hunting. Maybe a woman died last night while I was sleeping. Maybe a woman died this morning while I drank my coffee and joked with Callie.

I force these thoughts from my head.

"Yes, sir. This is a very methodical individual. He's confident and a risk taker, but he's not crazy. He's not fighting sexual urges or hearing voices. He's pursuing a course in the direction of a known goal. Exactly what that goal is, we haven't figured out yet."

He leans back in the brown leather chair that he's had since I've known him. It is worn and cracked in places. He's been told on more than one occasion to get rid of it, orders he's ignored. He can be stubborn like that. He gets away with it because he's good at what he does.

"Okay," he says, "then what's left? What's the plan of attack?"

"Callie and James are dealing with the trace. Perhaps we'll get a break there."

"But you don't think so."

"No, sir, but . . ." I shrug. "Assume making an ass of u and me and all that."

"And? What else?"

"Alan and I are returning to Father Yates. We're going to interview all of Rosemary's known associates and see where that takes us."

He taps his fingers on the desk. Nods. "I'll fill in the Director. Keep me in the loop."

"Yes, sir."

"And call Rosario Reid, Smoky. Keeping her in the loop and on our side is a good idea."

"That was the very next thing, sir."

"NOTHING NEW? NOTHING AT ALL?"

Rosario's voice sounds far away. I don't hear the strength I'd seen in her car that night.

"No, I'm sorry. But it's early, Rosario, very early. Sometimes this is how it goes."

"And that other poor girl he murdered? Does she have a family too?"

"Not that we've found. She did have her church, though."

Silence.

"Lisa's funeral is tomorrow."

I hear the edge in her voice, the desire to crack warring with her own control.

"I'm sorry."

"Can I ask you something, Smoky?"

"Anything you like."

"How was it? Burying your Alexa?"

The question has scalpel precision; it cuts through my defenses in a blink.

How was it? The memory is as vivid now as then. I buried them at the same time, Matt and Alexa, my world. I remember that the day was beautiful. California sun lit up the coffins till the metal on them gleamed. The sky was cloudless and blue. I heard nothing, felt nothing, said nothing. I marveled at the sun and watched as my life was put into the ground, forever.

"It was like a horror movie that wouldn't end," I tell her.

"But it did end, didn't it?"

"Yes."

"And that was even worse, wasn't it? That it ended."

"That was the worst of all."

I promised her truth, always, and I have no qualms about delivering it. Rosario Reid and I are sisters in spirit. We don't really have it in us to take our own lives in despair, or to turn into raging alcoholics. We're built to grieve and scream and then, when it's over, to carry on. Changed and heavier, but alive. She wants to know what is going to happen; I'm telling her. I can't save her from it, I can only prepare her for it.

"Thank you for keeping me up-to-date, Smoky." A pause. "I know, you know, that finding him is not going to make it better. It's not going to bring her back to me."

"But that's not the point, Rosario. I understand, believe me. He has to pay."

He has to pay for what he did, not because it will bring Lisa back, not even because it will diminish any of the pain her death leaves behind, but because he killed Rosario's child. No other reason is needed, it stands alone. Eat a mother's children and pay the price, a law of the universe that must be enforced.

"Yes. Good-bye."

"Good-bye, Rosario."

I realize, after we hang up, that I had been lucky, in a way. I got to kill the man who killed my child. It changed nothing. My Alexa was still dead. But . . . when I think of him, dying at my hand, a lioness purrs inside me, satisfied and terrible. That blood on her whiskers always tastes divine.

18

with its last gasp. The air this morning had been crisp, cool but not cold, and now the temperature is heading into the high sixties.

The traffic is not bad. Alan is able to keep the speedometer above seventy-five. This can be a minor miracle on the 405 freeway any time of day. You're never lonely on the 405, no matter when you drive.

I watch as Los Angeles proper morphs into the San Fernando Valley. It's a subtle change but a change nonetheless. If Los Angeles were an apple, it would be rotting from the inside out, with downtown as its core. The Valley is blighted as well, but flowers still grow through the cracks in places. There is just a little bit more space, just a little less dirt.

We pull into the parking lot of the Holy Redeemer.

"Not much to look at, is it?" Alan observes.

I hadn't gotten a good look at the church last night; it was dark and I'd been tired. Alan is right. It's small, probably poorly funded. No rich parishioners to keep Father Yates in real butter, here. This place is strictly margarine. Water from a tap, not a bottle.

"I trust it more this way," I say.

Alan smiles. "I know what you mean."

We learn, in our line of work, that clothes don't make the man. You can kill in a T-shirt or a three-piece suit, you can be rich and kill or poor and kill. A knife is a knife is a knife. I don't trust any church completely, but I trust the gold and gilded ones the least of all. Piety, in my opinion, is an ascetic activity.

"I called ahead," Alan says. "He's expecting us."

I GET TO SEE THE interior of the church with new eyes as well. And a new nose; I smell bleach. The pews are wooden and well worn. The floor is concrete, not marble. The altar at the front is small. Christ hangs in his usual position looking down on us all. Our savior needs a paint job, he's flaked in places.

His image still makes me quiver inside. I don't know if I believe in Him anymore, but I believed in Him once. Him and the Virgin Mary. I prayed to them, begged them to cure my mother's cancer. Mom died anyway. That betrayal was the end of my relationship with God. How could He forgive me for my sins when I'd never forgiven Him for His?

Father Yates sees us and comes toward us with a smile.

"Agent Barrett, Agent Washington."

"Hello, Father," I say. "It's pretty empty in here. Slow day?"

I wince inside. I seem helpless to censor my own bitterness in this place. Alan looks at me strangely. Father Yates takes it in stride.

"Every day is a slow day at the Reedeemer, Agent Barrett. We're not saving souls by the bucketful here. One at a time."

"Sorry, Father. That was uncalled for."

He waves a hand. "You're mad at God, I understand. If He can take it—and I think He can—then so can I. Now, I have someone I'd like you to meet. Agent Washington told me why you've come, and the woman I'm about to introduce you to is the only person I could think of. So far as I know, she was Rosemary's only friend. Rosemary had no living family. But perhaps this person will be helpful."

"Why?"

"Because she used to be a police officer. A detective, in fact. In Ohio."

"Really?"

"Cross my heart." He smiles. Priest humor. "She's waiting for you in the sacristy."

*   *   *

LIKE EVERYTHING ELSE ABOUT THIS church, the sacristy is small but clean. Simple shelving provides a place for the chalice to rest when not in use. I can see the wine and the bag containing the host wafers.

"They're made by nuns," my mother had told me when I asked.

I was not a fan of nuns at the time, but I had to admit that I liked the wafers even less. They should have been a reward for surviving the endurance test of Mass, but they tasted like Styrofoam.

I see a closet with no doors, wood painted white. Father Yates's vestments hang inside.

There is no desk in this small room, just a window and three battered wooden chairs. A woman sits in one of the chairs, waiting.

"This is Andrea," Father Yates tells us. "Andrea, this is Agent Smoky Barrett and Agent Alan Washington."

She nods but does not speak.

"I'll leave you alone for now," the priest says, and takes his exit.

I examine Andrea. She's not a small woman but not big either, about five-four and maybe a hundred thirty pounds. Her face would be average if not for her eyes and her hair. The hair is long and shiny and so black that it's almost blue. Her eyes are large and limpid and darker than the hair.

They are intelligent eyes. I can see the hint of cop in them. Her gaze is frank, direct, guarded, that mix of contradictions only found in law-enforcement professionals and hardened criminals. She takes in my scars without a perceptible reaction.

She's wearing a yellow T-shirt that's maybe a half size too big for her and a pair of faded blue jeans and tennis shoes.

I hold out a hand.

"Pleased to meet you, Andrea," I say.

Her grip is firm and stronger than I expected. Her palms are dry. I manage to cover my own surprise at the scars I see on her wrist and arm. Two cuts, one horizontal, one vertical. The mark of the truly dedicated suicide.

"Likewise." Her voice is low and throaty, the voice of a phone-sex operator. "And yeah, I tried to kill myself once." She turns up her other wrist, and I see more scars. "They're a matching set."

"Been close myself," I say, though I'm not sure why.

She gives me a mild look, and nods for us to take a seat.

"Why does Rosemary's murder rate the attention of the Feds?" she asks.

Right to the point. I try out the standard answer.

"I'm not at liberty to say."

She gives me the most mirthless smile I've ever seen, followed by a chuckle that says we're funny if we think she's going to be that easy. "Then I'm not at liberty to help you. Put up or shut up."

I glance at Alan. He shrugs.

"Fine," I say. "Rosemary is not this killer's only victim. If you need to know more, then we're done."

"Nope, that makes sense. And I'm glad to hear it."

"That he's killed others?"

"Of course. Multiple murders are easier to solve than single instance homicides."

She has no concern for the bigger picture. If the death of others will help solve the murder of her friend, so be it.

"You want to tell us about it?" Alan asks.

I glance at him. He's entirely focused on Andrea. Alan is possibly the most gifted interrogator I know, so I keep my mouth shut and take a moment to study her.

It takes me longer to see it than he had, but I catch on. It's in her eyes, in her face, in everything about her. She's *sad*. It's not the short-term sadness of someone having a bad day. It's not despair. This is something in between, a weariness that carries weight. Andrea is someone with a story to tell, a bad one, and you have to let her tell it before you can ask her what you really want to know.

Andrea doesn't respond right away. She continues to assess me with those big, dark eyes for a few moments before turning them onto Alan.

"I used to be a cop," she begins. "Back in Ohio."

Alan nods. "Father Yates told us."

"I was a good cop. I had the gift. I could smell the lies a mile away, and I could make connections where others couldn't. I ended up in homicide five years in."

"Fast track," Alan notes. "All ability, or did you have a rabbi?"

Someone higher up who shepherded her career, he is asking.

"Both. I was good, real good. But my dad had been a cop too, so I had people looking out for me. It's the way of things there."

"Here too," he says. "I was in LAPD homicide for ten years. Ability wasn't always enough."

"Yeah. Well, I managed to juggle it all pretty good. I got promoted fast, married a great guy—not a cop—and had a baby. A beautiful boy named Jared. Life was good. Then things changed."

She stops talking. Stares off into the distance.

"What things?" Alan prods her.

"There was this guy. He killed families. Wholesale. He'd come into a suburban neighborhood and recon until he found the right family. His requisites were: multiple children aged ten or above, preferably with some boys and girls in their teens, and at least one parent. Single moms were the best, but he always wanted a boy as a part of the equation, whether it was the dad or a son, brother, whatever.

"He'd come at them when it got dark. He'd make them all strip and then he'd spend the night doing his thing. He'd force them to have sex with each other. Sisters to sisters, Mom to son, dads to daughters. You get the picture. Then he'd fuck his favorite or a few of his favorites. When he was done, he'd leave all of them alive except for one that he would strangle while the others watched."

She swallows, remembering all of this.

"A task force was put together. I was on it as second in command. I was hot for it too. Something about this one got to me. Still don't know why. It was bad, sure, but I'd already seen gruesome."

"Sometimes it's easier to deal with dead victims than living ones," I offer.

She looks at me with renewed interest. "Funny you should mention that. These families were permanently fucked up. Most ended in divorce. Some of the fathers and kids killed themselves. None of the mothers, though. Still not sure why."

"For the kids," Alan murmurs.

"What?" she asks.

"The mothers didn't kill themselves because they needed to be there for the kids."

She stares at Alan for a moment, then continues.

"The ruin of those poor people is what he got off on. That was his real fix. Once I understood that, I knew that's why he kept them alive. He wanted to go back and watch them be miserable. We posted surveillance around his victims' homes and, sure enough, the fucker showed up. Ohio has the death penalty so he sucked down cyanide gas a few years ago."

"That's good work," I say.

"We caught him," she agrees, "but it didn't help me. I couldn't get the victims' stories out of my head. The things he made them do. How it affected them. I started to have trouble sleeping and in true cop fashion, I kept it all to myself and turned to the same therapist my dad had always used in rough times. Dr. Johnnie Walker." Another one of those mirthless smiles. "Dr. Walker was cheap, he could keep a secret, and he always went down clean."

"Seen him myself," Alan says.

"Really?" she asks.

"Sure. Lots of cops have."

Bitterness spasms across her face. "The thing is, he's not *really* cheap. He starts out low, but that back end is a bitch."

"Almost cost me my marriage," Alan replies. "What did it cost you?"

Those eyes close once and open again and turn to me and then Alan and then the ceiling. I see a storm in them, wind and rain and thunder, pain and rage and something more terrible but undefined.

"Everything," she says. "It cost me everything." Her voice is a monotone. "Maybe if I'd reached out, asked for help, I could've changed things. But cops aren't too big on that anyway, and I had the added pressure of being a woman. Someone was always waiting for me to show weakness. I kept it to myself, and I hid it good. One thing a cop can do, man, is lie." She looks at Alan. "I drove drunk with Jared in the car. We crashed, he died."

Silence. She's not looking at us now.

I have a bitter taste in my mouth, like blood. This is just one more terrible story to add to my catalogue of useless and terrible stories. What happened to her did not happen because she was a bad person or a bad cop or a bad mother. Something about that case got to her where others hadn't and drove her to the bottle. One day she was in the car with her son and the bottle made her zig instead of zag. That was the end of her, at least for a little while. The fact that she'd caught the monster didn't matter. She was his last victim.

"I tried to kill myself twice. Once with pills, the other time with a razor. I got put on disability from the force. My husband left me. I was about to give suicide a third whirl when I realized the truth: death was too good for me. What I needed to do was suffer." She's still talking in that laconic monotone. "So I moved to LA and I became a whore."

I flinch at this revelation.

"Why?" I ask.

The large eyes find me, pin me. "Penance. I killed my son. I deserved to suffer. I figured letting myself get fucked by strangers for four or five years for money would be a good start." She barks a laugh. "The capper? A guy I had arrested in Ohio had gotten out and moved to LA. Fate sent him my way. He really got off on having the female cop who busted him down on her knees sucking his cock."

I am aghast. I can't find the words.

"You're not doing that now," Alan says. "How'd you come to be here?"

"Time does one thing, Agent Washington. It keeps on going. The world moves on. You get changed by that, whether you want to or not. Doesn't matter how much pain, doesn't matter how much you hate yourself. Sooner or later, even if just in little ways, your soul moves on. I was happy to suffer for what I did to Jared. It was right. But one day I woke up and had the idea that maybe it was enough." She shrugs. "I needed a place to turn. I was raised Catholic, so I found my way here. Father Yates did what he does, and I quit being a whore."

I realize this is about as abridged as it gets. The gap between whoring herself as penance for her dead son and who she is now is a big one, but this woman is only going to share what she wants to. She's not going to cry, or get touchy-feely, or look toward heaven with a beatific light in her eyes. She might have been a soft flower once—who knows? That rose had long since turned to stone.

"How well did you know Rosemary?" Alan asks.

The smallest quiver in the cool facade.

"Well. Real well. We'd become best friends."

"Sorry."

"Life's a bummer sometimes."

"You met here?"

"Yeah. We both did volunteer work on Saturdays. Helping other down-and-outers, whatever. I wasn't very talkative. Rosemary drew me out. She had a way about her, a kind of helpless happiness that was hard to resist. Like, she knew everything was fucked up, but she couldn't help laughing anyway. That's what attracted me to her; she never stopped hoping for a reason to be happy."

Something about the way she's talking makes me ask the question.

"Were you lovers?"

Her eyes narrow, then she sighs.

"Briefly. It wasn't about sex for me, really. I just wanted to be with someone. And I liked Rosemary. We ended it in a good way. I'm not that into women, and neither was Rosemary. We dropped the sex and kept the love. It worked for us."

"I understand," Alan says. He moves in gently now, with the question we really want answered. "Andrea, is there anything you can tell us that you think might help us? Anyone you noticed taking an undue interest in Rosemary? Anyone new working around the church? Anything at all."

She shakes her head in frustration.

"I've been racking my brains, believe me. When I heard Rosemary had been killed, I went a little crazy. I never cry anymore, but I destroyed some furniture. I haven't thought about too much else since then. The thing is, Rosemary kept herself on a tight, tight leash. She was addicted to fucking. I'm not saying she was addicted to sex, that's the wrong phraseology. She liked fucking. The more degrading the better. The way she kept things under control was to have a routine and to not change that routine. She'd get up, exercise, work, then come here. Other than spending time with me, that was it."

"And no breaks or changes in that routine prior to her death?" Alan asks.

She spreads her hands, helpless. "No. Nothing."

"What about here?" he prods. "New male arrivals?"

"I considered that, believe me. But no, nothing. Sorry, I wish I could be more help, but the only thing I can say for sure is that it wasn't someone from her past."

"Why do you say that?" I ask.

"Rosemary told me everyone she ever knew was long dead and gone. Killed off by age, illness, or drugs."

*   *   *

ALAN AND I ARE DRIVING back to the Bureau. I'm feeling restless and discombobulated.

"This is fucked up, Alan," I say.

"How's that?"

"We're nowhere. Nowhere. We have three victims—and we only have those because he gave them to us—no reliable description, no fingerprints, no nada. I have an idea of what's driving him, but it's too incomplete. Nothing's vivid, nothing's standing out."

He gives me a look.

"What?" I ask.

"This is how it goes sometimes. We work the case until we find something that breaks it. You know that. Why are you getting so worked up about it just two days in?"

"Because it's personal."

"How?"

"We think this guy has been creeping around for years killing people, right? We think that the numbers on those crosses designate the number of victims. If that's true, he's going to turn out to be one of the most prolific killers ever. And he's been doing it right under our noses. The Lisas and Rosemarys of the world have been dropping like flies and he's been laughing about it the whole time."

He nods. "The victims got to you."

It's an incisive observation, a word-knife.

"I always care about the victims."

"Sure, of course. But sometimes you care more than others. This is one of those times, isn't it?"

I stop resisting.

"Yes."

"Why?"

"For the same reason that Atkins was upset about Rosemary. Most people let life carry them along. They accept what they get. Lisa Reid and Rosemary Sonnenfeld swam against the current. Even though they knew it might be hard, might even be futile, they swam anyway. Then, after they'd made it to shore, this guy came up behind them, slit their throats, and dumped their bodies back in the river."

He's silent for a little while, just driving. He clears his throat.

"Yeah. They got to me too. Made me think of you."

I look at him in surprise.

"Really?"

He smiles, gives me a sideways glance.

"When it comes to swimming against the current, Smoky, you're the hands-down gold medal winner."

19

"NO USABLE PRINTS," CALLIE BEGINS. "ALL THE BLOOD ON the cushions belonged to Lisa Reid. We found a black hair on trace that did not belong to Lisa, but there was no root. We're not going to be able to get DNA from it."

"Great," I say. "What about the cross?"

"It's not pure silver," James says. "That is, it's sterling silver. About ninety-three percent silver mixed with copper. Very common. He picked a good metal to work with if he wanted to make the crosses himself. Sterling silver melts at approximately sixteen hundred forty degrees Fahrenheit, it's harder than gold, and very malleable."

"What you're saying is that he could have grabbed up a bunch of spoons and melted them down to make his crosses?" Alan asks.

"Easily."

"What about the tools needed to do that? Anything unusual that we could track?"

" 'Fraid not," Callie says. "If you're not melting large amounts, the right kind of gas torch will do the trick."

"Lisa's apartment? We know he touched her diary, and I bet he spent a while roaming through the rooms."

Callie shakes her head. "Again, no prints. I even brushed the keys on her keyboard. He's a careful boy."

"As expected," I admit.

"Got a call from the local detective," Alan says. "Passengers on the plane describe our perp as a talkative white guy with a beard. He had roughly the same appearance as Ambrose. Unhelpful."

I walk to the dry-erase board in frustration. I begin to rattle off what we know, little as it is, searching for something cohesive or helpful.

"It's not about sex, it's about him seeing them as sinners—repentant or not."

"Repentant," James says.

I turn to look at him. "Explain."

"The story the cop told you about herself tells us something about Rosemary. They were friends because these were people who had devoted themselves to walking the straight and narrow. They kept themselves under tight control. They took care to reduce any catalysts in their environments that might drive them back into addiction-seeking behavior. The point being, everything about these people says repentance."

"What about Lisa?" Alan asks.

"Lisa's own diary shows her repentance," James points out.

I nod. "Good, James. Let's go with repentant. Back to methodology: the coup de grace is a poke in the side just like Christ got on the mount. He leaves crosses in the wounds, and inscribes them with numbers, which may or may not be a counting of his victims up to now. If it is a count, he's very prolific and thus very accomplished. VICAP doesn't come up with earlier similar crimes, which means he's only just decided to step into the limelight."

"Another contradiction," James murmurs.

"How do you mean?" I ask.

"The cross. It's his symbol, its placement is ritualistic. When ritual is involved, it's everything. If he has killed over a hundred people, how did he resist placement of the cross prior to this point? We would have heard about corpses turning up with crosses in their sides. We haven't."

It's a good point. Murder is always an act filled with significance for the organized serial killer. How it is done is specific, important, sacred. She must be blonde, she must never be more than a C cup, her toenails must be painted red when she dies—this is a signature and once developed, it is never deviated from. Our killer stabs them in the side and places silver crosses in the wounds. If he really has been killing for years, this should not be a new behavior.

"Only a few possibilities in that case," Alan notes. "He's changed his pattern, the numbers are a bluff, or he disposed of the bodies of his past victims so they'd remain undiscovered."

"I think it's the last," James intones.

"Wonderful thought," Callie says.

I stare at my own writing on the board, willing something else to jump out at me. Anything. Nothing does.

"Well, that's all well and valid, but we're dead-ended," I admit.

"That's it then?" Alan asks.

"For now. I'll go brief AD Jones. Use the time to get your paperwork up-to-date and keep your fingers crossed that we'll get a break that doesn't involve another dead body."

"SO BACK OFF IT FOR now," AD Jones tells me. "Sometimes that's what you have to do, give yourself some distance."

"I know, sir, it's just . . ."

"I know, I know: he's not taking a break. That's tough, but that's how it goes sometimes." He examines me, speculative. "You've been spoiled the last few years."

Annoyance flares up at this observation. I can barely keep the edge off my voice.

"How do you figure that, sir?"

"Don't get your back up. What I'm saying is, you've had a good run breaking cases quick. A real good run. It's not like that all the time. Everyone has their Zodiac, Smoky. The one they never catch. I'm not saying that's what this is, I'm just saying that you won't win them all."

I stare at him and try to keep it from becoming a glare.

"Sir, I don't mean to be disrespectful, but I don't want to hear that right now."

He shrugs, unsympathetic. "No one ever wants to hear it. The stakes are too high. But you better be ready for the day that you fail, because that day is going to come, guaranteed."

"Wow. Great pep talk, sir."

He barks a laugh. "Okay, okay. I'll keep running interference with Director Rathbun. Do what you have to."

"Thank you, sir."

I SURVEY THE OFFICE. CALLIE is chattering away on the phone with her daughter, Marilyn, about the wedding. The fact that Callie has a daughter, much less a grandson, is still a little disorienting. She was always the picture of a female bachelor, enjoying men like a gourmet meal. Her only permanent ties were here, with us, the job.

She'd buried a moment in her past, along with the pain it had caused her, until a case and a killer brought her and her daughter together again.

It irks me, now and again, that a mass murderer was responsible for giving Callie this gift.

Alan is out of the office and James has his nose buried in a file.

I stare at the white board until my eyes burn.

"A whole lotta nothing," I mutter underneath my breath. "Oh well for now."

Putting a case aside is not like placing a file folder in the "to do" pile. You open your arms and close your eyes and fling it as far away from you as possible. It sails away and you head into your normal life at a dead run and pretend it's not out there, circling like a bat.

It *is* out there, though. Tethered to your wrist with sticky-string, tugging and chuckling and waiting for the wind to change. Sometimes I'll wake up in the night to find it there, perched on my chest, staring at me with those big black eyes and smiling at me with a mouth too wide for its face. It loves me. It's horrible that it loves me.

I'm about to go see Bonnie, so I open my arms and fling. Force of will works, again, for now.

20

everything. Bonnie and I always choose the weekly recipe together. This week we're feeling ambitious and are trying a steak with a Madeira-balsamic vinegar sauce. The mere fact that it involves the unlikely mixing of wine, balsamic vinegar, and Dijon mustard is a little terrifying, but we had agreed to stray outside our comfort zone.

I read the list back to myself in a mutter: "Delmonico steaks, cracked pepper, olive oil, yep, all there."

Satisfied, I head toward what is always the highlight of my day, week, month, and year: picking up my adopted daughter to bring her home with me.

"SMOKY!"

It's a cry of sheer delight, followed by a twelve-year-old crashing into me. I return the hug and marvel, with a mix of amazement and regret, at just how tall Bonnie has gotten. At twelve, she's five feet one, which might seem reasonable to an outside observer. It means she is taller than me. The fact that two years ago I could look down and see the top of her head emphasizes the changes she is going through.

I never got to experience this with Alexa, watching her morph subtly from girl to young lady. Bonnie teeters on the cusp of becoming a teenager and she is definitely her mother's daughter. Annie was a beautiful, blonde early bloomer. Bonnie has that same blonde hair, the same striking blue eyes, the same slender frame. She is changing from awkward to coltish before my eyes. I note again, and always with the same mix of sadness, anxiety, and helplessness, that her chest is no longer boy-flat, that her walk has become less clumsy and more loping.

A dark thought comes to me: the boys. They'll start noticing you soon. They won't know why, not exactly, but you'll be more interesting. You'll catch the eyes of the normal ones, but you'll also catch the eyes of the hungry ones, because they'll smell you like a dog smells meat.

I shove this thought away down deep. Worry later. Love now.

"Hey, babe," I say, grinning. "How was school?"

She pulls away and rolls her eyes. "Boring but okay."

"She did fine," Elaina says. "A little distracted maybe, but she's ahead of her grade level."

Bonnie smiles at Elaina, basking in the praise. I can't blame her. Praise from Elaina is like sugar cookies or a patch of warm sun. Elaina is one of those genuine people, who always mean what they say, say what they mean, and err in the direction of kindness. She's been another mother to Bonnie and to me. Our love for her is fierce.

"Goddammit," Alan mutters.

He's sitting on the couch in front of the TV, and appears to be having troubles with the remote.

"Language," Bonnie scolds.

"Sorry," he says. "We just got TiVo and I'm having some problems figuring it out."

Bonnie gives Elaina and me another eye roll and walks over to Alan. She grabs the remote from him.

"You're such a Luddite, Alan," she says. "Here's how you do it."

She walks him through the steps of picking programs to record and how to watch them when they have, answers his questions with patience. Elaina and I look on, bemused.

"And that's all there is to it," she finishes.

"Thanks, kiddo," Alan says. "Now beat it so I can watch my programs."

"No hug?" Bonnie admonishes.

He smiles at her. "Just testing you," he says, and reaches out to engulf her in those massive arms.

The affection between the two is a constant. If Elaina is another mother, Alan is a second father.

"Okay, *now* beat it," he says.

"Come on," I tell her. "We've got a steak to ruin."

She grabs her backpack, gives Elaina a final hug, and we head out the door.

"Luddite, huh?" I say as we reach the car.

"Vocabulary. See? I listen," she says, and sticks her tongue out at me.

"MAN'S GUIDE TO STEAK," I complain. "Why did we choose this cookbook? Hello—two women here."

"Because it's made for cooking retards like us," Bonnie replies. "Now come on, we can do this. What does he say?"

I sigh and read aloud from the cookbook.

" 'Rub the surface of the steaks with salt and pepper.' "

"Check."

"We're supposed to use a half tablespoon of olive oil in the skillet."

"Check."

"Uh . . . then we heat the olive oil to high heat. Whatever that means."

Bonnie shrugs and turns the knob to high. "I guess we just wait till we think it's hot."

"I'm going to cut the slit in the middle of the meat."

This is our cheat. The first few times we tried to cook steaks, we followed the various dictates of a cookbook. "Three to four minutes on each side," or whatever, and ended up with meat that was either too cooked or too rare. It had been Bonnie who suggested slicing the meat all the way through in one place so we could actually watch the color of the center change. It wasn't pretty, but it had worked for us so far.

"I think it's ready," Bonnie says.

I grab the two steaks and look at her. "Here goes nothing." I throw them on the pan and we are rewarded with the sound of sizzling.

Bonnie works the spatula as I look on, pressing the meat to the pan. "Smells good so far," she offers.

"I have microwave mac and cheese in the freezer if we really screw it up," I say.

She grins at me and I grin back. We really have no idea what we're doing, but we're doing it together.

"How does that look to you?" she asks me.

I bend forward and see that the center is brown, but not too brown. We have managed to do this without turning the outside surface of the steaks into charcoal. Miraculous.

"They're done," I decide.

She uses the spatula to remove them from the skillet and onto the waiting plates.

"Okay," I say, "now comes the scary part. The sauce."

"We can do it."

"We can try."

She holds up a stick of butter. "How much?"

I consult the cookbook. "A tablespoon. But first it says to reduce to medium heat. Maybe we should give it a second to cool down. I think butter can burn."

We wait a few moments, still mystified.

"Now?" she asks.

"Your guess is as good as mine."

She digs into the butter with the spoon and drops it onto the pan. We watch as it bubbles and turns liquid.

"I don't know," Bonnie says. "Doesn't seem like much butter to me."

"You think we should add more?"

She frowns. "Well . . . it's just butter. It's probably safe."

"Do another tablespoon."

She does so and we watch it melt and become one with its brother.

"Now what?" she asks.

"It says we're supposed to stir in the shallots . . . oh crap." I look up at her. "I don't remember anything about shallots."

"What's a shallot?"

"Exactly."

We stare down at the pan of now bubbling butter. Look back at each other.

"What do we do?" I ask.

"I don't know," Bonnie replies. "Maybe the extra butter will make up for it?"

"Works for me," I say. I giggle.

Bonnie points the spatula at me. "Get it under control, Smoky," she says in a stern voice. Then giggles herself.

Which of course gets me giggling again and now this train is really in danger of leaving its rails.

"Oh Lord," I manage to sputter, "we'd better finish this up or the butter is going to burn."

Bonnie giggles again. "Because butter burns."

"So I hear." I consult the cookbook. "Back to high heat."

She turns the knob.

"Now we stir in one cup Madeira wine and one-third cup balsamic vinegar."

We pour the cups in and are rewarded with an acrid, stinking cloud of vinegar fumes.

"Wow!" Bonnie sputters. "That smells terrible! Are you sure that's what the book says?"

I blink my eyes to clear them and consult our current bible. "Yep."

"How long do we cook it?"

"Stir it until . . . let me see . . . till it's reduced by half."

Three minutes later, to our amazement, the mix has done exactly what the cookbook predicted.

"Now we're supposed to whisk in three teaspoons of Dijon mustard," I say.

We plop the mustard into what is beginning to look somewhat swillish. Bonnie whisks away. The odor is not as strong as it was before, but it doesn't smell great.

"Are you sure this isn't some kind of a practical-joke cookbook or something?" she asks.

"Oh, hey," I say. "Turns out we're supposed to use three tablespoons of butter after all. The two we already did, and add another one now, just until it melts."

The butter does not make our witch's brew look any more appetizing. A few moments pass. Bonnie frowns at me.

"Think it's done?"

I peer at the concoction. It's a yellowish gray color. It smells of butter, mustard, and vinegar. "Too late for prayer."

We take the skillet off the stove and spread the sauce over each steak as the cookbook directs. Bonnie takes our plates to the table as I pour us each a glass of water.

We're poised over our steaks now, forks and knives in hand.

"Ready?" she asks me.

"Yep."

We each cut off a piece and pop them into our mouths. There is silence and chewing.

"Wow," Bonnie says, amazed, "that's actually . . ."

"—really good," I finish for her.

"No, like *really* good."

"As in delicious."

She grins at me, a spark of mischief in her eyes.

"Shallots?" she says. "We don't need no stinking shallots."

I'd taken a drink of water and I choke on it as I laugh.

"I THINK NEXT TIME WE might even try adding a side of vegetables," I say.

We'd had just the steak and some dinner rolls.

"Maybe some shallots," Bonnie jokes.

I smile. We're sitting on the couch, barely watching some reality talent show. Dinner had been great, and the evening has been wonderful. Normal. I crave normal a lot, but get it rarely.

"So, I want to talk about school," Bonnie says.

So much for normal.

I chastise myself for this. What could be more normal than a kid wanting to go to a school with other kids? I can see from the anxiety in her face that she's so *worried* about how what she wants will make me feel.

Oh hell.

I focus on her, give her all of my attention.

"Yes. I'm listening, babe. Tell me."

She shifts her legs up under her, and pushes a lock of hair back behind her ear while she searches for the right words. This gesture gives me a strong feeling of déjà vu; the ghost of her mother. Genetic possession.

"I've been thinking a lot, lately." She glances at me, smiles a shy smile. "I guess I think a lot all the time."

"It's one of your better qualities, bunny. Not enough thinking in this world. What's been on your mind?"

"What I want to do when I grow up. Well . . . when I'm an adult, I mean."

Interesting distinction.

"And?"

"I want to do what you do."

I stare, at a loss for words. Of all the things she could have said, of all the professions she could have chosen, this I like the least.

"Why?" I manage. "What about painting?"

She gives me a smile that says I am deluded but nonetheless charming.

"I'm not that good, Momma-Smoky. Painting is something I'll always enjoy. It brings me peace. But it's not what I'm meant to do."

"Baby, you're twelve. How can you be meant to do anything?"

Her eyes snap to mine and fill with a coolness that shuts me up fast. Right now, she looks anything but twelve.

"Do you know the first thing I see, every time I close my eyes?" Her voice is calm, soothing, almost singsong. "I see my mother's dead face. Just like I saw it for those three days when I was tied to her." She stares off at nothing and everything, remembering. "She was stuck in a scream. I cried on her a lot the first day. I remember feeling bad about that, because some of my tears went into her eyes and I thought that that just wasn't right, she couldn't brush them away or anything. Then I stopped crying and I started trying to sleep. I pretended like she wasn't dead, and she was just holding me. It even worked, for a little while. Until she started to smell. After that, it was all grays and blues and blacks. I paint those colors sometimes and think about that last day, because that last day wasn't real, but it was the most real day of all. When I dream about that last day, all I dream about is screaming and rain."

These words transfix me. When I can speak again, my voice is rough with grief. "I'm sorry, Bonnie. So so so so sorry."

She comes back to the present. Her eyes lose that faraway cool-ness, that *deadness,* and fill with concern for me, instead. "Hey, hey, Momma-Smoky, it's okay. Well, I mean, no, it's not okay, but *I'm* okay. I could have been really messed up forever, you know? I wasn't sure I was going to be able to talk again or stop having nightmares. I even thought about killing myself. But now, I like my life. I love Elaina, and Alan, and most of all, I really love you." She grins. "Like tonight. We made steaks."

"Yes," I manage. "Good steaks."

"Yeah, and that's small, but it's also everything, you know?"

"I do, babe."

"But the thing with my mom *happened,* Smoky. It *happened,* and it's always there and in a way it always will be. I know you know what I mean, because stuff happened to you too. And you know what? I don't want to forget. I think the day I can't remember how my mom looked in that room is the day I'll really be in trouble."

The simple mature wisdom of what she's saying takes the keen edge off the saw blade that had been attacking my heart. She's right. I used to think that if I stopped mourning Matt and Alexa, I was killing them all over again. I came to realize that suffering was not a require-ment, not even guilt; remembering was enough. But—and here is the ocean-sized caveat—remembering is *required.*

"I understand," I tell her.

She smiles at me. "I know you do. So you should understand why I want to do what you do."

"Because of what happened to your mom."

Those cool, oh-too-speculative eyes are back. The twelve-year-old is gone again.

"Not just my mom. Because of what happened to me. Because of what happened to you. Because of what happened to Sarah."

Sarah was the living victim of a case I'd been involved in a few years back. Even though she is six years older than Bonnie, they have found kinship in tragedy and remain close friends.

"Everyone I love most knows that the monsters are real, Momma-Smoky. When you know they're real, you can't pretend anymore, and you have to do something about it."

I stare at her. I don't want to hear these words coming from that mouth.

God, I hate this conversation. And you know what? I'm going to lose this argument. Because these wheels were put in motion the moment Bonnie was tied to her gutted mom and left there to change into what she is now.

It makes me sad. I've been living in a fantasy world, hoping that Bonnie would grow into a normal life, a normal job, get the white picket fence and the dog. Who had I been kidding?

Not her, that's for sure.

I sigh. "I understand, babe."

I may not like it, but I do.

"Going to a regular school is a part of that. I can't understand the monsters, not really, if I don't understand normal people, you know?"

And you're not one of the normal people, babe?

I think it, but do not ask it. I don't want to hear her answer.

"I thought maybe it was so you could make some friends your own age."

"But *I'm* not my own age, Momma-Smoky."

It finally happens, against my will. That little tidbit is enough to bring a tear. Just one. It rolls down my cheek in a straight line. Bonnie's face scrunches up in concern and she reaches her hand out to wipe it away.

"I'm sorry, I didn't mean to make you sad."

I clear my throat. "I don't ever want you to tell me anything less than the truth. However it makes me feel."

"But you shouldn't feel bad. I could be dead. I could be in a mental institution. I could still be screaming in the middle of the night—remember that?"

"Yes."

We both used to do it, sometimes in stereo. Nightmares would walk us into memory and we'd wake up screaming ourselves hoarse.

"So things are better, see? I don't want you to think I'm not happy."

She manages to drill down with that, to put words to the greatest, most basic mother-fear.

"Are you, babe? Happy?"

I'm a little shocked at the miserable, desperately hopeful sound of my own voice.

She gives me a new smile now, one that's unfettered, unadulterated, no fog, no screams or rain or cold, cold eyes. Just twelve-year-old cloudless blue-sky sunshine, the most beautiful sun there is.

"Eight days out of ten, Momma-Smoky."

I remember what Alan said earlier, and know that he was right. Count your blessings is a cliché, but only because it's so damn true. Bonnie is here, Bonnie is beautiful, intelligent, talented, she talks, she doesn't fear life or wake up screaming in the night. Yes, she's been changed by what happened to her, but she hasn't been broken, and in the end, that's the biggest blessing of all. Almost a miracle, really.

I grab her and hug her to me.

"Okay, okay. But can you wait till next fall? Finish out this year with Elaina?"

"Yes, yes, yes, thank you, thank you!"

I know the decision is the right one, because those squeals of delight are pure twelve-year-old again.

We spend the rest of the night wrapped in normalcy, doing nothing much, just enjoying each other's company. For a little while, I don't worry if someone's dying.

Somehow, the world turns on without me.

I WAKE UP TO THE insistent buzz of my cell phone. I check the caller ID with bleary eyes. Alan.

"It's five A.M.," I answer. "Can't be good."

"It's not," he says. "The shit's about to hit the fan."

PART TWO

THE
STORM

21

"I GOT A CALL FROM ATKINS. HE SURFS A LOT OF THOSE VIRAL video sites—"

"Come again?" I ask.

"Websites that allow users to post video clips," James explains. "They can be self-made, or they can be thirty-second to three-minute clips people encoded from the news or a DVD or whatever."

I frown. "What's the point of that?"

"Entertainment," Callie says. "Voyeurism. Socializing. You have everything from skateboards crashing into the sidewalk and breaking wrists to cute just-legal somethings talking about world events while sitting around in their bikinis."

I sigh. "Bonnie probably knows all about this stuff."

Callie pats my head. "Everyone does except you, honey-love."

Alan opens up a browser and types in a url: user-tube.com. A moment later, the screen fills with a series of neatly arranged thumbnail photos. Each thumbnail has text aligned beneath it.

"Wipeout," I read below one.

The photo shows someone flying off a motorbike as it crashes into the ground.

Alan clicks it and a new page loads. The video clip begins to play. Sure enough, we see a motorbike hit a ramp, fly into the air, and miss its mark. The rider does a real-life Superman as the bike crunches into the ground. He lands, bounces a few times, and ends up in a tangled heap.

"Ouch," I say, wincing.

"There's more," Alan observes.

Whoever made the clip did us and all other viewers the service of rewinding to the moment before the crash and replaying it all in glorious slow motion. We get to hear the crunches and crashes in that long, drawn-out ohhhhhhhhhh-nooooooo druggy reverb, get to watch the hapless rider arrow through the air and bounce like a human basketball.

"Gross," I observe.

"Modern day Roman arena," Callie says.

"What's all that posted below the clip?" I ask.

"User comments," Alan says. "You create an account. That lets you upload your own clips and allows you to comment on stuff other people have posted."

He scrolls down a little so I can read some of the witticisms.

Motherfucking WIIIIIPEOUT!
Who says a man can't fly?
Holy shit, did you see him *bounce*? Holy shit!
We all saw the same thing you did, you dumb fag . . .

"Highbrow," I remark.

"It's not all mayhem," Alan says, navigating back to the home page. "They have categories, see?"

I read. Family Fun. Animals. Romance. I start to understand the attraction.

"So anyone can come on here, upload a video clip, and have others talk about it?"

"Yep. You get a lot of crap, but you also get some pretty creative stuff. Short movies, comedians and musicians trying to get heard, all kinds of things."

"And sex, I'd imagine?"

"Actually, they police that pretty hard. No nudity allowed."

"No problem with gore, though," James observes.

"Nope."

I glance at Alan. "And you frequent this site?"

He shrugs. "What can I say? It's addictive. Each clip is a snack, not a meal."

"You can't eat just one," Callie chirps.

"Okay," I say. "I understand the structure. Now show me what it has to do with us."

Alan points to the listing of categories.

"There's a religious category. Generally, it has a few different uses. Preachers or would-be preachers giving three-minute sermons, a far-righter talking about the sins of abortion, a far-lefter talking about the sins of organized religion in general."

He clicks on the category and a new row of thumbnail images fills the screen.

"The top ten are the ones you need to see."

He clicks on a thumbnail. There is a black screen. White, block letters appear: *The Beginning of the Opus—A Study of Truth and the Soul.*

The letters fade into another few seconds of blackness and then open to the mid-body shot of a man. He is seated at a simple brown wooden table. He is only visible from the shoulders down to the table-top. The wall behind him is blank gray concrete. The light source comes from above, just enough to illuminate him and some of his surrounds. The word *austere* comes to mind. Snow on a treeless field. His hands are clasped in front of him, resting on the table. They are draped with a rosary. He wears a black shirt and a black jacket.

"The study of the nature of truth," he begins, "is the study of the nature of God." The voice is low, but not bass, more alto. It's a pleasant voice. Calm, measured, relaxed.

"Why is this? Because the basic truth of all things is that they exist as God created them. To view the truth of something is to view it exactly as it is, unlayered by your own views, your own preconceptions, your own additions to its composition. To view the truth of something is to see it not as you want it to be, but as it is. In other words, to see it exactly as God created it to be, at the moment of its creation. Thus, when you see the truth of something, you are, in fact, allowing yourself to see a piece of the face of God."

"Interesting. Cogent," James murmurs.

"What, then, prevents us from perceiving this truth? We were all born with eyes to see, with ears to hear. We all have a brain to process the input of our senses. Why, then, do two men witness an automobile accident and have entirely different versions of the truth? Why, further, does a video camera recording of the same accident demonstrate both men's observations to be incorrect?

"The answer is obvious: only the video camera records without alteration. What, then, is the difference between the man and the camera?" He pauses for a moment. "The difference is that the video camera has no filter of 'self.' It has no soul, no mind. One can then extrapolate that where errors in judgment occur, the soul and the mind are the sources of the flaw.

"But if God created all things, and He did, then we must acknowledge that He created the soul and the mind as well. God does not make mistakes. Therefore, the soul and the mind, at birth, are perfection, capable of perceiving exact and basic truth. One could argue that, at birth, no filter exists at all between the truth of the world and the self. What, then, is this 'filter'? This thing that changes man over time, that makes his recollection less reliable than a video camera?"

Fade to black again, followed by those same white block letters proclaiming, *End Part One.*

I turn to Alan. "This is fascinating—but what does it have to do with us?"

"Keep watching."

He clicks on the next thumbnail and we go through the black screen, white letters, and return to the narrator.

"The filter is sin. The catalyst is power of choice. God gave man the ability to choose between heaven and hell. To choose between everlasting glory 'or eternal damnation. From the moment we're dragged from the womb, we begin to make choices. The nature of our choices, over time, are what decide our fate when Death knocks.

"From the moment we choose sin, we create the filter. We pull a veil over our eyes, create a barrier between ourselves and the basic truth of things as God created them. Do you see? As we alter the basic truth of us, that truth that God created, we change, thus, our perception of all of the other truths and works of God. This is described in many places within the Bible, such as in the story of Saul.

" 'As he was traveling, it happened that he was approaching Damascus, and suddenly a light from heaven flashed around him;

and he fell to the ground and heard a voice saying to him, 'Saul, Saul, why are you persecuting Me?' And he said, 'Who are You, Lord?' And He said, 'I am Jesus whom you are persecuting, but get up and enter the city, and it will be told you what you must do.' The men who traveled with him stood speechless, hearing the voice but seeing no one. Saul got up from the ground, and though his eyes were open, he could see nothing; and leading him by the hand, they brought him into Damascus. And he was three days without sight, and neither ate nor drank.

"You see? Saul could not see Jesus even though Jesus was before him. And later:

" 'Ananias departed and entered the house, and after laying his hands on him said, "Brother Saul, the Lord Jesus, who appeared to you on the road by which you were coming, has sent me so that you may regain your sight and be filled with the Holy Spirit." And immediately there fell from his eyes something like scales, and he regained his sight, and he got up and was baptized; and he took food and was strengthened.'

"Saul repented his sins and came to Christ and was thereafter no longer blind. There are those, I know, who will see only the literal in this and no metaphor. I see it as a direct message, an example of the paradigm I have been discussing. Saul was a sinner, and thus, he was blind to God even when God was before him. Saul was filled with God, and his sight was restored. What could be more obvious, more basic, more true?

"And so I say to you, as someone who has worked all his life to be an observer of God's truth, that your sins, your secrets, your lies, these are what prevent you from seeing the simplicity of the love in the world around you.

"Perhaps you hear this and you agree and you have decided, now I will live in truth. I will be honest, I will sin no more. I applaud and encourage you in this, but I must be honest and tell you—you will fail unless you come to understand this fact: truth is not a striving, it is an immediate arrival.

"What do I mean by this?

"It is explained in our next discussion: the nature of the truth that hides a lie, and the example of Lisa/Dexter Reid."

Fade to black.

"Oh shit," I say.

"It gets worse," Alan replies, grim.

He clicks the next thumbnail. I watch and fight the unease that's coming to a slow bubble inside my belly.

Again the hands. They haven't moved once since we began watching.

"Lisa Reid was born Dexter Reid, son to Dillon and Rosario Reid. Dexter became unhappy with the body God had given him, and chose instead to alter that body in an attempt to become a woman.

"All can agree that this is an abomination against the Lord. But it is here, with this misguided soul, that we most vividly illustrate the phenomenon of the truth that hides a lie. The phenomenon goes as such: a person reveals a secret, a sin, a lie. It is not a small thing that they reveal. It requires courage to do so, and it garners them both relief and admiration. They receive praise for having 'come clean.' All of which would be well and good . . . except for the fact that they had a deeper, darker, as yet unrevealed secret.

"You see? By revealing one great sin, they remove all suspicion that there might be another. We watch them tell the truth, cry tears of relief along with them, and wish we had their strength of character, their newfound courage and virtue. Unbeknownst to us, something more terrible remains unseen.

"This is what I meant when I said that truth was not a striving, but an immediate arrival. One either comes to the truth all at once, or not at all. There is no halfway mark on the path to God. You are either with him or you are not.

"Dexter Reid became Lisa Reid. He came into the open, he revealed his secret—the desire to become a woman—to the world. He accepted all the disgust, chastisement, and blame that would accrue with this. He walked this path unflinching, refusing to be deterred by the disapproval of society. Some—many, even—saw this and admired him for it. Dexter's life was difficult, even dangerous, but he did what he did because he felt he must, in spite of the obstacles. The definition of courage."

Another pause. The hands move this time. One thumb comes free and rubs the beads of the rosary.

"But Dexter had another secret. He detailed it in his journal. I have those pages of the journal here, as I stole them after I killed him."

Fade to black. The white letters *Continued in next clip.*

"Dammit!" I say.

"It's a hard medium to get used to," Alan allows.

Alan clicks on the next thumbnail. When the video begins, the screen is filled with a page of paper. I recognize Lisa's handwriting. The narrator pulls the page away from the lens and holds it in his right hand so he can read it. The rosary remains draped in his left, and he moves the beads between thumb and forefinger with reverence, a motion I can tell is as natural to him as walking. He begins to read.

THE SIN
of
DEXTER REID

22

IT WAS A GREAT SUMMER DAY. GREAT. HOT AND NOT TOO muggy and filled with the promise of everything *but* school.

Dexter stood on the porch of the house and surveyed his neighborhood. It was a good neighborhood, no doubt about that. Not the good that came of new homes, but the comfortable good of old homes kept up to snuff.

The sky was blue and visible in that way Mom called "Texas Sky." Texas was flat and rolling and Austin was not all that fond of skyscrapers, so in many places you could see blue from horizon to horizon. It was all right.

Dexter had awoken this Saturday to do his usual routine. It was precious to him, and growing more so as he got older and began to get the hint that times were changing. He was eleven, and already he could see the lines between the sexes—once so blurred—being forced into focus. Guys only a year older were talking about things like "pussy" a lot more and with a genuine interest and hunger. It was disconcerting.

Dexter had been able to wake up at 5:30 A.M. on Saturday mornings with no alarm since he was six years old. He'd discovered that some of the best cartoons, the old black and whites that you never saw anywhere else anymore, were on in those early hours.

He'd get up and head down to the kitchen and treat himself to homemade cinnamon toast. His version included huge hunks of butter, unhealthy helpings of sugar, and just enough cinnamon to give it all a little bit of bite. In it went to the toaster oven, out it came with the butter bubbling. He'd watch it cook, stare at the heating coils turned orange by their temperature.

He loved these mornings, loved that no one else was awake, that he had the house to himself, at least in illusion. It was a feeling of freedom and safety, not so much as if nothing bad would ever happen— but the certainty that nothing bad would happen now, at this moment. The times between 5:30 and 8:00 A.M. were an armistice in Dexter's heart.

He'd grab the toast once it had cooled enough (but not too much) and put it on some paper towels and head into the living room where the TV was. He'd switch on the set and put it to the right channel and plop down on his beanbag. Mom hated the beanbag, and Dad wasn't all that excited about it—he called it a seventies throwback—but Dexter had stood firm on keeping it. It was a talisman, a part of the ritual.

Sometimes they'd still play "Inky and the Mynah Bird" in Texas in those early morning hours, but most of the time, it was "Huckleberry Hound" or some old unclassifiable cartoons. These turned into "Tom and Jerry" and from there to the "Bugs Bunny/Road Runner Show." He'd watch them all, and make mental lists during the commercials of the cool new toys to bug Mom and Dad about.

The first part of the magic ended at about 8:00, as Mom and Dad got up. He loved them both, but the ritual was all about solitude; their presence broke the spell. He'd hit the shower and get dressed as they stumbled through their first coffees. A kiss on Mom's cheek and a mumbled good morning from Dad and he was out the door by 8:30.

Now here he was, cartoons and cinnamon toast behind him, the whole day before him. What to do? He had a few bucks in his pocket, the result of lawn-mowing industry. He could head to the Circle K and buy some comics. He could grab his bike and ride to the pool. Heck, he could do anything he wanted!

He opted to walk, an unusual choice, but the day was just so great and he wanted to feel the ground underneath his tennis shoes. He headed down to the junction, which is what he called the top of the T where his street met another at a stop sign. Right took you to the park and the pool, left took you to Rambling Oaks, what the kids called the "woods."

It was not exactly a "woods," more like a copse gone wild. It was the edge of development, dirt not yet turned by tractors in preparation for new home construction.

Most times he didn't like to go to the woods alone, but today was different. Dexter was a social boy, but he didn't feel like company right now. So he turned left and not right. It was a simple decision that would change his life forever, which is the way it usually goes.

The street dead-ended in dirt. The dirt ended at the trees. Walk through the trees a little and you came out to grass, which then led to more pavement and new homes. The woods were a kind of last stand and all sorts of things happened there.

First cigarettes had been smoked in the woods by more kids than could be counted. First kisses had been tasted, and of course there were the rumors of first blow jobs and such, though Dexter wasn't sure about that. He wasn't brilliant or anything, but he had a little more wisdom than most of his peers, and he had the sneaking suspicion that getting a girl from this neighborhood to suck on your Johnson involved better surrounds than a place like the woods. A car, at least.

Dirty mags had been read here, and Dexter had seen a few in the last year, though his reactions were ambiguous in a way that didn't seem to match up with his friends'. So he'd leered and joked with the rest of them, tossing off verbal gems like "hairy clam" and "furburger" with snickering confidence and aplomb. None of it made sense to Dexter, as the girls in the pictures he saw were hairless down there, and what did a burger have to do with it, anyway?

People had wept in these woods too, Dexter was aware. Nice neighborhood or no, kids still got beat, from time to time. Abuse existed, though it wasn't talked about much. The woods had been a sanctuary, a haven, a place for the simple, the illicit, the groping, and the sad. Even at eleven, Dexter understood that the woods was going to be one of those places he'd never forget. It would always have power, even if just in memory.

He took his time walking down the street. Enjoying the sunshine and the sounds. No one was crazy enough to be out mowing this early, but two people were out washing their cars, which Dexter thought was a fine idea. He stuck his hands in his pockets and found a white stone in one of the gutters to kick. It was going to be a hell of a day!

The pavement ended and he hit the dirt. There were two kinds of Texas dirt. There was the dark, dry, clumpy sod, the kind that grass grew in and came out in chunks. Then there was the tan, almost granular kind, that soaked up the sun and was generally filled with detritus, stones and such. This was the second kind.

The trees weren't too far off, and Dexter decided that he would really make a morning out of his walk. He'd head through the woods, out the other side, and into the neighborhood next door. He'd circle around and be back at home in time for some bologna or peanut butter and jelly and probably some Kool-Aid. Then maybe a trip to the comic store and the pool.

Why not? The day was his.

He quickened his pace toward the trees, excited by all the prospects unfolding before him.

That's when he heard them.

"Kiss it, you fucking retard," the voice said.

Dexter recognized this voice. Any kid in the neighborhood would. It belonged to Mark Phillips, bully and all around evil individual. Mark's story was as unoriginal as the Texas dirt under Dexter's tennis shoes: he grew fast, he grew tall, he grew wide, and he liked the power this gave him over others.

He had various protection rackets running, as bullies will. Some lunch-money graft, comic-book offerings, allowance percentages. Noncompliance was met with punishment, and it was here that Mark truly excelled. He was a cut above, willing to go that extra mile.

The average bully would smack you around, maybe give you a titty twister, or hold you down while dripping a stream of spit into your mouth. Mark used these standbys as well, but the difference was in how far he was willing to take it. Tears were generally a sign that your point had been made. Not so for Mark.

Dexter had been on the receiving end one time. For some reason— he still didn't know why—he'd refused to turn over a comic that Mark had asked for. Mark's response had been instant and savage. He'd slapped Dexter's face so hard it made him feel like his eyes were rattling around in their sockets. Mark had followed it up with a shot to the solar plexus that drove Dexter to his knees, gasping for breath.

Mark had swarmed on top of him in an instant, pinning him to the ground, arms trapped under Mark's knees.

"Faggot grew some balls, huh? Bad idea, faggot. Now you gotta pay."

Dexter had felt he was already paying. His inability to catch his breath had panic rising in his chest like a flood. He was sure that he was dying. He wasn't, but it felt like it.

"Gonna show you something I learned watching a martial arts program, faggot," Mark said. His tone was almost happy, and Dexter looked up at the boy and removed the "almost" from that equation.

Mark put a thumb to either side of Dexter's face, digging into a spot just under the upper cheekbone. He pressed up. Not hard, which made it all the more terrifying, because even that little pressure hurt.

"It's a nerve someajigger or a pressure point or something. Whatever they call it, it hurts worse than a kick in the balls."

Then he really dug in, turned his thumbs into steel rods and pressed with all of his not inconsiderable strength.

Dexter couldn't help it; his eyes bugged out and he didn't just yell, he screamed. The agony was instant and terrible and everywhere. It felt like Mark had driven spikes into Dexter's jaw.

He could see Mark through his pain, white-edged now, grinning away. Mark's eyes were shining and Dexter became aware that the boy actually had a hard-on. Mark was making Dexter scream, and it was giving the bigger boy a woody.

It should have stopped there. With another bully, it would have. But that was the day Dexter learned that Mark was willing to go that extra mile, to really put his heart into it, so to speak.

Because he didn't stop. He pressed harder. He pressed and grinned while Dexter screamed, and kept on pressing until Dexter pissed his pants. In the end, Dexter was begging the older boy to stop.

"Is your momma a whore?" the older boy asked.

"Yes, yes, yes!" Dexter screamed.

"Say it, then. Tell me your momma is a dirty old wetback buttfuck-loving, cock-gobbling whore!"

Again, that dim awareness of Mark's hard-on, throbbing now.

To his credit, Dexter actually paused for a moment at this demand. But then Mark pressed harder.

"Okay, okay, okay! She's a dirty old wetback cock-gobbling whore!" he screamed.

"Buttfuck-loving, cock-gobbling whore."

"Buttfuck-loving, cock-gobbling whore! Please stop please stop please stop please stop please—"

And then Mark did let up. He removed his thumbs. He didn't get right up and off Dexter, though. He stayed where he was, staring down at the smaller boy, eyes half-lidded and predatory, hard-on throbbing against Dexter's stomach. Drunk on power, the power of might-makes-right and the dispensing of pain.

"Listen up, faggot. You ever tell anyone I did this to you, and I'll find you and tear your cock off. You think I'm kidding?"

Dexter couldn't speak. He was shivering, the throbbing in his cheeks wouldn't stop, it was almost as if Mark had never pulled those thumbs away. He shook his head no, and began to weep, big, long, ropy sobs. Mark looked down at him in disgust.

"Fucking pussy faggot."

A moment later the bully was gone. Dexter turned on his side and vomited into some of that good old Texas dirt. His cheeks were on fire. It took almost two days for the throbbing to die down completely and he couldn't eat right during that time.

It was Dexter's first brush with full-on gibbering terror, and it had left a mark. He had no doubt the bully would make good on any threat. Mark *liked* handing out a hurting. Handing out a hurting put some air in Mark's tire, put a little bit of bone in the old hot dog.

Mark was evil. Dexter understood this. Kids don't look for shades of gray. Moral ambiguity is something that comes later, when they need to start justifying their own misdeeds. Mark was a monster, black and white, and Dexter took that at face value.

So, hearing the boy say "kiss it, retard," was not a good sign, not a good sign at all.

In later years Dexter would wonder why, knowing this, he didn't just turn around on that tan Texas dirt and head right back to where the pavement began again, back up to the junction and the way that led to the park, the pool, and still being an eleven-year-old.

He moved forward that day, toward the voice, filled with dread but unable to turn away.

Once through the first line of trees, a small clearing opened up. Dexter saw Mark there, standing above Jacob Littlefield.

Jacob was older than either Mark or Dexter, almost seventeen, but Jacob was smaller than Mark and mentally slower than either of them. Dexter now understood that Mark's use of the word *retard* was not figurative. He was using the unkindest cut as a matter of course, an insult that Jacob had surely heard before and probably understood.

Jacob was down on his hands and knees, and he was crying like a lost baby. He had a big round face and short cropped blond hair. His skin was milky white. Dexter had always thought privately that Jacob had the most beautiful skin he'd ever seen on another guy. Jacob was a sweet kid, always smiling, very trusting. His mom usually kept a close eye on him. Dexter wondered what the hell had happened.

Mark pointed at his right foot, which Dexter noticed was bare. It looked fugly and toe-jammed and altogether unappetizing.

"I said, kiss it, you stupid retarded fuckup. You drool enough already, you shouldn't have any problem working up the spit to clean up between my toes."

"But I don't wanna," Jacob blubbered. "Please don't make me."

Mark slapped the boy's face. Hard. Dexter heard the smack and shivered.

"Do what I tell you or I'm gonna beat the shit out of you, you fucking retard! You hear me?"

Mark slapped the boy again, and now Jacob was really bawling, full bore, the way a baby does, total abandon. Dexter watched with a mix of horror and fascination as Jacob bent forward and began to kiss and lick Mark's nasty foot.

Motherfuck was all that came to mind. Dexter didn't swear too often, but *motherfuck* was a versatile word. It just fit right in some places. This was one of them.

"That's right, retard, clean 'em up good."

Dexter recognized that look on Mark's face. Savage joy. He was just as certain that Mark had *pitched a pup tent,* as they liked to say during sleepovers. Its usual witticism seemed to fall flat here. Dexter's throat was dry and his mouth tasted like dust. He was witnessing the worst thing he'd ever seen in his life right now. He was sure of it.

He was just as sure that he needed to get the fuck out of there. The *motherfuck* out of there. Otherwise, he was pretty certain he was going to find himself right down there on his hands and knees with Jacob, licking the toe-jam and grime from Mark's feet until they gleamed.

But what about Jacob?

The thought came, of course. Dexter was a decent boy, after all. The answer followed, fast and shameful:

Sorry, Jacob. Sucks to be you.

Not noble, maybe, but even the thought of what Mark had done to him before made his bladder feel loose and jiggly. Jacob was on his own, which was a motherfuck, but that's the way it was going to have to be.

Dexter turned to go and that's when it happened. It was like something from a bad movie, the oldest cliché around: he stepped on a stick. It had been a dry summer, so the wood snapped like a firecracker.

The thing about guys like Mark, Dexter would ponder later, their double whammy, was the singular lack of hesitation that having no moral code gave them. The stick cracked and Mark was on him in seconds. He heard the older boy's movements first and felt one of Mark's big, meaty hands grip his neck a moment later, all before Dexter could get the idea of *run* translated into motion.

"Well, lookee here," Mark chortled. "Looks like we got ourselves a regular retard convention going."

"Let me go, Mark," Dexter said, more from force of habit than out of any real hope that the older boy would listen. "I was just walking. I don't care what else is happening, I promise."

Mark squeezed a little harder and Dexter squirmed. It wasn't exactly pain, but it was the promise of it.

"I don't think so, fag," Mark said. "I'm having a little party here and I think you need to join in."

He turned without another word, still gripping Dexter around the neck, and marched them both back into the clearing. Jacob was still down on his hands and knees. He was shivering and blubbering. Dexter didn't wonder why the boy hadn't run away. Mark had probably said if he did he'd kill him. Better the foot slobbering in front of you than the unknown promise that kept you looking over your shoulder. All small kids who got bullied understood this logic.

Mark let go of his neck by tossing him forward. Dexter stumbled and fell, landing at an odd angle on his wrist so that he couldn't catch his fall, only slow it. He ended up clipping his chin against the ground. His teeth clacked together so hard he felt it in his skull, like a brutal rap with a big wooden spoon.

"Get back to licking, retard," Mark commanded Jacob.

Jacob kept sobbing, but his resistance had been broken. He went back to using his tongue to clean between Mark's filthy toes. Dexter brought himself to a sitting position and wiped his mouth. His teeth ached.

The sun was hot, but no longer in a good way; it was more surreal now. It kind of made Dexter feel like he was being baked alive. The noise of bugs and birds in the air had a sluggish feel to it.

That bad dream syrup, it's everywhere . . .

That's what Nana called the quality of those nightmares, the ones where you needed to run but felt like you were moving through mush. She called it bad dream syrup, and had pointed out to Dexter that the bad dream syrup had the habit of appearing at times when you were wide awake.

Mark turned a sleepy-eyed, lizard smile to Dexter. He was well pleased. This was it, for him, right here. Subjugation, degradation, power. Mark knew what he wanted and he wasn't conflicted about it.

"Listen up, faggot. You got a choice here. You can do what I tell you to do, or I'll give you some more of what I gave you those months back."

The words gave Dexter a chill. Sweat actually broke out on his forehead. His mouth went dry.

Whatever he wants, it can't be as bad as that was. Nothing could be that bad.

"Here's the deal. You're going to whip out your tiny little dick and you're going to make the retard suck on it. I want him to choke on that Oscar Mayer." Mark smiled, another lazy, happy, unconflicted smile. "He sucks and you come, fuckwit. No come, and you're getting the thumbs again." He wiggled said thumbs and grinned wider.

Dexter would wonder, years later, how guys like Mark knew exactly where to stick the knife in so that it would hurt the most. It was an uncanny ability, like a shark smelling blood in the water.

Dexter wasn't a perfect boy, but he tried to be a good boy. He had his moments of anger and selfishness, but up until that moment, he'd never done anything truly ugly. He'd never taken his rage out on someone weaker than him, he'd never harmed a defenseless animal, his lies were white and not big. Somehow, Mark knew this. He wanted to change this because he knew it would hurt Dexter a lot more than gobbling Mark's toe-jam or writhing under Mark's iron thumbs.

"And if I don't?"

"Keep licking, retard!" Mark snapped down at Jacob. He turned the sleepy gaze and the lizard smile back to Dexter. "I'll make you scream, fag-boy. I'll make you scream until you lose your fucking mind."

Dexter fought his fear. He allowed himself that truth, when he remembered this day in later years. He tried. But courage in the face of torture, he found out that day, was for comics, not eleven-year-old boys being offered a way out.

He stood up and walked over to where Mark was. He looked down at Jacob, who had stopped crying so much. He was still licking Mark's feet, which were starting to look pretty clean.

Good job! Dexter thought, on the edge of hysteria.

Jacob stopped for a moment and looked up at Dexter. The boy really did have beautiful skin. He had the eyes of a child; big and trusting. He had snot running from his nose and his cheeks were tracked with tears.

"Now before you make him suck, I want you to slap his face," Mark said. The bully's voice was languid, lazy.

Don't do this, a voice in Dexter's head boomed. This is something, if you do, you can't undo.

Dexter couldn't take his eyes off Jacob's face. His round, stupid face. He felt anger rising, an irrational anger that said it was Jacob's fault that Dexter was in this position, that it was Jacob's fault that Dexter was being forced to do something so terrible.

If you weren't such a fucking retard, you wouldn't be here and I wouldn't be here and I'd just be taking my walk on a great Saturday morning.

Rage rose in Dexter. He'd realize later that the rage was really just fear and shame come together.

He pulled his hand back. It hung in the air, trembling.

"Do it, fag," Mark goaded, gloating like a toad.

Dexter was in hell.

He closed his eyes so he couldn't see Jacob's face anymore. He hugged the rage to him, hard, and brought his hand down.

23

"I SLAPPED THAT POOR BOY, AND I . . . DID WHAT MARK TOLD me to do, and I watched as Mark threatened him after," the man on the video continues to read. "He told Jacob he'd kill him if he finked, and that afterward, he'd fuck Jacob's mom in the ass.

"That was the end of my childhood Saturdays. I tried waking up again in those quiet hours, but the cartoons seemed washed out, and the cinnamon toast never tasted as good.

"I never felt the same about myself after that. You have ideas about yourself, particularly as a child. Ideals. You assume that you'd be courageous when needed, that you'd make the right decision in a tough situation. Mark shattered that illusion for me. I realized that I was capable of harming, even raping, another person—a helpless person—to save my own skin. I wasn't heroic when the chips were down, and whatever else happens, I'll always know that about myself.

"I told Nana about what happened. I told her and I cried and she held me for a long time. She was quiet for a while, thinking through it in that way that she had. In the end she told me this: 'Everyone has a little bit of ugly in them. Remember yours the next time you think about judging theirs.'

"Nana was the only one who knew, until this year. I found a priest, a good man, who was willing to hear my confession. I talked, he listened, and then, miracle of miracles, he absolved me. He told me that

God would forgive, and I believe him. God, I am finding, is not really the problem. I'm just not sure if I'm ready to forgive myself.

"But I'm trying. I really, really am."

The man puts the page down on the table in front of him and refolds his hands, thumb and forefinger still rubbing away at the rosary.

"So Dexter Reid revealed one secret to the world, his desire to be a woman. But he held one back, something even more shameful, perhaps. Certainly more shameful to him. As they say, the whole truth, nothing but the truth. Easy to say, difficult to do, necessary for salvation. Another example follows in the death of Rosemary Sonnenfeld."

The clip fades to black.

"Is the bad feeling I'm getting justified?" I ask Alan.

"Yeah."

"Go ahead."

He clicks the next clip. The lettering this time reads: *The Death and Sin of Rosemary Sonnenfeld.*

"Rosemary was a sinner's sinner," the man intones. He doesn't sound especially judgmental about it. Just telling it like it is. "She spent her youth having sex indiscriminately and for money, embroiled in drugs and perversion. At her lowest point she accepted God into her life and confessed her past to Him. She revealed her secrets and tried to walk a righteous path. But, as with Dexter, she had a second secret, a deeper sin. Observe."

The clip cuts to a woman, her face hovering above a pile of cocaine, straw in hand. She's naked and shaking. The sound of her snorting coincides with the pile getting noticeably smaller. I recognize the woman as Rosemary.

"Again," a voice commands. It's the man who's been narrating the clips so far.

Rosemary looks up. Her eyes are a little unfocused, but I can see the fear in them.

"If I keep snorting, I'll die," she says.

"Indeed," the man replies. "But if you don't, I'll shoot off your kneecaps and cut off your breasts. You'll still die, but it will be far more painful." A pause. "So, again."

A look of resignation crosses her face. She bends over the pile and takes a huge snort. It seems to go on forever. The straw falls from her fingers, and her head snaps back, eyes fluttering, hair trailing down her back. It's a kind of hideous art, the aesthetics of death and death to come.

"Lay back now," the man says, his voice soothing. "Lay back, my child."

A gloved hand comes into view and he pushes her shivering, shaking body back onto the bed. She's smiling, biting her lower lip. Fine drops of sweat bead her brow. She's the picture of a woman in the throes of something ecstatic and wonderful. She clenches her upper thighs together again and again, as though she's fighting an orgasm.

"Tell us about Dylan, Rosemary."

The clenching stops and she seems to find some focus. She frowns and then shudders. She's started to sweat.

"H-how d-do you know . . . ? H-how? Only told people at my . . ."

"I know, Rosemary," he interrupts. "You're dying. Go to meet God with the truth on your lips. Tell us about Dylan. He was your brother, wasn't he?"

"Y-yes. Brother. Beautiful brother."

"How old was Dylan?"

She spasms once and she closes her eyes.

"Thirteen," she hisses.

"And how old were you?"

"Fifteen fifteen fif-fif-fifteen," she says in a singsong.

"Tell us, Rosemary. Tell us, tell them, tell God, what it was you did to beautiful Dylan."

A long pause, and now she's really trembling. Her breathing is getting shallower and faster.

Not much time now, I think.

"I came into his bed one night and I sucked his cock!" she crows. "Sucked him and he couldn't help but let me. And then I got him hard again and fucked him."

"And what happened the next day, Rosemary?"

Silence. Spasms. Sweat.

"What happened the next day?"

She shakes her head back and forth, back and forth.

"No no no no no no no."

"God is love, Rosemary."

These words bring a change upon her that I don't quite understand. She begins to weep.

"He killed himself. He went into the bathroom and cut his wrists and he didn't leave a note because he knew I'd know why. No one else ever knew, not Mom, not Dad, but I knew I knew I knew. The evil hungry in me had killed sweet Dylan, had made him do bad against his will, had eaten him alive. The evil hungry had killed him dead."

I grimace at the pain in her voice, and at the idea of someone having a name for something about themselves that they despised. *The evil hungry.*

"Very good, Rosemary," the man says, and I'm surprised at the depth of compassion apparent in his voice. He actually seems to care. "I'm going to give you peace now, I'm going to send you home to God. Would you like that?"

She begins to recite the Lord's Prayer.

"Our Father, Who art in heaven."

A long, metal rod with a sharp and pointed end appears in the camera view.

"Hallowed be Thy name," he answers.

The film cuts back to the man seated at the table. Just as well. I know what happened next. He stuck her in the side, angled the point up and into her heart, delivering the quick death he'd promised.

"Again, you see? One secret, revealed, hides the other, unrevealed. Truth is not a striving, it is an immediate arrival."

For the first time, his body language changes. He places the rosary to one side of the table and lays his palms flat on the surface.

"I have spent my life building up to this moment, preparing for this reveal. I haven't done this for myself. I haven't done this because I enjoy killing."

"Right," Callie says, sardonic.

"I have taken this time to build an absolute, airtight, irrefutable case for truth. Because the most basic truth is this: live with lies, live in sin, and you will deny yourself the fruits of heaven. Live with the truth, confess your sins, hold nothing back, and you will sit at the right hand of God when you die. *It is that simple.* It requires no debate or endless figuring. What it does require is operation at the level of an absolute.

"We love our little sins. The secrets we hold for ourselves, some-times they are the only things we have that we can truly call our own. I understand this. I know life can be hard. The mother who is working three jobs and raising four children on her own sneaks off for an hour affair with a married man. It gives her a rush of life and excitement and a stolen, momentary sense of freedom that perhaps she feels she might die without. Sin can be as water in the desert sometimes.

"The truth remains: she can work those jobs, raise her children well, live a life that is otherwise clear of wrongfulness, but if she dies without full and unfettered confession of that sin, *she will not arrive in heaven.*

"So ask yourself: are those stolen moments worth an eternity?

"I have spent two decades killing, not for the thrill of it, but so that I could arrive here and now and share with you the truth of what I have seen. I selected my sacrifices carefully, as you will see. Each had a secret, a darkness, something they could not reveal. All now sit at the right hand of God and enjoy the wonders of heaven. In the end, they gave their lives so that you could understand. Not willing mar-tyrs, but martyrs nonetheless.

"I am no messiah. There has been only one messiah—Jesus Christ, the son of God. But I humbly submit that I am a prophet for the modern age. We are living in times that are drenched in sin. Godless-ness is almost a given. If you are watching this, listening to what I say, then it's time to wake up. There is good and there is evil. There is a God. There is a heaven and there is a hell. The road to heaven is a road of absolute truth. The road to hell is a road of lies, of non-revelation, of holding tight to those treasured secrets. Which road will you take?

"If you choose the road to heaven, then watch the rest of my movies, and listen. Perhaps you'll see your own sin revealed by others. Perhaps you'll come to terms with that great and simple truth: the worst thing that you have done can still be forgiven by God. You just have to ask him.

"Twenty years ago, I realized that sharing this truth with the world was what God had called on me to do. Sin is omnipresent. We begin to sin from the moment we are born. But if you are watching this, understand: you can be saved, so long as you admit all to God and hold back nothing for yourself.

"Some will ask how I can justify murder. I answer simply that murder is not what has happened on these video clips. Sacrifice is what has happened. They confessed their sins to me, they were contrite, and thus all will have been allowed into heaven. Consider the facts—many in history have said before what I am saying now. Yet people do not listen. They continue to clutch their secrets close. They hear the words, but they do not feel them in their hearts.

"Words, it seems, are not enough. Man, it appears, needs to see his fellows weep, and bleed, and die. He needs to hear the dark secrets of others, to realize, perhaps, that he is not alone, that others have done terrible things as well. Those I sacrificed were given up to God so that I could make certain, this time, that you would *listen* and *hear* and *feel* this primary truth: be honest with God and achieve eternal salvation; hold back the smallest thing and burn in hellfire forever."

These last words had come out in a rush, a quiet thunder, passionate. This is it, I think. Why he does what he does. Or at least, why he thinks he does what he does.

He's been building a case for truth before God. The deaths were necessary to proving this ideal and were justified by the potential salvation of others who'd watch and learn the lessons he was trying to teach. He didn't have to feel guilty. They'd confessed, right? That meant he was sending them to a better place. Heck, he was doing them a *favor*.

What a crock of shit. What about Ambrose? How had he justified killing him?

Psychotics, however brilliant, will always have blind spots. Their systems of rationalization, however logical at first glance, can never hide the basic motivation: they enjoy the suffering and death of others.

He picks up the rosary again, and begins rubbing the beads.

"I offer myself as a final demonstration of the tenets I espouse. To the members of law enforcement who will watch this: everything you need to know to find me is on these and the other tapes. Everything. But you will have to be clear-minded. You will have to have the ability to see the *truth*. Practice what I preach and you will find me standing right in front of you. Hold on to your lies, keep the veil over your eyes, and it will take you that much longer. In this case, time is life, Officers and Agents.

"I am not done. I have names on a list, and I have put things into motion to bring them first to me and then to the right hand of God. I will kill again in the next two days, and this time, it will be a child."

"Shit," Alan breathes.

That frozen moment again. The world stops turning, the cicadas return. I have no doubt that he's telling us the truth, even less that he'll keep his promise.

"That's all for now. I realize in this day and age I'll be given a nom de plume of some kind. I don't want someone's clever creation to distract from the purpose of my message. So let's agree to keep it simple: you can call me the Preacher."

Fade to black.

Everyone's quiet.

"The Preacher," Callie finally says, with a little bit of a sneer. "What an overblown ego."

"Rosemary said she 'only told the people in my . . .' In her what?" I ask.

"Church?" Alan posits.

I frown. "That wouldn't make much sense. Did you see her face? Zero recognition. She had no idea who this guy was. It's a small church, with a tight-knit congregation."

"Puts Father Yates in the clear," Alan points out. "But how about a support group?"

"What, like Coke Fiends Anonymous?" Callie asks.

"It'd be a bigger collection of people. Harder to remember a face that way."

"It's a thought," I agree.

"Shitty thought." Alan sighs. "I've had to follow leads into groups like that before. It sucks. They take the 'anonymous' idea pretty seriously."

"Still, let's keep it in mind. What about the rest of the clips?"

"I haven't viewed any past this last one," he says, "but it looks like he's been true to his word. There are another six clips or so on this page, and then . . ." He clicks on a link that says *Next Page* and a new page loads into the browser, filled with thumbnails of clips. "If you look, you'll see that the information on each clip includes the author. These are all him."

I lean forward and sure enough I see *Author: The Preacher* below each thumbnail. I examine the thumbnails themselves. They are a mix of images. Some simply have a black screen, others have the now familiar white lettering he uses for his "opening credits." Some show women, young and old. Some look dead, some appear terrified, a few have gags tied around their mouths. There's no recognizable victim type here.

"How many thumbnails to a page?" I ask.

"Ten rows of five," Alan replies.

"How many pages?" I dread the answer.

"Almost three."

"So if each is a separate victim," Callie muses, "then the numbers on the crosses he left in Lisa Reid and Rosemary Sonnenfeld were a body count, after all."

"There's another problem," Alan says. He navigates back to the front page of the religious section of the website. "These make it to the front page based on popularity. In other words, the number of times they're viewed."

"Great," I mutter. "And I'll assume that there's an overall popularity index too, right?"

He nods. "If these are viewed enough, they'll end up not just on page one of the religion category, but page one of the website itself."

"Someone will make the connection with the Reid name soon," James observes. "Not to mention his threat to kill a child. This is going to hit the news."

The anxious feeling in the pit of my stomach widens into a chasm.

"This is going to turn into a shit storm," I say. "We need to try and get ahead of it." I begin pacing, talking out loud to organize my thoughts. "The media is going to splash the story and then we're going to start getting calls from all over about the victims. The fact that he's kept himself hidden until now probably means that most of his victims are unsolved disappearances. That's potentially a lot of families that will be clamoring for confirmation."

"Good Lord," Callie says, now really seeing the truth of what I'm saying. "Those poor people will be crawling out of the woodwork."

"Them and the crazies," Alan observes.

High-profile murders, particularly those that garner media attention, call forth the loonies like throwing meat in front of a hungry dog. People line up to confess. The more unusual the crime, the longer the line. I rub my forehead, still pacing.

"We need to get the clips pulled," I say.

"Yes," Callie agrees.

"Wait a moment," James says, and begins typing in website addresses, one after the other, each in a new browser window. He leans back after a moment, shaking his head. "I thought so."

"What?" I ask.

"The key term here is *viral*," he replies. "User-tube is the most popular site for the sharing of video clips, but it's far from the only one. I typed in the URLs for ten others. See for yourself."

We all lean forward as he cycles through the various browser windows he's opened. Each one is filled with rows of video-clip thumbnails.

"This is . . . ?" I ask.

He nods. "The Preacher's clips. Re-posted by users to other similar websites around the world." A shrug. "The feeding frenzy starts a lot faster on the Web."

Alan rubs his face with both hands. "Holy fuuuuuuck."

"So what?" I ask. "You're telling me it doesn't matter if we get them pulled from user-tube?"

"No. User-tube is the most popular video-sharing site on the Internet. Getting them pulled will make an immediate difference, but it won't stop them from spreading. It'll only lessen their visibility."

"How's that?" Alan asks.

James shrugs. "The clips are everywhere now, including people's hard drives. They'll be burned onto CDs and DVDs, viewers will e-mail them to each other, share them on forums and newsgroups. There are a ton of video-sharing sites that are run outside the U.S. Most won't listen to a word we say. Even some of the ones run from within the states will resist removing the clips without a court order. Then there's the hierarchy of user-tube itself. All the content is user provided. For every clip we pull, someone else will probably repost it, in the name of free speech or voyeurism. It's the perfect medium for the Preacher, really."

Alan throws up his hands in disgust. "What the fuck should we do, then?"

"Get them pulled. We'll have Computer Crimes liaise with user-tube and monitor any attempts by the Preacher to post future clips. They'll intercept them and let us know. We'll also have Computer Crimes contact the other video-sharing sites that we know will be co-operative. Beyond that . . ." He shakes his head. "The main thing you have to understand and accept is this: the clips are out there. That ship has sailed. Families are going to see them and there's nothing we can do about that."

I stare at him for a moment, blinking. "I have to call the AD," I say. "We're going to need additional personnel."

James nods. "A task force."

"Yes."

Alan groans. "Great. Bunch of newbies tripping over their own feet and trying to steal my desk."

"We'll use them primarily to field the phones and to help collate information. Following up any leads—and the primary investigation—remains with us."

"They do the grunt work, we get the glory." Callie nods her approval. "I like it."

"First things first," I tell them. "We need to watch these clips. He told us the names of Dexter and Rosemary. Maybe he followed the same formula throughout. We need to make a list and then start searching the databases for similar crimes nationwide."

"Look for commonalities of location," James provides. "Hopefully he'll give us some clues in that regard that will help us identify the victims and narrow down our geographical target area." He looks at me. "We're going to end up sending this victim list out to local police municipalities. If we can reduce the radius, it will help."

"Good thinking. Divide up the clips. I'll take the last set and start viewing once I've called AD Jones and Rosario Reid."

Alan grimaces. "Think she knew? About what her son had done to that kid Jacob?"

I feel tired and rumpled and half put together and far, far too electrified at the same time.

"No. Let's get to work."

24

wait him out. "This is going to be everywhere," he says.

"Already is, sir."

I had called him on his cell phone. It's always on.

"Do we have any idea at all who the kid he's promised to kill might be?"

"No, sir."

More silence.

"Have you spoken to Rosario?"

"Not yet, sir. I called you first. But I will."

"This is going to be hard on them." He sighs. "I suppose you want a task force?"

"We're going to need the extra manpower, sir. Once this gets out past the Internet, to the mainstream media, the families are going to need a number to call. If we can't prevent the media from doing its thing—and we can't—then we can use it to our benefit."

"Agreed. You'll need someone who's done this kind of thing before, who can hit the ground running."

"Any ideas?"

"There's an agent working in public affairs who's run a phone bank before. Jezebel Smith."

"Jezebel? Really?"

"Yeah, I know. The religious references are running wild on this one. She's been on the job for about eight years and she's a self-starter. We used her on the '07 terror scare. People were calling in sightings of al Qaeda from a hundred miles around. Total bullshit and a waste of time, but she did a good job of sorting out the wheat from the chaff."

"At least she's not a newbie. I imagine the agents we use to man the phones will be a bunch of greenie-weenies?"

" 'Fraid so. What else do you need?"

"Do you want me to call the Director?"

"Yeah, but I won't make you do it. I'll deal with him and I'll make sure he knows to call me and not you. We'll need his resources to help deal with the media."

"Thanks."

"Better get rolling, Smoky. I'll round up Agent Smith when I get in and send her to see you. Should be within the next hour. Call Rosario Reid."

"Yes, sir."

He hangs up and I take a moment to procrastinate. I don't want to call Rosario, I really don't. I hate having nothing but bad news to give to the survivors.

"Suck it up," I tell myself.

I dial the cell number she'd given me. She picks up after just three rings.

"Smoky?"

"Hi, Rosario."

"It's bad news, isn't it?" No hesitation. This makes it a little easier for me, that she's expecting it. Not a lot easier, but a little.

"Very bad."

Again, no hesitation. Her voice is firm. "Tell me."

So I do. I explain about the Preacher, the video clips, and the pages he'd torn from Lisa's journal. She is silent throughout and after I am done.

"I remember Jacob Littlefield," she says. "A sweet boy. And I remember Mark Phillips too. A little monster who grew into a big one. He was in jail by the time he was twenty. Poor Dexter. My poor, poor son."

Her voice cracks, the first time I've heard it do so. This is how loss hits us sometimes, I know, by making an irrelevance of time. She hadn't lost her composure when her child was murdered, but she loses it now, thinking of her young son and the death of his Saturday mornings.

"Are we any closer to knowing who this monster is?" she asks after a moment.

"Yes, in the broader sense. He's provided us with video recordings of his earlier victims. The more data we have, the greater the odds that we'll catch him."

"Why would he do this? Why would he tell Lisa's secret to the world? Wasn't it enough to murder her?"

She wants to understand, and I try to help her, though I know it won't give her any comfort.

"It's always about power, Rosario. Power over life and death and all the components thereof. I can't give you an exact picture of his motives, not yet, but the short answer is—no, murdering her wasn't enough. He wants to feel in control of everything that was the most personal, the most private, the most guarded. That's sex for him. Great sex."

"And his speech about 'truth' and God?" Her voice quivers with distaste.

"He believes that he believes. I'm sure of that. But he's insane, so he misses the real truth."

"Which is?"

"He tells himself his joy comes from using the deaths to forward a purpose. The real truth, the ugly bottom line, is that the deaths are the only purpose he needs."

She is silent for a moment. "How do you know something like that?"

I consider the question. It's not the first time I've been asked it.

"I guess I let myself feel what they feel."

More silence.

"And what is he feeling right now? This monster that killed my baby?"

"Joy," I reply without hesitation. "Joy at its apex."

When she speaks again, her voice is rough and husky. "I want him to feel agony, Smoky, not joy."

"I know. All I can do is catch him."

"Don't worry about me or how this getting out will affect my family. It will be difficult, but we'll deal with it. Concentrate on find-ing this . . . *thing*. Please."

"I will."

ALAN HOLDS UP A SHEET of paper as I walk back into the office.

"He's giving us the names in every case," he says. "Some of these go back a long way, I'm thinking up to twenty years based on the clothes, hair, stuff like that."

"It's all the same basic format too," Callie says. "He gets them to admit to a deep, dark secret and then makes it clear he's going to kill them."

"But each clip ends before the actual death," James notes.

"Strange," I murmur. "You'd think the moment of death would be more important than that to him."

"Perhaps it's a part of his rationalization framework," James says. "He's telling us, and himself, that he's doing what he's doing to for-ward a concept of truth that brings one closest to God. He's trying to share this truth with the world so that others can be saved. Showing the murder, perhaps he feels it would make him look voyeuristic."

"I bet he did film the murders, every one of them," Alan says. "He just didn't include them in the clips. He probably sits at home and jacks off to them regularly."

"I don't know," I say. "I think he'll be into self-repression. The holy man who resists his own vices successfully, that kind of thing. That fits with the identity paradigm he's trying to assert to us. Let's keep going through the clips and noting the names. If he's willing to give them to us, let's use them."

I fill them in on Jezebel Smith and the rest of my conversation with AD Jones.

Alan checks his watch. "We should be seeing her soon. She'll be setting up the number?"

He's referring to the tip-line phone number that we'll be putting out.

"Yes. She'll run that whole show—and knows how to, apparently. Anything else?"

No one says a word.

"Then let's keep at it."

Moments later I am back in my office. James had downloaded all of the clips, and split them up between us. I pop in the CD he'd given me. The clips are in number order, four digits each. I sigh and click on the first one. I watch as the black screen appears, followed by the white letters: *The Sins and Death of Maxine McGee*. I note the name down on the pad. A woman's face appears. It's a pretty face, though not a beautiful one. She's got brown, shoulder-length hair, and it's feathered in a style that tells me this was probably shot in the 1980s. She has big brown eyes and her face is just short of chubby. Those brown eyes are surrounded by black, the eyes of a raccoon, because she's sobbing and terrified and her mascara has turned her tears to dirt.

I note down her physical characteristics next to her name. I try and use this to distance myself from the fact of what I'm seeing. This is a woman who once was alive and now is dead. She's living her last moments, she knows it, I'm watching it. It makes me tired.

"Maxine McGee," the Preacher says, in that pleasant voice I'm growing to hate. "Tell the people watching about your sin."

Maxine can't stop sobbing.

"W-w-what are you talking about?" she blubbers.

"Maxine." The voice has a chiding tone, the verbal equivalent of a friendly but cautionary finger wag. "Don't you want to sit at the right hand of God? Tell them about your baby. Tell them about little Charles. How old were you then? Sixteen?"

The change in her demeanor is instant and amazing. Her eyes go wide, her tears quit, and her mouth drops open. She's become a caricature of shock and surprise.

"You see? You *do* know what I'm talking about."

That chasm of unease in my stomach has opened back up.

Maxine blinks rapidly. Her mouth closes, opens again. Closes.

She looks like a dying guppy.

"Come, Maxine. Charles. You remember Charles, don't you? Little baby Charles, who gasped his last in an alley trash can, thrown away like garbage."

The expression that passes over Maxine's face horrifies me. It is violation, so deep and so profound, so absolute and authentic, that I almost stop the clip right there. He's hurt her by knowing this and by showing her he knows. He's slipped past her most entrenched defenses, and this is worse than being tied to a chair, maybe even worse than knowing she's going to die.

This, I realize, this right here, is what he craves. That moment of abjectness.

She begins to cry again, but it's a slower, deeper grief. This is shame, not fear. Her head hangs forward and those black, dirt-tears patter onto her naked legs, staining them.

"I was only sixteen," she says in a small voice.

She sounds sixteen saying it.

"True," he says. "But then, how old was baby Charles?"

"Minutes," she breathes. "He was just a few minutes old."

"What did you do with him?"

"I—I was only sixteen. I got pregnant from Daddy. He and Mom pretended not to notice. I was skinny and my stomach didn't get that big, but kids at school noticed. It didn't keep Daddy from coming to see me at night." She's lifted her head back up. She's staring off, remembering. She's regressed and speaks with the voice of a child. "I hated the thing inside me. It came from Daddy being with me and I remember thinking it was like having a devil in me, a demon. A creature, growing, with fangs and claws. It would move sometimes and I'd start to shake. I was so afraid of it. Toward the end, Daddy stopped pretending it wasn't there. He touched my stomach one time and he said, 'If it's a boy, we'll call him Charles.' " She shudders. "That made me hate the baby even more. I was sure it was the son of Satan or something.

"I woke up one night and my bed was wet. My water had broken. I was in a lot of pain. One thing I knew for sure was I didn't want to have it there, at home. So I got dressed and I took Daddy's car and I drove out to where all the abandoned factories were. I found a place in the dark so I wouldn't have to see him when he came out, with his fangs and his tail and his claws."

She stops. Her face twists in pain.

"What happened then, Maxine?" the voice asks.

"I had him. He was born. He just laid there on the dirt and I was kind of out of it, but I knew one thing, I was scared. I didn't want to look at him. And then—he cried." I hear wonder in her voice. "He sounded so normal. Not like a demon at all. He sounded like a baby. So I looked at him and he was so small and he was just crying and crying like he was mad at me and mad at the dirt being cold and just mad at the world. He had my blood on him and I just grabbed him and really looked."

"And what did you see, Maxine?"

She closes her eyes. "I saw a baby. Just a baby."

"And? What else did you see?"

Her eyes open. They're filled with endurance, a pain at its purest. "That he'd belong to Daddy. Daddy would use him up somehow, would infect him or abuse him. He wasn't born a demon, but Daddy was the devil, and Daddy would turn him evil in the end. So I did"—she draws in a single, whooping breath—"I did the only thing that I thought it was right to do. I took Charles and I found a trash can and I put him down in it, and I covered him with garbage until I couldn't hear him crying anymore."

"What happened after?"

"I went home. And you know what?" Her eyes look toward the camera now. They're full of pleading. "Daddy never asked what happened to the baby. Never, not once."

"It was worse that your mother didn't ask, wasn't it?"

"Yes," she whispers, "that was the worst of all. It was like he never existed for them, and maybe he never did. Maybe they were those kind of people, able to live without feeling guilt or worrying about anyone else, ever."

"You weren't 'those kind of people,' were you, Maxine?"

She squeezes her mascara-ringed eyes shut again and wails. "No! I never forgot. Never! I ran away a year later and came here to California. I whored for a while, did some drugs, and hated myself. But—but then I found God, and I turned my life around." The eyes open, again, suffering, again. "Don't you know that? I changed. I got away from my devil and I gave my soul to God. I work with children now, I help them, all to make up for what I did to Charles. Don't you see that?"

She's asking for mercy, but the murmuring I can make out tells me what I already know: he had none to offer. The murmur is his be-ginning recitation of the Lord's Prayer.

"Our Father, Who art in heaven, hallowed be Thy name . . ." Then a pause. "God is love, Maxine," he says.

Fade to black.

My mouth has filled with bile. Adrenaline races through me and makes my heart jitter and skip beats. My skin feels flushed. I'm dizzy.

I'm flying apart, I realize. Right here, right now, with no warning at all.

I feel a cackling thing running through the night in my mind, scrabbling at great speed to try and jump from the darkness into the light.

See me, it cackles and snarls and growls. You know what I am. See me.

I clench my eyes shut and shake my head.

No no no no no!

The phantom from the night is back, grown to a monster this time, and he's caught me by surprise.

I find myself longing for that bottle of tequila, longing for it with a level of savage naked need that terrifies me. This, I realize, is what drives the alcoholic to his next drink. The feeling that if he doesn't, he'll die a long, lingering, screaming, painful death.

I hold out my hand, palm down over my desktop. It's shaking.

See me, the voice demands again, more strident and certain this time. No question, all command.

I feel nausea rising inside me. I realize it's going to keep coming, I can't fight it back.

Jesus Christ, I'm going to puke!

I bolt from my office and race to the bathroom in the hall. The door can't be locked, but no one else is in it, thank God.

I fling the door to one of the three stalls open and I drop to my knees on the tile without ceremony. My gorge rises and my stomach twists and a brief, sweet pain spikes through my head and I'm puking my guts out in the next millisecond. It's brief, but it's violent. I can feel how flushed my face is, and the force of it all squeezes tears from my eyes. I grip the sides of the toilet bowl and wait to see if it's over.

See me.

I'm twisting like a rope in a pair of strong sailor's hands, bending like a violin bow, muscles spasming as I vomit again. It goes on a little too long, and puts spots behind my eyes.

This time I know I'm done and I fall into a sitting position, back against the wall of the toilet stall. I sit there for a moment and breathe, hand against my forehead, working to stuff the monster and his claws back into the box.

Now is not the time, I tell myself. There is a time, but it's not now. Please.

I close my eyes and lay my head back against the stall wall and let myself drift. Time goes by in internal fuzzy flashes. Pictures come to me. They're all unrelated, jumbled, no rhyme or reason. I see Matt, I see Bonnie, there's Tommy telling me he loves me, and there's Maxine with her raccoon eyes.

I open my eyes again and find that the voice is gone. I take advantage of the lull to stand back up on wobbly legs. I flush the toilet, and as I do, I realize that tears are running down my face.

"Goddammit," I mutter.

I hate crying, always have.

I seem to be a little more stable now. My stomach has stopped flip-flopping, and the yammering in my head has died down to a background whisper. My mouth, however, is filled with the acrid taste of vomit. I open the door to the stall and totter out.

"Better?"

I'm so surprised that I almost draw my weapon. I whirl on the voice and nearly fall over doing so, as my legs remain a little rubbery. Kirby is standing there, arms crossed, leaning against the door to the bathroom. She's chewing gum and is staring at me with a look I can't quite fathom.

"What are you doing here?" I ask.

"I was making sure no one came in while you were falling apart." She shrugs. "I came up to see Callie and watched you run into the bathroom. Got curious."

I turn to the sink so I don't have to look at her. I turn on the water.

"I wasn't falling apart," I say, defensive.

She cracks her gum. "If you say so. But you were sitting in that stall for almost twenty minutes."

I stand up straight, shocked.

Twenty minutes? That long?

I sneak a look at Kirby. She's just standing there, chewing her gum. Her expression is a mix of the patient and the bland. She seems to read my mind and holds up a wrist to show me her watch.

"I checked the time."

I turn away again and splash water on my cheeks, which are now burning with embarrassment.

"And what the fuck is it to you?" I snarl.

"Well, I don't respect too many people in this world, Smoky, but I do respect you. And I figure if you need to fall apart, then you deserve some privacy while you do it, you know?"

She says all of this with that same careless, happy-go-lucky tone she uses to talk about the weather or the dead.

La-di-dah, how about this heat? Sorry I have to kill you, but it could be worse, it could be slow instead of quick, you know?! Ha ha ha! Blam!

I rinse out my mouth enough to clear the taste of puke away and spend a moment taking stock of myself in the mirror. I look tired but I don't look crazy. That's something, at least.

"Thanks," I manage.

"You're welcome."

I stare at myself one final time.

Secrets.

You can even keep them from yourself. Just not forever.

BACK AT DEATH CENTRAL I find a woman waiting for me. She's very tall, about six foot, and, unbelievably, could give Callie a run for her money in the beauty department. She's probably close to thirty-two, with long, straight, blonde hair and one of those fresh-scrubbed apples and oatmeal complexions. She has clear, intelligent blue eyes and a slim, athletic body. I want to hate her on sight, but then she smiles. It's not the perfect white teeth that disarm me, but the genuine openness of the grin. She holds out a hand.

"Jezebel Smith," she says.

I shake her hand and ignore Kirby's chortling behind me.

Jezebel nods to Kirby, unfazed. "Yeah, I know, it's some namesake. Mom was kind of an anti-fundamentalist, so . . ."

"Hey, my dad named me Kirby, so I know how *that* can be. There should be a law against parents naming kids whatever they darn well feel like, you know?"

"Amen." Jezebel smiles.

"Kirby—" I say, turning toward her.

The assassin holds up her hands. "Say no more, boss woman. I'll let you get back to what you're doing. I just need to see Callie-babe about some wedding stuff."

She saunters off after giving Jezebel a final wink and wave.

"Interesting woman," Jezebel muses.

"You don't know the half of it, and don't want to know the rest. So did AD Jones fill you in?"

She nods, grave.

"Can I see one of the clips?" she asks. "I like to know what I'm a part of."

I don't ask her if she's sure or if she's seen this kind of thing before. If she has, the question will insult her. If she hasn't, she won't be prepared anyway. I take her to my office and I bring up a random clip. I look away as it plays. Jezebel bends over to watch. She's silent throughout.

"Monster" is all she says when it's done.

"Yes."

"I deal with the victims regularly, doing what I do. I see them, talk with them—I've sat with them in their homes. This, what he's doing, is going to hurt a lot of families."

"He knows that."

She straightens up. "Okay. So, I will set up a phone bank in the conference room on the floor just below this. I'll man it with six agents—I'd like more, but that's all that AD Jones can spare for now. We have a set of phone numbers reserved for tip-line situations like this one. I'll choose a number and let you know what it will be. I know the woman at HQ who is going to be the contact for media inquiry on this, so I'll arrange with her how we go about getting that number out."

"We should take a proactive approach on this," I say. "Get ahead of the media."

Her smile is gentle. "Trust me. They're already way ahead of us on this one. I can guarantee you that media outlets all over the country have already been contacted. Think of it like a tsunami: it's coming, it's inevitable, and resistance is most definitely futile."

"Swell."

"The good news is, I'm really, really good at what I do. And so are the people that will be working on this at headquarters. You shouldn't have to deal with the media at all except to refer them to me. My team will filter all the calls that come through the tip line. You'll only get real leads."

Her confidence is inspiring. I scribble my cell number on a Post-it and hand it to her.

"Call me with updates, please. I'll be asked for regular reports—I'm sure you know the game."

"I'm familiar with shit and the way it rolls," she says with a grin. The smile fades. "Let's get this guy."

It would be more melodramatic if it weren't exactly the right sentiment.

25

rate. The tidal wave hits at around two o'clock in the afternoon.

I've been continuing to watch my assigned helping of video clips. We all are. It's quiet in the offices, but the air is thick with anxiety and the need to find him before he carries out his promise.

I'm noting the name of a particularly terrified brunette woman when my phone rings.

"The story is hitting the five o'clock news everywhere," Jezebel says without preamble. "And it's already five on the East Coast."

"What are they saying?"

"That a guy calling himself the Preacher has posted video clips on the Internet of purported murder victims. That they've been able to confirm the identities of two of the victims already."

"Great."

"We knew it was going to happen, and we're ready. I've been in contact with the media relations director at Quantico and she'll be doing a press conference within the next half hour. That will be picked up nationwide and she'll announce the tip-line number then."

"Can you get me the names of the two confirmed victims soonest?"

"Within the next half hour. Do you want to see the press conference?"

"Nope."

"Really?"

"It's not that it's not important, it's just not my part of this. My team and I need to stay on identifying the victims. It's the best thing we can do right now."

"I understand. I'll get you those names and will keep you updated. I expect the tip line to go crazy in the next few hours."

"I'll be here."

I put down the phone, pick my pen back up, and click to continue the clip I was watching.

"Please," she begs.

Please, please, it's always please. The one-word lyric of the victim's song.

ALAN IS AT THE DRY-ERASE board, writing down names and, where known, locations. I hand my list to him and take a moment to examine the data we've collected so far.

"All women," I say.

"A sexual link after all," Callie notes.

She's right. If this was all just about truth and his opus on the subject, we'd see some men in there. He probably has no awareness of this, and would be surprised if it was pointed out to him. Murder is murder and it's always an act of anger. The anger could be direct—he hates women—or it could be misplaced—he hates himself because of something that involves women. It's intriguing.

"Common age?" I ask.

"We don't know for sure without actual confirmation of their identities, but based on physical observation, I don't see anyone older than the age of thirty-five. Most are younger than that."

"How much younger?"

"All adults. Twenty or older. If he does kill a child, it looks like it would be a first for him."

"Were all the victims attractive? No, scratch that. Not all the women I saw were classically beautiful. Some were pretty plain."

"I can confirm that as well." James nods. "One of the women in my group was obese. Another had a bad case of acne. Appearance is not a crucial part of his criteria."

"But gender is," I muse. "Okay. How about locations? How spread out has he been?"

"I'm getting a map printed out so that we can see it graphically," Callie says. "He's been a traveler, but with few exceptions so far, he's stayed within the western United States, primarily California, Oregon, Washington, Nevada, Arizona, New Mexico, Utah, and Colorado."

"Interesting. So Virginia was well outside his common stomping grounds."

Callie nods. "None of the other victims have been linked that far east."

A thought occurs to me. "No other transgendered victims?"

"No," James says.

"So Lisa Reid was another anomaly. She's the only transgender victim and the only one found so far outside his normal killing zone. Which means that's exactly why she was chosen."

"He's decided to come out into the open," Alan agrees. "He figured she'd help him make the biggest splash. Killing a child, same thing."

"Why now?" I wonder. No one answers. "What other commonalities?"

"He stops the clip before the actual murder of every victim," James says. "As discussed before, he's showing us that his overall message is more important to him than the deaths themselves. The murders were committed for a purpose, not titillation."

"He cared for them, or wants us to think he did," I say. "In one way he strips them naked—the whole secrets thing. But then he pulls the curtain over their last moments. He respects that privacy, preserves their dignity."

"He never gets angry," James notes. "He's firm, but calm with every victim. He's not above threatening them to gain compliance, but it's detached. A means to an end, not a fantasy."

"I take it the secrets theme has been consistent?"

" 'Fraid so," Callie says, "and not just in fact but in form."

I frown. "Sorry?"

"She means there haven't been any 'I stole twenty bucks from Mom's wallet' kind of secrets," Alan provides. "It's all dark or twisted or sad or all three." He consults notepad Ned. "Lot of it has a sexual component, of course. There's some accidental murders that were then hidden, but there are a few premeditated killings in there as well. One woman had been beaten by her husband for years, so she took it out on her baby. With lit cigarettes." He looks back up at me wearing a humorless smile. "A ghastly fucking gallery."

My stomach twists once and I feel that voice again, not vocalizing yet, but stirring. Thinking about making itself known. I push it away and force myself to focus on the list of names and what they can tell me.

"He videoed every crime, obviously," James says, "but the changes in video and sound quality show us that he's been at this for some time. He probably started out on super eight or a similar medium and graduated up to better technology as the years rolled on. He'll be fairly proficient technically, nothing earth-shaking, but more knowledgeable than the average computer user. He'd have to be to digitize old mediums and to create the various video clips, edit them, and so on."

"It gives him credibility," Callie observes, her tone grudging. "He's been documenting his actions from the start, waiting for the day he'd bring his 'case' to the world."

"How could he be sure?" Alan muses.

I look at him and frown. "What do you mean?"

"Well, when he started this, the Internet didn't exist, at least not for public consumption. He always planned to show his face and it's pretty clear that he planned to use the videos to do it. Go back a few decades and we'd have gotten a stack of VHS tapes."

"So?"

"Well, that would have been direct. Him to us. But this?" He gestures at the computer. "He put these clips up on a public website. How could he be sure he'd get our attention?"

"He chose carefully," James answers. "The website he posted those clips on is the most viewed viral video site on earth. I imagine if we hadn't taken notice on our own, he would have followed up with an e-mail or a letter."

Alan nods, seeing it. "Maybe even a phone call."

"Any way to track the clips themselves?" I ask.

James shakes his head. "No. CDs, DVDs, even printer pages can be traced to some degree, but a digital clip doesn't have a watermark or buried signature by default."

"What about the upload? He had to contact the Web somewhere to get these clips onto user-tube."

"I already have computer crimes checking on that, honey-love," Callie replies. "They're rolling on the warrant as we speak."

"Probably a dead end," Alan observes.

"Probably," I agree, "but . . ."

"Yeah," he says. "Sometimes the bad guys are stupid."

"Sometimes. Anything else?"

"Yes," James says. "Again—where is he getting his information?"

The biggest part of the mystery. Lisa Reid left her story in a diary, fine, but the others?

"Maybe he's a priest," Alan muses.

"A traveling priest?" I say. "I don't think so. Again, too high profile. Even if he was just posing as one, Father Yates didn't mention anything about visiting clergy. Rosemary didn't recognize her attacker." I shake my head. "Not a priest."

"It's the question to answer, though," Alan says.

"What about my earlier suggestion?" I ask. "Support groups? With these kinds of secrets, we'd see plenty of substance abuse problems."

"Like Rosemary and Andrea," Alan agrees. "And look at how quick Andrea was to spill her guts."

"It doesn't have to be a single pool he's drawing from," Callie points out. "He could find the kind of person he's looking for in any number of places. Churches involved in heavy community outreach, Alcoholics Anonymous, Narcotics Anonymous, choose your poison. He'd infiltrate as a fellow addict or alcoholic or whatever, gain the confidence of his peers, and lend a sympathetic ear."

"Good point," I say. "We need to look for that as a point of commonality in the victims."

"Let's list out what we do know about him," James says.

I nod. "Sure. I'll start: He's high functioning and probably attractive.

He'll be confident around women. They're not a threat to his self-image. They don't make him angry, at least not overtly."

"He might be a virgin," James murmurs.

I raise my eyebrows. "How did you arrive at that?"

"Think about it. He's rational. His attitude with the victims is always calm. Any threat of violence against them is as a means to an end, not self-excitement. Of the victims whose bodies we've been allowed to find, there's no evidence of sexual violation or unnecessary violence. His fantasies are cerebral. They revolve around religion and truth and thus, by extension, purity." He shrugs. "The act of sex isn't just absent, it's nonexistent."

"Madonna and the whore," Callie muses.

"Come again?" I ask her.

"Oh you know, that old saw. Men want to marry Madonnas, but they want to have sex with whores. A wife who likes sex is not a wife, blah de blah."

"Right—but where's the connection here?"

"He doesn't have sex with these women. Why? Because he reveres them."

There's a shutter click inside my head, like the rapid fire of a high-end camera. It is the feel of something shivering into place from out of nowhere.

"Yes," I say, staring off. "That feels right. But how can he revere them with the kinds of secrets they're carrying around? How?"

I walk over to the dry-erase board and stare at it hard, trying to force the thing that eludes me to show its face. My team is silent, waiting. They've seen this before.

"Well?" Alan finally asks.

I exhale in frustration. "I can't get my hands around it yet."

"Then move along, go to something else," Alan prods. "It'll come."

I know he's right. Try to remember where you left your keys and you'll never find them.

"What's the next plan of attack, oh Great One?" Callie asks.

"Missing persons," I say. "If he's stayed off our radar for this long, he's been hiding the bodies, making sure they wouldn't be found and that we wouldn't know about him until he was good and ready." I turn and look at the rows of names. Name after name, so many. Too many. "I'm guessing we're about to break a hundred plus unsolved missing-persons cases in the worst way possible. We need to find out who these people are."

"Fast," Alan agrees.

Death's promise isn't on the horizon anymore. It's standing next to us. Every now and then it checks its watch and grins.

26

"PARDON MY FRENCH, AGENT BARRETT, BUT IT SEEMS TO ME like we're now in the middle of a grade-A, eight-cylinder cluster fuck."

"That's a fair assessment, sir."

I'd answered my cell phone to find the Director of the FBI at the other end. I'd wondered for a moment how he got my number, but only for a moment. He is the Director of the FBI, after all.

"It's bad, sir, and it's only going to get worse."

"I guess you missed out on the executive reassurance seminar."

"I prefer the truth."

"Fine," he retorts. "Dazzle me with some truth."

"The truth, sir, is that this is huge and messy and I don't envy you the media side of things. But it's also true that this frenzy exists because he came out into the open. He's provided us with a list of his victims' names through the video clips. He's got a unique MO. If we don't catch him with what he's given us, we should all be fired."

"Don't give me any ideas." He sighs. "You're saying by cursing us with his publicity, he's blessed us with the way to catch him."

"Yep. And a very pithy way to put it too, sir."

"Leave the smart mouth to Agent Thorne, she does it better."

"Agreed and understood, sir."

"Tell me what you see, Smoky. Bottom lines."

I consider my answer for a moment. This conversation seems simple enough, but I am talking to Sam Rathbun. He's not just the

Director of the FBI, it's rumored that he was a gifted interrogator once. Maybe he's being sly, putting me at ease so I'll give him enough verbal rope to hang me with later.

I sigh to myself. I don't have time for Machiavellian strategizing, and I've never been any good at it anyway. I understand evil men, not ruthless ones.

"I see one hundred and forty-three dead women, sir. I see a lot of families that are going to get the worst news possible. I see that he's made a fatal mistake by showing himself. We'll catch him, and we need to do it before he kills again."

He takes a moment. Mulling things over, I guess.

"Get back to work, Agent Barrett."

He hangs up before I can get the "yes, sir" out.

I dial AD Jones right away. Politics may not be my strong suit, but even I know this rule: when the boss of bosses talks to you, you let your boss know about it, posthaste.

"What?" he answers.

"Is this a bad time, sir?"

"Yes. But you wouldn't have called without a good reason."

"I got a call from the Director."

"He called you personally?"

"Yes, sir."

I hear him muttering, cursing under his breath.

"What did he want?"

I relay the content of our conversation.

"Okay. I know what's going on there." He sounds mollified. "He's got someone asking him questions. Probably the President."

I thought I was fairly immune to the whole concept of people in powerful positions. They fart in private just like the rest of us, even if it is through silk. The President of the United States, I find, still gives me pause.

"Not sure how I feel about that, sir."

"Feel nervous, it's an appropriate response. Thanks for the heads-up."

Again, I'm hung up on before I can get my "yes, sir" out. Frustrating.

I check my watch. It's 7:00 P.M. The night is young. I still have a lot to do, but I want to check in with Bonnie before diving back into the maelstrom.

"Hi, Smoky," she says. Her voice is troubled.

"Something wrong, babe?"

Silence.

"I watched some of those video clips."

I sag in my chair. *Dear God.*

"Oh baby. Why?"

"I—I—just what we talked about before. I want to do what you do. I saw the stuff on the news and I went and found a site that had them and watched some."

"How many did you see, honey?"

I hear her swallow. "Just one at first. It was this girl. Her name was April. That guy made her talk about hurting her baby. I got sick. I'm such a dork," she mumbles. "I was really upset with myself about getting sick, so then I went back and watched some more."

"How many more?"

"Maybe thirty."

"Jesus, Bonnie!"

"Don't be mad, Momma-Smoky. Please don't be mad."

Mad? That's the last emotion I'm feeling. It hadn't even occurred to me until she mentioned it, but in the midst of my concern, it's an idea that gives me pause. Should I be mad at her?

I realize that I've never really disciplined Bonnie. Not because I've been lax with her, but because she's never needed it. I think maybe, just maybe, she needs it now.

"I'm not mad, Bonnie, but . . ." I think fast, looking for an appropriate punishment. "I'm going to restrict your computer privileges for a while. You should have asked me or Elaina about this before doing it, and I think you know that."

She sighs. "Yeah. I knew."

"And?"

"I knew you wouldn't let me."

The honesty of this makes me smile.

"That's generally a tip-off, babe."

Another sigh. "I know."

"Okay, so no Internet other than what you need for schoolwork for the next two weeks. Got it?"

"Yes."

Okay, okay, enough of that, how is my baby?

"How are you doing, sweetheart? Are you okay?"

"I don't know. I think the thing that bothered me the most was the things he said, that they made sense. That stuff about truth. A man like that, who does things like that, he shouldn't make *sense*, you know?"

"I do, babe."

"That's what really stays in my mind. The women, the things they went through, the things they did, sure, those were bad, but the worst thing is agreeing with him on *anything*."

"If you do what I do, you're going to run into that a lot. Actions—the things people do, like murder or rape—can be in black and white. But people themselves? All kinds of shades of gray there, babe. That's why it's actions that matter the most."

"What do you mean?"

"You can have a guy say that he believes that being a good father is the most important quality that a man can have, who then goes home and beats his kids. Or, even more complicated—maybe that same guy counsels other people's children, perhaps he's a therapist. He's done that for years, and maybe he's even helped a lot of kids. But the only thing that matters, from the perspective of my job, is that he goes home and beats his *own* children."

She's quiet, mulling this over.

"I need to think about that some more."

And she will. Bonnie is like a waveless lake, placid and still. But there's a lot happening underneath, where the sun can't reach and the crayfish hide.

"Will you talk to me about this some more? When you're done thinking?"

"Okay."

"Promise?"

"I promise, Momma-Smoky. I feel better now. I'm sorry for doing something you wouldn't want me to do."

I note the bending of phrase to her will. She's not apologizing for the action itself, she's apologizing for the fact that the action upset me. I let it pass.

"Apology accepted. But remember—two weeks."

"I will."

"Now let me talk to Elaina. Too much."

"Way, way too much," she replies.

A moment passes and Elaina comes on the line.

"Oh, Smoky." She sounds so miserable, I want to reach through the phone and hug her.

"Don't beat yourself up, Elaina. We've been lucky up to now with Bonnie. I think we were due."

"I suppose you're right, but still—I feel so guilty. She was on her laptop, using the wireless Internet connection. I haven't been sleeping well, and I decided to take a nap and it really got away from me. I slept for a few hours. She watched the clips while I was sleeping. I'm so sorry, Smoky."

"Elaina, please. You're her second mother. You've taken on her homeschooling, you keep her there when my hours get crazy—you do a *lot*. Don't be so hard on yourself."

"Appreciated, but how would you feel if you were in my position?"

I'd feel like crap.

"Point taken. You know, Bonnie's not a baby. It's not like we forgot to lock up the laundry detergent when she was a toddler and she ate it or something. She knew we wouldn't approve of what she was doing, and she deliberately hid it from us." I tell her about the two-week moratorium on Internet usage.

"I'll help enforce that, you can be sure."

"Somehow I don't think it'll be an issue. She didn't raise a fuss about it. Not a peep."

"Hmmm." I'm happy to hear some amusement leak into Elaina's voice. "Maybe that should worry us more than anything else."

"Good point. Now stop beating yourself up. I love you."

She sighs in agreement. "I love you too. Give my husband a kiss for me. Bonnie wants to talk to you again."

"Put her on."

"I forgot to tell you something," Bonnie says, a little breathless.

"What's that?"

"That man? The one who calls himself the Preacher?"

"Yes?"

"Catch him and put him in jail forever. I want him to die there."

It's not a request, it's a pronouncement. Bonnie saw what he's done, and whatever else she's wrangling with about it, the blacks and the grays, the moral maybes, one certainty has arrived: his freedom is unacceptable.

"I will, sweetheart."

"Good."

She hangs up without another word. I stare at the phone for a moment, bemused and disturbed. Bonnie has always been both a simplicity and a complexity in my life. The simplicity is my love for her. It's unfettered, it's depthless, it's pure. The complexity is Bonnie herself. She's got the brightness of a child, but she's also layered like an adult, full of private places I'm not sure I'll ever get to see. She's learned how to keep her own secrets and, perhaps more significant, how to be comfortable about it. Sometimes this bothers me, most times it doesn't. It just is.

Now she's about to turn into a teen, like a werewolf under a full moon, and with that, it seems, comes the ability to sneak and the willingness to lie. This by itself wouldn't bother me; it's the way of things. The problem is Bonnie hasn't chosen to sneak or lie about smoking or kissing or driving too fast; she applied her stealth to viewing the last, terrible moments of all those poor women.

There's nothing, I reflect, quite like motherhood to make you feel more helpless or inept.

I head out of my office. The maelstrom awaits.

"THIS KIND OF CASE REALLY exposes all the holes in our missing persons system," Alan grouses. "Did you know that NCIC contains about a hundred thousand missing persons cases, but AFIS has less than one hundred of those on file?"

NCIC is the National Crime Information Center. AFIS is the Automated Fingerprint Identification System. The other two major databases that figure into what we do are CODIS, the Combined DNA Index System for missing persons, and VICAP.

"You only got about fifteen percent of unidentified human remains that have been entered into NCIC. CODIS has been around since 1990, and it's growing, but it's still just a drop in the ocean."

CODIS was a stroke of brilliance. If someone goes missing and has not turned up within thirty days, a DNA reference sample is obtained. This can be either a direct sample from something belonging to the missing person (hair, saliva from a toothbrush) or a comparison sample from a blood relation. The DNA gets analyzed and the profile is loaded into the database. If a body turns up, it can often be identified via CODIS. There have also been cases of a child missing for years being located alive because of CODIS.

The problem with all of these databases comes down to cooperation, time, and money. They're all voluntary. If the local departments don't fill out the forms or collect the DNA, it doesn't end up in the right database. Even when the information is provided, someone has to enter it.

It's a flawed and incomplete system, but it's better than nothing for sure. We've broken cases using these various databases. They might be limping, but they're still assets.

"What have we found?"

"We have name matches on forty so far. Computer crimes is assisting on this flat out. They're extracting still images of the victims' faces from the clips, which we'll then shoot to the respective local law-enforcement agencies. They'll take the photo and name to the families and get positive IDs. My guess is we'll be looking at ten out of ten on that. Too big a coincidence that the name from one of these videos would match up with a missing persons case."

"I agree. By the way, your wife says to give you a kiss."

"Thanks."

"Keep on it. We're going to go till about eleven."

"Joy."

I head over to James, who is just hanging up the phone.

"The tips Jezebel is fielding to us are paying off," he says. "We've had almost eighty people come forward to identify victims on the clips."

"Wow."

Some might wonder why so many so fast. I don't. In many ways, the missing are far far worse than the dead. The missing are a maybe: Maybe they are still alive. Maybe they are not. The missing prevent closure, disallow true grief. That maybe ensures that the families are always looking, forever grasping at straws of hope.

I brought the news to a mother, once, that a daughter who'd gone missing three years earlier had been found dead. She wept, of course, but it's what she said that cut me the deepest.

"It's been so hard not knowing," she'd stammered through her tears. "One time—oh God—one time I remember being weak, and just wanting it to end, even if that meant she was dead."

I had watched her eyes widen as she truly saw what it was that she'd just said, that she'd wished, however briefly, for her daughter's death. The impact of this realization on her is something I'll never forget.

Keening is a kind of vocal lament that is traditional in Scotland and Ireland. In older days, before it was outlawed by the Catholic Church, it was done as a part of the wake. A woman or women would be hired to list the genealogy of the deceased, to praise them, and to emphasize the pain of the survivors. She (or they) would do this vocally, often wailing, and using physical movements such as clapping or rocking back and forth. It was a verbal expiation, designed to do justice to the fact of the loss of life. I thought of this then, because that's what I watched this woman do. She keened.

I think of it now, all those families. Keening. Eighty, just an incredible number, impossible to really get your mind around in terms of the human impact.

"I'm following up with all of the local law enforcement," James says. "I've made myself the sole point of contact. I'll have them assume any of our confirmed missings are a homicide, and get them to put their best detectives on it. Anything found will get funneled through me, and I'll collate it and add it to our database on these victims."

"We have a database?"

He points to his computer. "I wrote one."

"Good work, James."

"I know."

He turns away from me, a dismissal.

The door to the office swings open and Callie comes marching in with a big map of the U.S., mounted on foam-core. Kirby is following her, jabbering away.

"So we're good on the flowers? The price is fine?"

"The price is wonderful, Kirby. How about the cake?"

"I'm not fucking the cake guy. He's got back hair."

"Very funny. The pricing?"

"It's under budget. Oh, and good news on the photographer. There's a guy I used to know. We worked together, stuff like that. He used to do surveillance, but he's good with a camera and, hey, it's kind of the same thing, right?"

I watch Callie mull over the wisdom of letting Kirby bring an old work buddy to her wedding, given Kirby's background.

"Fine."

"Bridal pragmatism wins again," Alan opines. "That's going to be some wedding. Kirby will have fucked or threatened half the vendors, and the rest will be a collection of ex-mercenaries she used to know."

"Not ex," Kirby says. "A lot of them are still on the market."

"I hate to break this up," I say, "but—Callie?"

"Hey, I'm outie," Kirby says, "I know what I need for now. See you later Callie-babe."

"Yes, please call me later."

"I'm only up till four in the morning," Kirby chirps. "Girl needs her beauty sleep, you know?"

Callie holds up the map for us to see.

"I got James to print out a list of all the locations of our victims for me, and I marked them with pushpins."

We crowd around to get a look.

"I see we have a few clusters," Alan says. He points to Los Angeles, where there are over twenty. "And here." Las Vegas, Nevada.

"Sun and sin," Callie says.

The rest are spread out among the Preacher's other target states. Some are in cities anyone would recognize, others are in small towns I've never heard of. The overall effect is sobering.

"Like a fucking forest," Alan growls, an echo of my own thoughts.

"Excuse me," Kirby says. She hadn't left, after all. "Why is this name on this board?"

She's pointing to one of the Los Angeles victims. Willow Thomas.

"Why?" I ask.

The smile she gives me is mirthless and terrible. It puts me on immediate alert.

"Please answer the question."

Her tone is mild. She could be someone asking about the weather.

But the leopard eyes have appeared, and they are cold, cold, cold. This is the absolute indifference of a hired killer, the kind who shoots a man not because he was a particularly bad man, but because someone wanted him dead and was willing to pay to make it so.

"Haven't you been watching the news, honey-love?"

Kirby flicks her gaze at Callie, then back to me.

"Now, if I'd been watching the news, I guess I wouldn't be asking the question, would I, Callie?"

The fact that Kirby uses Callie's name without adding any twist to it heightens my unease. Her voice is still mild, the chide she throws at Callie just a languid "pshaw" of a slap, but the air feels electric and dangerous.

What the hell?

"There's a man," I say, watching her for a reaction. "We think he's been killing women for the last twenty years. We're pretty sure the names on the board belong to his victims."

"Victims? As in dead?"

"Yes."

She walks over to me and puts her arm around my shoulders. It's anything but friendly, an intense and uncomfortable closeness. "And?" she whispers, her mouth near my ear. "Do we know who this man is?" Her words could have been carved from ice, they're so cold.

"Not yet." I pull away and look at her directly. "Not sure I'd tell you if I did."

She stares at me for what seems like forever with that arctic gaze.

"Can I talk to you?" she asks me. "Alone?"

She walks toward my office without waiting for an answer. I turn to Alan, Callie, and James.

"Not a clue," Callie says.

"I never know what's going on in that psycho's head," Alan says.

Only James is silent.

WE'RE SEATED IN MY OFFICE with the door closed. I am waiting for Kirby to start talking. The fact that she's not is unnatural. The wind blows, Kirby talks; it's one of the axioms of life.

She's sitting in the chair that faces my desk. She's picking her lip and looking off. She gives me a lopsided smile.

"If you're waiting for me to lose it, you're going to be waiting for a looooooooong time, Smoky."

The attempt at flip, something she's normally so good at, right now seems less than genuine.

"I think I already did see you lose it."

She scrutinizes me, flashes a smile and shrugs.

"Well . . . maybe I had a little bit of a reaction there."

"Cut the shit, Kirby. I appreciate what you did for me in the bathroom. Let me return the favor."

She shakes a finger at me. "Now, now, I don't let anyone behind the curtain, Smoky. You should know that."

"Tell me about Willow Thomas. Who was she? Who was she to you?"

Again, the lip picking. I've never seen Kirby this wordless or evasive. She's generally about as subtle as a two-year-old.

"Willow was . . . a friend of a friend. She was a civilian. Always. She was born innocent and probably died that way. She was a puppy dog, a kitty cat, too bright eyed and bushy tailed for the world you and I live in, you know? She wasn't like me or my friend. We were never civilians. We came out ready to rock and roll, prepared for the shit and shinola the big ol' bad ol' world dishes out. Not Willow. She was weak."

"What was your friend's name?"

Another finger wag and lopsided smile. "Nice try. But no. I'm not sharing that particular information right now."

"Is it germane?"

"If I thought it would help you figure out who this future dead man is, I would tell you."

Future dead man. It has the ring of utter certainty coming from her mouth.

"You're sure?"

"Willow made the right choice. She left us for a nice, normal life. We never spoke again, but I checked in on her every now and then to make sure no one was taking advantage of the puppy dog. One day I checked and she was gone. I used some of my—ah—resources to try and track her down, but she'd vanished. It was like she swam out into the ocean one night and never came back."

"When was this?"

"About ten years ago."

"Does she have any family?"

She takes a long time to answer.

"No. She was an orphan."

"I see."

I wait for more. Kirby smiles.

"Hell will freeze over first. She was an orphan, she disappeared ten years ago from sunny Los Angeles, she never deliberately hurt a person in her life besides herself. That's all you need to know."

"She was hiding something, Kirby. That's how this guy operates."

I explain the video clips to her. I watch her face as I do, looking for a tell, some crack in that Kirby-facade. She just listens, twirling a strand of blonde hair with one finger while she does.

"I understand," she says when I'm done.

"Kirby, did Willow have any problems you know about? Drinking, drugs? Did she go to meetings, anything like that?"

"Actually, yeah. She drank. She kicked it, though. Big AA attendee."

Bingo, I think.

"Anything else you can tell me about her?"

"Nothing that will help you." She leans forward. Again, there's that feel of something predatory and electric in the air. "So you don't have any idea yet who he is?"

"Nope."

She nods. "Well, okay then. I guess we're done here." She stands up to go.

"Kirby. Do you want to see the clip?"

She pauses, her back to me, hand on the doorknob.

"No. I know the secret that she was hiding."

She turns the knob and leaves.

A CIVILIAN. THAT'S WHAT KIRBY had called Willow Thomas. I understand the reference, watching the woman on the video in front of me.

She had the look. She would have been surprised by the cruel cuts of life, would never have failed to feel betrayed by them. She'd have survived on a plane of hopeful fairy tales, idealizing and dreaming until something smashed into her and brought her back down to earth.

It would have been a never-ending cycle, started as a result of some great harm done to her that she never really recovered from.

She'd been beautiful, in a limpid-eyed kind of way. She had straight dark hair and she was thin, painfully so. The gauntness brought out her beauty, the way it will in some women. She had pale, pale skin, with color at the cheekbones. Her lips had been full and red.

"Tell me about the scars, Willow," the Preacher says to her.

She is shivering. Her eyes dart every which way; at him, right, left, then staring straight into the camera so that I feel like she's looking right at me. Her tears aren't constant. The corners of her eyes take a long time to fill before releasing single, huge drops that careen down her cheeks and plop almost immediately onto her naked thighs. I am hit with a wave of queasiness when I realize she is covered in goose-flesh. He must have been able to smell her horror.

"Willow," he prods, gentle as always. "The scars. Or I'll have to hurt you again."

This prompts a shiver so powerful I hear the chair legs rattle against the floor.

"No!" she cries.

"Then talk, please. Tell me about the scars."

"But, but you already know," she whines. "I know you do, you told me."

"Yes, but I need you to say it on camera."

Her shivering stops. She heaves a single, huge sigh. Then another, a lung-filling whoop of breath in, a noisy rattling out. Her head drops so that all that straight hair hangs down and tickles the top of her tear-spattered thighs.

"We used to cut each other," she whispers.

"Who, Willow? You and who?"

"Me and Mandy. Mandy was my sister. She was two years older than me. We went into foster care together because Mom and Dad beat us so much. Mandy told me about cutting, how it could make you feel better when you hurt a lot."

"And did you? Hurt a lot?"

"Yes."

"Go on."

"We used a razor. Most of the time we'd cut on the inside of our legs, above where you'd ever see it if you wore a skirt. Sometimes, we'd do it for each other."

"That's what you were doing that day, isn't it? Cutting each other?"

"Yes." It's the smallest voice I've ever heard. Barely audible.

"What happened?"

"She'd cut me first. It felt . . . wonderful. I can't describe it. Before you cut, you're feeling numb and hurting at the same time, it's all un-real, but then you cut and the pain is *real*, it's sharp and sweet and *now*. No future, no past. Just now. Cutting made everything only about that moment. It made you real, it made you matter."

"Go on."

"I was feeling kind of hot and good, you know. She'd cut me pretty deep. She saw how great I felt, and she told me to cut her deep too. Real deep. So I did."

"Did you cut too deep, Willow?"

Her face comes up and I'm shocked at how white it is. This is a corpse face.

"I cut into the artery," she whispers. "She was always so thin, we both were. I was pushing and I wasn't paying enough attention be-cause I was still feeling the adrenaline rush and endorphins from when she cut me and I just cut too deep. She started to bleed so fast, so much."

She stops talking.

"Tell the rest of it. What did you do then?"

I see the first hint that there'd been any strength in this woman; her eyes gleam with pure hate for the Preacher. If she could have, I think she would've cut him deep too.

"I told her she was bleeding bad. She looked down at it and—and—she smiled. She smiled. She told me to get out and not to tell anyone I was the one who'd cut her. I told her no, she needed help, but she told me it was too late, she was going to die, and that it was okay, she didn't mind, kind of liked it, really, but she didn't want me to get into trouble so I needed to leave and come back and act like I found her and like it was a big surprise so I did and I counted to five and I came in and she was already going unconscious and I screamed and there was blood everywhere and—" The torrent only stops for her to draw in another one of those whooping breaths. "I was holding her and try-ing to stop the blood, but it was too much. I was in a pool of it, I could have gone swimming in it." A beat of silence. "She died."

"Did you do what your sister told you, Willow? Did you pretend?"

She nods. She's gone even paler. Her eyes sparkle with her hatred, naked and pure.

"Say it, child," he tells her.

She shakes once, another one of those chair-leg-rattling shivers. "I killed my sister and let everyone think she'd killed herself." She spits the words out, bitter, venomous.

"And did you garner sympathy for this?"

"Yes."

"Did you tell people about your own cutting?"

"Yes."

"And the last thing, Willow. Did you tell them your sister led you down that path? Did you let them think she was the one who made you do it?"

"Yesssss." It comes out in a moan. Her eyes are fluttering. Her facial expression morphs from hate to despair and through all the per-mutations in between.

He waits. I get the sense he's well satisfied, and I feel a little bit of my own hatred rise.

"Thank you, Willow. Remember: God is love."

Fade to black.

I didn't realize I'd been holding my breath. I exhale and lean back in my chair.

So that was Kirby's friend, I think.

I wonder if this really is the secret Kirby seems to think she knows.

A knock on the door interrupts. James pokes his head in.

"We have a lead."

27

an IP number to the uploads of the video clips," James says. "We wanted to find out if he was stupid enough to lead us to his Internet connection. Given the sophistication of this perp, it seemed unlikely, but he put up a lot of material, so it was worth a try."

"And? You're saying he left a trail?"

"Most connections operate on the basis of a dynamic IP number. The Internet provider assigns a new IP to the user machine every time they connect, or every day. Some people prefer what they call a static IP—a number that never changes. The number associated with these uploads is static."

"Which means it couldn't belong to anyone else but that particular bill-paying user."

"Correct."

I pace, thinking about this.

"Seems really *really* strange. It doesn't make sense he'd be so smart about everything else and so stupid about this. Is it possible this isn't our guy?"

"Very. If the owner of this IP uses a wireless router, and he didn't password protect it, then someone could conceivably park a car in front of his home with a laptop and hijack his connection for the uploads."

"Is it really that common for home wireless networks to be insecure?"

"Yes. A lot of people buy a router and just plug it in and go. They never bother to secure the connection, mostly because they don't understand it themselves."

"Show me the guy."

He taps a key on his keyboard and points to the screen. A picture of a California driver's license is displayed.

"Harrison Bester," I read. "Age forty-one, black hair, blue eyes. Normal enough looking. Do we know anything about him yet?"

"We do now," Alan says, walking in the door, waving a manila folder.

He plops down in his chair and reads aloud.

"Harrison was a systems engineer who parlayed a pretty good severance package into purchasing a franchised shipping store. He doesn't make big money, but he's definitely middle class. Lives in Thousand Oaks. He's married, wife's name is Tracy. They have two kids, both daughters, aged seventeen and fifteen."

"Which, again, sounds all wrong," Callie observes. "Harrison and Tracy were sitting in a tree k-i-s-s-i-n-g at a fairly young age to have a seventeen-year-old. That doesn't fit with our boy's timeline. He's the dedicated sort. No time to be a family man."

"I agree," James says.

"Me too," I reply. I think for a moment and come to a decision. "Callie, I want you to take a laptop and your car and park in front of the Bester house. See if Bester has a wireless connection and if he isn't up on his security. In the meantime, I'll coordinate with AD Jones and get this guy put under twenty-four-hour surveillance."

"Safe than sorry?" Alan asks.

I shrug. "I don't *think* Bester is the Preacher either, but thinking and knowing are two different things. Even if he isn't, that doesn't mean they don't know each other. Maybe they're in cahoots. Or maybe they're just longtime drinking buddies and Harrison has no idea his friend is a serial killer. There's always the possibility—slim, but possible—that the Preacher will decide to come back and steal some more wireless time. It's our best lead, for now."

"Cahoots," Alan snorts, teasing me.

"I'll go and see about Mr. Bester," Callie says, grabbing her laptop bag and heading toward the door.

"Call me with what you find," I yell after her.

"Only if you promise you won't keep me from going home afterward for a quickie with my husband-to-be," she calls back, and then she's out the door.

"I looked into the support group Rosemary attended," Alan says.

"And?"

I guess he hears the hopefulness in my voice, because he shakes his head in the negative. "She went pretty regularly to a Narcotics Anonymous in the Valley. I spoke to the director there. It's a high turnover meeting, with people from every spectrum. There's no roll call and no application or screening. Long as you talk, you're welcome."

"Perfect hiding place."

"Yeah. Anyway, he sympathized, but he wasn't willing to give me information on anyone. Par for the course." He shrugs, frustrated. "Guy's smart. I'll bet he was there."

"And I'll bet you could question every one of them and no one would remember anyone who stuck out. Just like the passengers on the plane."

AD JONES ASKED ME TO brief him in person rather than on the phone. I knock on his office door.

"Come in," he barks.

He's seated behind his desk as I enter. He looks beat. His tie is loosened and his cuffs are rolled up. I plop down in one of the leather chairs. He cocks his head, appraising me.

"You look terrible," he says.

"Likewise, sir. And thanks."

The ends of his mouth curl up in the barest hint of a smile.

"Yeah. It's been a hell of a day. It's been all Preacher all the time up here. The media is going nuts, which means the Director is going nuts. I've had to field calls from the police commissioners of Los Angeles, San Francisco, Vegas, Carson City, Phoenix, Salt Lake City . . . you get the idea. I've managed to get them all to agree to total co-operation. No turf wars."

"How'd you pull off that miracle?"

He rubs his forehead. "They have families screaming for answers or blood or both, along with plenty of media coverage. Commissioners have to play politics, and they need answers quick. They recognize the best chance of that is for all of us to just get along."

"Thank you, sir. It will help."

"Your turn to help me. Where are we at on this?"

I brief him on the IP number lead. He makes a face.

"I agree that it has to be checked out, and I'll authorize the surveillance, but I doubt it will be our man."

"I agree. He's spent a lot of time building up to this moment. It's important to him. Too important to trip up over something so elementary."

"Where does that take us, then?"

"I think we're going to solve this by finding the most basic common denominator, sir."

"Clarify."

"It's a logic problem. He's smart, but he's a creature of habit. All his victims have been women with the exception of Lisa Reid. They all had a deep, dark secret to disclose, and we can deduce that he killed them all the same way. We have to distill the pattern down to the one thing that'll lead us to him."

"Where do you think that's going to lie?"

"Everything for him is about secrets and truth. The question we need to get answered: how does he know what he knows? I think if we figure that out, we'll have him."

"Ideas?"

"We think he's picking his victims from AA meetings, support groups, and churches. He probably infiltrates as a fellow member." I shrug. "I mean, he could be acting as a counselor, I guess. Or in the case of a church, as a priest."

"But you don't think so."

"It's too direct, too risky. He needs to hide in the crowd, and he needs the freedom to fade away when the time comes. He can't do that if he's someone people build a relationship with. Addicts and sinners trust their counselors and their priests. They notice when they go missing."

"Right," he says, thoughtful. "So how do we use this to find him?"

"I don't know yet." I can hear the frustration in my voice.

"There's two things to do in that situation, Agent Barrett. Either you take your attention off it, or you immerse yourself in the environment."

"Yes, sir."

"Figure this one out soon, Smoky. From what I can tell, he wants us to catch him. Let's give him what he wants. Get going."

I leave his office with the words he'd spoken ringing in my mind.

Immerse yourself in the environment.

When I get back down to Death Central, I stand in front of Alan's desk.

"Let's go see Father Yates."

28

IT'S ANOTHER LATE NIGHT ROAD TRIP TO THE VALLEY. THE moon is hiding now, punching through the clouds in places with silver fists.

"Never see any stars in LA," Alan mutters.

"It's all the city lights reflecting off the sky." I smile. "That and the smog."

The wheels hum on the uneven pavement as we barrel through the dark.

FATHER YATES IS DRESSED IN a pair of jeans and a pullover shirt. His hair is rumpled. His eyes are tired. He yawns once.

"Forgive me." He smiles, shaking first my hand and then Alan's. "I'm early to bed, early to rise, as the saying goes."

"Don't sweat it," I tell him. "We're in the same boat, except that it's more like late to bed, early to rise."

He gestures to the front row of pews as a place to sit.

"You said you needed my help."

"Have you watched any of the video clips he made?"

"Just the first few where he's laying out his argument for truth. I have no interest in watching him murder anyone."

"And? What did you think?"

He leans back in the pew and studies the large crucifix of Jesus. It is his anchor in this place, I can see it in the way some of the worry and tiredness leaves his eyes.

"Are you at all familiar with the catechism of the Catholic Church, Agent Barrett?"

"Uh, sure. I was raised Catholic."

"What about the official catechism?"

"I don't think I know what you mean."

"Hold on a second."

He disappears into the sacristy area and returns holding a small, thick hardback book. He hands it to me. I read the title: *Catechism of the Catholic Church.*

"Everything you ever wanted to know about the Catholic Church but were afraid to ask." He smiles. "There is a paragraph in here that I use to guide my actions. I went and read it again not long after I watched those video clips." He takes the book back from me and flips to a page near the front. "Here it is. 'The whole concern of doctrine and its teaching must be directed to the love that never ends. Whether something is proposed for belief, for hope, or for action, the love of our Lord must always be made accessible, so that anyone can see that all the works of perfect Christian virtue spring from love and have no other objective than to arrive at love.'" He closes the book. He touches the cover with affection. "I love that paragraph. It's a piece of truth. Whatever else might occur with my church, whatever mistakes are made by overzealous or intolerant parishioners, whatever crimes might be committed by evil men masquerading as men of God, I can read this and know the problem lies with men, not with the church or with my faith. Those who fail the church are those who don't align their actions to the purity of purpose contained in that simple paragraph, the idea that we have 'no other objective than to arrive at love.'"

"It is a nice idea," I allow. "Too bad it's not put into direct practice more often." I wince. "Sorry again, Father."

He smiles. "I happen to agree with you. Confrontation and attack are not the way to bring someone to Christ. You don't tell them they are stupid and hell bound; you show them Christ's words, or set an example yourself through your actions. Or just lend a helping hand when someone needs it. Faith is an act of choice, it's not something you can foster at gunpoint."

"I see where you're going with this," Alan rumbles. "The Preacher isn't exactly embodying the whole love concept."

Father Yates scowls. "Murder is never an act of love. This man is deluded at best."

"What about his ideas?" I ask. "The things he said about truth?"

He sighs. "I will be honest. The ideas themselves are powerful. I've been taking confession for a long time, and I've seen the phenomenon he talks about. The hardest thing isn't for people to tell the truth—it's for them to tell the *whole* truth. I'm sure there are plenty who will agree with what he's said. You can count on him having supporters."

"Are you joking?" I'm incredulous.

"Afraid not. A lot of people in the Christian world believe in black and white and operate on a principle of 'you get what you deserve' when it comes to God and the Bible. If you didn't own up in the confessional, then you were going to hell anyway. Some will see these poor victims as victims of nothing more than their unwillingness to confess to God."

I look at the crucifix, that paint-chipped, color-faded Christ. I search for the same comfort Father Yates seems to find. I come up empty, as always. How can I believe in a church or a faith that would produce people like that?

"Don't forget the good that's done," he says, breaking in on my thoughts. "The millions of children who eat every day because of Christian charities, the houses built for the homeless, the mission food lines. Not long ago a group of Christians from South Korea went to Afghanistan. They knew it was dangerous, and it was probably ill-advised, but the point is, they had no ulterior motive. They went there to help. They were taken hostage and while the majority were released, a number of them died. Religion has always and will always be a double-edged sword. It's how you use it that makes the difference, and that always depends upon the individual.

"It's no different than anything else. If there was no Internet, there'd be less pornography and child exploitation. But what about all the good done because the Internet exists? Commerce, free flow of information, breaking down culture barriers and xenophobia because people can talk to each other across the world? Anything can be used for good or evil. That includes the church and interpretations of the Bible."

"Talk to me about confession, Father. Tell me what it means to you."

His eyes find Jesus again. "In my opinion, holy confession is the most important service the church can offer. The real reason that monster's words are going to hit home to people is not because they're particularly revolutionary, but because the fact is, most of us walk around with secrets that eat away at us every minute of every day. I have had confessors sob with relief after confessing just a minor misdeed."

"Most of these people did some really awful things. What about that?"

"I've heard some terrible things in my time, yes, it's true. Terrible things. And there have been those who weren't particularly repentant. But the vast majority struggle under the burden of the bad things they've done. Most people judge themselves much harder than you or I would. Hearing confession hasn't jaded me, it's had the opposite effect. I truly believe in the basic decency of humanity."

"That's a tough sell with me, Father," I say.

"Amen," Alan mutters.

He smiles. "That's understandable. You spend your time with men and women who sin without remorse—worse, with enjoyment. I promise you, the more common example of man is the mother who has to be coaxed into forgiving herself because she got tired and raised her voice at her child. We're flawed, not evil."

"Do you hear about everything?" I ask.

"Most things. People hold things back sometimes. Taking confession isn't a rote activity. It's an art form. You have to build trust in your parishioners. They have to know you won't treat them differently after you hear about their sexual peccadilloes or petty crimes, or worse."

"There have to have been times you've heard something really bad. Murder or child molestation. How do you treat that person the same afterward?"

He shrugs. It's not a "who knows" kind of shrug. It's a motion that says, "I have no other answer than the one you're about to hear." "It's my sacred duty."

"Must be tough sometimes."

"There have been moments," he allows.

"How do you deal with it when you hear about something happening right now?" Alan asks. "A father who's molesting his kids, for example. Or a guy who confesses that he has HIV from sleeping with hookers but continues to sleep with his wife?"

"I pray, Agent Washington. I pray for strength. I pray that the act of confession itself will prevent that person from continuing to sin. Yes, it's tough. But if I break the seal of confession because of the sins of one man or woman, I make myself unavailable to the hundreds of decent people who need me as Father Confessor. Should I make hundreds pay for the sins of one?"

"That's it? No exceptions?"

"I am allowed to urge penitents to turn themselves in to the police if it's a criminal matter, and I can even withhold absolution if they refuse, but I can't break the seal of confession."

Alan shakes his head. "I don't envy you your job, Father, especially since I can see that you're a thinker. Must keep you awake at nights."

Father Yates smiles. "Some survive on the strength of faith. Some survive intellectually, their thoughts guided by scripture. I fall somewhere in between. I have crises, all priests do. Nuns for that matter. Mother Teresa struggled with personal darkness and doubts about God for most of her life."

"Have you seen real change in people?" I ask.

"Of course. Not always, but enough to keep me happy."

"What's the common thread? For those who change?"

He considers my question. "Contrition. True contrition. It's one thing to confess to a sin. True contrition, in my opinion, requires change as a basic component. If you are contrite, you change. If you are not, you won't."

"Was Rosemary contrite?"

"I believe so, yes."

The glimmering in my mind is getting stronger. There's something here, in what we're talking about. It's not just a flicker at the corner of my eye anymore; it's an itch I can't reach.

"Can I see the inside of your confessional, Father?"

He pauses for some time, studying me. I don't feel uncomfortable or violated by his scrutiny. There's too much kindness there.

He stands up. "Follow me."

"I'll wait here," Alan calls after me. "Maybe do a little praying about getting enough sleep tonight."

I give him a halfhearted wave as I follow Father Yates toward the confessional booth. Two things are happening at the same time here; the thing I'm trying to see is getting clearer, stronger, brighter, and the voice in my head, the one that makes my stomach do loop-de-loops, is back.

I feel a cold, greasy sweat break out on my forehead.

"Let's give you the full experience," Father Yates says as we approach the confessional booth. "I'll take up my normal position and you take the place of the penitent."

"Sure," I say, but I can hardly hear my own voice. Too many bat wings flapping around in my head.

I open the door and enter. There's little light here. The booth is small and sparse, made of dark, poorly stained wood. A kneeler is set on the floor below the lattice screen that divides priest and penitent. I close the door and stare down at the kneeler.

In for a penny, in for a pound, I think. I want to laugh and cry at the same time.

This time the voice speaks out loud: See me.

I kneel in an instant. For some reason, this makes the voice go silent.

Father Yates slides the window open.

"Smaller than I remember," I say.

"I take it you were much younger the last time you confessed," he replies, amused.

"Well, let's see . . . bless me, Father, for I have sinned. It has been—hmmm—about twenty-seven years since my last confession."

"I see. Do you have anything to confess, my child?"

I freeze. I feel something rising inside me. It's angry and ugly and bitter.

"Is that what you were thinking when you were looking at me back there, Father? That you'd get me in here and I'd spill my guts and find my faith again?"

"Just the spill your guts part," he says, calm. "I think it's a little too soon for the last."

"Screw you."

He sighs. "Agent Barrett, you are here, I am here, and inside these small walls, you're safe. You can rage in here, you can weep in here, you can tell me anything, and it remains between you, me, and Christ. Something is troubling you, I can tell. Why not talk about it?"

"The last guy I told all my secrets to tried to kill me, Father." I'm surprised at how cold my voice sounds.

"Yes, I read about that. I can understand your misgivings. Perhaps if you can't extend your faith to God, you can extend it to me? I've never broken a confidence."

"I believe you," I allow.

I do. I can't deny that with this environment comes a yearning. It's deep and piercing and the fact of that is the cause of a lot of my anger.

See me, the voice had said. The problem was not that I couldn't see what it was asking. The problem was that I could never *stop* seeing it.

The need to tell someone my secret, finally, to get it off my chest, the possibility that it would bring me some peace—God or no God—promises a relief so strong that I can feel it crawling across my skin like an army of ants.

I breathe in and out, fast. My heart is racing. My hands are clenched together, more in desperation than supplication.

"I don't know if I believe in God anymore, Father," I whisper. "Is it right to confess if I'm so unsure He even exists?"

"Confession, so long as you are truly contrite, can only be a good thing, Agent Barrett. I truly believe that."

"Smoky. Call me Smoky."

"All right. Smoky, do you have any sins to confess?"

I have many sins, so many, Father, sins of pride, sins of envy, sins of lust. I have murdered men. In self-defense, it's true, but some part of me enjoyed killing them. I love that I got to kill the man who took my Matt and my Alexa from me. It pleases me forever.

Sins?

I have sinned against my family, my friends, those who loved and trusted me. I have lied—a lot. I drink in the night. I have only lain with two men in my life, but I have done it with abandon. Sometimes for love, sure, but sometimes just for the pleasure they could give me. Is it a sin to have taken joy at the feel of cock in my mouth, to have whispered into Matt's or Tommy's ears "fuck me fuck me fuck me, dear sweet God, fuck me"? Does God appreciate my bringing Him there, making Him a part of that sweaty moment?

I have gazed on the suffering of others, on their victimization, on their murdered and mutilated corpses, and I have taught myself how to turn away. How to shut off the images and the emotions, to go home and eat spaghetti and watch TV as though their pain never existed or didn't matter. I have made a job out of hunting evil men. I get paid a salary because people die.

Are these sins?

I shift on the kneeler. All those things that had run through my head may or may not be sins. None of them are the thing that wakes up the monster in my mind.

See me, it says, but the voice is gentle this time, and the voice, of course, is me.

I feel tears running down my face. I'm going to tell him, I realize. I was always going to tell him, I knew it the moment I walked in here. That's why the sweat and nausea went away.

"I did a terrible thing, Father," I whisper. "I think because I did this thing I'll never let myself feel real joy. I'll never let myself really love someone again. Because I don't deserve it."

Saying it aloud brings out the anguish in earnest. The grief-monster tries to crawl up and out of my throat as a wail. I fight him down, let him detonate inside me. It's too quiet here; Alan would hear me. I clench my hands together in a single fist and I push it against my mouth. I bite down till I break the skin. I taste a little of my own blood and shiver with my own pain.

Father Yates has been quiet, waiting. He speaks again. His voice is gentle. Safe. He reminds me, for a moment, of my real father, not God, but my dad, who always kept the creatures under my bed at bay.

"Put it into words, Smoky. Just let it go. I'll listen, I won't judge. What you say here will never be repeated by me to another. Whatever burden you're carrying, it's time to put it down."

I nod, tears still running down my face. I know he can't see me nod, but my throat has closed up, and I can't speak. He seems to sense this.

"Take your time."

I sniffle and he waits. As the moments pass, the hand clenching my throat loosens. I'm able to speak again.

"After the attack, I was in the hospital for a while. Sands had cut my face down to the bone in most places. He'd sliced me on other parts of my body and had burned me with a cigar. None of it was life threatening, but I was in a lot of pain and they were concerned about infection because some of the wounds were so deep.

"I was set on dying, Father. I had absolutely, positively, one hundred percent decided that I was going to be blowing my own brains out. I was going to get out of that hospital and I was going to go home, get my affairs in order, and kill myself."

"Go on."

"This is all stuff everyone knows. I had to see a shrink—and you know how that turned out. The point is, people know I wrestled with the whole suicide thing. They know about the rape, and they can sure see the scars. That's all safe stuff. Stuff they can understand and excuse. 'Of course she was suicidal, look at what she went through, poor thing!' You understand?"

"Yes."

"And some part of me, Father, some part of me ate it up. All that sympathy. Poor, poor Smoky. Isn't she strong? Isn't it admirable how she overcame and went on?"

The bitterness is rising in me like black coffee, or sour milk. I can almost taste it in my mouth. It's the flavor of self-loathing. No, that's not strong enough. Self-hate.

"So tell me that thing they didn't know, Smoky. The thing that wasn't admirable."

The rush of hostility makes me a little dizzy with its ferocity. Heat blooms in my cheeks and forehead. Pure anger, the do-or-die of an animal with its back against the wall. This secret is going to go down fighting. It can see the light, and the light makes it rage and scream.

"Fuck God," I breathe, and love the taste of the words, the thrill of them.

"I'm sorry?"

"Fuck God and His forgiveness. Why should I ask that asshole to forgive me for anything? What did my mother need to be forgiven for? Did you know that in the last days she begged us to kill her? She was in so much pain, she begged us to do it, to take her life. And she was the most devout Catholic I knew!"

"And did you?" he asks, his voice calm.

"What? Fuck you. No." The rage is a tidal wave, it has swept me up and I am helpless against it.

"Then tell me what you did do, Smoky. You don't have to ask God for forgiveness, if you don't want to. But you do have to ask yourself."

I grind my teeth and grip my hands together until they're numb.

"Forgive myself?" I snarl in a whisper. "What, just because I say it out loud here, it's suddenly going to all be okay?"

"No. But it'll be a start. I can't tell you why it makes a difference to tell someone else what we've done, Smoky, but it does. It's only words, but yes, you will feel better. You need to tell me what you did and then realize that the world didn't end because you told me."

That calm is unstoppable. It's a little juggernaut of faith, patient and inexorable. If he had to empty a swimming pool with a spoon, he'd do so without complaint, however long it took. It makes me feel safe and hostile in tandem. I want to hug him and slap him all at once.

"I was pregnant," I blurt out.

Silence.

I think, for a moment, that he's judging me already, but I realize he's just waiting.

"Go on," he says.

"Just a few months. It was a big surprise. I used a diaphragm. Matt and I weren't old, but we weren't exactly spring chickens either. It just . . . happened."

"Did your husband know?"

You're too smart for me, Father.

"No. I wasn't sure I was going to tell him either. I wasn't sure I wanted to keep the baby."

"Why not?"

"I don't know. Selfishness, I guess. I was in my late thirties, career on the rise, all the usual excuses. Don't misunderstand, I hadn't de-cided to get rid of it, not for sure. But I was thinking about it, and I was hiding it from Matt."

"Did you have a lot of secrets in your marriage?"

"No. That's the thing. Well, part of the thing. Matt and I, we were lucky. I know all about the ways a marriage can go off the rails. Men cheat, women cheat, men lie, women lie. Mistresses kill the wives, wives kill the husbands, or maybe they're fine, but cancer kills them both anyway. Sometimes it's a long, slow death. Years of little secrets turn into big distrusts, and the marriage is less about love than endurance.

"Matt and I? We never had that. We had fights. We could spend days not talking to each other. But we always came back together in the end, and we loved each other. I never cheated on him, and I'm sure he never cheated on me."

"This moment then—hiding this from him—this was unusual."

"Very. You hide little things. It's part of living with someone. You have to keep some things for yourself. But you don't hide big things. You don't hide a pregnancy, and you sure as hell don't hide an abortion. That's not who we were."

"Did he know before his death?"

"No."

"Do you think you would have told him?"

"I like to think so. But I'm not sure."

"What happened to the baby, Smoky?"

It's THE question, of course. *See me,* the voice said. I do, I do, in bright neon, under the light of 10,000 times 10,000-watt lamps.

"It's not so much that I aborted the baby," I say, "but why." My voice sounds empty. I am exhausted. I think I'd rather be anywhere than here, right now. "See, I wanted to kill myself, but I knew I could never do that with a baby inside me. So I asked the doctor to take care of it." Tired, tired, so tired. "It was the last little bit of Matt, right there inside me, ready to grow and be born and live. He didn't have to end there, we didn't have to end there, do you understand? Sands didn't take that from me. He didn't kill my baby. I did that. Me."

I start to weep.

"Is there more?" Father Yates asks.

"More? Of course there's more. I'm here, don't you see? I got rid of that baby so I could kill myself, but in the end I didn't even *do* it! The baby died for nothing! For no reason at all! I—I—" I don't want to say the words, but I need to. "I murdered that baby, Father. M-m-murdered."

I can't talk anymore. All I can do is cry. I don't cry for myself. I cry because one of the last actions in my marriage was to lie. I cry for the idea of Alexa having a baby brother or sister. Most of all, I cry for that child. She, or he, had been a chance to put something back of the things Sands had stolen. I threw that chance away in a moment of agony. It's not about the right and wrong of abortion. It's about the reasons for the decision, the pain, the selfishness, the maybes, might-haves, could-have-beens. It's about the misery of realizing you've done something terrible you can never take back, can never make up for.

I cry and Father Yates lets me. He doesn't speak, but I can feel his presence, and it comforts me.

I don't know how long it goes on. The grief blows itself out, not gone, just quieter.

"Smoky, I'm not going to throw a lot of scripture at you, here. I know that your faith isn't up to that. I'll simply say, yes, what you did, why you did it, was wrong. You know this. But what is the real sin? What is it that makes what you did so terrible? It is the fact that you threw away the gift of life. I don't care where you think that gift came from—God, primordial soup, a little bit of both—but life is a gift, and I think you know that. I think you know it more than most people, because of what you do."

"Yes," I whisper.

"Then, don't you see? Continuing to deny yourself forgiveness, continuing to deny yourself love, is to continue the same sin—because all of it means to deny yourself *life*."

"But, Father—how can I let myself be happy, really happy? I can't change what I did."

"You atone. You don't forget. You don't justify. You *change*. You're raising the daughter of your friend. Raise her well. Be a good mother to her. Teach her to love life. You have a man in your life? Love him. If you marry him, don't keep secrets from him. You have a job that lets you imprison those who would take life from others. Do that job well, and you'll save countless lives. It's right that you've suffered for this sin, but you're not evil, Smoky, and it's time, if you won't forgive yourself, to let someone else forgive you. I've given you your penance. Maybe it will take you a lifetime to do it. Now, I absolve you of your sins in the name of the Father, and of the Son, and of the Holy Spirit."

They're just words. I'm not right with God, and I'm not sure I ever will be. I may never see the inside of a confessional booth again, and I secretly think Jesus might just have been a carpenter. But Father Yates had been right: saying it to someone else, out loud, and seeing that the world didn't end as a result, gives me a relief I had never expected. I feel . . . clean. The sorrow is still there and that's okay. Only the men I hunt don't regret.

"Thanks, Father."

I don't know what else to say.

"It's my pleasure." I can almost feel him smiling. "You see? There's plenty of adventure to be had, doing what I do."

"No kidding," I agree.

Some people explore the outer world. They climb mountains, sail the oceans, hunt with the natives, so to speak. Some find their adventure in excess, as Hemingway did, running with the bulls, downing the booze, living larger than life. Then there are the Father Yates and me types, we spend our days spelunking through the inner world, where something new and maybe terrible always lies beyond the bend. "Here there be tigers" the old explorers used to put on the maps. That warning applies most to the territory between the ears and inside the heart.

To think that you could come inside this wooden box and talk to another human being about the things you could never tell anyone else . . .

"Holy shit," I whisper.

"Smoky . . ."

"Oh my God."

Immerse yourself in the environment. I sure as shit had done that. And the answer had been staring me in the face. It was simple, it was direct, it was right.

"Smoky, are you all right?"

I stand up. Where did he get access to their secrets? Where else?

"Father, I think I have some bad news. I think someone else has been inside your confessional, and I'm not talking about God."

29

"IT IS KIND OF A PERFECT ENVIRONMENT FOR PLANTING A

"IT IS KIND OF A PERFECT ENVIRONMENT FOR PLANTING A bug," Alan observes. "It's dark inside, and people have their attention fixed on themselves, not on what's around them."

We're standing just outside the confessional. I'd rushed out with my tears still drying on my face.

It makes sense. We'd looked at the idea of support groups, AA meetings, things like that, but why cast such a wide and imperfect net, if secrets were what you were after? The Preacher was all about religion. If you're a religious person, who do you tell your deepest, darkest secrets to, the kinds of secrets we've been seeing on those video clips?

Your priest.

You close that confessional door and let it all hang out. I had, and I was the ultimate lapsed Catholic. The obvious worry in terms of confidentiality would be the priest, that's where the penitents' concerns would lie, not on the esoteric possibility of someone bugging the confessional.

Father Yates paces back and forth. He is troubled, angry, perhaps a little sick. I understand. I think about what we just did in there, and I shiver a little thinking about someone else listening in. It must be ten times worse for him, because he'll feel responsible.

"If this is true, it's terrible, just terrible," he mutters. "Parishioners won't feel safe coming to confession. The ones that have are going to feel betrayed. There will be crises of faith."

The poor man looks more agitated and upset than anytime since I met him. It's disturbing; I've become used to the comfort of his unflappability.

"Father, I need to ask you something."

He stops pacing. He runs a hand through his hair.

"Of course. Anything."

"I need confirmation. You said you hadn't watched any of the video clips of his victims. What about the one of Rosemary? He included that in his initial 'thesis.'"

"Absolutely not. I skipped through it. I couldn't watch that."

"I need to ask you about the secret she revealed in that clip. It was something pretty bad, and it was something he already knew. I'm going to tell you what it was, and I need to know if she revealed it to you in confession."

"I can't break the seal of confession," he protests. "Her death doesn't absolve me of that."

"Come on, Father! Even if it helps to catch her murderer? He's told us he's going to kill a child soon if we don't catch him!" I stab a finger at him. "You don't get off the hook that easy. This is a difficult issue for you, I understand, maybe some advanced canonical interpretation is required, but you need to take a hard look at the right and wrong here. Her big secret is already sitting out there on the Internet for everyone to see. How can you make that worse? Seems to me you can only make it better."

"Really?" His voice is harsh. "Let me ask you something, Smoky. If you died tomorrow, would you want me to reveal what we just talked about inside the confessional?"

The question takes me aback. My immediate, visceral response: *Fuck no.*

Touché, Father.

"Under normal circumstances, of course not. But if I'd been murdered like Rosemary? Forced to tell it all again, and then had it exposed to the world?" I move in close to him, make him look down to meet my eyes. "I'd want you to do whatever it took to bring that fucker to justice."

I can see the struggle going on inside him, can understand it. Father Yates is a man of conviction, a true believer who practices what he preaches. He lives his life by certain inviolate concepts. The stability of those concepts, the black and white of them, are what keeps him anchored to his faith while he toils away in the gray areas. The Rosemarys of the world are complicated. Dealing with them must be difficult. I can understand his need for certainties.

"Fine, tell me," he says. "If I think your theory has merit, I'll give you a sign. I won't speak directly to the content of Rosemary's confession, but I will give you a sign."

I can see that even this compromise has cost him.

"Thank you, Father."

I tell him about Rosemary having sex with her brother, and about how Dylan then took his own life. Father Yates's face is a mask throughout. When I finish, he looks right into my eyes and makes the sign of the cross.

"In the name of the Father, the Son, and the Holy Spirit," he murmurs. "Amen."

Excitement thrills through me, overtaking everything else.

"I need access to the confessional tomorrow, Father. First thing in the morning. I'm going to get someone over here to sweep the confessional booth and the rest of your church for bugs."

He sighs. "Of course."

"Alan, can you give us a moment?"

My friend nods. "I'll meet you out by the car."

When we're alone, I gesture to the front pew. "Take a seat, Father."

He does. I sit down beside him.

"I know this is bad for you."

He's gazing at Jesus again. He doesn't seem to be finding that same peace and contentment I'd seen earlier.

"Do you?" he asks. "Do you really?"

"Yes. You feel violated. You feel like the one thing you could always count on has been shattered."

He turns to look at me, still troubled but intrigued. "That's a fair assessment."

"I know all about it. My profession betrayed me, led a killer to my house who took away my family and my face." I open my jacket to show him my weapon. "I always believed in my gun and my FBI ID. I was sure they'd keep me safe. I was certain of it, no doubt allowed." I shrug. "I was wrong."

"So what do you do then, when that happens?"

"You go to sleep, wake up the next morning, and get back to work. The work matters, Father."

He smiles now, and I'm glad to see it. He's still sad, but this is better.

"You're saying that my work matters, Smoky. Does that mean you've reconciled with God?"

"Don't get ahead of yourself. I'm still plenty pissed at God. I don't know about"—I gesture to indicate the church that surrounds us— "all of this. What I do know is you helped me. Real help, no bullshit. So yes, if that's any indicator of what you do, your work matters."

Those troubled eyes, again. "I let the devil into my church."

"So? The first time you get knocked down you give up? Where's the tough guy from Detroit? Yes, it's fucked up. Acknowledge it, take a drink or pray or whatever it is that priests do to blow off steam, and then get back to work."

Another smile. I get the feeling it's in spite of himself. "I'll consider what you're saying. In the meantime, you need to stop swearing in my church, Smoky."

"I'll promise to stop swearing if you promise to stop feeling sorry for yourself."

He actually laughs. "It's a deal." His face gets somber. "Please catch this man."

"I'll catch him."

"Good. Now, leave me alone. I need to pray."

ALAN IS LEANING UP AGAINST the car, staring up at the starless LA sky.

"Ministering to the minister?" he asks.

"He's okay."

"How do you want to play this?"

I glance at my watch. It's after eleven.

"Let's wrap it up for tonight. I'll call Callie and James and tell them to go home. We'll hit the ground running in the morning."

"Sounds good to me. I'm beat. You call, I'll drive."

* * *

"MR. HARRISON BESTER IS APPARENTLY not a security-conscious Internet user," Callie says. "I'm sitting in front of his home right now, choosing the paper stock for my wedding invitations."

"Did the surveillance show up yet?"

"No."

"They'll be there soon, I imagine. I need you to stay put until they arrive."

She emits a long, loud, noisy sigh. "You really have no respect for the pressure I'm under. Planning a wedding, working this case, riding herd on Kirby, and trying to fit in my nightly sex-a-thon with Sam. Very stressful."

"Poor baby." I smile.

"Thank you, honey-love. That's all I need, just a little sympathy now and again. How did it go with Father Yates?"

"It was positively enlightening. I'll fill you in tomorrow. We need to start early."

"I'LL GO TO BED WHEN I feel like it, thanks. You're my superior, not my mother."

"Have it your way, James. I have a lead, though, a good one. I want everyone in early."

"I'm always early," he retorts, and then hangs up.

I shake my head as I close the phone.

"How's Damien?" Alan asks.

"Charming, as always."

"You know what the strangest thing is for me about James being gay?"

"The idea of him being intimate with anyone?"

He grins. "That's right. Before he said he was gay, I honestly kind of thought of him as a eunuch. Sexless. I can't imagine anyone putting up with his shit long enough to hop in the sack with him."

"Takes all kinds to make the world go round."

"I'm glad about it."

"Why?"

"He's an irritating little fucker, and sometimes I want to punch his lights out, but he's still family. I'm glad he's got something going on in his life besides the j-o-b."

I smile at him as he drives. "You're a big old softie, Alan."

"Don't tell anyone. Hey, I was watching Father Yates when you were telling him about Rosemary and the video clip. The guy is good. Really good. I couldn't read his reaction at all."

Alan reads people the way others read books. Pupil dilation, changes in breathing pattern, even something simple like the nervous turning of a ring around a finger, all have their place in ferreting out the truth. He's saying that Father Yates is very, very good at restraining these reactions.

"Kind of interesting," Alan observes. "Maybe we should take a closer look at the priest. That kind of control is rare unless you've been trained to do it."

"He's not the guy," I say.

"You sure?"

I shouldn't be. I've been fooled before, trusting angels who turned out to be devils in disguise. But I am, this time.

"I'm sure."

"You seeing things clearly on this one?"

This is as close as Alan will ever get to asking me what happened inside that confessional booth. He knows to leave it alone, just as I would if our roles were reversed.

"Go ahead and pull his background, Alan. Dot the i's. But I'm telling you, he's not our guy."

"Okay, okay." He goes quiet as we continue to drive through the darkness. The city lights are everywhere, like dirty diamonds on a gray velvet background. This is LA, beautiful and flawed. Rough-cut forever, somehow endearing in all its shallow fumbling for greatness. "So does this mean you're going to start going to Mass and taking Communion and all that stuff?" he asks.

"Watch that crazy talk. He helped me. He didn't fix things between me and God. I have a feeling by the time this case is over I'll have had about all the Catholicism I can stand for a while."

"Amen to that."

"What about you?"

"I haven't talked to God since the second time I saw a dead baby."

We see too much, doing what we do. The problem with believing in God, for us, is this: if God is real, either the devil's got him on the run, or he just doesn't give a damn. No God is better than a God that doesn't care.

30

"WELCOME BACK, TRAVELER," I SAY TO MYSELF AS I WALK through my door.

The words don't seem quite as futile as they had the day before. My confession left me feeling hollow, but not in a bad way. This is not a black hole inside me. It's an empty table, waiting to be set.

What do I place on you? New china or the old silverware, handed down?

A little bit of both, I think.

I open up my phone and call Tommy.

"Hey," he answers.

"Were you sleeping?"

"Nope. I was thinking about you, actually."

"Good. Because I'm ready to talk, and I need to tell you something. Bonnie is staying at Alan and Elaina's. Can you come over?"

"Silly question," he says. "See you soon."

HE SHOWS UP AT MY door looking more rumpled than I've ever seen him. Tommy is not a neat freak, I've never gotten the idea that he obsesses over himself at the mirror, but he's always brushed and shaven and smelling of soap. Right now he's sporting a growth of stubble, his hair looks like it received only haphazard attention, and his shirt has a tiny food stain on the front. I reach out and touch his cheek with my palm.

"You okay? You look like hell."

"I've been waiting to hear from you."

I step back, dumbfounded. "This is about me?"

His smile is lopsided. "Strong and silent is a cliché, Smoky. I'm Latin, we wear our hearts on our sleeves. I feel things with all of me or none of me." He shrugs. "It's a problem sometimes."

I stroke his cheek again, amazed at the idea of this man losing sleep and peace of mind over me.

That's because you've been thinking you're worthless for a long time, my voice-friend is kind enough to point out. And maybe he'll agree once you tell him what you told Father Yates.

"You want a beer?" I ask.

"Sure. But I might end up sleeping on your couch if I do. I've already been partaking; I was fine to drive here, but maybe not after one more."

I smile at him. "I'll take that chance."

I grab us each a beer from the fridge and sit down on the couch, my legs curled under me. I pick at the label on the bottle with a thumbnail.

"I need to tell you something, Tommy. It's something I did, and it's pretty bad. I'm afraid that once I do, you're not going to want me anymore."

He gazes at me with those dark eyes and takes a thoughtful swig of his beer.

"Is it something you have to tell me?"

I frown. "What do you mean?"

"It's okay to keep some secrets, that's what I mean. I don't need to know everything about your past to love you right now."

The hand holding my bottle trembles for a moment. "I agree with that for the most part. But I need to tell you this. This is the thing that makes me feel like . . ." I search for the words. "Like I'm not the person people think I am."

Simple, succinct. He takes another swig, puts the bottle down on the coffee table, and takes my beer from me and places it next to his. He grabs my hands and traps them between his own. He looks into my eyes.

"So tell me," he says.

And I do. I tell him all of it. How I felt lying in that hospital bed in the dark. The desire to die. The ultimate selfishness, killing my baby so it wouldn't prevent me from putting a bullet through my head. He listens as I talk, doesn't say a word, doesn't stop holding my hands, doesn't turn away. When I finish, he is silent for a time.

"Say something," I whisper.

He brings my hands up to his lips and he kisses them slowly. It's not a sexual act, not even a sensual one, but it's very intimate and comfortable. He kisses every finger on the knuckle, ends with the thumb. Turns my hands over and kisses my palms with dry lips, then traces the lines in them with a finger. He brushes a lock of hair behind my ear, and smiles.

"I love you, Smoky. Maybe you were expecting something else, but that's the something I have to say. I need you with me, and not halfway. I want all of you, every inch, every scar, every perfect part, and all the defects too."

"Are . . . are you sure? I'm not easy, Tommy. Ten times in the last two years I've told myself I was all done with my past, with the things that happened to me. I'm a lot better, it's true, but I always seem to find some new pocket of fucked-up-ness waiting to mess me up. What if that never changes? You want to love someone who might always have a little bit of her past she can't let go of?"

"You are who you are because of everything that's happened in your life up to this point, Smoky. Not just the good things. I love the you that you are right now."

"And Bonnie?"

"I love her too, and she knows it."

"She does?"

"She told me she loved me a few months ago. We were watching cartoons, and she said, 'Tommy, you know I love you, right?'" He shakes his head, bemused. "She didn't even take her eyes off the TV. I acted like it was no big deal, of course I knew, and I told her I loved her too. We kept watching cartoons like nothing had happened."

"Wow." I grin. "You have all the bases covered."

He goes back to turning my hands over in his. His hands are rough, with the calluses and oversized knuckles of a boxer.

"I'm a decent guy, Smoky. I don't cheat. I'm essentially honest. I'm loyal. But I have my moments. I can be arrogant sometimes, truly self-righteous. It doesn't happen often, but when it does, I can guarantee you it'll make you crazy."

"I know you're not perfect, Tommy. You don't have to do this."

"Let me finish. I don't do drugs and I don't smoke, but once or twice a year I do like to get good and drunk. Maybe I shouldn't, but I do. It's my one excess. You've never really seen me like that."

"I'm sure I can handle it."

"I'm sure you can too, but you need to know about it. When I get that drunk, I get horny, but the sex is selfish, and of course I'll throw a tantrum when you tell me you're not interested in sleeping with a drunk. But I'll feel bad about it the next morning."

"What else?"

He's silent. Tracing my palms, over and over and over. "I've killed five people doing my job, Smoky. At least twice I've been pretty happy about it. I'm not talking about simple satisfaction, I'm talking about something that fell just shy of joy." He looks back up at me. "Of all my faults, that's probably the one that bothers me the most."

I examine this man, finding some of myself in him. For me, Tommy has always been strong but gentle, slow to anger, prone to thinking before acting. These things are true, but he also has a little bit of savage in him, the ability to get his hands sticky with the blood of an enemy and feel well satisfied about it.

"I can tell you from experience, so long as it still bothers you, you're probably okay."

"That's what I tell myself."

"Me too." Our eyes meet again. "I do love you, Tommy."

Saying the words brings me a kind of bone-shuddering relief. I've been walking under a crushing weight, the whole time thinking I was flying. This isn't the love Matt and I had. Matt met me before I was a killer, he knew me as a child, gave me my very first kiss. He was my tether to the world outside what I do, he and Alexa, and that was a beautiful thing.

Life has hacked away at me with an axe since then. Parts of me have been amputated or crippled. I've done terrible things to men who probably deserved it, and I have probably enjoyed doing these things far too much at times. I've observed the monsters, and been

observed by them. They came away unchanged. But me? There's a little bit of monster in me now, and I doubt I'll ever get rid of it.

Tommy sees that in me, and in himself, and shares the burden.
The understanding that all that darkness is like a drug, that taking
life gives you a feeling of power like no other, that the line between
good and bad can be microscopic at times.

"Well, cool," he replies, grinning at his own understatement.

"But I have one other surprise to pull on you," I say. "You might
not like it."

"What's that?"

"I want everything, Tommy. The whole shebang. I want my home
back. So what I'm saying is, as long as all this love is in the air, then I
want us to live together too."

He blinks in surprise. For a moment I'm afraid. Then his lips
curve into a smile. He kisses me.

"I can agree to that."

My turn to blink. "Really? Just like that?"

"We've been together two years, Smoky. I wouldn't call it sudden."

"Good point. So that's a yes?"

"Of course it's a yes."

He takes my face in his and the kiss he gives me this time contains
all the passion we've been withholding.

I come away breathless and needy. "Now that the love stuff is out
of the way, can we get down to the fucking?" I growl.

"So romantic," he murmurs, kissing my neck, feeling my breasts.

I pull his head away and make him look at me. "I mean it, Tommy.
The last two days have been rough. I don't need tender loving tonight. Think cat in heat."

He answers with action, sweeping me into his arms and heading
up the stairs to the bedroom. He dumps me on the bed without ceremony and starts to get undressed. I do the same, overwhelmed with
need and the simplest desire of all: closeness.

Within the half hour, I am using God's name in proximity to the
profane again, as I reach for more, more, more. In this moment, all
things considered, I somehow don't think He'll mind.

31

across my belly and bedsheets that smelled of last night's sex.

Most of all, I woke up happy. I was at the crest of a case that was about to get even more explosive, chasing a killer with the biggest body count of my career, and I felt good. Focused. Ready for the challenge.

I bounded from bed to the shower, washing Tommy off me with some regret. I was almost done when he joined me. He bumped against me with his morning erection.

"I know what you want for breakfast," I said, moving into him. "Make it quick. I have to get in early today."

He obliged with gusto and ten minutes later he was washing me off him while I ransacked my closet for clothes to wear. I pulled my hair back into its customary ponytail, and whistled while I fastened the straps on my shoes. Tommy appeared at the door of the bathroom, toweling his hair. I took a moment to look him over from head to toe.

"Yum, yum," I said, and he laughed.

"You out the door?"

I checked my watch and bounced off the bed. I went to him, leaning up to give him a kiss on the lips while letting my hand luxuriate in his chest hair for a moment.

"Yes, gotta run." I headed to the door of the bedroom before remembering the most important thing. I turned around. "I love you," I said.

He grinned, and that became the most beautiful part of him to me. "I love you too. Call me later."

I agreed by blowing him a kiss and went downstairs, inhaled a cup of coffee, and hit the road.

I'm almost to work now, and I allow myself a moment to bask in the fact that I've told a man that I love him again, and meant it. I remember Callie's smiling when she told me she was sure about Sam.

You were right, Callie. It does feel great. I'd forgotten.

The internal voice that'd been bugging me is nowhere to be found. Matt's ghost isn't around right now, though I'm sure he'll show up again at some point. I understand that hoping to dispel him and Alexa permanently is an unrealistic expectation. They'll show up forever, off and on, and not always in a good way. I imagine they'll be there at my deathbed.

It occurs to me that I've been helped by a monster once again, however indirectly. The Preacher had preached about the value of truth. I'd done what he said and sure enough, I was better for it.

I am not grateful.

I ARRIVE TO FIND JAMES already there, along with Jezebel.

"Just who I wanted to see," I say. "I think I know how he's been getting his information."

I explain.

"It makes sense," James agrees. "It fits with the religious paradigm. He likes technology. Infiltrating support groups and hoping to strike up a conversation with the right victim is too hit and miss; bugging the confessionals would be precision targeting."

"If I'm right, the common denominator to all victims will be that they were practicing Catholics. We need to figure out a way to verify that without giving away the reason we want to know."

"What do we want to know?" Callie enters with her coffee in one hand, donuts in the other. Alan follows behind her.

I lay out my hypothesis again.

"Me oh my," she says when I finish. "That's going to make some waves."

"I want to avoid that if we can."

James frowns. "There's an ethical question here. We have some idea of how he chooses his victims. Perhaps we should go public with this, to warn anyone who's come clean on something major in confession."

It's an interesting point, and one I hadn't considered.

"We'll cross that bridge when we come to it," I say. "For now, we need to find out if the victims were Catholic. If they are, then we can strategize from there."

"We could do it as a questionnaire," Jezebel muses. "Call the families and ask them a series of general questions, tell them we're just looking for any and all information that might help. One of the questions could address religion. It won't raise any flags that way."

"Great idea," I say. "Draft it with James right now."

"Callie, I need you to go over to the Redeemer. Father Yates is expecting us. We need to sweep the confessional for bugs."

"That's not really my forté. Forensics, not electronics, remember?"

"Call Tommy. He's an expert in the area. He can tell you what you need."

She raises an eyebrow. "Are you two speaking again?"

"You could say that."

"I thought you had that self-satisfied 'I've just been laid' aura about you," she says.

"It's a lot more interesting than that, but I'll tell you later, not now."

She grabs her coffee and her purse, points a finger at me. "Don't think I'll forget."

"Last of my worries. Oh, and, Callie?" She stops and turns. "Call me right away with what you find."

Because I'd like to be sure my own confession isn't sitting on a tape somewhere, I don't say out loud.

I think it's unlikely; the smart money is on them removing the bugs once they finish up, so as to avoid detection, but better safe than stupid, Mom always said.

She tips me a two-finger salute.

"What about me?" Alan asks.

The office door flies open before I can answer. AD Jones walks in. His face is pale.

"We're too late."

* * *

"VALERIE CAVANAUGH, AGE TEN. FOUND dead in her bedroom this morning. Stuck in the side like the others."

We're in the AD's office. Alan is seated. I am pacing, back and forth. I want to scream or shoot something; I'm sick with guilt.

"Do we know if she's Catholic?"

AD Jones frowns. "What does that have to do with it?"

I haven't had time to bring him up to speed on my theory. I do so now.

"It would explain everything," he agrees. "How he gets his information, the religious tie-in. It all fits."

"I want to keep it under wraps, for now." I explain about the questionnaire.

"Good. Get them going on that and then I want you and Alan to head over to the Cavanaugh home."

"Could be a copycat," Alan says. "Using it for cover."

"The parents?" I ask.

He shrugs. "Anything's possible."

I have to allow that he could be right. One of the parents, or both, could have seen the news coverage about the Preacher and killed little Valerie in the same way, hoping to blame it on our serial killer. Most child victims are murdered by a parent.

But I don't think so. Not this time.

"Be discreet with that theory," AD Jones orders. "As I understand, they had to sedate the mom."

"THE FORMAT IS SIMPLE," JEZEBEL says as I read the questionnaire. "We'll keep two people on the tip line. We've confirmed the identities of all the victims anyway. James and I will supervise the other four and we'll start calling the families. It will take us into the late afternoon, but we'll get it done."

"This is good," I say.

The questions are designed to fit with the cover story of collecting "background" information on the victims. They are broad and innocuous. "Did she ever attend college?" "Did she have any children?" "What social groups was she a part of?" And, buried among them all, the question we really want answered: "What, if any, religion did she practice?"

"The media won't alert on this," Jezebel says, "and the families will be eager, for the most part, to answer."

"Do it."

"THERE ARE NO BUGS IN this church, hallelujah," Callie tells me on the phone. "However, I did find a spot inside the confessional that looks to have been wood-puttied recently."

"Prints?" I ask, hoping without really expecting.

"Sorry, no. And the wood putty, while intriguing, isn't decisive. There's no way for me to confirm how long it's been there. Could be months, could be years."

"Not days?" I ask, thinking again of my own confession.

"No, older than that."

"Big coincidence that it's there at all," I say.

"What do you want me to do?"

"I want you to meet us at a crime scene." I explain.

She's silent.

"He did it? A child?"

"Looks that way."

"Give me the address."

32

THE CAVANAUGHS LIVE IN ONE OF THE SUBURBS OF BURBANK, in a two-story home built in the early eighties that has since been updated. It's on one of those small residential streets that are unique to Los Angeles; quiet, secluded, tree lined, but just three blocks away it's all concrete and steel and rush, rush, rush.

"Media vultures are already circling," Alan observes.

"Young, white, middle-class, female, and dead," I say. "That's a lead story anywhere in the USA."

We are let in past the cordons put up to keep the media at bay. Neighbors stand outside on their lawns, horrified at the idea that a monster came so close, thankful he didn't choose their child, and unable to look away.

"Three black and whites," Alan points out. "Probably crowd control. Two unmarkeds. One's a town car, probably brass come out because of the media. The other will be the detectives in charge." He shakes his head. "Wouldn't want to be them right now."

I snort. "Them? What about us?"

"It's different when you're a cop. We're the FBI. We can do our thing here and walk away. These detectives have to stay right here in the limelight."

"I never looked at it like that."

"How do you want to do this?"

I examine the scene. Most of the media is involved in setup shots, filming the home, the surrounds, the police presence. Helicopters circle above. News reporters clutch their microphones and practice snappy summations of what they know so far. It's not them I'm worried about right now. I continue scanning and find what I was afraid of.

"Shoot," I mutter. "We have some smart ones."

I'm referring to what I consider the "real newspeople," the ones who spend more time looking than talking, noses to the air, sniffing for the slightest scent of the real story. The one I spotted is a woman. She's a blonde, in her mid-thirties, well dressed in a tailored jacket and matching dark slacks. She's not watching the house, but is looking right at our car. I can see her talking to her cameraman, and pointing toward us. She can't have seen who we are through the tinted windows, but somehow she knows anyway.

"Can't stay away from the cameras on this one forever," Alan says.

"I guess not." I sigh. "Let's just find whoever's in charge, see what we need to see, and get out of here."

We exit the car and head up the walk. I try and keep my face turned away from the cameras, but give up when I remember they'll just catch me coming out. We reach the door and are stopped by a cop in uniform.

Older, I think, more experienced. They want someone who can think on his feet standing post here.

"What's up, Alan?" the cop asks, unsmiling.

He's a big guy. Not as big as Alan, but broad. He has white hair and a rough, heavy face. I'd peg him as a meathead if not for the eyes. They're sharp, intelligent, and unfriendly.

"Need to see whoever's running the show, Ron," Alan replies.

The cop sneers a little. "What does the FBI want with this scene? Isn't this a little beneath you now?"

Alan smiles. It's as unfriendly as Ron's eyes. "Still an asshole, I see. And still blaming me for getting you busted back to uniform."

The sneer threatens to become a snarl. I decide it's time for me to step in.

"Hey—Ron, is it? You know who I am?"

He tears his eyes away from Alan with some reluctance. He examines my face, nods.

"I know you."

"Then you know there's only one reason I'm here. That dead little girl. Can you help me out, and maybe pick this up with Alan at a later date?"

His eyes flick back and forth between us. He gives off a grumbling sigh. "Hang on." He unholsters his radio and presses the transmit button. "Detective Alvarez?"

A moment's pause and a reply comes back. "Go."

"I got two feebs out here. Alan Washington and Smoky Barrett. They're asking for access."

A longer pause this time. "Let 'em in."

"Roger that."

Ron reholsters his radio and opens the door to the home without another word. Those hostile eyes follow Alan all the way in.

"What was that about?" I ask once we're inside the foyer.

"Short version? Ron Briscoe was a homicide detective. Pretty good one. He ran a case where a guy was strangling little girls. He knew who the guy was, but couldn't get the evidence he needed. So he cut corners. Planted evidence. I found out about it and spoke up. The guy walked and Briscoe got busted back to uniform."

"What happened to the bad guy?"

"The father of one of the victims blew the perp's brains out. Father's in prison now."

I stare at my friend, fascinated and aghast at this revelation. He'd said it all so matter-of-factly, but I know it has to be a burden for him.

"Here comes a suit," Alan murmurs to me. "Police Commissioner Daniels himself."

Fred Daniels has been the LAPD commissioner for over ten years now. He's in his late fifties, but remains more vital than men younger than him. He's tall and thin, with a grizzled, military haircut and the hard face of a drill sergeant. He's reputed to walk the line between fair and ruthless, with ruthless winning more often than not. He approaches us and puts out a hand to shake mine.

"Agent Barrett," he says.

"Commissioner."

He shakes Alan's hand as well.

"You used to be LAPD, Agent Washington, is that right?"

"Ten years in homicide, Commissioner."

"Nice to know some of the people at the FBI come from the streets. No offense, Agent Barrett."

"None taken."

"You're here because you think this is connected with the Preacher?"

Straight to business.

"We're examining the possibility," I reply.

"Crime scene is upstairs," he says, pointing to the staircase. "Alvarez is a good detective. Don't step on his toes." He'd been holding his police cap under his arm. He pulls it out and fits it onto his head. "I'm going to go feed all the piranhas with cameras."

He heads out the door, almost running into Callie as he leaves.

"Wooo, the commissioner," she breathes, batting her eyes in faux-groupie fashion. "I feel special to be here already."

"Do you know Alvarez?" I ask Alan.

"Only his name."

I sigh. "There's no use in putting this off. Let's go find him and see the scene."

RAYMOND ALVAREZ IS A SHORT man, no more than five-five. He's handsome enough, and I see a wedding band through the latex glove covering his left hand. He's full of energy and he talks with his hands, pointing and gesturing.

"Dad's with Mom at the hospital. She freaked out. Started destroying the kitchen. Like, throwing chairs through the windows, smashing dishes. She cut up her hands pretty bad, bleeding all over the place, they had to forcibly sedate her."

"You see it?"

"Her? Yeah. Seemed real."

Sometimes the guilty feign hysteria to throw us off. It's difficult to do well. Real grief, the kind that comes from finding out that a loved one has been killed, is spontaneous and anything but rote. Some people scream, some wail, some go wooden, some faint dead away.

"Can we see Valerie?" I ask.

"This way," he says.

He doesn't ask why. There simply is no substitute for seeing the corpse at the scene of the crime. He leads us down the hall, past a master bedroom with beige carpet and white walls. The carpet continues everywhere, as do the walls; safe, unimaginative California at its best. We pass photos hung on the walls, every frame black, each one the same style. The Cavanaughs are a handsome couple, he with the short blond hair, she with the long blonde hair, both with the whitest teeth I've ever seen. They smile and show all those teeth in every photo. Beautiful people. A girl I assume to be Valerie appears in a number of them, also blonde and smiling with the white teeth passed down to her by her parents.

I catch my own cynicism and try to rein it in. There's nothing in any of these photos or those smiles that says their happiness was ungenuine or that the people themselves are shallow.

They're not smiling now, I think. It occurs to me that Alexa was ten when she died, that Bonnie was ten when she came into my life.

A magic number.

"Here we go. Glove up and put on the paper booties," Alvarez says, pointing to the boxes placed outside the room.

We each comply, and I smell that smell now, the singular mix of latex and blood.

We enter the room. It's pink everywhere, little princess to the max. The walls are pink, the bed is a canopy with frilly pink bedsheets and comforter. Various stuffed animals decorate both bed and floor. There's a small desk—pink—with a computer set up on it. The monitor, I note, is on.

Valerie is what commands our attention, the attention of everyone in this room. She is lying on her back, arms folded across her chest. Her eyes are open wide. Her blonde hair fans out around her head. Blood has run from the hole in her side to soak the pink bedding and the beige carpet with a bright contrast of burgundy. Her mouth is closed, the white teeth not in evidence here.

"She's naked," Alan observes.

"The posing is still not sexual," I point out. "It's more like he's sending them out as they came in."

"Yeah."

I turn to Alvarez. "Who found her?"

"The dad. She didn't come downstairs for breakfast, he came up to check on her, found her this way."

"The father didn't touch her," Callie says. "Strange."

She refers to the fact that Valerie remains posed as she died, something we can tell by the pattern of blood flow from her side.

"I asked him about that," Alvarez responds. "He said he could tell she was dead. The way her eyes are open, and how white she is."

"I can see it," I admit.

There's no spark of life evident in Valerie. She has the appearance of a cold, soft mannequin.

"Evidence of a point of entry?" Alan asks.

"Two. There's a door that leads from the backyard into the garage, and there's a door that leads from the garage into the house. Both show evidence of skilled tampering. If he did it, he opened the gate that leads into the backyard, forced door number one, then door number two and gained access."

"No alarm system?" I ask.

"No. And no dog. Bad luck."

"Still, pretty bold," I say. "Coming in here at night, killing her while the parents were sleeping."

"That fit with your guy?" Alvarez asks.

"He's a risk-taker and he warned us he was going to kill a child."

He indicates the bed and Valerie.

"What about this? Does it seem authentic?"

"I only have two other scenes to compare it to. It presents the same, except for the age of the victim, which is troubling. We held something back regarding his MO." I tell him about the cross the Preacher inserts into the wounds postmortem. "If it's not there, this is a copycat."

"In which case we'll have to take a hard look at the parents." Alvarez sighs. "Great. I'm not sure which is better."

"Can we get this checked out now, honey-love?" Callie asks. "The coroner on-site?"

"He's out front getting the body wagon ready. I'll call him in."

"HOW FAR IN WAS THE cross placed in the other victims?"

Dr. Weems, the coroner, is a middle-aged man with a precise, fastidious air about him.

"Just under the skin, against the rib cage," Callie answers. "You should be able to feel it if you palpate."

"It would be irregular to remove it here," he muses.

"But not illegal," I point out, "and if you film it, you'll have things covered from an evidentiary standpoint. Time isn't on our side, Doctor."

To his credit, he doesn't hesitate for long. "Very well. Detective Alvarez, if you can get the crime scene recorder in here, I'll examine her and remove the cross if it exists."

Recording crime scenes and their processing with video cameras has become common practice in many investigations, especially the high-profile ones. It is a double-edged sword; if procedural mistakes are made, they're caught on camera and become fodder for defense counsel. The reverse is true as well, though; if the camera says it's so, it's so.

The man wielding the small camera is introduced as Jeff, a young, brown-haired man who doesn't look old enough to be here. He's unfazed, however; he turns the camera on Valerie's corpse without blinking.

Dr. Weems kneels down to examine the wound in Valerie's side.

"Appears to be a hole, approximately one-half inch in diameter, not ragged. The instrument used would have been pointed but very sharp. Incision marks extend out from the sides of the initial puncture. These are clean cuts, probably made by a scalpel or similar blade." He uses his fingers to feel around the wound, gently. "I can feel a hard object underneath the skin."

Adrenaline rushes through me. I am excited, then ashamed by that excitement. Her death should have affected me for longer. All I can think about now is what she can give me, not what was taken from her.

Dr. Weems looks up and into the camera. "Photographs have already been taken of the wound pattern. I'm going to try and retrieve the item." He grabs a small satchel I hadn't noticed before. It's a black medical bag. It looks like a throwback to the 1950s.

His kit, I think.

I find this self-conscious nod to style via retro accessory a little creepy. Things that deal in the dead should have their aesthetics confined to function.

He opens it up and hunts through it until he finds what amounts to an oversized pair of tweezers.

"If anyone here is squeamish," he says, bending toward the wound, "please look away or leave. We don't need vomit contaminating the crime scene."

No one moves. Jeff films away, unperturbed.

Dr. Weems sticks the tweezers into the hole without hesitation or ceremony.

"I'm contacting a hard object," he confirms. "I need to rotate it to pull it out without damaging the skin further. Wait a moment . . . there." He pulls the tweezers out slowly.

"Son of a bitch," Alan breathes.

A silver cross. It has the same approximate dimensions as the others.

Weems deposits the cross into an evidence bag after photographs and video have been taken.

"So it is your guy," Alvarez says.

"It appears that way," I agree. "The question now is: Why her? He goes for people with big secrets. What kind of a secret could a ten-year-old girl have?"

"I had a fair number by the time I was ten," Callie says. "But then, I was always ahead of my time."

My cell phone chimes.

"Barrett."

"It's James. Three things. We're moving well on questioning the families. So far, it's a hundred percent on the victims as practicing Catholics."

Another adrenaline rush.

"That's excellent, James. What else?"

"We need to consider pulling surveillance from the Bester home. I checked into his whereabouts during the Lisa Reid murder. He was on a business trip in San Francisco."

I frown. "We need more than that . . ."

"More ties into the third thing."

"Go on."

"Someone from Computer Crimes has been coordinating with the user-tube staff every half-hour or so to check for attempted new postings by the Preacher."

"And?"

"They caught one. Concerning Valerie Cavanaugh."

"Damn it!" I rub my temples.

"Back to Bester: this new clip wasn't posted from his IP. Surveillance says he was at home and in bed when Valerie Cavanaugh was killed. It's not him, Smoky."

I sigh. "Agreed. Pull the detail." I lean forward a little, feeling something inside me narrow to a focus. "Now, tell me about this new clip."

He pauses. A little too long, I feel. "It's different. He didn't film her just before killing her."

I'm perplexed. "I don't understand."

"I e-mailed you the clip. Watch it. It's bad, very bad. It's going to devastate this family."

The usual acerbity is absent from James's demeanor. He sounds quiet, troubled. This, more than anything else, replaces that rush with a slight chill.

"How bad?"

That too-long pause again.

"It's a nightmare."

THE CAVANAUGHS HAVE A WIRELESS Internet connection and Callie has her laptop, so we find ourselves in the living room, checking my e-mail and downloading the clip James had sent me.

I am sitting next to Callie on the couch. Alan is next to her, Alvarez stands behind us all.

"Ready?" she asks.

I nod. "Go ahead."

She clicks to begin and the familiar black screen and white lettering goes by. We arrive at the hands and the rosary, the stark light and the spare wooden table.

"I realize this is, now, most likely going straight to law enforcement officials," he begins. "A temporary problem, let me assure you. There are too many ways to get the truth out. Having said that, let us discuss the relationship of truth and time, as it is apropos here. Truth is not concerned with age. A child is a child, yes, but a soul is a soul is a soul, and truth applies to all. The devil can come in many guises, and whether you are ten or eighty, confession and contrition will always be your one and only salvation. And that is the purpose of this particular part of my opus, to demonstrate two things: truth is ageless, but that truth without contrition is a lie all its own." He rubs the rosary with a thumb. "Valerie Cavanaugh comes from a good family. She has God-fearing parents. They demand much from her, and by all appearances, she has provided. Valerie has always been a straight-A student. She practices her piano lesson one hour a day, every day. She is on a swim team, and has brought home trophies. She has been active with her parents in volunteer activities, helping those less fortunate."

"All true," Alvarez notes.

"Appearances can be deceiving," the Preacher continues. "And confession to the greatest crimes without remorse makes a lie of confession itself."

THE SINS
of
VALERIE CAVANAUGH

33

"LOOK AT ME, KITTY," VALERIE SAYS.

The cat turns toward her voice, meows once. The cat has beautiful green eyes and Valerie smiles.

"Good kitty," she says, and pets the cat behind the ears.

It's a pretty nice day. The sun is out but the heat isn't oppressive. Daddy calls it a "California fall." There's a slight breeze. Valerie closes her eyes and turns her face up to the sky, letting the breeze cool her skin and ruffle her hair with its wind-fingers. She continues to rub the cat behind the ears.

Valerie is in the backyard of her house. Mommy and Daddy are out for the day, and Emma, the babysitter, is snoozing on the couch. It's one of the few times Valerie finds herself alone, and she cherishes the moment.

The backyard is large. They have a patio and a pool and a lot of green green grass. Mommy spent a lot of time designing the land-scaping herself and supervising the workers. (Do things halfway and you'll end up a halfway person, Mommy always says.) Valerie is sitting behind a line of hedges that forms a barrier between the rest of the yard and one of the tall, painted cinder-block walls that divides them from the world outside.

"Good kitty," she murmurs again.

The cat meows. It's not a happy meow, and Valerie can't really blame the poor kitty. She's all wrapped up in a towel, after all.

"Sorry, kitty," she says, "but I can't have you scratching me all up."

Valerie wants to wait longer, to enjoy the solitude for a few moments more, but she knows she can't count on Emma sleeping forever. She sighs.

"Better get to it, kitty. Do things halfway and you'll be a halfway person."

She places the towel-wrapped cat on its back in her lap and puts her hands around the cat's neck. She begins to squeeze.

She doesn't squeeze too hard or too fast—she doesn't want the kitty to die too quick, after all. Part of the fun is savoring the moment.

Valerie keeps her eyes on the cat's eyes the entire time. She's not sure what it is she's looking for. Maybe that exact moment of death, when the spark of life goes out. Who knows? But it's an endless source of fascination. *Something* happens in there, that's for sure!

She can feel the cat struggling against her, trying to escape the towel.

Sorry, kitty, but I know what I'm doing. You'll never get free.

She giggles, once.

Valerie is aware of her heart beating fast in her chest. There's a somewhat undefinable sensation running through her. A kind of excitement she can't classify. She doesn't try all that hard to figure it out. The doing of the thing and the feeling it gives her is enough.

The cat's struggles become frantic. Valerie's heart beats and that excitement keeps pace. Another moment passes, and the cat expires. Valerie continues to squeeze, unaware that her eyes are wide and that her tongue is protruding from between her lips.

The moment passes. The cat is seeing nothing. Valerie relaxes her grip. She'd been holding her breath; she exhales.

"Good kitty," she says again, and scratches the dead cat behind the ears.

She likes that there is no meow in response now. She likes that a lot.

Valerie gives herself a minute to relax, to luxuriate in this brief moment of being her true self.

It's hard acting like a normal girl all the time, she reflects. This is when I feel the most free.

But Valerie knows, even at ten, that she has to keep her real face hidden. She's been very careful, since she started killing the cats. She's paced herself, and she's made sure to bury the bodies here, behind the hedge. It's been difficult, true, but she can wait. She's seen the future. She'll get older, and someday she'll have a lot more freedom. Some-day, she thinks, she'll even be able to drive.

Who knows what she'll be able to start killing then?

She's unaware that these thoughts have brought a grin to her face. Those white teeth flash in the sun and her blonde hair flutters in the breeze, and she pets the dead cat in her lap as she dreams.

"JESUS CHRIST," ALAN MUTTERS.

I'm silent, as is Callie.

It was obvious that Valerie was unaware she was being videotaped. The video itself was black-and-white and high quality. The angle it had been shot at gives me an idea. I stand up and march to the sliding glass door leading into the backyard.

Once outside, I stand and look. I see the pool, clean and blue. The grass is green and cut and perfect. I see the row of hedges on the right and left. They form an unbroken line going from the front of the yard to the back on either side. There's about a one foot space between the hedges and the cinder-block walls that act as a fence.

Not much space, but enough for a ten-year-old.

I choose the line on the right and walk over. Short as I am, I have trouble seeing past the hedge tops, so I lean forward, placing my hands against the wall and stand on my tiptoes.

The grass ends at the hedges, which come all the way down to the ground. Beyond the hedge line is plain dirt. I can see little patches of turned earth that had been patted flat.

Eight or ten, I think. Probably all dead cats.

Valerie Cavanaugh, sweet blonde Valerie of the perfect hair and teeth, had been a little psychopath.

I close my eyes and recall the video, that angle. I open them again and turn to the right. I march along the hedge line to the end and lean forward. I see what I was looking for.

*   *   *

"**THERE'S A PINHOLE CAMERA PLACED** near the end of the hedge line," I say, walking back into the house. "She had no idea he was watching her."

"How'd he know where to put it?" Alvarez asks.

"Not sure," I lie.

Callie raises a single eyebrow but says nothing. Alan studies his fingernails.

"Let's finish the clip," I say, taking a seat again.

Callie had paused it when I went into the backyard. She hits play again now.

We watch as Valerie digs a hole with a gardening trowel. She removes the towel from around the dead cat. She holds the cat's corpse up by the scruff of its neck, stares into its eyes for a moment, shrugs, and drops it into the hole. She fills it back in and takes care to feather the dirt and pat it flat. She folds the towel. We see her face once before she stands up to exit the hedgerow. She looks blissful and beautiful, untroubled and at peace.

The video holds for a minute, recording the cinder-block wall, the hedges, that slightly turned earth, before cutting back to the Preacher and his ever-present rosary beads.

"You see?" he says. "Evil can be ageless. If evil can be ageless, then so can the necessity for truth. Take note, parents. Young Valerie was an extreme example, but she serves as a warning. What are your children doing that you'd least expect?"

He shifts his hands again, laying them flat on the table.

"To the second part of this particular lesson—the fact that lack of contrition can make confession itself a lie."

A still image appears. It's from the video of Valerie strangling the cat. He's plucked this image from the instant where her mask slipped the most. We see the wide eyes, the dark joy, the tip of her pink tongue in the corner of her mouth. It's a moment of ecstasy.

The Preacher continues talking as a voice-over, keeping this image of Valerie on the screen. "Imagine this child confessing to this crime. Imagine her weeping crocodile tears as she sobbed about the dark thing inside her, about her battles against the temptations Satan had thrown her way. Can you see that? Now, look again at this picture, and ask yourself: Could the monster you see here ever be truly contrite?"

No, I think. She would have used her youth, those white teeth, that angelic face, would have used them to manipulate and hide. But she wouldn't have felt sorry, not ever.

"Remember: truth alone is not enough, because truth is still a lie unless it is accompanied by regret and the desire to right the wrong."

The clip ends abruptly.

"Jesus." Alvarez whistles. "No pun intended. This is going to kill her parents. You ever seen anything like that? Like Valerie?"

"It happens," I say. "Some psychopaths become what they are because of environment, while others appear to be born that way. They grow up in good homes, with no abuse, lots of love and opportunity, but still end up twisted. We don't know why."

"Gives me the creeps."

I stand up and examine the downstairs area. The couch is a dark brown, the beige carpet and white walls continue. It's all very clean, all unremarkable. Not the home of a child-monster. My eyes roam the walls until they find what I was looking for: a wooden crucifix.

There you are, I think. She hid behind you and all this beige. Catholicism, confession, this is the answer.

"We need to go," I tell Alvarez.

"That's it?" he asks, surprised.

"We know who killed her," I say. "Now we need to find him."

WE WALK THE GAUNTLET. CAMERAS flash and newsmen and -women shout my name. I've been recognized; they smell blood.

"You're a regular celebrity, honey-love," Callie says.

We climb in the car and shut the door.

"Why'd you hold back on the Catholic angle with Alvarez?" Alan asks.

"Because it's unconfirmed and it's a bomb waiting to go off."

"True," Callie muses. "I suppose a lot of people will be upset to find that they've been on candid camera during their private confession."

"Would she have gone to confession so young?" Alan asks.

"I did," I reply. "It's all about the 'age of discretion.' The point where the child starts to struggle with and consider right and wrong, good and evil. It's a contentious issue. Some people feel that pushing a child into confession too early is tantamount to stealing their child-hood; others feel that if you wait too long, you run the risk of letting them settle into bad moral habits. Seven or eight is generally consid-ered an acceptable median age."

Alan shakes his head. "Thank God I was raised Baptist. You Catholics have too many rules for me."

I scowl at him. " 'You Catholics'? Bite your tongue. Let's get back to the offices. James and Jezebel should be done questioning the vic-tims' families soon. If I'm right, and I'm almost certain I am now, we need to plan out just how to let the shit hit the fan."

ALAN DRIVES. CALLIE FOLLOWS US in her own car.

"Weird, isn't it?" Alan asks.

"What?"

"We came to the Cavanaughs' all ready to feel messed up about a little girl getting killed. Now? After what we saw her doing, I don't know what to feel."

I think about an older Valerie, beautiful, breathtaking and formi-dable, wrapping those fingers around a human throat, white teeth flashing as she peered into her victim's eyes and grinned and grinned and grinned.

Good kitty, she might whisper. *What a good, good kitty you are.*

34

"WE'RE MISSING CONFIRMATION ON TWENTY-ONE," JEZEBEL says. "Either because we can't reach the families, or there are no families to reach. Of those we have questioned, it's confirmed. All practicing Catholics."

I knew this already, at some level, but the full meaning only hits me now that it's been confirmed. I sit down in a free chair near Alan's desk and take a moment to stare at all those names on the dry-erase board.

"Wow," I manage.

"I did a little research," James says. "There's never been a violation of the Catholic confessional on this scale."

"I'm sure that's true," I murmur.

I'm thinking about Father Yates pacing in the church last night and am transposing onto this action an image of the Pope.

I hate this case. It's put me in direct contact with the Director of the FBI, in proximity to the President of the United States, and I'm sure something of this magnitude will, factually, reach the Pope's ears.

I stand up and make sure I have everyone's attention.

"We've worked high-profile cases before, but this is a whole new playing field. This goes nowhere. Nowhere. No pillow talk with spouses or partners, don't tell your dog if you have one. Got it?"

They all nod. No one shows any signs of disagreement. Maybe the sober truth has hit them too.

"James, I want you to sit down with Callie, Alan, and Jezebel and I want you to start going through that database you made. Look for and list the most probable churches each victim would have visited."

"Where are you going, honey-love?" Callie asks.

"I'm going to see AD Jones to give him the bad news."

"YOU SURE ABOUT THIS?" AD Jones asks.

"Yes, sir. We have corroborating data now. We know from the Cavanaugh scene that he likes to use covert surveillance. We have confirmation on the Catholic connection with the victims' families we've been able to reach. How else could he have known what he knew about these people? Besides, he led us there."

"How's that?"

"That note in Lisa Reid's journal. *What do I collect? That's the question and that's the key.* And then in those first video clips, he tells us that everything we need to know to catch him is right there in the clips. Plus, the affect of most of the victims fits; they seemed shocked to find out that he already knew what their secrets were and there was no evidence of recognition."

I'd missed this before, and I kick myself for it now. They'd all thought their secrets were still secret. Why hadn't I seen that?

Was it because I was still too blinded by my own?

AD Jones doesn't say anything for a little while. He laces his hands behind his head and stares off, thinking.

"This is a political nightmare, Smoky. Not something I usually care about, but in this case it'll probably hamper catching this guy. If we go to the Catholic Church and we go in heavy they're likely to tell us to fuck off and close ranks."

"Yeah," I say. "Priests touching boys? Bad, bad, bad. Bugs in the confessionals? Wow. I think we need to show them we'll play ball. Make them allies, not enemies."

He frowns. "How do you propose to do that?"

"This doesn't affect the entirety of the United States, as far as we know. We clamp down on this locally, keep it confined to my team and you and the Director. No one else. The Director gets hold of someone in the church who has some juice and briefs them. He gets them to arrange access for us and we agree to keep the whole thing quiet. We don't even need to let the local priests in on it if they don't want us to."

"What about Father Yates?"

"He has no interest in this getting out, believe me. He's loyal to his church, and I imagine they know that."

"It could work," he allows.

"It will work. I doubt the Catholic Church is different from any other bureaucracy when it comes to some things. People guard their territories and their budgets and work hard to keep shit from rolling uphill. I'll bet even money that they won't want to let the Pope know if they don't have to."

"You make them sound like us," he says, only half joking.

"It's survival of the species taken to the level of the group organism, that's all."

"True enough."

"I like this approach better anyway. The Preacher's whole deal is shaking things up. He thinks he's a prophet, preaching about the truth, getting people to think and talk and wonder about God. The less chaos we allow him to create, the better I'll feel."

"Agreed. I'll call the Director now."

"YOU'RE ON THE NEWS," JEZEBEL tells me when I walk back into the office.

"Good thing there's no TV in here."

She smiles. "Not to worry, I can access a feed right here on the computer." She points to Alan's monitor. "May I?"

"Sure."

She taps a few keys and enters a password. A moment later a different desktop appears on the screen.

"This is actually my computer we're looking at. I'm controlling it remotely." She opens a program and a video player fills the screen. The video begins to play.

The newswoman looks familiar.

"She was at the Cavanaugh home," I say, placing her. "The smart one."

The one who'd noticed us pulling up and who had directed her cameraman to point his lens our way.

I watch as we climb out of the car and the newswoman begins her voice-over.

"This morning a young girl was found dead in her own bedroom, in this quiet suburb of Burbank. It didn't take long for a large police presence to develop, which is not, in and of itself, surprising. What *is* surprising is the arrival on scene of this woman: FBI Special Agent Smoky Barrett."

"Hey, what about me?" Alan jokes.

"Special Agent Barrett became known to most Californians and many Americans almost three years ago. She herself became the victim of a home invasion. Joseph Sands, a serial killer Agent Barrett was hunting, turned the tables on his pursuer. He entered her home at night, murdered her husband and ten-year-old daughter, and raped and disfigured Agent Barrett herself."

A photograph of me, scars and all, appears on-screen.

"Agent Barrett recovered and continued her job with the FBI, a move debated by many at first. The debate seems to have died down; results tend to do that. Agent Barrett has continued to do her job and do it well. Which brings us to the burning question: why is the lead serial murder investigator in Southern California at the Cavanaugh home? The only conclusion this reporter can come to is that the death of ten-year-old Valerie Cavanaugh is tied to the man who calls himself the Preacher."

A recap of the Preacher's exploits follows, along with his promise to kill a child if we didn't catch him first.

"Stroke of luck," Callie observes. "They haven't seen Valerie's clip."

I consider the Preacher's promise that he'd find a way to promulgate the truth in spite of us. *I wouldn't count on that luck lasting.*

"How much coverage has the Preacher been getting?" I ask Jezebel.

"A lot. Worldwide. There's plenty of dialogue about truth, religion, the topics he soapboxed about. He's got a surprising number of supporters."

"Supporters?" Alan says. "What the fuck is there to support? He's a murderer."

"It's not so shocking," James says. "There's plenty of precedence, and it's not confined to Catholicism. He's preaching a totalitarianism of faith, an all or nothing 'giving of self to God.' That'll always have support among the faithful. Extremism and fanaticism go hand in hand with religion. They always have."

"The connection's also been made between you and the Reids," Jezebel says. "Someone was nice enough to let a reporter know that you and your team were in Virginia."

"Nature of the beast," Alan says.

"Have any of them mentioned the victims' Catholic connection?"

"No. Only the Preacher's."

"Good."

I brief them all on my conversation with AD Jones and my proposed handling of the confessional information.

"Probably the best move," Alan agrees. "They're a little touchy about scandals."

"My mother is Catholic," James says, out of nowhere. "She loves going to confession. The idea of someone violating that would kill her. The big question now is, how is he doing it?"

"Finish making that list."

"AGENT BARRETT?"

I'd answered a call on my cell phone from a number I didn't recognize.

"Yes?"

"This is Cardinal Adam Ross. Of the Archdiocese of Los Angeles?"

"Oh. Hello, Cardinal." I frown. "Is 'cardinal' the correct form of address?"

"Cardinal is fine. So is Adam, if you like."

"Let's stick with cardinal, then. How can I help you?"

"I think that question goes both ways, Agent Barrett. I received a call about ten minutes ago from the Director of the FBI. A very disturbing call. I'm in my car on the way to your office right now. Can you see me?"

The man's manners are impeccable in spite of the obvious tension in his voice. I had expected imperious; he's the picture of politeness.

"I'll be here, Cardinal."

* * *

AD JONES WHISTLES. "THAT WAS fast. I got off the phone with the Director less than a half hour ago."

"How did that go?"

"He agrees with your plan. He says to keep it under wraps permanently if at all possible."

"Do you know Cardinal Ross, sir?"

"I've never met him. I'm not exactly the churchgoing type. But if he's on the Director's speed dial, he's a mover and a shaker. Try and treat him accordingly."

"We play well with others as long as they return the favor, sir."

"ISN'T CARDINAL ONE OF THE stepping-stones on the road to wearing the Pope hat?" Callie asks.

"Technically, any Catholic male who fit the criteria could become Pope," James says. "In practice, it's reserved for the cardinals. The last time a non-cardinal was elected Pope was 1378."

"How does someone become a cardinal?" I ask.

"You're appointed by the Pope. They're called 'the princes of the church.' It's a big deal, obviously, and it comes after years of service. You'd be a priest first, then probably an auxiliary bishop, then a full bishop and then an archbishop—which is also a position appointed by the Pope. Cardinals are then chosen from the archbishops.

"The cardinal electors are the most powerful individuals in the Catholic Church other than the Pope himself. They appoint the new Pope when the old one dies. There are usually about a hundred twenty of them, which is a very, very small per capita when you consider the overall size of the Catholic Church. Roughly one or two cardinals per eight or nine million Catholics."

"I'd imagine they have a direct line to the Pope?" I ask.

"Yes."

This gives me a better picture of the man who's on his way up in the elevator to see me. He'll be smart, hard-nosed, and used to the accoutrement of power and command. Most important, for our purposes, he'll be someone who can make decisions and issue orders that others will listen to.

Hopefully he's not an asshole.

"Do you think they wear anything under those robes?" Callie asks.

"Slacks, dear, we wear slacks."

We turn to the voice, which is as rich and baritone as any of us could have imagined coming from a cardinal.

Cardinal Ross is very tall, nearly six foot four. He's got silver hair and is thin, though not unhealthily so. He has a long face to go with his height, and while it's not unattractive, it has recorded the years. I estimate his age at just over sixty. He has dark eyes that sweep over us with a certain weight, a definite gravitas. He's dressed in simple clerical black; slacks, shirt, jacket, and the white collar with a large silver cross hanging down. The simplicity of his garments don't lessen his presence; the man fills the room.

He's come alone, it seems, which surprises me.

I hold out my hand. "Welcome, Cardinal."

He takes the hand and shakes it, smiling down at me as he does. He holds the grip for a little longer than needed, letting his eyes take in my scars.

"Thank you for having me."

I introduce him to the rest of my team. He looks around the office with some interest.

"So you catch murderers here."

"We try, yes."

He walks over to the dry-erase board, examines the names. Paces around the desks, nodding in what seems like approval.

"The most important jobs always seem to get done in the humblest surroundings." He glances our way and smiles. "Before anyone takes offense, I'm not knocking your offices. I mean it as a compliment."

"We're a simple folk," Callie drawls.

"Somehow I think that statement is both true and false, Agent Thorne. You have a narrowness of focus and a terrible simplicity of purpose, but you understand complexities of evil that are beyond me."

Callie grins. "You can certainly lay it on thick."

He laughs. It's a nice laugh. Rich and unself-conscious. "Occupational hazard. I'm not being dishonest with my praise, I assure you."

"That's nice, but can we cut to the chase?" James asks.

He's put my own words to voice, though with more hostility than I'd have liked. Cardinal Ross takes it in stride, unruffled.

"Indeed. Your Director called me. He briefed me on your suspicions regarding this man bugging our confessionals. I'm sorry to ask, but can you please explain how you came to this conclusion?"

I tell him about the Preacher, still holding back on the matter of the crosses in the wounds. I mention the conversation with Father Yates, his unspoken confirmation regarding Rosemary Sonnenfeld. Cardinal Ross rubs his forehead when I am done, and looks very, very troubled.

"Do you mind if I sit down?"

Alan gives him a chair.

"I understand. And agree, of course. There's no other way he could have known. This is terrible, terrible, terrible. If this got out it would shake the faithful badly."

"You sure you're not just worried about more lawsuits?" James sneers. "Your church did a fine job of hiding pedophiles for many years."

"James!" I snap.

The cardinal holds up a hand. "No, Agent Barrett. I've come to accept that I deserve any chastisement about that matter sent my way. I never personally hid a pedophile priest, but members of my church did, and it was shameful. My concern isn't with public relations, in spite of what you might think. This is a matter of faith. Have any of you ever given confession?"

"I have," I say. "But not since I was younger."

Alan keeps his face bland at my little white lie.

"Not me," Callie says. "A good thing too. I'd have made some poor priest blush."

James doesn't reply.

"Can you imagine how you'd feel if you found out someone besides your priest and God was listening in? It goes beyond scandal—it is a violation of one of the most basic, beautiful, and trusted bastions of Catholicism. Priests have died rather than break the seal of confession."

"Cardinal," I say, "we're not on a crusade here. We don't need to make this public. What we do need is cooperation and access."

"You'll get it, of course. You'd get it regardless. But I do appreciate the reassurances. The truth is, it will come out sooner or later. I'm sure someone else will consider the facts as you did and come to the same conclusion. What you will be giving me is time."

"It wouldn't hurt if the man responsible was captured either," I point out.

"I can't deny the truth of that. What do you need from me?"

"We've made a list of all the victims and have cross-referenced their geographical locations with nearby churches. I need to reach every one of these churches, and I need to find out if these victims were parishioners. Once we confirm they were, we need to speak to the priest in charge and see if they remember our man."

"I can provide you with three members of my staff immediately. They can make the call and tell each priest to cooperate fully, and then pass the phone to you."

I blink, taken aback.

"That'd be perfect."

"I'll arrange it the moment I leave."

35

JEZEBEL, CALLIE, ALAN, AND JAMES ARE IN THE PHONE ROOM with the three priests the cardinal provided us. I observed for a little while. The cardinal's men are all business, no questions; serious men, used to serious tasks. They are there to do what they've been told to do.

There's a definite "when I say jump . . ." phenomenon within the church hierarchy, apparently. The cardinal's men would call and get someone on the phone without much delay. They'd relay in terse words that they were passing the phone to a member of the FBI and that the priest at the other end was to answer any and all questions. One of my guys would take the phone and do the interview. They'd pass it back to the cardinal's man, who'd make it clear that not a word was to be spoken about this, ever. Then they'd hang up. Simple, no muss, fuss, or complaints.

I've left them to it and taken a moment for myself inside the now empty Death Central. So much change has happened in the last few days. I've flown apart and come back together again. The Preacher let the world know he existed and I've followed his trail to the dark of the confessional booths.

I need a moment to step back, to look at the forest, not the trees. I need to try and see the man we're after.

He is smart. His ideas are not new, but his take on them has depth, care, a certain reverence. He's not hiding another motive behind the words he's saying. He believes them, they are what drives him.

So what are those words?

They come down to truth, lies, and sin, and they are wrapped in religious significance. He hasn't taken a philosopher's path, where truth is a generality. His take on truth revolves around the specificity of salvation. What does it tell me?

He was raised Catholic.

I nod to myself. Yes. He grew up around the imagery, the back and forth of guilt and worry and hope mixed with mild self-loathing and self-forgiveness. He grew up seeing Christ on the cross and with the obligation to feel something about that.

Fine. Why, then, does he need to tell the world about it?

Because he thinks the world is not listening.

The world? No. That's the visible manifestation. We're dealing with a serial killer here. This isn't a man who had a strong belief and devoted himself to getting the word out. This is a man who's spent twenty years or more looking for those with the worst secrets so he could murder them on camera. However you slice it, whatever the supposed belief system constructed around it, murder is still always an act of anger. It may or may not be anger at the person being murdered. In fact, in the case of serial killers, it's most often misplaced rage. Mom or Dad, killed over and over and over again.

Someone or something was not listening at some point in his life. Someone or something intimate to him, someone or something important and entwined with his sense of self. The consequences of this angered him, and now he's making sure that this particular message never gets swept under the carpet again.

What's the message?

Simple words. He's said them in various ways; I hear them now like a bell: *Don't lie to God.*

There's a flaw in his logic, I realize, a huge, gaping hole in his argument: the people he's murdered had already confessed their sins. They'd done what he said they should, they'd knelt down in the confessional and they'd struggled with the words until they found the courage to say them.

Maybe he doesn't consider that his victims were flawed. Perhaps they weren't examples of what not to do, but examples of what should be done. Maybe the fact that they'd already confessed and were thus guaranteed a place in heaven let him kill without guilt, provided him with the system of rationalization he needed to violate that commandment we all seem to agree on: thou shalt not kill.

Or maybe, I think, this is where the rubber leaves the road with him. Maybe this is where he stops making sense and starts making crazy. He's built himself a church of ideas, but it was built on murder, with the bones of his victims.

Maybe, I think, for all his speeches about truth, he's the one lying the most.

I smile at this idea. I like the idea of him failing himself and his principles. I like it a lot.

You're no different. I look at all these names, and that's what I really see. Just like all the monsters; you're not talking to God, you're not talking to me, in the end, you're talking to someone you used to know, and however much you scream, they'll probably never listen.

IT'S TEN O'CLOCK. EVERYONE IS back at Death Central, listening as James briefs us on the results of the phone calls.

"We were able to confirm specific churches for approximately ninety percent of victims killed within the last five years. Beyond five years the percentages go down because the priest running the church has changed."

I hadn't thought of this, but it makes sense. The Catholic Church has personnel turnover like anyone else.

"It's worth noting that of those we were able to confirm, the priest involved generally remembered them without much prompting. They were almost invariably hard-luck cases who made good. Some exceptions, of course, but true in most instances."

"It'd fit with his manifesto," I say. "Those who came clean reversed the course of their lives."

"He chose the churches well. The ones he went after, with few exceptions, were similar to the Redeemer here. Churches run by priests who tried to help those having the most troubles."

"The most likely to have bad shit in their past," Alan points out. "Also least likely to be missed."

"Now for the bad news. None of the priests we talked to—not one—remembers anyone strange hanging around at the times our victims disappeared."

"Nothing at all?" I ask.

"No. We were very specific with our questions. 'Do you remember a man who would have left around the same time that particular victim disappeared?' for example. Not one answer in the affirmative."

I'm dumbfounded. It wouldn't have surprised me to find most saw nothing. He'd have been careful, people aren't that observant—but no one remembers anything at all? That's very strange.

"What about cleaning people?"

"We asked, of course. Most of these churches are too poor to pay for someone to come in and clean. They do the work themselves."

I shake my head. "Let's break it down. He'd need access and he'd have to fit in. Especially in these environments. These churches would be small, the parishioners tight-knit. It'd be difficult for a stranger to come in and not stick out."

"He could have pretended to be a parishioner," Callie says. "A down-and-outer like the others."

"Then why wouldn't these priests remember that? He wouldn't have stuck around, he'd have left once he had his victims. Plus, based on Father Yates, I think we're dealing with priests used to keeping their eyes open. They know they're not preaching to a congregation of innocent little lambs."

"Frustrating," Jezabel observes.

James's cell phone rings.

"Yes? What? Okay. Thank you." He snaps his phone shut. "That was computer crimes. We have a new attempt by the Preacher to post a clip on user-tube. They intercepted it and are e-mailing it to me now. They said it's different."

"Different how?" I ask.

"There's no victim in this one. But he's letting us know there will be another one soon."

"I SEE THAT THOSE IN law enforcement continue to work diligently to remove my video clips from the website I chose to share them on. That's understandable and certainly not unexpected. It doesn't matter all that much now anyway; the clips I posted have already found their way to hard drives around the world. They're being shared via newsgroups, e-mail, and other viral video websites. It's the nature of the Internet, and the reason I chose it as my first medium.

"From this point, I acknowledge, it gets a little more difficult. Law enforcement will likely be preventing my message from getting out at all. Again, not unexpected. For that reason, this particular clip is directed to you, to whoever it may be that is hunting me. I've given you everything you need to find me. If you do not, then sometime in the next forty-eight hours, I'll kill again." He pauses. His thumb stops moving on the rosary beads. "I'll say it again: I have given you everything you need to find me. You should know by now: I never lie, and I will keep my promise. Find me."

The clip ends.

"Why does he want to be caught?" Callie asks.

"It's the next step," I say. "You think he's got an audience now? Wait till he's in prison. He'll be a bonafide celebrity. Soapboxing away till they put a needle in his arm."

"Which will make him a martyr. Something I doubt he'll mind," James points out.

"Back to the drawing board," I say, pacing again. "He told us we can find him with the information we have. He says he never lies. I doubt that as a generality, but in this case, I'm buying it because he *wants* to be captured. We're missing something. What is it?"

Alan sighs. "I was never any good at logic problems. Give me a list of suspects to interview and I'm happy to beat my feet all day long. This is your territory, Smoky. You and James."

"It will be something simple," James says, studying the ever-present list of names on the dry-erase board. "We'll be missing it because it's obvious. Like the confessional as the source of his knowledge. It was there in front of us, which is why we didn't see it at first; it was a part of the landscape."

"*Too* apparent," Jezebel says.

"Exactly. Hide it in plain sight, just a little disguised. It belongs where it is while we're looking for something trying to be secret."

I remember my original words to AD Jones about the Preacher. I'd said he would have used a disguise on the plane, something simple with perhaps a single striking feature.

Something shutter clicks inside me.

I've tried to describe this phenomenon to others, the thing that always seems to herald a sudden realization on my part. It's like losing time, as though some part of my consciousness grays out, for just a millisecond. I'm left wondering what happened in that millisecond. What did I miss? The answer is simple: the thing I needed to see came into view, but I was not yet ready to understand it. I regain that lost time when I do.

That's what just happened, and I'm left to wonder: What is it that I need to understand? What's that thing that wants to be seen?

"Talk to me, James," I murmur. "List out the component parts of the problem one by one."

He doesn't ask me why; we've been down this road before.

"He chooses his victims based on their confessions. He's able to do this because he's been bugging confessionals in churches that cater to the more troubled sections of society. The congregations of these churches tend to be tight-knit communities."

"Stop there. Why do they tend to be so tight-knit?"

"Common experiences."

"Simpler than that," I say. "All they have in common is each other. No one else accepts them as they are, faults and all."

"Fair enough—which leads us back down the same road: people are watched closely when they come into a group like that, and noticed when they leave. No one remembers a guy leaving around the same time as the victim's disappearance."

Plain sight, plain sight, plain sight . . .

The words roll through me like waves that never crest. It's maddening. I try to be the moon, pulling them toward me with my gravity. They come close, but vanish before they ever hit the shore.

"Go on," I say.

"He needed access, so he had to be there. But no one remembers him being there."

I bolt upright.

The waves hit the shore.

Plain sight . . .

"Because he *wasn't there*," I say, excited. "He understood the mechanics of a group like the ones he needed to infiltrate."

The intimacy created when you admit that you're a fuckup and the people you admit it to accept you anyway, because hey—they're fuckups too.

"Someone working with him, you mean," James says. "How is that any different? They'd still be missed if they left when the victims did."

"That's exactly right. But they didn't disappear when the victims did. They waited for a while, maybe a few weeks, maybe even a month, and then they slipped away. They'd never need an alibi because they were right there with the rest of the congregation while the victim was being kidnapped and killed."

James frowns. "A lot of supposition."

"Logical supposition, though, don't you think?"

"It makes sense," he allows. "We need to make the same calls again, but this time we need to broaden our questions. Ask about men that left not long after the victims went missing, but not immediately."

"And who had been close to the victims," I add. "It'd be a part of it for them. Gathering intel, getting familiar with the victim's life."

"You know," Alan says, "it'd make the most sense for them to be linear in their actions."

"I don't follow," I say.

"Their victim pool is going to be filled with people who tend to be transient or unstable. They'd need to plant the bug, find the victim, and make their move. They couldn't afford to leave and come back, they'd run the risk that their chosen victim had moved on. They'd need to stay focused and remain on-site until the deed was done."

"So?"

"So there should be a lot of time between murders, right? Pick a vic, grab her, film her, kill her, move on to the new locale. That's a lot of logistics. But we have three dead in less than two weeks. Lisa Reid, Rosemary Sonnenfeld, and Valerie Cavanaugh. Seems to me it's possible he would have had to pitch in directly on at least one of those in terms of gathering intel, don't you think?"

"It's a good point," Callie says, "but which one?"

"Lisa Reid." James says it as I think it. "Has to be. She's the one departure, the only victim who wasn't born a woman. She's also the one he used to get our attention."

I feel the excitement rising in me again. The waves are rolling, moving, cresting, and they all threaten to reach the shore together.

"We need to focus on those two, right now—Lisa and Rosemary. How did he choose Lisa, anyway? How'd she come on his radar? She wasn't in his usual stomping grounds, he went after her, she didn't come to him. So how'd he even know about her? Rosemary is one of our most recent victims and we have an in with Yates. He'll remember something, someone close to her who—"

I stop talking as a big wave, a *huge* wave, comes crashing into shore, roaring for what seems like forever.

Hiding right in plain sight . . .

"He told me early on," I whisper.

"What is it?" Callie asks.

"Yates. We asked to talk to Rosemary's known associates. She only had one. Andrea." I swallow. I look at Alan. "Call Yates. Find out Andrea's last name and check into her background. I have a feeling we'll find it's bogus and that she's long, long gone."

36

"LISA REID WAS A BIT OF AN INTERNAL SCANDAL FOR THE church," Cardinal Ross tells me. "The priest running that particular church is a younger man, Father Strain. He's part of a small but growing group of priests who are young, smart, and willing to disagree—albeit respectfully—with Rome on certain issues."

"I assume taking confession from a transsexual would fit the bill?"

"Yes and no."

I frown. "Sounds complicated."

"The church's stand on homosexuality remains as it has been. Homosexuality is regarded as a sin. Transgendered individuals are considered to be effeminate, i.e., homosexuals who have used the benefits of modern technology to change their outward appearance to match their inner desires. The fact of that change is not considered by the church to remove the truth that they were born as God created them."

"So a transgendered person is basically considered to be a homosexual."

"Yes."

"You said 'effeminate.' What about women changing to men?"

"Both are held to the same standard. Homosexuality is a sin."

"So what does a homosexual who wants to be a Roman Catholic do?"

"They can receive confession, and are urged to do so, until such time as they change their ways and become as God created them and the Bible demands. If they're unable to become completely 'straight'—to marry a member of the opposite sex, for example—then they are expected to practice chastity. Until either of these things happen, they are not to take part in Holy Communion or various other sacraments."

"Then . . . I don't understand. Where's the conflict with Strain?"

"Twofold. Strain was giving Communion to Dexter Reid, for one."

"And the other?"

"Parishioners complained. It can be a different experience depending on where you are, Agent Barrett. A homosexual walking into a church in Los Angeles might expect different treatment than one walking into a church in Texas, for example."

"Ah. I understand."

"Father Strain was cautioned, nothing more. He was told to stop giving Holy Communion to Dexter Reid and to be more circumspect about his dealings with Dexter. He refused."

"What happened to him?"

"Nothing."

There's a quality to that "nothing" that makes me think there are two words missing from it: *for now*.

"What will happen to him?"

"That's in God's hands."

I chuckle and shake my head. It's comforting, in a way, to see that a bureaucracy is a bureaucracy the world around. Something tells me that Father Strain can expect no further advancement. Maybe he doesn't care.

"Cardinal, I'm looking for a connection. How would Lisa Reid have attracted the Preacher's attention? Was it newsworthy?"

"It didn't appear in any major news outlet that I'm aware of. There were some mentions of it on Catholic blogs and in some newsletters. There is debate even within the church, at times, on homosexuality and how best to bring homosexuals into God's grace. A heated topic, as I'm sure you can imagine."

"That could be it," I murmur. "Maybe he was monitoring religious blogs."

"Agent Barrett, do you think Father Strain is in any danger? This man, would he go after the Father for allowing Dexter into the congregation?"

I notice that we continue the debate he mentioned in the here and now; I say Lisa, he says Dexter. Tomato tomahto, except that we're talking about a person. It seems like such a casual dismissal on his part of everything Lisa was trying to do and be and feel about herself.

"I don't think so. Lisa was a tool for him, a way to draw our attention to what he was doing. He wanted to come out of anonymity with a splash. Lisa fit the bill in spades; her family's political connections, her controversy. Virginia was way out of his normal stomping grounds. I think he did what he intended to do, and then left. I do need to speak with Father Strain, though."

"I understand."

Alan pokes his head into my office. "Got something," he says. He seems excited.

"Cardinal, I have to go. I appreciate your help."

"I'm available when you need me, Agent Barrett."

I bet you are, I think as I hang up. Don't need more scandals now, do you?

The discourse on homosexuality and his refusal to use the name of Lisa has stirred up some of my old angers with the Catholic Church. There was a time I loved the purity of prayer. Just me and God. It was simple, and there was a kind of peaceful truth to that. I never understood or enjoyed what I perceived as the intolerance, the unwillingness to think beyond, to look beyond. Not much seems to have changed.

"What is it?" I ask.

"Andrea told Father Yates her name was Andrea True."

"True? Are you kidding?"

"I know, big funny on their part, ha ha ha. You were right. It was a false name. No Andrea True ever worked for any police department in Ohio. No Andrea True in AFIS, CODIS, etc., etc."

"Perhaps she's just a transient who gave a fake name," Callie observes.

"That'd be some coincidence," Alan says. The tone of his voice is more than doubtful.

I shake my head. "No way. She's a part of it."

Here we go, I think. Here comes the downhill side. Everything picks up speed now.

"Callie, you're coming with me to the Redeemer. Bring your forensics kit. Alan, get on the phone with Father Strain in Virginia. Grill him again on anyone he might have seen associating with or interested in Lisa Reid. Go in the other direction this time—look for the last person he would have suspected of anything."

"Got it."

FATHER YATES STILL LOOKS TROUBLED. I feel bad that I'm about to make things worse for him.

"Andrea True is a false name, Father," I tell him.

"That's not so unusual here."

"There's no Andrea True that ever worked for any police department in Ohio."

He runs his hands through his hair. His eyes find Jesus again. How many times a day does he look to that paint-chipped savior for comfort?

"You think she was working with the Preacher, don't you?"

"I do."

I explain to him how I came to this conclusion. He begins to sag, and it only gets worse as I lay out the probable MO: infiltrating the congregation, bugging the confessional, picking a victim and getting close to her, passing the victim off to her partner, sticking around for a while after the victim disappeared to throw off suspicion. He doesn't want it to be the truth, but Father Yates has worked too close to the hard parts of this society for too long to ignore evidence of evil when it's presented to him.

"Everything you say makes sense, God help me. Andrea moved the day after you spoke to her. She said that it was time for her to go home and restart her life again." His voice is bitter. "I trusted her. I took her in, I gave her Communion and confession. I held her when she told me about her dead son and she wept for him."

Callie has been silent throughout until now.

"Sometimes they're wonderful actors," she says. "It's not that you were blind or stupid, it's that they can give Oscar-worthy performances when they need to."

He gives her a halfhearted smile of agreement but he doesn't seem to take much true comfort from her words.

"How can I help?"

"I think Andrea left something behind for us on purpose. This is coming to an endgame for them. They want us to catch them, but they want us to have to work for it. He said everything we needed to find them was there."

"Is there anything in here that Andrea was in regular contact with?" Callie asks. "Anything she touched a lot, anything she paid an undue amount of attention to?"

His eyes widen.

"What is it, Father?" I ask.

"The chalice. She asked to be given the job of cleaning it. She said that she loved touching the chalice, that it made her feel closer to God."

"That was probably true," I say.

"Can we see it?" Callie asks.

"Of course. Wait here, please."

He leaves and comes back in a moment carrying a blue drawstring bag. He motions for us to come forward to the altar.

"Put it down, please, Father," Callie asks.

He does.

We both watch as Callie puts on a pair of gloves. She doesn't reach into the bag to remove the chalice, but instead opens the top of the bag and then pulls it down toward the base. The chalice is gold and it gleams even in the poor night light of the church.

Callie takes out a fluorescent flashlight and proceeds to examine the outer surface.

"Nothing on the exterior at all," she says. "Not even any smudges."

Disappointment rises, but then an idea occurs to me.

"Check on the bottom, underneath the base. I bet that spot gets missed during cleaning by most. If she wanted to leave us a clue, she'd want to make sure that it couldn't get wiped away by accident."

Callie upends the chalice and applies the light. She looks at me and smiles.

"Bingo. Nice big thumbprint, clear as day."

That electric feeling, all over again. It's not the endgame, but we're on our way there.

Callie makes the print visible with fingerprint dust and raises it with clear celo-tape. She attaches the tape to a white card. She takes digital pictures of the print as well, so we have a backup in case something happens to the print card.

The camera flashes seem alien here, man-made lightning strikes. Jesus and the altar appear in a moment of daylight before returning to the shadows caused by the candle flames. The chalice lights up like it's been set on fire.

I stare at it and wonder, when exactly did this happen? How did I arrive here? When I was a girl, I sipped from the lip of a similar cup and it meant that I was close to God. Now it means I am close to a monster.

Is it a choice? I ask myself. The monsters or God? Is it possible to get so near them, to understand them as well as I do, and still have room for a concept of the divine?

The flash fires and I wince against its painful brilliance, a light that has nothing to do with God, nothing at all.

"That's all I need for now," Callie says.

I turn to Father Yates. "We need to take the chalice, Father."

He grimaces. "Feel free. It's not fit for use anymore, as far as I'm concerned."

"Her thumbprint erases God's presence? Seems like a lot of power you're granting her."

He finds that smile, the one he's been giving me all along as I've challenged him with my own disbelief and bitterness. One-part tolerance, two-parts compassion, and kindness, through and through.

"No, it's not that. I simply won't allow any part of them to coexist with that holy moment. They don't deserve it."

I realize that I've been projecting. Father Yates has been troubled by recent events, true, but his faith has never been shaken. Uncertainty about God is my bailiwick; he's always remained loyal.

"What are you going to pray for now, Father?"

"Justice, of course."

My mouth twists as some more of that dark bitterness rises inside me. It seems like there's no end to it.

"My kind of justice, or God's?"

"I don't have to pray for His justice. His justice is certain. So I guess I'll pray for yours."

* * *

"WE'RE CLOSE NOW," CALLIE SAYS as we drive back. "We'll know who they are soon."

"Yes."

"Must be nice, to have the kind of faith that man has."

"I suppose. I take it you don't?"

She laughs and pops a Vicodin she'd had waiting in her hand.

"I believe in me and a select few and that's hard enough as it is."

A-fucking-men, I think.

"What about you?" she asks.

"Ask me after we catch him. I will tell you one thing, if you can keep your big mouth shut."

"The unkindest cut." She sighs. "But tell me."

"Tommy and I are going to move in together. In the middle of all this, that's one thing I was able to figure out, and I'll admit, Father Yates played a part."

She's quiet.

"I'm so happy for you, Smoky."

Her voice is thick with relief, a release of tension that puzzles me until I study her and understand.

"You worried about me too much, Callie. I was always going to be fine."

"That's—" She swallows, shakes it off, flashes me one of those mega-watt smiles. "That's one of the many things good friends do."

I reach out to touch her, but pull my hand back. Intimacy with Callie is a dance all its own.

"Let's go catch a killer, friend."

That we can share. No problem at all.

37

"FATHER STRAIN WAS PRETTY SHARP," ALAN SAYS. "WHEN I explained what I was looking for and why, he remembered something right away. A cripple. Guy in a wheelchair came in, had been a drunk and stumbled out into traffic one day, ended up paralyzed from the waist down. He hit it off with Lisa Reid."

"Clever. Why didn't his name come up if he left when Lisa was murdered?"

"He was smart. Made up some story about a daughter he was reconciling with. He was scheduled to fly to California to meet her a few days before Lisa's trip. I'm guessing he'd already killed Ambrose before he left the church. He probably hung out at Ambrose's until Lisa left and then followed her to and from Texas."

It all makes sense and it reinforces our image of him; intelligent, decisive, organized. In all the prior murders, he sent "Andrea" in to locate the victim. She was their public face. With Lisa he could come out into the light. It must have been very satisfying.

"Alan, I need you to switch places with Callie and run the print we got from the Redeemer through AFIS. Callie, I need you to get on the phone with forensics in Virginia. I need them to go to Strain's church and see if there's a print there too."

"Do you think it'll be on the chalice?"

"It's the first place I'd look."

He couldn't have resisted. No more hiding, right? He probably grinned without knowing it as he left his mark for us to find.

"HERE WE GO," ALAN CALLS out.

I hurry over to his desk. On the screen of his computer is a photograph of Andrea True. She's younger in this picture, her hair is shorter, but there's no denying that it's her.

"Frances Murphy," I read. "Why is she in the database?"

"Past criminal record." He scrolls down. "Get this: arrested for assaulting a Catholic priest. That particular priest was later arrested for child molestation and, let's see . . . no dispensation from the judge because she wasn't one of those the priest had molested. He liked boys."

"Known associates?"

He taps a key and three words appear that take my breath away.

"Brother, Michael Murphy," I read aloud. "Look him up."

Michael Murphy's photograph appears on the screen. He's a male version of his sister, with the same big, sad eyes. He's handsome enough, not a pretty boy. He has a strong face and a certain intensity; he'd have had no problems with the ladies.

"He took part in the assault on the priest," Alan notes. "Twenty years ago. No dispensation. He wasn't one of the molested either."

"What else?"

A few more taps and their rap sheets appear.

"A familiar pattern," Alan observes.

The list of offenses starts at the age of eighteen and continues forward for about four or five years. Petty thefts, larceny, check-kiting—nothing huge. The convictions taper off at about twenty-two for both of them. There's nothing after that other than the assault on the priest.

"Check out the birthdates," Alan says.

"January twenty-second and . . . January twenty-second?" I blink. "They're twins."

"Think they'll look good in matching jumpsuits?"

Kirby's voice startles me. She'd crept up behind us. I'd been so engrossed that I hadn't noticed her coming in.

"Twins acting as a killing team?" I mutter. "How does that work?"

"He'll be the one in charge," Kirby says. "Look at her. She's weak around the eyes." Her voice is filled with contempt. "I ran into a brother/sister killing team once down in—well, somewhere else. Killing just seemed to run in the family. Even the dad was a good hitter. Kind of cute too."

I glance at her. She grins.

"I can take a hint. I'll talk to Callie later. Have fun with Dick and Jane."

I murmur something in reply as she leaves.

Weak, huh? I consider her act as Andrea, her commitment to that persona, and have to disagree with Kirby's assessment. I wonder, were the scars on her arm fake? Or had she cut herself sometime in the past, so that she could play the part of a failed suicide to perfection? The probable answer is as disturbing as everything else about these two.

"Let's find them, Alan."

Coming up on the end of you, Preacher. You and your sister may have shared everything, but you'll die apart. I'll make sure of that.

"GOT A PRINT SCANNED IN and on its way to me via e-mail," Callie says. "Give me a sec to match it up with our Mr. Murphy and we'll have all the confirmation we need."

"Alan, where are we on possible current locations for these two?"

"Still working on it."

The door to the office swings open and James walks in with Jezebel. Both have grim expressions on their faces.

"We have a new message from the Preacher. I only watched the beginning of it, but he's showing his face and congratulating us on figuring out who he is."

"Shit," Alan and I say in unison, looking at each other.

"He had eyes on the Redeemer somehow," I say. "He knew there's only one reason we'd show up there, and he knows they left the thumbprint there."

"Think he'll run?" Alan asks.

"I don't know. I think he wants to be caught, but now that it's come down to it . . ." I shrug. "They could be having a change of heart. Let's see the clip, James."

He sits down and we all crowd around the monitor to watch, with the exception of Callie.

There's no lettering at the beginning of this clip, no fancy editing. He's communicating to us in as close to real time as this medium allows. The other difference is that we can now see his face.

I examine him and see that Michael Murphy is a man at peace. He's certain. He is doing what he was meant to do and doesn't go to bed at night worrying about whether he's on the side of right or wrong. He's calm, composed, happy. His voice is almost friendly.

"It's come to my attention that those in law enforcement responsible for tracking me down have finally found out who I am. I can't tell you how happy this makes me. My sister and I have been building to this moment for twenty years. Twenty years of hiding, twenty years of planning, twenty years of sacrifice.

"Many will ask: why? If you had something to say, why not just say it? I think the answer to that question is self-evident. Look around you at society today. We live in a world where, more and more, the idea of the soul is scoffed at if it's even thought of at all. Mankind revels in the flesh, and the flesh, I am afraid, only believes what it can see.

"Talk to the flesh of truth and it will sniff and say: 'Truth? What truth? I don't see truth. I see sex. I see drugs. I see sensation.'

"I knew if we were going to prove our point and bring people back to God, that we would have to show them. They would have to see with the eyes, hear with the ears. Only then would they be able to know with the heart.

"And it's working, praise God. The impact of the opus is already being felt. Discussions have opened around the world." He picks up a paper from the table and reads. " 'The Preacher has opened my eyes again to the idea that I could get rid of that space I put between me and God, the space made up of the lies I've been unwilling to let go of. I listened to what he had to say and I walked to my local church and gave my first confession in ten years.' "

"Disgusting," Callie says, curling her lip in scorn. "Did you also confess to agreeing with a murderer?"

Discomfort wiggles inside me. I too had been driven to the confessional by the Preacher.

I'll make up for it by catching him.

"That is one of many. Not all agree with me, of course, but the point is—they are talking about it. They are discussing the subject of truth, lie, sin, God, confession, and salvation. The flame has been lit again, praise God. Attempts to block my message are a hopeless activity in today's world. Copies of this and all of my other videos have been put on CD and are being mailed worldwide to media outlets, authors, religious scholars, and skeptics. The message can be slowed; it can't be stopped."

"He's right about that," James says.

"I feel certain that my sister and I will be captured soon."

"He's right about that too," I growl.

"We welcome this. It's the next step on the path we've chosen. It is time that we preach in person, that we be available for discussions, questions, and interviews. Before that happens, I thought it was important to show that we are able to practice what we preach. Come here, Frances."

Frances, who I met as Andrea, steps into the camera lens. She too looks peaceful. Almost radiant. They are more attractive together than apart, light and mirrors reflecting back at each other. She smiles down at her brother, and turns to the camera. He continues speaking.

"Frances and I were born as twins. We were born healthy and have lived healthy, which, as you will come to understand, was God's first gift to us. It could have been much, much different. We lived a difficult life, and it was not without sin or lies. We strayed from God's path on more than one occasion. It's time for us to do what we asked others to do: it's time for our confession."

"This I want to hear," Alan murmurs.

"Our father," he says, "was a Catholic priest."

THE SINS
of
MICHAEL
and
FRANCES MURPHY

38

MICHAEL CROUCHED DOWN BEHIND THE CURTAIN AND CARE-fully, oh so carefully, put his ear to the wall of the confessional booth. Mrs. Stevens was in there, she of the blonde hair and the large bosoms. Mrs. Stevens specialized in sins of lust, which made for exciting listening indeed.

He closed his eyes and opened his mouth a little. It took a moment, but the voices began to filter through the wood.

"I can't seem to stop touching myself, Father."

A pause. Michael could imagine the priest covering a sigh.

"And where do you touch yourself, my child?"

A sharp breath, indrawn.

She likes this question, Michael thinks.

"Between my legs, Father. Under the panties, and inside the lips of my pussy."

Michael's mouth dropped open farther. What kind of harlot uses the word *pussy* in a confessional?

He chastised himself for his own hypocrisy. Hypocrisy was a form of pride, and pride was a sin. The truth was, the whole thing had given him a raging hard-on. The idea of Mrs. Stevens (she of the blonde hair and the large bosoms) touching herself *there*—heck, the idea of her in *panties*—was an image that boggled the mind's eye.

The downside to this, of course, was that he'd have to come clean in confession. He'd have to admit—again—to hiding behind the curtain against the wall, to putting his ear up against the confessional booth, to listening to that most private of moments. In this case, he could add his own lustful thoughts to the quality of the sin.

It made it more difficult that the priest he'd be confessing this to was his own father. Not Father Confessor, but Father Dad. No way around it, though. Confession was a must, and Michael would never allow himself to withhold a confession, whatever the price. Failure to confess was a one-way ticket to an eternity in hellfire. Michael believed in hell. No secret was worth that.

One of the many things Michael admired about Dad was that he kept the separation between his job as a priest and his job as a father absolute. There was never a hint to Michael in real life that his dad had any personal opinion about what Michael had revealed in confession.

As Michael listened to Mrs. Stevens getting more graphic about her sin of masturbation *(wet, wet, she whispered, so very, very wet)*, he experienced a moment of admiration and love for his father. Dad was the best man Michael knew, the most decent, the most honorable. It was a question of character, and Frank Murphy had it in spades. He needed no priest's collar to prove it either.

Dad was the reason Michael wanted to become a priest. Dad was the reason he'd decided to enter the priesthood as a virgin. If he was honest with himself (and Michael prized honesty above all other things), that pledge was what he used to rationalize this moment. He was never going to know the touch of a woman, so was it really so bad to take a gander into the world of Mrs. Stevens and her wet white panties? Just a tiny, dirty peek?

Not so bad, no, he thought, but still a sin. Still to be confessed.

He was amazed at his father's patience sometimes. Mrs. Stevens didn't sound all that sorry to Michael. She sounded pretty excited, as a matter of fact. Even at thirteen, Michael could tell she was using this moment to sin some more, that she was getting off on confessing her masturbation to a handsome and celibate priest. She probably had wet panties right now.

Pubic hair as blonde as the hair on her head, glistening as she gasped . . .

This image both repulsed and excited him.

"Who's in there?"

The whisper would have shocked him to his bones if he hadn't sensed her coming. It was nearly impossible for them to sneak up on each other. He wasn't sure why. Maybe it was because they were twins.

Michael pulled his ear away from the booth with great care and some reluctance, making sure the wood didn't creak. He turned to his twin and smiled.

"Mrs. Stevens."

She made a face. "That whore? Why do you like listening to her, anyway? Does it make your pee-pee hard?" she teased.

"No," Michael whispered in protest. "Of course not."

Frances just smiled back. It was a knowing smile. Michael reflected that lying was the other thing they couldn't do with each other.

He sighed and shrugged.

"I'll go to confession."

"Good."

That would be the end of it, he knew. The final thing they shared, the thing in his life he was most certain of, other than his faith, was that his twin would always love him, no matter what.

"Let's move away from here," he whispers.

They pad away from the confessional booth like master thieves. They head back to the living quarters, and their shared room. It was a small room. Some might even call it bleak, but it was home to them.

The room was separated by a curtain hung from the ceiling that they could draw shut when they needed to. Father had put it up when Frances had begun to develop breasts.

"This is a wall," he'd said. "A wall with no door. When you draw it closed, only the person who drew it can open it again. You understand?"

"Yes, Father," they'd agreed, not really understanding the need for it at the time.

They understood better now. Michael masturbated at night, sometimes, after Frances had fallen asleep. He'd fight the urge, but it could become overwhelming. In a hidden place, inside a dark grotto that he wasn't quite ready to peer into yet, it was somehow more exciting to do it while thinking of his sister there, an arm's length away and yet untouchable. He tried to be silent, but knew, sometimes, he gasped louder than he should. Had she heard him in those moments? He thought maybe. Yes. Maybe she had.

He'd heard her too. Late at night, when she must have thought he was sleeping, he'd heard her little sighs and muffled moans, and had realized that she was touching herself. It shocked him at first, then intrigued him, then brought forth something he decided not to look at.

He'd never touch his sister, not in a million years, but he admitted something to her once.

"I'll never have sex," he told her. "But . . . if I was going to, it would be with a woman just like you, Frances."

"I know," she'd said and smiled. "I feel the same way."

Some might call it twisted; they called it love, and were careful not to look too deep. Besides, nothing ever happened.

Frances was going to become a nun. It was their plan. The fact that it would separate them was difficult, very difficult, but wasn't suffering one of the things that God demanded of the faithful?

There was a reason for everything, they both believed that. Father had a twin sister as well. Father had not gone to the seminary a virgin. He'd lain with a woman, and had gotten her pregnant. She'd died in childbirth. It was difficult, but, as in all things, Father was up to the task God had placed before him. He had raised them and had convinced the church to allow him into the seminary. His twin, Aunt Michelle, had cared for them while he was in the seminary. When father returned as an ordained priest, he took them back, and Aunt Michelle joined a convent and became a nun.

It was an unusual life, they knew that, but Father was a good father. He was kind, he was wise, he was hard but fair. He raised them to love God above all things, but he also demanded that they test their faith with intellect, putting them into public, not private schools, and exposing them to the sinful world outside the walls of the church.

"There are far more people in this world who do not believe in God than do," he'd told them. "If you want to spread the word of God to the faithless, you have to understand them. Understanding breeds compassion, compassion breeds love, and love is the best way to bring Christ into a sinner's heart."

Michael and Frances did as he said, and entered that world

together. They viewed it like two soldiers who'd been sent on a mission. They hung out together, socialized little but were not unfriendly. They were both so attractive that other oddities were forgiven. Michael's refusals of advances drove the girls crazy, while Frances's refusals convinced the boys that she was the most desirable creature on earth.

They had no real friends at school, only acquaintances, and that was fine with them. They were content in the path they saw before them and had no doubts about their future.

Father and Aunt Michelle were twins, and had become a priest and a nun. Frances and Michael were twins, and shared the same destiny. What else could this be but a sign from God?

They sat down on their beds to do their homework. Michael was uncomfortably aware that he still had an erection. The image of Mrs. Stevens was a vivid one. He glanced over at his twin and was shocked to see that she was looking at him.

She knows. She always knows.

It excited him, it disgusted him, it filled him with guilt and something far darker.

The expression on her face was one of speculation. She smiled and reached for the curtain. Before she drew it between them, she said:

"Be sure to go to confession tomorrow."

He swallowed and nodded.

"I will."

"I love you, Michael."

"I love you too."

She drew the curtain closed.

MICHAEL AND FRANCES WERE SIXTEEN when everything changed.

There was no evidence that their world was about to come crashing down around them. The world—and God—were strange and cruel like that. This was something Michael had always known and accepted, until it happened to him.

They were asleep when the sound of voices woke Michael up. He glanced over and saw that Frances was still sleeping. Years later, he'd wonder why he'd been awoken. He'd come to understand that God had called him from sleep, because God had a plan.

The voices weren't loud, but they had a sense of urgency to them. The fact of them was strange; it was 2:00 A.M. Father went to bed at 9:30 and woke up at 4:30.

Michael stood up and went to the door. He put his ear to it as he had done so many times to the wall of the confessional booth. He closed his eyes, and he listened.

One of the voices was female, and strangely familiar, though he couldn't quite place it. The other belonged to his father.

"They don't need to know!" his father whispered. "There's no reason. This was our sin, our secret. They're fine, they're healthy, and they both plan to lead holy lives, devoted to God. Why burden them with this now?"

"God spoke to me, Frank. I've spent the last sixteen years praying to him, asking him for forgiveness. I have calluses on my knees from praying. He finally answered. Do you know what he said? He said just one word: *truth*. I heard it in my heart, clear as a bell. God is love, Frank, remember? Love can only come from truth. I agreed to hide this in the beginning because I was ashamed. I was certain God would never forgive me. But he spoke to me, he told me he will forgive me. All I have to do is obey him, to tell the truth."

"You're hearing things! Do you really think that God would want you to ruin their lives by telling them the truth, by telling them you are their mother?"

Michael's head shot away from the door like he'd had his ear pressed against a hot iron.

What had he said?

Mother. The word was *mother*.

How many times, in early years, had they pressed Father, had they asked him about their mother?

She died in childbirth, he'd told them. She's with God now, she's the reason I joined the priesthood. Let her be.

One day they stopped asking, but they never stopped wondering.

And why did her voice sound familiar?

"What is it?"

He started in the dark. His twin stood behind him. He realized he was shivering.

"Michael?"

She put her arms around his waist and hugged herself to him, cheek against his shoulder blades. He continued to shiver, but even in his fear he was aware of her small breasts against his back. He chastised himself in silence.

Lust is the devil's work, and the devil is tireless.

"F-father is arguing with someone. A woman. I heard him say she's our mother."

He felt her stiffen against him.

"What?"

He wanted to turn around. He wanted to turn around and tell her to forget it, they should go back to bed and wake up the next morning and realize that it had all been a dream. He couldn't turn around right now, though. She'd see his lust.

The devil is tireless . . .

"I heard him. Listen."

She continued to clutch him as they strained to hear. He marveled at the dexterity of Satan. Michael was terrified of what they might hear, angered at what they'd already heard, he was a little bit dizzy, he was trying to hear more but didn't want to hear more, and through it all, he was never unaware of those small breasts against his back, the hint of what might (*just might*) be her nipples. Lucifer could walk and chew gum at the same time, no doubt about that.

"I forbid it!" Michael's father raged in a whisper.

Silence.

The woman's voice was calm, sure, certain. He still couldn't quite place it; the whisper was disguising it.

"You can't forbid me to do what God's ordered, Frank. I am their mother, and God has said it's time they knew everything."

Michael knew something was very wrong when Frances gasped. She buried her face in his back and moaned. It was a sound of horror. Her arms left him and he felt her back away. He turned around and saw that her face was milk-white, her eyes so wide he thought they'd pop out of their sockets, her fist stuffed in her mouth to stifle her moans. She pointed a shaking finger at the door, but couldn't seem to say anything coherent.

"Frances? What is it?"

She pulled the fist from her mouth. He was shocked to see that she'd bitten it hard enough to draw blood in places.

"Her . . ." she whispered, still horrified. "Don't you recognize her voice?" She began to pull her hair. Some of it ripped away from her scalp. "Don't you recognize her voice?"

Michael grabbed her wrists to keep her from hurting herself more. He'd always loved her hair. Other than her eyes, it was the thing that made her the most beautiful.

"Frances! Get hold of yourself!"

She yanked her wrists out of his grasp and sat down against the wall. She pulled her knees up to her chest and put her forehead against them. She began to rock, back and forth.

"Go and see. You'll understand."

He could barely hear her.

But something was starting to swim up from a very deep, very dark place. Something that caused a greasy sweat to break out on his forehead.

He took a last look at his twin and opened the door. He padded down the hall toward the voices, which were coming from the chapel. The sweat was really coming now and he started to run, because that dark thing was swimming with a vengeance, and he wanted to get there before it broke the surface, so he could prove it wrong, wrong, wrong . . .

He burst into the chapel barefoot, in his underwear, covered with sweat and shivering like a naked man in a snowstorm.

The thing burst through the surface. Laughing.

Do you see? it asks. Do you seeeeeeeeeeeeeeeee hee hee hee hee?

He did see. He saw his father, the great and honorable Frank Murphy, standing next to the woman who'd said she was their mother.

The woman was a nun, and he knew her well.

Aunt Michelle.

39

"MY FATHER AND MY MOTHER HAD BEEN BROTHER AND SIS-
ter, twins like my sister and I. They'd lain together and the result had
been us." His face is sad, somber, grave. "They conspired to hide my
mother's pregnancy. It wasn't so hard. They were both eighteen.
They'd gotten drunk and had let the devil lead them.

"How do I describe what that was like for us? The two people we
respected most in the world had spent our lifetime lying to us. Our
birthright was incest. We were the result of the forbidden coupling.

"I asked my father, that night, if he'd ever confessed this sin to another. He said that he had not." Murphy's expression is incredulous.
"Can you imagine? He'd kept his sin to himself, had consigned himself to hellfire. Why? To protect us? No. Any priest he'd confessed to
would have kept his secret. He did it because he was ashamed.

"Of all the things I learned and heard, that was the one that was
unforgivable to me. Not the incest, though that was bad enough. Not
the lying to my sister and me, I could even understand that. The one
thing I could not forgive him for was his deception of God.

"They told us they'd devoted their lives to God and had raised us
to fear God as penance for their sin. I couldn't hear this, couldn't see
past that most basic deception.

"My sister and I fled the church that morning. Father tried to stop
us, but I struck him down." He smiles, once. "No, I didn't kill him. He

died of cancer ten years ago. I have no idea if he ever confessed to his sin. I like to think he did."

"She never talks," Alan says.

"He's in charge," I reply. "It's his show."

This is common in serial killer teams. One acts as the dominant, calls the plays, provides the rationalization for their actions. Kirby hadn't been so far off the mark after all.

"We were troubled for a number of years, I will admit. We lost our way. The only thing we never lost was our love for each other." His sister places a hand on his shoulder. He reaches up to hold it while continuing to speak. "It took us some time to come back to God. I won't bore you with the ins and outs of that right now. There's time for our full story later. All that's important now is that truth: we did come back to God. I came to realize that the ruination of our lives was the result of a lie, a refusal to bare all to God, a refusal to confess in order to receive salvation.

"We have since applied this to ourselves, without mercy or restraint. I admitted to sexual longings for my sister. She did the same. We did our penance for our actions, for so nearly following in our parents' sinful footsteps. And we came, once again, to understand what God's purpose was for us."

He glances up at her, she down at him, and they smile. It's an image made terrible because it is beatific. Monsters with halos and blood on their teeth. They return their gaze to the camera.

"God had tested us, from the moment of our conception. He gave us every reason to give up on Him. He provided us with betrayal, doubt, and suffering. He wanted to be sure we were strong enough. God tests all His prophets thus.

"I came to understand that the face of my father was the face of far too many. The holy man, devoting his life to God and others. The admirable soul who is yet willing to consign himself to eternal damnation because he is willing to reveal some of his secrets, but not all of them. My father admitted to having children out of wedlock, but not to the ultimate truth—that it had been his sister he slept with.

"I came to understand that it was our duty to bring others to the full light of God by ensuring they understood that God accepts only absolutes in His truth. Be truthful about all, be factually contrite, ask

Him to forgive, and He will cleanse the sin from you. Admit to nine sins of ten, hold back the one, and you will burn forever.

"We have devoted our lives to this work. It has been difficult. Thou shalt not kill, one of God's most basic dictates. But all those we killed had confessed to their sins, and all save one were truly contrite. How else could we know about them? We only took souls who had admitted their sins to a priest in holy confession. They were martyrs, all but one, pierced in the side as Christ on the cross, and the contrite now sit at the right hand of the Lord." He pauses. "The child is the exception, of course. I have no doubt that she is burning as I speak. She died to illuminate the other half of the sacred agreement: contrition. Because of these deaths, millions more will understand that they are not alone, that we all have shameful things inside us. We all have a darker side we must admit to if we're to experience the fullness of the love of God. And oh, how wonderful that love is. God is many things, but most of all, God is love."

The first visible hint of insanity reveals itself. It's subtle. A certain shine to the eyes, a higher pitch to the voice. But it's there. Behind it will be the truth of what he's doing and done and why. Shame at the circumstances that caused their birth, betrayal by those they trusted, all of it wrapped in the religion in which they were raised. I don't care how flowery the phrases are, how carefully thought out the rationalizations; serial murder is sublimated rage. There are no exceptions.

I consider, again, the fact that the victims were all women and realize that Callie had been correct when she spoke about the Madonna and the whore. Michael Murphy blamed his aunt/mother more than he blamed his father, and the women he murdered had paid the price.

"That stage of our work is done. We're ready now, to move forward, to take the next step on the path God has laid for us. Come find us. We are ready. We will go willingly, and will not fight back."

Fade to black.

"Isn't that nice of them?" Callie says, scorn in her voice. "Poor babies, boo-hoo for them. Daddy was an asshole, join the club."

I tend to agree with her sentiments; we all do. Life is rough, even cruel and unjust. That's no excuse for turning on your fellow man. The nature versus nurture argument has raged for years, and will rage for more. I think there is truth in the need for a good environment. Our future is informed by what we experience as children. Statistics bear this out too often to be discounted.

Approximately one-third of the abused go on to become abusers. But what about the other two-thirds? All those abused, mistreated, beaten, and betrayed, who went on to lead normal lives? Haunted for-ever by their experiences, maybe even permanently damaged, but—and here's the point—still decent? For every victim of molestation who goes on to offend against children as an adult, we can find examples of victims who went on to become kind and loving parents. What is the difference between the two? Are some of us just born able to carry bigger burdens than others?

Michael and Frances had been dealt a bad hand, true, but it was hardly crippling. Not even close to the worst I'd ever heard. The fact that they'd managed to spin their misfortune into a rationalization for twenty years of murder is, for me, more a testament to their weakness and their guilt than a reason to sympathize.

"I don't really care why," I say. "I just want to put them in jail."

"I can get behind that," Alan agrees.

In the end, this is the simplicity that saves us. Looking for reasons why, trying to get down to that deep, dark bedrock, is just a serpent eating its own tail. In the end, you won't find truth, you'll just devour yourself. At some point we have to stop trying to understand why and accept that our only job is to remove them from society. It's easier with some than others.

"Let's get a current address," I say, "and give them their wish."

AN HOUR HAS PASSED SINCE the discoveries began to come so fast and furious. AD Jones is in our offices, along with my team and the FBI SWAT.

The head of our SWAT is Sam Brady, Callie's fiancé. Brady is in his mid-forties and he's a tall, lanky man, standing around six-four, with close-cropped hair and a face that can be as grim as his profession calls for. I've seen other sides to him and have come to know a man at peace with who he is. He loves Callie quietly, but he loves her deeply and he seems to bring this approach to everything in his life. He's solid and all man and utterly unintimidated by Callie.

Brady has watched the last video clip of the Preacher.

"I don't recommend going in hot," he says. "I'm not the expert, but it seems to me that they want to be taken into custody. Need it, even."

"I agree," I say, "but I'm not confident enough about it to go knock on the front door. I think we should set up a perimeter and talk them out via phones or bullhorns. If they want to come quietly, we'll let them. If not . . ." I shrug. "Tear gas time."

He considers this and nods. "I'll get my team geared up. Give us twenty minutes."

"We'll meet you in the parking lot."

I AM CHECKING MY WEAPON and readying my mind. We all are.

"Hey," Alan says, ratcheting back the slide on his weapon, "if you know the death penalty is on the table and you plead guilty—is that suicide?"

"I think in their case they're confident that it's martyrdom."

He holsters his weapon and sighs. "Yeah. So, do you think they meant it about coming quietly?"

"I think so. But you can never be sure at the end."

Suicide, by self or by cop, is an oft-preferred solution for a criminal when the jig's up. Most accepted from the beginning that they would die if discovered.

"Seems strange they have a house in the Valley," he muses. "Probably drove by it once or twice and never knew."

James's cell phone rings. He answers, listens, and frowns.

"What's that?" he asks. His face goes white. "Send it to me now."

"What is it?" I ask.

"Bitch," he breathes, but it has an odd sound to it. More desperate than insulting.

"James?"

He looks at me.

"Kirby got there first. Now they've got her."

40

KIRBY APPEARS ON CAMERA, NAKED AND TIED TO A CHAIR.
Michael Murphy stands next to her. He's furious.

"I told you we'd surrender peacefully! I didn't expect any of you to agree with our actions, but I did expect you to uphold the law." He takes a deep breath. "I am very, very disappointed."

"Oh, for God's sake, shuuuuuuut uuuuuuuuup," Kirby says, rolling her eyes.

"Stupid fucking kid," Brady murmurs. "Can never learn to keep her mouth shut." I'd called him back once we knew what we were looking at.

Michael steps in front of her. All we can see is his back and her legs.

"You're in no position to take the Lord's name in vain," he says.

"Bite me, bozo," Kirby replies, "and your God can bite it too. Hard."

I brace myself, expecting him to slap her, but he draws his arm back and hits her in the face with his closed fist. The smack of flesh against flesh cracks through the computer speakers and Kirby goes over backward in her chair.

"Motherfucker," I whisper.

The camera had been stationary. It begins to move now, jiggling a bit with the motion. Frances must have picked it up. It zooms in on Kirby's face. She's lying against a hardwood floor, blonde hair sprayed

out around her. Her eyes are having trouble focusing. Her lips have
been split open in two places and blood runs freely down her chin
and left cheek. She shakes her head to clear it and laughs.

"You hit like a girl."

"Oh, Kirby," Callie says. "Stupid girl. Shut up now."

She won't, I think. This is who she is.

Michael grabs her by her hair and uses it to heft the full weight of
her body, to bring her back into a sitting position. Kirby turns her
head to the right and spits to clear the blood from her mouth. She
turns back to the camera and we all see those cold, awful killer's eyes.

"I'm going to kill you and your sister," she says. "Just wanted you
to know that. And no one sent me here. One of the people you murdered was an old friend of mine." She grins. Her teeth are red with her
blood. "Thought I'd return the favor."

"Murder is a sin," Michael scolds her. "We killed for God's purpose. If you kill us for vengeance, you'll go to hell."

Really? I think. What about Ambrose, the man you murdered for
his identity? God's purpose?

It's a useless question; his answer would be yes, of course.

Kirby shrugs. "So sue me. I'm good at it." Another torn-lipped,
red-toothed grin. "You'll see."

"You really came here on your own?" Michael asks.

"I'm a solo act, asshole, and I always have been."

"Unfortunate for you," he says, "that you missed the backup security camera. We were waiting for you when you came through the
door."

"Yeah, well. Nobody's perfect. You should have killed me, though.
Tasers are for pussies."

"Knocked you down fast enough," Frances snarls.

Kirby smiles. "Down, but not dead, dummy. Bad move on your
part."

"What's your name?" Michael asks.

"Since we're on a religious bender, why don't you call me . . . Eve."
She chuckles. "I always liked her style, you know? Eat that apple.
Yummy."

"Very well. Are you Catholic, Eve?"

She rolls her eyes.

"Supreme beings are for suckers. I believe in guns, good beer, masturbation when I don't have a man, and a nice hard cock when I do." She winks. "Know what I mean?"

"Blasphemous bitch," he observes.

"Why, thank you, asshole."

"Why don't you stop calling me that, Eve. My name is Michael."

"Nah. Asshole is just fine."

He sighs. "I can see getting you to confess is going to be a lot of work, Eve."

"Ohhhh, torture? Coolio."

"Why isn't this clip ending?" I ask.

"This isn't a clip," James says. "This is live."

"Sam?" I ask, turning to him. "We need to get over there now. This is your show. What's the game plan with something like this?"

He examines the video feed. "Looks to me like they're in the living room." He grabs the house plans from a desk. "There's only two ways in. Front door and back." He cups his chin, thinking. "Flash-bangs through the front windows, and we breach through the front and back doors. Go in hard, take them down while they're still reeling. Simple is the best way. Get more complicated and you increase the possibility of screwing the pooch." He nods to the computer. "They've been kind enough to provide us with ongoing video surveillance. We'll use it. Bring a laptop with wireless capabilities and execute at the most opportune moment."

Sounds good to me. I glance at AD Jones. "Sir?"

"Do it. Shoot to kill if necessary. And figure out a way to make sure this video never gets seen. The last thing we need on a high profile case like this is association with a killer like Kirby Mitchell."

"I have a high speed connection via a cellular network on my laptop," Callie says. "I just need the URL for this feed."

"I'll provide that," James says.

Brady nods. "I'll meet you in the parking lot."

"Before I'm done," Michael says to Kirby, "you'll experience the wonder of confession to God. You'll learn what it's like to be purged of lies. Truth is a light, Eve, a light like no other."

"Bring it on, asshole. But can you stop hitting me in the face, at least? Girl's got to be able to get a date, you know?"

"Let's get moving," I say. "If she keeps talking like that, she might not have much time."

41

"START SMALL, EVE. THAT'S THE BEST WAY, SOMETIMES. BE-gin with the small things and work up to the most shameful. Do you think you can do that?"

We're all in the same car. Alan is driving, following Brady and his team in their van. I have the laptop.

Kirby smiles.

"Sure. I got one for you."

"Yes?" He sounds pleased, maybe a little surprised that she's agreed so easily.

"The first blow job I ever gave."

Michael nods. "Lust, oral sex. Very good. Go on."

"Well, it was this really cute guy, hunkalicious, you know? I'd heard he had a big old cock, and while I'd seen pictures of them, I'd never seen them in the flesh, so to speak. *Turgid,* you know?"

"Yes, yes, continue." He doesn't seem to appreciate Kirby's use of the descriptive.

"Anyway, I told him I wanted to see that big ol' hot dog, and hey—coincidence—he wanted to show it to me." She rolls her eyes. "Guys are funny that way. He had a car, so I snuck out that night and I met him out front and we drove to a parking lot near the beach. I told him to whip that sucker out, pun intended. Turns out someone had added a few inches. I mean, it wasn't small, but I've sucked bigger, you know."

"Get to the point, please."

"It was kind of cute. Wearing its little army helmet, all washed up and shiny and standing at attention. 'Sergeant Cock reporting for duty, ma'am!'" She giggles.

"This slut is wasting your time," Frances says from behind the camera.

"Hey, it's my sin, right? As long as I end up telling the whole truth, it shouldn't matter how I tell it."

Michael nods. "Fair enough, Eve. Go on."

"Okay. So I decided it was time to play turkey—you know: gobble gobble gobble! I opened wide and put the train in the tunnel. That's when he started screaming."

There's a moment of silence. Michael frowns. "Why was he screaming?"

Kirby heaves an exaggerated sigh. "Hey, I was only twelve. He was sixteen, and hot. I was nervous. I was really worried about bad breath, so I gargled with mint freshener for like an hour beforehand. Then I chewed up a bunch of breath mints right before I started . . . you know." She clucks her tongue and looks regretful. "Poor guy. Almost blistered his wee-wee. He started screaming and yanked my head off. From experience, things have to be pretty bad for a guy to do that. He jumped out of the car and was running around in circles saying, 'It burns, it burns, it burns!' That, right there, that's the *real* sin."

"What, exactly?"

"That I gave a bad blow job." She bats her eyes sweetly. "Will the Big Guy forgive me? I never did it again, and I'm a much better cocksucker now, I promise."

"Oh, Kirby," I say. "Why can't you just shut up and play along?"

I half-expect Michael to fly into a rage. He just shakes his head in regret.

"I'm sorry you've decided to be difficult," he says, "but perhaps your journey will help others understand the folly of holding on to sin. Because in the end, you will confess, Eve. You might have no eyes, your nipples may have been cut off, perhaps your kneecaps will be broken, but one way or another, you will confess."

Kirby yawns. "Here's a tip on torture for you, asshole. It's a lot scarier when you just do it as opposed to talking about it beforehand."

"If you insist. We'll start small, as I had suggested you start with your sins."

He steps out of the camera lens. I can hear his footsteps on the hardwood floor. Frances continues to focus on Kirby.

"You'll break, you know," Frances says.

Kirby blows a kiss into the camera. She moves her eyebrows up and down. "Hey . . . we've got a camera going . . . a hot naked babe . . ." She spreads her legs. "I'm ready for my close-up, director. Want to join me?"

"Jezebel!" Frances hisses.

"Hey, I have a friend named Jezebel, so be nice."

"I think she really is insane," Callie says.

"Either that or she has a death wish," I reply.

"Fearlessness is a common trait in sociopaths," James says. "Look, he's back."

Michael Murphy is carrying a rod, approximately three feet long, with a copper tip and an insulated handle. A wire runs from the base of the rod and out of frame. He shows it to Kirby.

"Do you know what this is?"

"Looks like a picana to me. Popular for use in electric torture in South America and other sorta-civilized places. What's yours run—about sixteen thousand volts?"

"Thirty thousand. Technology has evolved. Since you're familiar with it, you know what it is capable of. I ask you again to confess a sin, a real sin, with true contrition in your heart."

"Hey, I did what you asked. I really did feel bad about giving a bad blow job. A girl has to have standards."

Michael sighs. "Frances, can you put the camera on a tripod, please? I need your assistance here."

"Yes, Brother."

The sounds of the camera jiggling and Frances doing as he's asked ensue. She appears in frame a moment later.

"Many people think application of the picana to the outside of the body, such as the breasts or genitals, is sufficient. It's painful, I agree, but I've found internal application to be far more effective."

"Me too," Kirby agrees. "So—where? In my mouth, my ass, or my punani?"

"A little ways down your throat," he says. "Try not to breathe in your own vomit. You'd die."

I see a twitch appear at the corner of Kirby's left eye. It's the first sign of a crack in her facade up to this point.

"Hold her head," Michael says to Frances.

Frances grips Kirby's head with a hand on each side to keep her from moving. Michael positions the picana in front of Kirby's mouth.

"You can either open of your own accord, or I will smash this into your teeth until they're no longer in the way."

Kirby doesn't smile or joke, but she does open her mouth wide.

"Last chance," Michael says. "Do you want to confess?"

Kirby sticks out her tongue and makes an ahhhhh sound, like she's having her throat checked by the doctor.

Michael doesn't hesitate. He slips the picana between her teeth and into her mouth. I can tell he's in the back of her throat because her face starts to get red and she begins to gag. Frances removes her hands from the sides of Kirby's head. It's a deft move; they've done this before.

That's when he hits the button in the handle of the picana.

The result is instantaneous and awful. Her body goes taut as the electricity causes her muscles to contract violently. Her eyes bug out and her teeth snap down onto the picana with such force I'm surprised they don't shatter. Urine runs down her legs. Her belly jumps; I realize that she's probably defecating against her will. It only lasts a moment, it seems like an hour.

Michael lets go of the button. Kirby's mouth flies open, he yanks the picana back. Vomit comes with it and the convulsions follow. Spasms rock Kirby's body as her muscles and brain try to figure out how to respond to what just happened. Her chair goes over sideways and she crashes against the hardwood floor again, twitching. Her eyes flutter. The spasms eventually die off and we can hear her breathing against the floor, deep, ragged, moaning breaths.

Michael waits a moment, just watching. He walks behind her, reaches down, and rights her in the chair. I can't believe how much different she looks now than just ten seconds ago. Her face drips with sweat, her chin and chest are covered in vomit, and her eyes are having trouble focusing.

Michael leans forward. He brushes a lock of sweat-matted hair away from her forehead.

"Now, my child? Are you ready to confess? Don't be afraid, God will forgive anything you are truly penitent for."

Kirby opens her mouth to speak, but nothing comes out. She closes it, swallows, struggles to compose herself. She lifts her head up and gives Michael the sweetest smile I've ever seen on a stone-killer.

"Let's go again."

"Jesus!" I say. "How much longer, Alan?"

"Ten minutes."

Ten minutes? The torture we just saw happened in two.

"I don't know if she can last that long."

"She'll last," James says.

Is that a hope or a prayer? I wonder.

"If you insist," Michael says, "but in the end, the result will be the same. We all break under God's will. God is love."

Frances grips Kirby's head again and Michael brings the picana back up.

"Drive faster," I tell Alan. "Please."

42

"CURTAINS ARE DRAWN," BRADY POINTS OUT. "WHAT'S HER
state? Can she take the flash-bangs?"

Kirby's received the business end of the picana three more times. She hasn't broken, but her smart mouth is gone, the surest sign that she's hurting. Only her eyes remain defiant.

"She can take it."

The house is in Reseda. It's an older ranch style home from the 1960s that hasn't seen much updating since. The blue and white wood trim is cracked and peeling. The lawn is full of dead or dying grass. The windows are dirty and the curtains look old. The Murphys don't care about this home; it's just a place to camp between murders.

Brady jabs a finger at the picture windows that lead into the living room.

"No finesse. On my go we're going to toss flash-bangs through the windows, and simultaneously smash open the front door and throw in a few more. Then we breach and take them down. My team will enter, we'll call you in when it's clear."

Brady's voice is low and urgent. His men are silent and still, but it's the tense motionlessness of a track runner waiting for the starter pistol to go off.

Kirby screams for the first time and we hear it in stereo; it plays from the computer speakers and filters out from the house.

"Wait for the next scream," I say. "That's when they'll be the most off guard."

In the end, the monsters are all the same. They live for the screams.

Brady looks at me and frowns.

"It's her best chance," I say. "Better another shock than a bullet. She can take it."

Brady processes this in a heartbeat; he nods and then signals to his men in the front to be ready. One is poised at the picture window. Another stands by the front door with a battering ram, while yet another waits next to him, flash-bangs in hand. Brady has his HK53 at the ready.

My team and I stand back by the cars. Everyone has their weapons out. The moon hangs above us all, silver and unforgiving.

We'd just arrived, so the neighborhood hasn't yet woken up to our presence. That will change in another heartbeat.

There is a sense of time passing by the second, or the millisecond, or the nanosecond. Everything hangs, a tremendous waiting.

Kirby screams and the world explodes.

Flash-bangs crash through the window. The battering ram hits the door once, the doorjamb is destroyed as the door flies open. More grenades are tossed inside and again that stereo-echo as they detonate. I see it happen from the outside, I hear it happen from the inside, and it all happens in the blink of an eye.

Brady rushes into the home, followed by his men. There's no hesitation in their motion; everything they do is committed, decisive, swift. The camera has fallen over and now faces a wall. I can't tell what's happening inside.

"Come on," James mutters. "Hang in there, Kirby." I don't think he's even aware that he's saying it.

I hear Brady and his men yelling at the Murphys.

"Get down on the fucking ground!"

Grunts and sounds of a scuffle follow. I hear thuds. A minute later Brady is at the door, motioning us in. We run.

The living room is to the immediate right. The Murphys are both down on their stomachs on the floor. They are looking at each other and their lips are moving.

" 'Yea, though I walk through the valley of the shadow of death,' "
Michael says.

" 'I will fear no evil,' " Frances replies.

"Shut the fuck up," Brady growls.

They ignore him and continue their recitation.

James moves to Kirby. The smell of feces and urine and sweat are
strong in the room. Her head hangs down, her hair brushes her
thighs. He kneels in front of her, puts a hand under her chin, and lifts
it up. It's a tender act, unexpected.

"Are you okay?"

"S-stupid . . . stupid question," she croaks.

She's talking to him, but her eyes are on me. They are pleading
with me.

"Everyone out of here except Callie and me," I order.

Hesitation and quizzical looks follow. The Lord's Prayer murmurs
in the silence, like flies buzzing against a screen.

"I mean it," I say. "Now, please."

Only James seems to understand. He stands up and heads for the
door without another word. Brady's men pull the Murphys to their
feet and begin to walk them outside. Michael stops in front of Kirby.

"You didn't confess. You're going to hell, you know."

"S-see you th-th-there," Kirby hisses. She tries to blow him a kiss
but fails.

"Get them out of here," I say.

Alan is the last to leave.

"I'll watch the door," he says, and pulls it shut behind him.

"C-can Callie clear o-o-out too?"

"I need her help, Kirby," I tell her, my voice gentle. "She was there
for me right after. You can trust her."

Callie remains silent as Kirby studies her with a weary eye.

"K, c-can you please get me out of this?"

"Of course, honey-love," Callie tells her softly, kneeling next to
the chair.

Callie pulls a pocketknife from her purse. As she begins to cut the
ropes, Kirby starts to shiver. I put one hand on her shoulder, move
the hair back from her brow with the other. When the ropes are off,
she rubs her wrists and sits there for a moment, shaking.

"C-can I t-tell you something?" she whispers to us.

"Anything," Callie says.

She smiles. "I'm ab-b-bout t-to run out of s-s-steam . . ."

We catch her as she topples forward from the chair in a dead faint.

This is what I'd seen in her eyes, that thing I'd understood. Kirby was about to fall apart and she wanted as few witnesses to that secret as possible.

KIRBY CLINGS TO ME, HER arms around my neck, as Callie washes her in the bathtub. We clean her like a baby, and she lets us. It's a moment of trust not likely to roll by again. Her muscles twitch and spasm, and her grip tightens as Callie (gently, so gently) wipes her private areas for her.

"Want to hear my confession?" she whispers in my ear, so faint I'm sure that only I can hear her.

I say nothing. I feel Kirby's lips smile against my skin.

"I had a friend, when I was sixteen, who got murdered by her boyfriend. He beat her to death and ran. I found him one year later and it took him three days to die. I wasn't even eighteen, but I never felt a lick of guilt about it."

I say nothing. I stroke her hair. She puts her head on my shoulder and sighs.

Everyone, even Kirby, needs to tell someone their secrets, sometimes.

Ego te absolvo, Kirby.

43

I sit in the room with Michael Murphy, as I have with so many others like him, trying to pry out his final secrets. The last confession. He examines me, my scars, tries (I guess) to look into my soul.

"Are you Catholic?" he asks me.

"Not anymore."

"Do you believe in God?"

"Maybe. What did you do with the bodies?"

He hid from us for twenty years. Where did the victims go?

He sits at this table as he sat at the one in his video clips. The rosary has been replaced by cuffs around the wrists, but the posture is the same. Michael Murphy is exactly where he wants to be. In his mind, jail was just the next best pulpit to preach from, the death penalty he and his sister had received was an opportunity for martyrdom. They confessed without prompting or the need for a trial.

In terms of the video clips, "viral" remained an apt term. They've made their way around the world and back again via the Internet. In most instances their use is voyeuristic, the opportunity to peer into the last moments of another human being, to put an ear to the confessional booth. But it can't be denied that they ignited a debate that will probably rage on for months or longer.

There are those who feel that their methods were inexcusable, but that the message still has merit. Murder, one person had said, is not a Christian virtue, but full truth before God is. In other words, we don't condone *how* they did it, gosh no, but as far as *what* they had to say . . . well . . .

There is a radical fringe who consider Michael and his sister to be heroic, revolutionary. I'd run across a website selling T-shirts with slogans like *Full Truth or Hellfire* and *Only God Can Judge the Murphys*.

All of this would sicken me if not for the most basic truth: support is in the minority. Most Christians, the majority by far, decry every aspect of what the Murphys did. Many have written open letters of apology to the families of the victims on behalf of all Christians and Catholics, and I am reminded of that section from the catechism of the Catholic Church Father Yates had read to me about the guiding principle of love. It's nice to see that for most, those aren't just words.

The Murphys remain a ball of contradictions for me. Understanding the monsters the way I do is like harmonizing with a dark melody. I can never duplicate it, not exactly, but I can hit the notes an octave or so above, and from that surmise their song. I've achieved some of that with Michael and his sister, but many aspects elude me.

Fanaticism, when it is applied to serial murder, is almost always a smoke screen. Terrorist leaders who preach death in the name of God aren't really interested in God; they're just getting off on making people die. Hitler spoke of strengthening the Aryan race; in reality, he was just another serial killer.

I've seen little evidence that either Michael or Frances took sexual pleasure in the crimes they committed. The physician at the women's prison where Frances has been housed confirmed that she is still a virgin. They never asked for the death penalty to be taken off the table.

True believers? Or is there some dark joy buried deep, hidden so well that even they'll never see it?

"Do you really want to know?" he asks.

"No, Michael. I just had some free time today to come and chat with you. Of course I want to know."

He folds his hands and smiles. "Then confess something to me. It does not have to be something huge, but it can't be something small either. Tell me and I give you my word, I'll reveal to you what happened to the others."

I consider this offer. It's never a good idea to trade in an interrogation. Once they have what they want, they don't need you anymore and they can shut down. Michael's drug of choice is truth.

"Swear to God," I say.

"I'm sorry?"

"Swear to God that you'll tell me if I confess to something."

He shrugs. "Very well. I swear to God."

I sit back in my chair and think about it. He's not going to be happy with something like masturbation. It has to be personal, it has to be difficult, it has to ring true, but my personal integrity needs to remain intact at the end of it.

"My mother died when I was twelve," I say.

"What of?"

"Pancreatic cancer."

"I'm sorry. That's a painful way to die."

"Yes, it is. Toward the end, all she did was moan or scream, day and night. The painkillers didn't help."

"That must have been difficult for you."

Difficult? It comes to me now like it was then, a glistening piece of horror. My mother's hair had always been long and full. The radiation had made her as bald as a baby. I'd always thought her eyes were one of the most beautiful things about her. Because of the pain, they rolled in her head, or she squinched them shut tight, or she cried. Her curves had been reduced to a skeletal waste, and her scent, that mother-smell that had once been as comforting and natural to me as breathing, was now alien and reeked of sickness and the Horseman.

My dad, bless him, was a good dad, a great dad. He was a wonderful husband to my mom. But he couldn't take it for too long in that room, next to that bed. He'd visit for an hour and spend the next two days recovering. So it was left to me. I sat by her side and stroked her forehead and sang to her and cried with her. She was at home, and we had a hospice nurse, but I got the nurse to let me help with most things. At twelve, I changed my mother's diapers and I both hated and cherished the moment.

"In the last weeks, she begged me every day—sometimes twice a day—to kill her."

Kill me kill me please, honey, kill me, she'd moan or screech, over and over and over. *Please, please, please, kill me and make it stop, make it stop, Oh dear God, make it stop . . .*

"Mom was Catholic. Her faith had always been strong. She raised me to believe. In spite of it all, there she was, begging to become a suicide."

"God tests us," Michael says.

I glance at him and I consider killing him. Just for a millisecond.

"I believed that suicide meant she would go to hell. One day, toward the end, she had a good morning. It happened sometimes. She'd come back to us. Her eyes would get lucid and we could actually talk for a bit. It never lasted long. That morning I could have called my dad in, but I didn't. I decided to talk to her alone."

"About her death wish." It's a statement, not a question.

"Yes. I told her that suicide was a sin, that if she asked for death and got it, she'd go to hell. I told her that she needed to tell me she wanted to live until the end. I needed to hear those words from her."

He cocks his head at me, and narrows his eyes.

Does he see where I'm going? Maybe. Maybe this is his talent, maybe he smells sins like a dog smells meat.

"She was lucid. She still hurt, but I was able to get through to her, and she showed me at that moment what real faith could be. She smiled and told me what you told me. 'God is just testing me, love,' she said. 'It will be over soon.' 'Say the words, Mom,' I asked her. She was a little puzzled, but she was tired, so tired. 'I want to live to the end,' she told me. An hour later, she was gone again, back inside the pain, begging for death."

"Your mother sounds like an extraordinary woman."

"Yes, yes, she was."

He leans forward a little.

"The sin, Smoky? What did you do?"

I hate that he's using my first name.

"I just needed to hear the words, you know? So that when I killed her, it wouldn't be a suicide."

There it is, I think. The truth of you.

Because his eyes had widened as I said those words, ever so slightly. Not the widening of shock or surprise, but *thrill*.

"You murdered your mother?" he breathes.

"I brought her peace," I growl. "The peace that your God wasn't giving her. She was being tortured daily. We don't let animals suffer like that. Why people?"

"Because, Smoky—people have souls."

I feel like spitting in his face.

"Whatever. The bottom line was I poisoned her with an overdose of morphine pills. I knew how; I helped with her medication. And it wasn't a suicide, so, against your beliefs, she didn't go to hell for it."

He taps a finger against the Formica top of the table, considering. "I have to agree with you on that, Smoky. Your mother went to heaven. Her last, lucid wish was not for suicide. You, on the other hand . . ." He shakes his head. "Unless you ask for God's forgiveness, you will never feel His grace."

"Maybe," I say, "but that wasn't our deal. I agreed to confess something to you. I think I've upheld my end of the deal."

He sighs. "Yes, and I did swear to God. But I hope you'll consider this in the future. I hope you'll wake up one day and ask for God to forgive you for murdering your mother. Don't you understand? *It's the only way you'll ever see her again.*"

"The other victims?" My voice is ice.

"Very well. Dermestid beetles. They're flesh eaters, used in taxidermy to clean the skin from bones. They're very efficient and easy to purchase. We used them to strip the bodies of their flesh, and then we ground the bones into powder and tossed the powder onto consecrated ground."

"You had them . . . eaten?" My voice is incredulous.

"The body is just a vessel, Smoky. Their souls are in heaven." He is calm, assured, certain.

"I'm sure their families will appreciate that."

"It doesn't matter if they do or they do not. The truth remains the truth."

I fight the desire to strangle him with my bare hands. Just a few more questions.

"How did you find out about Dexter Reid?"

"Dexter's . . . situation became a controversial topic on a number of Catholic blogs. We monitored worldwide Catholic-oriented news via the Internet daily."

I picture Michael and Frances as ghouls, crouched together in the dark, faces lit by a computer screen as they licked their dead lips and sifted through cyberspace.

"Let's discuss your method of operation. Was it always the same? Frances infiltrated the congregation and bugged the confessionals?"

He nods. "We'd listen to the tapes together and make our choice. Frances would befriend them, learn their patterns."

"And you'd do the killing."

"She helped at times, but generally, yes. That was our division of labor."

"Then she'd stay with the congregation for a while after, so no one would suspect her of taking part in the disappearance."

"Correct."

"You started your . . . work before the Internet existed. What did you plan to do originally? With the tapes you made?"

"We weren't certain. We knew we needed to record our work, but I'll admit it wasn't clear to us at first just how those records would be used. Would we send them to a news organization? Direct to the people?" He glances up and smiles. "We trusted God would show us the way, and in His time, He did."

"Why did you change tack with Lisa Reid? You infiltrated her congregation personally."

He shrugs. "Eagerness, I suppose. We spent twenty years building our case. We knew our work was nearly done, and didn't want to wait a second longer than was necessary. As we were going to come out into the open, there was no further need to be so careful. Besides, it gave me the opportunity to leave my own thumbprint on the chalice."

"Weren't you concerned that Lisa would recognize you on the plane?"

"I wore a beard, and changed the color of my eyes. She'd always seen me in a wheelchair before. When someone is handicapped, quite often all people remember is the affliction."

True enough, I think.

"How did you know that your work was done?"

This is a key question for me, the behavior that makes Michael and Frances unique. Serial killers like to kill. They kill until they are stopped by capture or death. The Murphys had effectively stopped themselves by revealing their hand.

"We'd always known, had always agreed, that we would understand the moment when we had done enough. A few months ago, it was given to us that that moment had come."

"How?"

Michael Murphy looks right into my eyes and smiles, and it is the sweetest smile I've ever seen, the most beatific expression on a human face I've ever witnessed.

"God told me."

His voice radiates with awe. This is no joke or test.

"He spoke to you?"

"Even better—He *appeared* to me. It was approximately three months ago. I'd been sleeping fitfully for some reason that night, which was unusual. I always sleep deeply, and well. I had dozed off for a moment. I was at the precipice, that place where you tumble into true unconsciousness, when His voice came to me."

"What did He say?" I prod, though I don't really need to. He's there, in that moment, hearing the voice of God.

" 'Michael,' He said, 'you've done well, my son. You've walked a difficult path at great personal risk to yourself, but the time has come for the next part of your journey.' "

I notice that only Michael gets the credit in this narrative; no mention of Frances.

" 'The time has come for you to reveal the truth to the world. It will not be easy. Many will revile you and reject the Word, but do not let that deter you. My way is the Way, and you must continue forward even though you walk through a field of broken glass.' " Tears are running down Michael's face now. " 'Yes, Lord,' I cried out to Him. 'Whatever You ask, I will obey. Whatever burdens You give me, I will carry.' " He pauses for a long time. I wait him out. "Then He was gone, and I felt energized and refreshed, even though I hadn't slept. I felt as though I could run for days, weeks, months, years." He comes back to the present, wipes the tears from his face without seeming to notice he's doing it. He focuses on me again. "God put us on that path. God told me we had come to the end of it. That's the way it's always been, for all the prophets since time began."

He believes it. Every word. I can see it on his face, hear it in his voice. The insanity is back in his eyes again, that bright and shining light. Why had they stopped? For the same reason they had started; the Murphys were insane.

"What about Valerie Cavanaugh, Michael? She was a break in your pattern. Each victim had an outward secret that masked something darker. What was Valerie's outward secret?"

He pauses, thinking. "You're right," he admits. "She didn't have one. But when we saw her confession . . . she did it to torment her priest, not because she was truly seeking God's forgiveness. You could hear the pride in her voice. Once, she even giggled. That poor man. He struggled with what to do, I'm sure, but the seal of confession is absolute." He shrugs. "Not the same as the rest, but her death still serves the greater message: the necessity for full truth before God. Confession without contrition is the worst kind of lie there is." His voice goes flat. "This world is better off without her."

I cock my head at him. "She made you angry, didn't she? She was the knowing antithesis of what you were trying to say. Your version of Satan."

He shrugs, not agreeing, but . . .

"Question, Michael. Why just women? Weren't there any men with secrets worth killing to make your point?"

He stares at me blankly, puzzled.

"What does that matter?"

I find myself at a loss for words. He doesn't see it, I realize. There it is, the blind spot, and it's willful, reflexive, and profound. Self-revelation, I'd come to understand long ago, real, deep and personal deconstruction, was a luxury the psychopath did not have.

"One last thing, Michael. The scars on Frances's wrists—they're real. When did she try to kill herself?"

He smiles at me, and shakes his head. "She never tried. She needed the scars to play her part. It was risky, but I got her through, with the help of God."

I stare at him. I wish, on some level, that I could muster up a look of shock, or disbelief, but I know I'm long past that. I'm reminded of something a seasoned profiler once told me, back when I was new and bright and could still be shocked: *sometimes only the worst stuff is true.*

I stand up. Right now, I want to get out of here, I want that more than anything. I remember, though, the final thing. I turn to him and smile.

"Michael?"

"Yes?"

"Everything I just told you about my mother was a lie." I smirk. "You really are stupid. Did you actually think I'd confess to murder? Here? We're being videotaped, for God's sake."

I leave the room without saying another word, his curses following me.

This is my thrill, the thing that widens my eyes: the suffering they feel when I deny them what they need.

"SO IT'S OVER THEN," ROSARIO says to me on the phone.

"It's over. They'll both be put to death, eventually."

She is silent, and I feel that silence, understand it. It's the silence of the unfulfilled, the unfinished sentence.

"Why doesn't it make me feel any better?" she asks me.

"You know why."

She sniffles. She is crying.

"Yes, I guess you're right."

It's not enough because her child is still dead, will always be dead, will never come back. Nothing fixes that, not ever.

"Thank you for calling me, Smoky. And for . . . well, everything."

"Good-bye, Rosario."

We hang up and I know good-bye means good-bye for good. The families of the victims don't seek me out; I am forever associated in their minds with the loss of their loved ones. Rosario is grateful, they always are, but I need to be their past, not their future. It used to bother me; I understand it much more personally now.

I drive to my next stop and consider the past weeks. Have I learned anything? As much as I despise learning because of my brushes against the monsters, I also know it's one of the main things separating me from them; I can learn and change, they cannot.

Secrets. They run through everything we do, everything we are. Religion calls them sins, and says they'll keep us from heaven. They can be big or small. We can hold on to them like they were bars of gold. Everyone has them.

Maybe religion has it right, but perhaps it's just a metaphor. Maybe, just maybe, we carry heaven and hell with us, right here on earth, all the time. Maybe holding on to our darkest secrets puts us in a living hell, and perhaps the relief we feel when we disclose them is a form of heaven.

* * *

"HI, FATHER," I SAY.

Father Yates smiles, happy to see me. The church is empty. He guides me to the first pew and asks me to sit down.

"How are you?" he asks me.

"I'm well, thanks. How are you?"

He shrugs. "Better. Some things have changed. Churches have been issued equipment to check for bugs in the confessionals. Issued with the PR edict of 'ensuring, in this age of technology, that the sacrament remains sacrosanct.' "

"Someone's going to put two and two together eventually."

"I agree. But the church is reluctant to admit its weaknesses." He grins. "Which is one of its weaknesses."

"Still not jockeying for a cardinal-ship, I see," I tease him.

"I'm not built for that kind of politics, so it's just as well."

"Yeah, me neither."

"Then I guess we'll both just continue to do what we do."

"I guess so."

"Interesting, though," he muses. "Michael Murphy said that he was about the truth, but in the end, he may do more damage to the safe haven of confession than anyone else in the history of the Catholic Church."

"He'll never see it that way, Father. Not in a million years. They can't deal with their own contradictions."

We fall silent. I look at Jesus, still paint-chipped, still suffering.

"Why are you here, Smoky?"

"I need something from you."

"What?"

I hesitate. Find Jesus again.

Am I sure about this?

"I need you to hear my confession again. It'll be brief."

He studies me for a moment and then he stands up and indicates the way to the confessional booth.

"FORGIVE ME, FATHER, FOR I have sinned. You know how long it's been since my last confession. I lied to a man today. It was a big lie."

"What was the nature of this lie?"

"I told him I had done something, something terrible. I later told him I had lied, that I hadn't really done what I'd said."

"But you had?"

The big question, with the big answer, the one that never leaves me. It's there with me when I wake up, when I go to sleep, as I go through my day. It played a part, I'm sure, in my career choice.

"Yes. I had actually done what I confessed to him."

"Do you want to tell me what you told him?"

"No, Father."

A pause. I can almost hear him thinking this through. I can sense his reluctance, and his suspicion.

"This thing you told him, do you think God heard it too?"

"If He exists, then it was really meant for Him, Father."

"I see. So you want to admit here that what you said was true, but you don't want to say it again."

"Something like that."

He sighs.

"Do you want to be forgiven for this thing?"

"I don't know, Father, to be honest. I just know I want to admit that it happened. That's a start, isn't it?"

"Yes, Smoky. It's a start. But I can't give you penance or absolution this way."

"Penance is under way and has been for a long time. As far as absolution goes . . . we'll have to see. I just need to know that you heard me, Father. I'm still not sure if forgiveness is a part of the picture."

I'd ask my mom, if I could.

"I heard you, Smoky. And if you ever want to tell me more, I'll listen."

"I know, Father. Thank you."

I HEAD DOWN THE HIGHWAY toward home and Bonnie and Tommy and I think of my mother. I remember her beauty, her smiles, her temper. I remember every second I spent with her, and I cherish those memories for what they are: times and places that will never exist again.

I killed my mother when I was twelve. I did it from love, true, but

I've always wondered: Is that why I can understand the monsters the way I do? Because there's a little bit of monster in me too?

What do you think, God?

He remains silent, which is my continuing and basic problem with Him.

Mom?

Maybe it's my imagination, but the breeze in my hair through the car window feels like a reassuring touch, and I am, for a moment, at peace.

44

"HOW IS SHE?" I ASK.

"See for yourself," Kirby says.

The hotel room Callie chose to quit Vicodin in has seen better days. She's lived inside this room for twelve days now and it reeks of sweat and vomit. She'd refused to go to a formal treatment center, which hadn't surprised me.

"Housekeeping is going to hate us when we finally let them clean this place up," I observe.

"I'll be sure and tip them well, honey-love, don't you worry."

Callie stands at the door of the bathroom. She's pale and she has the shadows of exhaustion under her eyes, but she looks more steady than she has so far.

"How are you feeling?" I ask.

"Like something approaching human. Finally. I think I'll be ready to leave this hellhole tomorrow."

Kirby and I have been taking shifts with her. We've taken turns holding her while she shook and sweated and cursed. We've held her hair back while she vomited. Once, I stroked her hair while she wept at the wanting.

"Geez, about time," Kirby says. "This has really put a crimp in my sex life."

"Mine too," I say.

"Yes, yes, yes," Callie replies. "I haven't seen my man in the buff since this began either. We'll all be returning to our respective lovers soon."

"How's your back?" I ask her. "Any pain?"

She comes and sits down on the bed.

"There hasn't been any pain in my back for a long time, Smoky. The Vicodin became about the Vicodin."

"Wow, so you were a bona fide junkie, huh?" Kirby says.

"I loved my little white pills, it's true, but thankfully, I love my man more. Speaking of which—where do we stand on the wedding?"

"All systems go. Your daughter has been helping with the last details. Brady tried to slip in an invitation to your parents, but I caught it and pulled it from the pile."

"Thank you."

"I aim to please. Anyway, no worries. Everything's set. You just need to get the heck out of here, hit the gym, maybe do a little tanning . . ."

"I don't 'do tanning,'" Callie says. I'm happy to hear some of the haughtiness back in her voice. It's a good sign.

"Whatever. You want to look like the corpse bride, it's your funeral. I mean wedding."

"All redheads are pale complected," Callie protests.

"There's a difference between 'pale' and 'junkie white,'" Kirby retorts.

"Is it really that bad?" She sounds distressed.

Kirby sighs. "You're going to make me be nice, aren't you? No, it's not that bad, I'm just giving you a hard time, Callie-babe. Truth is, you look great even though you've been sweating and puking and stuff. I kind of hate you for it."

Callie smiles. "Made you feel bad, made you say it." She sticks her tongue out at Kirby.

"Bitch," Kirby observes.

There's a lull in the conversation. Callie stares down at her hands, obviously working up to saying something.

"Listen close, because you'll only hear it once," she says. "Thank you both for this. I couldn't have done it alone."

"You're welcome," I tell her.

"No problemo," Kirby chirps. "Besides, I got to see you down on your knees, praying to the porcelain god." She chortles. "Wish I could have gotten *that* on camera."

Callie makes a face, and more good-natured bickering ensues. I listen with half an ear, smiling in the right places.

Three women, all proud, all a little damaged . . . the burden of our secrets becomes heavy so easily. We don't trust enough to share, and there are parts of us that we keep for ourselves, things our men will never know, however much we love them. Things we prefer, most of the time, not even to share with each other.

But it's nice to know, if those burdens become too great, that we have someplace to go, someone who'll listen to our whispers in their ears and take our secrets to their graves.

"I COULD GET USED TO this, babe. What do you think?"

"Finding a man who can cook is definitely easier than having to learn yourself," Bonnie agrees.

Tommy is making us an Italian dinner. The meat sauce has my mouth watering, and the smell of homemade garlic bread wafts through the house.

"My mom made me learn," he calls from the kitchen. "She said cooking for a woman is a fast way to impress her."

"Smart mom," I say.

"Yes, she is."

"When are we going to be meeting her?" Bonnie asks.

I glance at Tommy.

"Why do you ask, honey?"

She rolls her eyes at me. "You must really think I'm retarded, Momma-Smoky. You guys are moving in together, right?"

I scowl. "Who told? Callie? Kirby?"

She smiles. "Give me some credit, guys."

I chew on my thumbnail, nervous. Tommy remains silent.

"Sorry, babe. We were going to tell you soon. How do you feel about that?"

This has been my final concern, the last worry. Bonnie may love Tommy, but it's been just her and me for two years now. We've built our life together. We've needed each other. I've worried how she'd feel about this change.

She walks back over to me and takes my hand. Her smile says everything I need to know.

"I think it's great. Really, really great. Besides—he can *cook*."

LATE AT NIGHT AND TOMMY sleeps beside me. Through that window I can see the moon again, that ageless, ancient moon. People have danced under it, fucked under it, killed under it, loved under it, died under it. The moon keeps shining; life goes on.

I'm thinking about my mom. I wonder why helping her die was less of a burden to me than the abortion. It's the one secret I'd never told, not even to Matt. Now I've told it to a monster, which seems to fit my life. It's never weighed on me that much. It is something that happened, that I don't think about often.

Was it wrong?

I look for the answer, and find the only one I've ever found:

I don't care.

She stopped suffering. That's all that really mattered to me, in the end.

I cried at her funeral. I haven't cried for her since. I don't cry now either, but I let myself feel her absence, just a little.

I miss you, Mom. Dad was a great dad, but I was always my mother's daughter.

Tommy stirs next to me. I smile.

He's a good man, Mom. Different from Matt. Not better or worse. Just different.

My life is messy. I realize I've been trying to put everyone away, to stuff them into their little boxes and cover them with earth. What a waste. The ghosts are there, they'll always be there, and they'll show themselves when they feel like it.

The trick is to continue without the pain of enduring. Like the moon.

It continues to shine and I tell the ghosts to go to sleep now. I turn into Tommy and let myself fall into his warmth.

Welcome back, traveler, someone whispers.

"Mom?" I mumble once before tumbling into a dreamless sleep.

The moon shines on.

One Final Thing:
THE SINS
of
KIRBY MITCHELL

NEWS ITEM, LOS ANGELES:

Michael and Frances Murphy were found dead in their prison cells this morning, apparent suicides. The twin killers became infamous for their recent postings of video clips on the popular user-tube website, detailing the last moments and intimate confessions of more than 140 women.

Michael Murphy was the spokesman for the duo. He claimed religious motives were behind the killings. His actions, though supported briefly by a radical minority, were widely rejected by the Christian community worldwide.

They died within a few hours of each other. The lack of suicide notes, along with the fact that the Murphys were Catholic and thus presumably against suicide, has some speculating that something more sinister occurred. This is not a theory currently being pursued by law enforcement.

ABOUT THE AUTHOR

CODY McFADYEN lives in California. He is the author of *Shadow Man* and *The Face of Death*. His website is www.cody mcfadyen.com.